PRAISE FOR MAUNA KEA RISING

"A lovely blend of multiverse and apocalypse played on a tropical stage." -- *Nathan Lowell, award-winning creator of the Golden Age of the Solar Clipper series.*

"I love the way Kelly weaves tech details—from sailing and power generation, to aviation and astronomy—into the action. SciFi fans will be very pleased with this read." -- *D.J. Ward, author of Seven Wonders of Space Phenomena*

"M. W. Kelly has crafted a science fiction novel that offers mystery, intrigue, subtle turnings, narrative twists and inner reflections that challenge the status quo. Mauna Kea Rising envisions new possibilities, strained relationships, fears, confusion, courage and curiosity. The story is multidimensional, alive, intriguing and not over. Read, reflect, engage and enjoy the ride…" -- *F. W. Rick Meyers, author of Mystic Travelers: Awakening.*

"In Mauna Kea Rising, Kelly weaves together multiple genres to create a story accessible to anyone. Containing adventure on the open seas, action on the islands of Hawai'i, romance between college sweethearts, history of the Polynesian culture, and glimpses into parallel universes, the story centers around the complex idea of how humanity survives in a crisis." – *amazon review*

"All the characters are interesting, but I loved Hellen because she was strong and was haunted by a secret she'd kept to herself for years. I was also hooked by the concept of this book: what if a solar storm destroyed the electricity networks, plunging our society into chaos?" -- *Alicia Clanet, Midgard's Writers*

MAUNA KEA RISING

M.W. KELLY

Hōkūlei
Press

This book is a work of fiction. Any references to historical events, real businesses, real people, or real places are used fictitiously. Other names, characters, places, and events are products of the author's imagination, and any resemblance to actual events, businesses, companies, places, persons, living or dead, is entirely coincidental.

 Hokulei Press

Printed in the United States of America. Hokulei Press LLC.;

2549 West Main Street, Suite 201; Littleton, CO 80120

www.HokuleiPress.com | www.mwkelly.com | twitter.com/mwkelly2001

Cover design by Ana Grigoriu-Voicu, www.books-design.com

Mauna Kea Rising / M. W. Kelly — 1st Ed.

First paperback edition, January 2019

ASIN: 1792779453 (Kindle ebook)

ISBN-13: 978-1-7346930-0-3 (paperback)

Library of Congress Control Number: 2019900674

v3.4_c6v

For questions and comments about the quality of this book, please contact us at mwkelly@HokuleiPress.com.

To Patty

"Three things cannot be long hidden: the sun, the moon, and the truth."

—Gautama Buddha

CONTENTS

PART I

KE KAI MOANA NUI LĀ

(THE GREAT OCEAN)

1

In early June of 2K25, Hellen stood on the floating dock along-side the forty-foot sailboat *Ohana*. The stern line in her hands, she waited for the signal to shove off. At the helm stood the most awkward surprise of the day. Brett Akamu. He put the diesel engine into gear and gave a quick nod. After releasing the dock line from the cleat, she gave the stern rail a good shove and hopped aboard, deftly clearing the widening space.

She released a long, taut breath. A part of her still stood on the dock, waving goodbye. In the way a stranger walks out of the mist, a lonely reality emerged. During their three-week sail to the British Hawaiian Islands, they would be off the grid, off the internet, and out of touch with everyone. The perfect opportunity to reconnect with Charlie, the son she lost to adolescent independence and infomania.

Her smartwatch chimed. She ignored the solar alert from the Space Weather Prediction Center. Such alerts had occupied her attention every day at the National Clean Energy Lab in Colorado. But no more. At least losing her job had one upside.

"Hey, Skipper," she teased, returning to the cockpit. "Aren't you forgetting the yacht ensign? We're underway."

Brett acted as if he hadn't heard her and picked up a nautical chart. Her brother, Donovan, set aside his beer and opened a cockpit lazarette and retrieved an American flag. "Here, knock yourself out."

Hellen unrolled it from a short wooden staff and set it into the transom holder. The ensign flapped in the breeze, six neat rows of eight stars each, a symmetry unchanged for over a century.

A distant sonic boom—felt more than heard—startled Hellen. She stood and shaded her eyes to search the sky. JAL's *Orient Express* arced far above San Diego's smog, reaching into orbit on its daily flight to Tokyo. The world's two superpowers had divided territories; Japan's Chrysanthemum Throne ruled space, and Britannia ruled the waves. The sun's glare swallowed the SpaceLiner, and she grinned at the irony. By the time *Ohana* left the harbor channel, the *Orient Express* would have already touched down at Tokyo Spaceport.

During the next two hours, *Ohana* chugged through the San Diego seaway. Brett briefed Donovan, Hellen, and Charlie on the watch schedule, practiced man-overboard drills, and delivered a long harangue about wearing a safety harness once they sailed offshore. After all the fun and games ended, Charlie retreated to his cabin and Hellen lay on the foredeck under a sky filled with the hazy shade of summer. *Ohana*'s masthead swept lazy-eights with the rolling swells of the incoming tide. The June sun hung above the milky skyline, sapping Hellen's energy. She both loved and hated the sun; it had powered her career and tortured her with sunburn. And today it baked her into a hot and sticky mess. To her relief, a marine cloud layer soon filled in from the Pacific. Pushed by the onshore breeze, its tendrils crept up to *Ohana* and stole the sun.

She ducked her head through the forward hatch, her hair cascading around her face. Charlie lay on the V-berth, immersed in his HoloSpecs. She waved her hand to get his attention. "Charlie, can you hand me my jacket?"

"I don't see it," he said without looking away from his HoloSpecs.

Squeezed partway through the hatch, she reached for the jacket without his help. She clutched the windbreaker closed with folded arms, insulating herself from the fog engulfing the sailboat.

"Come topside and sit with me, love," she said. "The fresh air will do you good. Besides, you might get seasick down there."

"No. I'm good."

Good grief, have it your way, she thought as she lay on the teak deck. Charlie seemed more sullen with each passing hour since their departure from Denver that morning. With only the four of them, the next few weeks at sea promised a welcome isolation.

Her eyes grew heavy. She fell into a warm bubble before the jib sail unfurled with a loud racket, making her jump to her feet. She dodged the flapping sailcloth as it chased her off the fore-deck. Its nylon rope snapped at her ankles like a yapping dog all the way aft to the cockpit.

At the helm, Brett cut the engine and let *Ohana*'s sails do the work. "The harbor channel's quiet," he said without taking his binoculars from his eyes. "There's one upside to your late arrival."

Hellen ignored the remark; it was the second time he mentioned it. Their flight from Denver had been delayed, so she and Charlie had been running ever since they landed, looking for the boat in a forest of masts floating in the busy marina, stowing their gear, and last-minute provisioning.

So far, this trip wasn't a sail into paradise. She pinched her lips, wondering how she'd navigate the next three weeks with her old college boyfriend in such close quarters. She needed to have a word with Donovan. Not telling her Brett was the skipper was beneath him. Then again, obfuscation was in his nature. Maybe sailing to Hawai'i was a mistake. Should've flown. She leaned back, took a deep breath, stretched her arms, and tried to relax.

Out of the corner of her eye, she caught Brett checking her out. Some things never changed.

"See anything interesting?" she asked.

He returned to his binoculars. "Inbound freighters."

All business now, Brett checked his watch, sliding it close to his wrist, the same little tick he had twenty years ago. He was the sort of man who aged gracefully, becoming more attractive through the years. His weathered skin, brown eyes, and close-cropped silvered hair gave her a sense of security. He knew the sea better than anyone, and this sailboat was his new home.

"So, how'd you find this boat?" she asked. "She's a lot more comfortable than the one we chartered back in '05. And she has a sweet name." *'Ohana* was Hawaiian for family, and the name fit this classic sloop with smooth lines, deep gunwales, and varnished trim. The boat's roomy cockpit and cozy staterooms made Hellen feel at home, which was saying a lot for a sailboat.

"A boat broker called last month and asked if I was interested in a cutter-rigged cruiser. I've long dreamed of owning a boat, but the Navy never let me settle down in one place long enough. Now I'm a free man, sweet dreams are made of this…"

Hellen warmed to his smile and winked at him. "Mind if I drive for a moment?"

She stood and nudged him away from the helm with her hip. The steering wheel trembled in her hand, driven by the sea movement against the rudder, as if the boat came alive. *Ohana* slid through the swells, driven solely by her sails, the only sounds coming from the wind and the boat's wake.

Hellen patted the wheel. "She's a solid boat."

"She has an ocean-friendly hull," he said, turning up the volume on the cockpit speakers. "The boat's designers had blue water sailing in mind when they built her; double-laid fiberglass, deep keel, and roller furling for the jib."

She sat and tapped her foot on the teak deck to the rhythm of

Sista Noland. Brett dribbled on in boat-speak, showing no awkward signs of their surprise reunion. Had he known of the unintended consequence of their brief affair almost twenty years ago, she would still be on the dock in San Diego.

"I love how the seats wrap around the helm station," she said, feeling the smooth leather seat cushions under her bare thighs. "I bet it makes for great parties. By the way, I brought a case of Tequila Tapatio to lubricate our voyage."

"Yet another reason I'm glad Donovan suggested you come out with us." A smile emerged from the corners of his lips, and this time his eyes didn't waver.

She shivered. "Can you take the helm? It's getting chilly. I need to get some pants on."

Elle opened the door to the forward stateroom and her heart sank. Sweat soaked Charlie's sheets. He stared back at her with sleepy eyes, a moist brow, and quivering lips. She reached up to the overhead hatch, released the clutches, and threw it open. The cool sea air blew into the cramped cabin and exhausted the nauseous stench. She poked her head through the open hatch and breathed in fresh air, relieving some of her own queasiness. Fog enshrouded the San Diego coastline behind *Ohana*'s stern, and the ruddy sun lay low on the horizon at her bow. This trip already looked like a bust.

She returned to Charlie and wiped his face with a wet towel. After she kissed his brow, his pleading eyes relaxed somewhat.

"You're just a little seasick, love. Here, let's move you to a dry bunk."

She helped her son into her berth, laying him on top of her clean bedsheets. With Charlie's soiled sheets bundled in her arms, she went to the head and soaked them in the shower stall. She then fetched saltines, water, and Dramamine and returned to Charlie's berth. Her throat tightened as he nibbled at the crackers. She recalled how close to death she once felt, seasick years ago on Hilo Bay. Sailing those racing dinghies with their flat bottoms didn't suit her stomach. After the seasick pills took hold, Charlie's eyes drew heavy and his head fell against his pillow. She twisted the cabin fan toward his face and wiped his brow again.

Aiva, her Artificial Intelligence Virtual Assistant, chimed on her smartphone. "Hellen, I'm sorry to disturb you," it said with a feminine lilt, "but my signal reception has degraded. Would it be possible for you to patch me into the ship's comm system?"

"Sure, let me look into it." Hellen went to the ship's nav station and inspected the system panel. After booting up the boat's LAN router, she yelled up to Brett in the cockpit. "What's the Wi-Fi password?"

"Rubberducky," Brett shouted back to her. "And select the 'UHF antenna' on the left panel. It should give you plenty of range, at least out to a hundred miles."

"Right—got it." She pinched the home button on Aiva and the device unfolded itself into a touch-screen tablet. After authenticating credentials with the wireless LAN, signal strength showed five bars.

"Thank you," Aiva said. "I see you have a VideoChat request from Elle. Want me to place the call?"

Hellen nodded and fitted her Bluetooth earpiece in place. "Sure, make it so."

Her tablet displayed a blurry close-up of a tattooed yin-yang symbol.

"Hello, Elle? Can you show me your face, not your arm? You're such a Luddite sometimes."

"Sorry. I don't know where the camera on this damn thing is pointed." The display jumped around until Elle's smile beamed back at Hellen. Although her hair had long since faded to gray, her Polynesian beauty took on more grace with every year, even into her late sixties. "Did you make it okay?"

"Yes, except Aiva can't retrieve my passport. Could you pull a few strings for us?" Losing her passport app was one of the string of mishaps since leaving Denver.

"Sure, I'll take care of it. I'm sure they won't give you too much trouble. After all, you grew up here. But I'll call the BHI Border Control just to be sure. Besides, they owe me a favor."

"You're always there for me, Mum. And thanks again for the airfare—I'm trying to stretch my severance pay."

Elle was more than her *hānai* (foster) mother, she was a shoulder to lean on and a bankroll for her education. Elle had come into her life when Hellen was only an infant, a child of a teenage mother. The sins of the mother shall be visited upon the daughter.

"I think it's wonderful you took my advice and accepted Donovan's invitation to sail to Hawai'i."

Her brother lay across from her, asleep in the cabin berth, his curly gray hair and bulging waistline a sight not to behold. Yet she needed him, a buffer to her emotions, a sage of wisdom to balance her temper. Someone to stand between her and Brett for the next three weeks.

"It'll give Charlie and me some personal time together. And celebrate his sixteenth birthday in hula style. The timing's perfect. I'm between jobs, as it were."

"I'm sure you'll find another position—just give it time," Elle said in a dismissive tone. "But look at yourself, darling. You're in serious need of a makeover."

"I'm just a bit knackered from the flight and feel'n a little green around the gills."

"You should be on the foredeck, getting Brett's attention."

Hellen cringed. "You confuse me for my younger self."

"Listen. It's been five years since you left Sam. You need Brett, someone you can trust."

Hellen set her tablet on the nav table and moved out of view from Aiva's camera. Brett had indeed been her man, but she let him sail off to Asia, too ashamed to share the unexpected aftermath of their summer sojourn.

"Hellen. You still there?"

"You knew he was the skipper of this little adventure—didn't you? No wonder you insisted I go."

Elle pulled back from her vidcam and closed her eyes. "It's for your own good, and his. I'm sorry I can't meet you when you arrive—I'll be at an astronomy conference in Hilo. But Suzu will pick you guys up at the airport."

Seeing Elle's partner again would be interesting, to say the least. The Iron Buddha was never one for small talk. "And Elizabeth? I can't wait to see her again."

"She's excited too. Your annual trips aren't enough. And it's time Elizabeth learns the truth. Charlie too. During your last visit, they grew a little cozy with each other…" Elle raised one eyebrow; her brown eyes bored into Hellen.

Hellen's skin tingled with pinpricks, and beads of sweat grew on her brow from the humidity. She asked herself, how much longer could she keep playing the act of "Auntie Hellen" for her daughter? Secrets tend to grow their own histories if they lived too long. But the path to the truth lay hidden in the past. "I know. I'll find a way."

"After Brett deployed, you did what you thought you needed to do, and your life was inexorably altered. But your children shouldn't pay for it. Don't dwell in the past, concentrate the mind on the present moment. Let go of your fear and share the truth with them. Two hands clap and there is a sound. What is the sound of one hand?"

Hellen glanced away from her tablet and rolled her eyes. "Yes, Mother Buddha. But honestly, the past is a bitter memory and the present is a constant struggle."

Elle smiled back at her, a teacher waiting for her recalcitrant student, allowing her to sit with the koan. Neither spoke and the space between them grew wider.

At last, Elle picked up a book and waved it toward the vidcam. "I've sent an advanced copy of my latest novel to you. It's a perfect companion for your voyage. It tells the story of a

Polynesian wayfinder taking his family across the Pacific to Hawai'i. Think of it as *da kine* literary compass, a story to guide your voyage."

"When will it be published?"

"Next month." She paused and glanced off screen. "Weren't Brett's ancestors Polynesian navigators?"

"Yes, I think saltwater courses through his veins."

The boat rolled deep into a long swell, throwing Hellen off balance. She caught a handrail and glanced through the open hatch at Brett standing behind the wheel, his eyes wild with excitement. His open shirt parted in the breeze, enough to reveal his lean abdomen. Hellen wondered why Polynesians had the best skin, smooth and honey-brown. He gave her a brilliant smile and a *shaka* sign, stirring up feelings she hadn't had in a long time. She shook it off. This trip was a chance to get closer to her son, not an old flame from her college days. The last thing she needed right now was to fall into a relationship.

"Rock and roll, baby," he called down to her.

"Remember when you and Brett last sailed together?" Elle asked. "You two were such a cute couple."

"That Hellen died years ago. Nostalgia isn't what it used to be."

"How's he look?"

"He's aged better than me, I'm afraid. Some men have all the luck."

"This trip will be a tune-up for your body and soul. Remember the red thread?"

"There isn't some mystical red thread tying us together. It's been too long." *And I've made too many mistakes.*

"It'll be good for Charlie as well," Elle said. "Maybe he'll even put his HoloSpecs down long enough to enjoy the fresh air."

"And a fresh perspective."

"Look, I have to run," Elle said. "But, remember, if you ever need anything, get a hold of Suzu. *Aloha no au ia 'oe.*"

"I love you too, Mum. *Aloha nui loa.*" Hellen wiped her eyes and stared at Elle's image as it dissolved on Aiva's screen. After she wedged herself into the cabin side berth, she opened Elle's book on her tablet. After the first chapter, she gave a bittersweet, hollowed laugh. The story started with 'Ehulani and Aukai, a couple filled with love for each other and a wanderlust for the sea, a fantasy bare of the multitude of problems facing her own life. She fought to stay awake, but the day's events exhausted her, and she fell into a light sleep.

Hours later, Donovan's snoring awoke Hellen with a start. Her quick motion sent the darkened cabin spinning. She rubbed her temples and took a deep breath to ward off her growing nausea. Heeled by the wind, the boat leaned over at a steep angle. After two Dramamines and a sip of water, she staggered to Charlie's stateroom and found him curled up and asleep. She adjusted the cabin fan to blow the sea air over him and made her way aft. Holding onto the companionway ladder handrails, she climbed the steps into the twilight to get some fresh air.

The full moon hung low in the eastern sky. Land lay far below the horizon, the ocean surrounding them in all directions. The cool breeze hit her, giving her goose bumps, but it settled her stomach. Brett stepped in front of the ship's wheel and held out his free hand. She grabbed it as another deep swell sent her sprawling onto the cockpit seat.

"Here, lie down." Brett sat next to her and slipped a seat cushion under her head. The boat's stern lurched high over a swell, shifting her weight. Her heart jumped, and she flailed her arms for a handhold. Brett caught her shoulder an instant before she rolled off the edge of the seat. She tensed at first but didn't have the strength to push his hand away. Instead, she grasped his wrist to steady herself, his skin warm and smooth, relaxing her muscles. The sea air engulfed her with a cool blanket and evaporated her nausea.

Thankfully, Brett sat in silence, studying the compass, his face glowing by the cockpit's red lights. He always knew when she just needed some quiet space. She recalled their first carefree days together in Lahaina, twenty years ago. Time acted like a warped drive, refracting her perceptions, compressing decades into the briefest of moments. Her fingers no longer tingled, her mind no longer spun with vertigo. She gave herself to a dreamless sleep, the heavy kind that came easy in childhood.

She later awoke to Brett squeezing her hand. Night had arrived.

"Hellen, wake up," he said. "Your smartwatch keeps chiming a message for you. Better pick it up while we still are in radio range."

He leaned over her to sheet in the mainsail, pressing his warm chest against her cheek. His bone-fishhook necklace tickled her neck. Tropical flowers wafted from his sunscreen. Her seasickness had disappeared, replaced by a gentle yearning to lie there forever.

She rubbed her eyes and lifted her smartwatch to eye level. Aiva chimed again and displayed a text glowing green in the night: "NOAA/SWPC Geoalert: X-class solar flare, 0607/0815UTC."

She sat up and showed the message to Brett. "The sun shot out a solar flare, a damn powerful one. Aiva, what's its trajectory?"

"The flare's vector is uncertain; however, SWPC reports it's along the ecliptic."

"And that means what to us?" Brett asked.

Hellen let her head drop back onto the seat cushion.

"The flare's path would cross the Earth's orbit but may miss us depending upon its velocity."

"You work for NASA or something?"

"Electrical engineer for NCEL—or was—until they laid me off last month."

She busied herself with Aiva, reviewing the latest data from the Solar Dynamics Observatory. She couldn't believe how large Sunspot 2532 had grown since last week. SDO's Subsurface Flow Map showed new and intense activity building in the sun's convection zone. The ceaseless dance between the sun's magnetic fields and high-energy plasma threw out frequent flares, but so far solar cycle 25 had been curiously quiet—up to now.

"Hellen, come back to me. What the hell is going on?" Brett whispered.

Her chest tightened. She took a deep breath before answering. "It's an X-class solar flare, a solar storm."

"That means nothing to me. Will a fireball hurl out of the sky and blast us with hurricane winds?"

"No, it's not a meteorological storm, more like a space weather storm. Every ten to eleven years, the sun becomes active with sunspots, flares, and coronal mass ejections. If this flare hits Earth, it'll create a geomagnetic storm matching the Carrington Event of 1859. Back then, most people didn't rely much on electrical devices. Even so, it blew out the Victorian-age version of the internet. Telegraph lines became amplifiers for electrical currents generated by the superflare. The currents blew up thousands of miles of wires and shocked telegraph operators."

"Imagine if this happened today. Our society can't live without the power grid and the internet. But you said the storm's track was uncertain. It could miss Earth, right?"

"Yes, let's hope so. The last Carrington-sized flare—the Halloween Storm of 2K03—just missed us."

Hellen focused on the star-filled sky. Her stomach churned, imagining the superflare shooting toward Earth at five-hundred thousand miles an hour. The SWPC data showed the solar storm might reach Earth's orbit within a week.

2

With the first five days behind them, *Ohana*'s crew had finally caught the west trade winds and sailed under a cloudy sky. After Hellen's warning of a solar storm, Brett made the habit of checking the GPS nav display, looking for any signs of satellite outage. But Hellen spoke no more about it and kept to herself and minded Charlie. Perhaps the hot sun evaporated her worries. She was difficult to read. He had accepted Donovan's suggestion of inviting her along with reticence. After all, it had been nineteen years since their summer together had ended on a sour note.

Ohana's northwest track would soon intercept the great circle course from Los Angeles to Hawai'i. The winds picked up before dawn, building large swells that tossed *Ohana*'s bow up and down. The wind whistled through the standing rigging, singing a chorus with the whirling buzz from the wind generator atop the stern rail. Alone in the cockpit, Brett lifted his ocular range-finder to his eyes and studied a British task force closing in on him, their lights shining like a floating city. The digital readout showed the closest ship tracked five nautical-miles astern. His mouth went dry at the menacing sight of a dozen warships, a surreal display of military might. When he had last stood on the

HMS Queen Elizabeth, the carrier task force had been his home. Now the precise formation of six ships threatened to run him over. He shook his head at his misfortune of crossing their path in all these thousands of square miles of ocean. Brett tacked the boat to avoid their converging track, thankful he had rigged the sail trim sheets to run aft to the cockpit, allowing him to control everything single-handed.

Charlie stumbled into the cockpit, breaking Brett's attention. In the red cockpit lighting, the kid peered around in a comical rendition of a pirate lookout. He stood a few inches taller than his mother, which wasn't saying much. While he had her auburn-red hair and elegant face, he lacked her grace and composure.

Charlie froze at the sight of the naval ships. "Like, where did they come from? Are we at war?"

Brett lifted the range-finder to his eyes again. "Probably just naval exercises, but we better keep our distance." He looked over to Charlie and grimaced. "Where's your life jacket? You know the rules." He raised the cockpit seat cover and retrieved a yellow life vest from the sail locker and handed it to the kid. Charlie scowled at it. "Gross—get it away from me."

"If you won't wear the life vest, then put on your safety harness and hook up to the cable, like I showed you."

Without comment, Charlie put on his HoloSpecs and sat under the cockpit dodger. The kid's phubbing wasn't a surprise. He seemed addicted to the gadget, an augmented reality device connected to eyewear and wireless earbuds. Charlie's blank eyes reflected the blue and green light beamed from the glasses. After a minute, he took them off and fiddled with his mobile data server. He threw the glasses under the dodger in frustration. "When do we get the internet back?"

"You'll have to wait at least three weeks until we reach Hawai'i."

"Wait—what?"

Brett let the boy's frustration simmer. "Look, kid, there's no internet out here. We're hundreds of miles from land and don't have a SatComm receiver. Now, get your safety harness on or go belowdecks."

Charlie glared at Brett with an adolescent bravado. His face held the sneer often worn by young boys, in their powerlessness, sometimes used to mask their vulnerability. He seemed on the verge of exploding, but retreated toward the hatch, tripped on its threshold, and stumbled into the cabin. A loud crash rang from below, followed by angry shouts between Charlie and his mother.

Brett winced at the kid's outburst. Ever since he stepped aboard, chaos had ruled the day. He had whined about his cabin, stood in the way while they stowed their provisions, and remained glued to his HoloSpecs. Regardless of Charlie's apathy toward shipboard safety, Brett had a ship to run, and he needed everyone to work together to make a safe Trans-Pac passage.

The ship's clock rang four bells—six a.m. Donovan joined Brett in the cockpit for his watch relief. He attached a harness over his foul weather gear and hooked its lanyard to the safety line running forward from the stern rail. With his frumpy khakis, bushy eyebrows, and rumpled tangle of gray, curly hair, he looked as if he had just climbed out of his bunk.

"Thanks for the wake-up call. What did you say to Charlie to get him so spun up?" Donovan asked.

Lost in his thoughts, Brett didn't reply.

"Well, Skipper, whatever it was, it sent him into a tailspin," Donovan said while avoiding any eye contact. "Give the kid some breathing room. You forget what it's like being a teenager, especially when you're out of your element."

"Yeah, I hear ya. But the kid has to understand he's a crewmember, not da kine cruise ship guest."

"There are better ways to get that idea across. I'll talk to Charlie, but you need to speak to Hellen. She's a little hot under her redheaded collar at the moment. The Irish are known for their strong women, and she's no exception."

"The kid needs to understand safety at sea. Besides, he's— never mind."

Donovan raised his eyebrows and waited. Brett looked away. He didn't understand how Charlie could be so obstinate, so unwilling to follow even the simplest protocol while at sea. Totally isolated now by thousands of square miles of ocean, they sailed beyond the help of the Coast Guard. Order and discipline were the DNA of safety at sea and Charlie acted like a virus, thwarting his every effort.

"Hellen said something about a solar flare alert she received after we left San Diego," Donovan said. "Will it affect us?"

Brett checked his heading and adjusted the mainsheet. "She didn't seem too worried about it—then again, she was pretty stoned on Dramamine that night."

"Damn. I wish she hadn't taken that stuff. I've got something safer in my med kit."

A familiar staccato of helo rotors resounded from astern. Six MQ-9 Fire Scout drones emerged from the murky, gray morning light, their rotors creating huge vortexes, curling ocean spray under their spotlights.

Their approach grew louder, and Donovan squinted in their direction. "They're flying damn low and fast. Do you think those flat-hatters see us?"

"Hell no, Doc. Those fatherless noodle-wingers will sooner clip our mast than pull up to a safe altitude."

Brett heaved the mainsheet and threw the helm alee. "Let's tack out of their way. Hard to lee."

After *Ohana* fell to leeward, Donovan eased the jib sheet. They surged forward, and the drones passed within fifty yards. The kerosene stench of their JP5 jet fuel exhaust hung around *Ohana* like a cloud.

"Damn it, they never altered course or altitude," Donovan said. "Don't drones have sensors or warning devices to prevent this from happening?"

Brett faced astern, watching the drones fly back to the carrier, remembering the sting of his early retirement. With its fleet of drones, the Navy no longer needed helo pilots. He checked the compass, then glanced up at Hellen as she came up the companionway ladder, joining them in the cockpit. No longer plaited, her long wavy hair danced in the breeze, sending a eucalyptus scent past him.

"And you're here to take the helm?" he asked, tipping his "Fly Navy" ball cap at her.

Hellen gave him a dismissive smile. "Only if you want me to get us lost. I came topside to see what all the racket was about. Are we under attack from those whirligigs?"

Brett settled back on the cockpit seat next to her and took a sip from his water bottle. "No, they're just surveillance drones from the British task force." He pointed to the gray warships dipping below the horizon. "We had to fall off the wind to avoid hitting them. Say, what happened to Charlie? You'd think the helos would've drawn him topside."

Hellen ignored him and faced the dawn. "Have you seen any lights in the sky?"

"Lights? Sure, plenty of air traffic flying the Pacific route."

"No, more like glowing colors in the sky—the Northern Lights."

"That's impossible," Brett said as he scanned the stars, "they never reach this low in latitude."

She said no more about it and tapped her brother's knee. "Charlie still hasn't found his sea legs. It's been years since we've done any sailing."

"I gave him a scopolamine patch," Donovan said. "More powerful than Dramamine and good for three days. But it makes him dopey, so keep an eye on him."

"Thanks. Having a doctor for a brother has its special privileges."

Hellen leaned forward and rested her elbows on her knees. A wedding ring popped out of her spaghetti strap shirt and swung on a necklace under her chin. An odd accessory to be wearing after five years on the leeward side of a stormy divorce.

Donovan leaned toward his sister. "Getting Charlie off those HoloSpecs might also help."

Hellen sat back and blew her bangs from her face. "Been trying for two years." She folded her arms and tapped the bottom of her chin, her elegant face framed by the rising sun. Minutes passed before she rose to her feet. "You'll have to excuse me, gentlemen, but I want to check in on my boy."

She climbed over him, squeezing past the helm pedestal, her hips brushing along his chest. Sorry to see her go, he sat saying nothing to Donovan. At least the kid's morning drama had dissolved into a muted retreat to the forward stateroom.

After Donovan relieved the watch, Brett went belowdecks and fixed scrambled eggs for his crew. They sat in the cabin while they ate, each in their own space. Brett eyed Hellen and Charlie, who finished their breakfast in silence. Donovan had a point; too many years had passed since he was Charlie's age. Back in the day, he wasn't a champion for following orders either. Even after graduating from the Britannia Royal Naval College in Dartmouth, he had a wild streak, a sense there was more to life than following rules. But he had learned you had to first learn the rules before you broke them.

Brett brought Donovan's breakfast topside. After Charlie cleaned up the galley—a job to which he had at last acquiesced— he came to the cockpit. His rumpled red hair danced in the breeze, hiding the scowl on his face.

"You need to get a life harness on." Brett had lost count how many times he had warned him. "We've discussed this, no one topside unless they are wearing a harness and latched in. If you fall overboard in these swells, we might never find you."

"I'm good. Stop worrying."

Brett's jaw tensed, and his chest filled with heat. His last commanding officer would've called this a teachable moment. "Okay pal, have it your way." He casually disconnected the autopilot, grabbed an orange life preserver, and threw it overboard. The saltwater activated its strobe light and its brilliant flashes overpowered the dawn. "Man overboard, port side," Brett shouted and put the helm hard over to windward.

Ohana spun into the wind. Just as they had practiced during drills before leaving San Diego, Donovan eased the mainsheet and took his station at the jib winch. Hellen ran topside and retrieved a boat hook from a cockpit lazarette. After much maneuvering, they reached the floating life preserver, and she scooped it up on the first try. Just like old times, she came back into her own. This part of the crew had proved to be an asset. She returned it to the cockpit and dropped it onto the settee next to her son. With sweat beaded on her brow, she grabbed Charlie's upper arm, making the kid cringe.

"Charlie, why didn't you keep an eye on the life jacket?" She pointed to the soaked, orange PFD. "You should know you are our spotter for the man-overboard recovery. And where's your damn harness?"

"Get off my case." Charlie flailed his arm, forcing her to let go. He nodded toward Brett. "He only threw this drill at us because I wasn't paying attention to him. Besides, why do we have to wear these giant-sized jock straps, anyway?"

"Look here Charles Callahan," Hellen said in her lilting accent, "we're in the middle of the frick'n Pacific, not sailing a dinghy in Chatfield Reservoir. If you fell overboard... You saw how long we took to retrieve the life preserver. So, *please*, pay a mind to Brett's instructions."

Charlie flinched away from his mother's words and rose to his feet. He stomped to the cabin hatch, making Hellen wince when he walked on her toes.

"Charlie, come back here. Dammit all to hell." She shut her eyes and did a palm smack. "Donovan, can you go and speak some sense into Prince Charles?"

Donovan busied himself with stowing the jib sheet. The compass needle danced with each passing wave. They sat for a long moment in silence.

"I'm sorry about Charlie's attitude," she said at last. "I know he can be a little difficult, but he's really a good kid. Just give him time."

"Sounded like you forgot that for a moment," Brett said, "but we need to follow certain protocols."

"Don't lecture me. You've never been a parent. He's a bit quirky, but no less than other kids his age. He follows his own ideas and carries a penchant for disrespecting authority. Seems you two might have something in common."

"I hear you," Brett said with a touch of remorse. "Okay. I'm sorry for riding him, but I swear he makes my toes curl in frustration sometimes."

She wrapped her hair around her neck, twirling a few strands in her fingers. She flashed a practiced smile at him. "Me too. But there're better ways of getting across to him. Let's both try to work on that, okay?"

A loud beeping alarm sounded from the nav display at the helm console. A message flashed on the screen, "GPS RAIM failed, position loss of integrity."

"What's the alarm for?" she asked with a hint of worry.

"GPS loss of position. It happens sometimes in the middle of the ocean. Do you think Charlie might want to practice traditional navigation? Maybe it'll get him more engaged."

She ran her slender fingers through her hair before answering. "Yes, he's always loved maps. You should see his collection of compasses." Her eyes lingered on him as if she questioned his sincerity. "Can you make him your little navigator?"

The way she said "little navigator" made him smile.

Days later, the sun returned. Brett left the hatches open to the breeze and stood on the dry deck in flip-flops. Glad to have put away the sweaters and foul weather gear, Brett let the sun warm his bare arms and legs. The days passed on their own inertia, unfettered by distractions. The ocean's remoteness gave him peace, void of the crowded intimacy of his life in Honolulu. The boat would make a nice crash pad once he moored in O'ahu.

Before relieving Hellen on watch, he engaged the wind vane autopilot and sat back against the cockpit coaming. She had settled into her own routine at sea, sometimes lingering after Brett relieved her watch. Her sexy accent meandered in musical tones, and her eyes brimmed with an energy he still found intoxicating.

And he and Charlie had finally come to speaking terms. They shared a common interest in gadgets and a wry sense of humor. After he taught Charlie about the autopilot mechanism, the kid compared it to a crazy steampunk relic from the Industrial Age. The Rube Goldberg device used a wind vane to sense the direction and controlled rudder movement through a chain linkage. Charlie had proven to be a quick student, memorizing guide stars, reading charts, and measuring distance made good along their track.

Charlie reminded Brett of his younger self, the time in his life when he had a perfect worldview. The adult world lay beyond the asteroid belt and was just as hard to penetrate. As a fifteen-year-old *keiki*, he had resisted his uncle's lessons on wayfinding, dismissing the ancestral teachings and preferring the company of his friends and the digital gadgets. But he later regretted his teenage rebellion against his surrogate father and grew to appreciate the knowledge of the "old ways."

Brett sat on the cabin roof, leaning against the mast after sunset. The wave direction had changed, allowing *Ohana* to glide along on a broad reach. The perfect evening for Charlie's navigation lesson. A transcendent time of day that conjured contemplation. The deep violet sky merged with the sea's gray horizon. His uncle used to call this time the "Twilight of The Gods," a definitive moment calling forth the key navigation stars, allowing wayfinders to get a celestial fix to guide their voyage across ten thousand square miles of ocean. After the sun dropped below the horizon, Venus shone bright in the western sky and the stars emerged one by one. He took a piece of Botan Rice Candy, his favorite, out of his pocket. He unwrapped the plastic wrapper and peeled away the fruit-flavored rice paper from the hard candy. A proverb printed on the wrapper read, *"ho'i hou ke aloha* — Let us fall in love again."

Brett's jaw twitched. The proverb fell too close to home. He had fallen in love with Hellen in Lahaina a lifetime ago. Her carefree younger spirit and elfin sexuality pegged high on the fun meter in those days. But it only lasted the summer. He deployed to the Far East, and she moved to Colorado. Their relationship wasn't strong enough to span a hundred degrees of longitude. After he sailed to the WestPac, she ghosted his DMs. And he had let their relationship fade into the thousands of miles between them, avoiding the complications and responsibilities of their love affair.

Charlie stumbled on the jib shackle block and plopped down next to him, breaking Brett's musings.

"Welcome topside, buddy." Brett handed him a Botan. Charlie unwrapped the candy and read the wrapper aloud but didn't make it past the first three words before giving up with an exasperating sigh.

Brett took the plastic wrapper. *"Haa ka mikioi i ke kai o Maunakea,"* Brett read. "It means 'It takes a skillful sailor to go to Mauna Kea'. Ready for your first lesson?"

"Sure. I'm amped up for it." Charlie took an antique, brass pocket compass out of his pocket and handed it to Brett. "It had belonged to my grandfather."

"So, I hear you're a math whiz," Brett said while examining the compass. "That'll make this easier for both of us."

He handed the compass back to Charlie. The kid moved it around in his hand, allowing its needle to swing back and forth.

Brett picked up his sextant. "Back in high school, I used to hang out with my uncle, listening to his stories of how our ancestors had sailed across the Pacific. Each generation's *kahuna* taught the next generation of wayfinders the 'knowledge of the old ways.'"

"Wait—what?"

"Self-reliant in their own skills, my ancestors navigated thousands of miles without a sextant or a compass. They used star positions, lunar phases, and wave patterns to determine their position." Brett pointed over Charlie's shoulder. "Let me show you. Now follow the line formed by those two outer stars in the Big Dipper and trace it downward. The next bright star on this line is Polaris."

"Like the North Star?"

"Yep. It's the most important navigation star."

He took Charlie's hand and traced out a downward arc with it from Polaris to the horizon. "And Polaris not only shows where true North lies, it can give us our latitude." Brett handed a sextant to him. "That's where this baby comes into play. We can measure star positions to a fraction of a degree with this instrument."

He allowed Charlie to play with the sextant before showing him how to take a sight through the ocular. Following Brett's instructions, the kid smoothly went through the steps to get a star fix. He seemed a natural at this, almost too good.

Charlie examined the micrometer wheel. "We have about twenty-three-point-four degrees elevation," he said with expectation in his eyes.

"Not bad," Brett patted Charlie's shoulder. "You're close. This tells our current latitude. Let's head below and mark this on our chart."

While the boys played at navigating the high seas, Hellen opened to the next chapter in Elle's novel, *The Wayfinders*. Reading it took on a whole new meaning at sea. Elle's first chapters described a voyage from Tahiti to Hawai'i by 'Ehulani and Aukai, two Polynesian navigators. Elle took great pains to make sure Hellen understood her message. The couple's mannerisms mimicked her and Brett. 'Ehulani also had red hair and Aukai had a Māori tattoo like Brett's, telling a warrior's story. Something about the heroine's name sounded familiar, but she couldn't place it. She pressed her index finger over the name and Aiva's word search came up with the dedication, "To Hellen, ko'u 'ehulani keiki (my heavenly, redheaded daughter)." A message popped up, "Do you want to view image?" She tapped the inquiry, and a photo emerged, showing her young trim body draped in a flowing white sarong, taken the summer she met Brett. "Tsk tsk," she said with a shake of her head. Elle had violated her own edict; a novelist shouldn't write about her own family.

Hellen returned to the point in Elle's book where Aukai teaches his son star finding, speaking of the gods and goddesses in the heavens. During his navigation lesson, Aukai's son points to Hōkū-pa'a, the fixed star in the north. Aukai's eyes widen at waving curtains of color bursting among the stars. First red, then green, and yellow, an aurora fills the entire northern sky. He looks over to 'Ehulani, her shock reflecting the changing colors. The waving light spreads over the sky and shifting colors dance on the canoe. Consumed by the colorful specter, she grips the mast.

The story dug up the constant ache resting in the back of her throat. The solar storm must have hit by now. Out of reach of any news, the long days at sea made the wait intolerable. Her mind went wild imagining widespread blackouts in the power grids, like those during the geomagnetic storm of 1989, when a superflare shot a river of charged particles into the ionosphere, inducing powerful electrical currents and tripping circuit breakers in HydroQuébec's power grid. Schools and businesses closed. Food spoiled in disabled refrigerators. Normal life had ended. Yet such events were rare south of Canada. She forced the air from her lungs. Perhaps the flare and its blast of high-energy particles might miss the Earth—after all, this had happened before.

Hellen glanced up from her book when Brett and Charlie came into the main cabin and sat at the dining table. Brett reached behind her and retrieved a nautical chart from the nav station desk. Her son pored over the chart, beaming as if it were a birthday gift.

Her curiosity piqued, she slid next to Brett. "You boys figured out where we are yet? Here, let me help." She swirled her finger over the chart before letting it drop on a random spot. "We're somewhere in this ocean, right?"

Brett grinned and took Hellen's hand, tracing their passage across the eastern Pacific Ocean with her index finger. She relaxed her arm and allowed him to pull her hand along the chart in a slow motion, bringing her body closer to him. She rested her chin on his shoulder and took a deep breath. The past week's tension seeped away. He always had a fresh smell—even out here in the middle of nowhere.

"Here's our last GPS navfix," he said. "I've marked our position every twelve hours since we left San Diego. We're tracking on a northwest course to intercept a great circle arc to the Hawaiian Islands."

Charlie leaned over the chart and traced the line with his finger. "Why are we going up there, instead of just sailing right from San Diego?"

"We're heading on an intercept with the shipping lanes from Los Angeles. It's the path most ships follow, so it'll give us a chance to hail somebody for help if we run into any trouble along our way to Hawai'i."

Charlie sat back from the table and frowned. "I don't get it. Why don't you just look at the GPS screen to see where you are going? Why use a paper map?"

"I guess I'm old school, but I like to keep a backup record on paper charts. Besides, the GPS is acting wonky."

Brett always had a Plan B. He reminded her of Kalino, Elle's plantation manager. Antique maps and nautical charts covered the walls of his study at Cloudcroft. More traditional than old-fashioned, Kalino had preferred fold-out paper maps over GPS screens. He claimed those clumsy, old wrinkled road maps gave him a broader perspective. During his many "misadventures," as she liked to call them, he claimed you had to know true north and stay the course. Same goes for life. For the past five years, her life had been a wreck. Divorced. Charlie's newfound rebellion. Losing her job. With her chin still leaning against Brett shoulder, now more than ever she yearned for her own Polaris, a star to guide her.

Charlie gave her a questioning smile and raised his eyebrows. Blood heated her cheeks, and she lifted her head off Brett's shoulder.

"I think it's been years since I used a paper map," she said. "Most people think they're obsolete. Years ago, a couple became stranded in Monument Valley after their smartphone turned stupid and told them to turn off the main highway." She laughed at the memory. "They were strung out and fit to be tied over the whole ordeal. After the story made its rounds at NCEL, we coined the phrase 'Death by GPS.'"

"Stuff like that happens more than you think," he scoffed. "I track our position on a paper chart. It gives me a better picture of place and time."

As Brett and Charlie continued their navigation exercise, she wondered how her life would've changed had she stayed with Brett and raised Elizabeth. Sometimes we make decisions which alter our lives in the same way a branch grows from a tree's trunk, she thought. Last March Elizabeth celebrated her eighteenth birthday. Now a young woman, she had never known her real parents. Elle had raised her to allow Hellen to finish grad school. Hellen's planned reunion never materialized. President

Jackson's alien exclusion act prohibited Elizabeth's move to America. Instead, Hellen later married Sam. Their divorce ended the physical and emotional abuse but left a gaping hole in her life, except for Charlie. After she rested her head against Brett's arm again, she gave a start at Donovan yelling from the cockpit.

"Guys—you better get up here. You got to see this!"

They raced up the companionway ladder and into the cockpit.

The northern sky blazed with rolling sheets of color, unfurling in the night with red diffusing into green bands, like a great hand dripping paint. The northern lights illuminated white caps on the waves and painted the mainsail with unearthly hues. *Ohana* rolled in the swells, veering off course. Donovan was absent from the wheel. Hellen ducked to miss the swinging boom just before it passed over her head. She reached for Brett to steady herself, her adrenaline sending pressure through her chest. A blue ghost danced at the masthead—St. Elmo's fire—sprites of blue lightening everywhere against the cloudless sky. Impossible. Her sense of awe mixed with fear. Now embodied in these celestial fireworks, Elle's book came to life and Hellen's chest stiffened at its foreshadowing.

The cabin lights blinked. A high-pitched alarm sounded from the helm console. The nav display flashed with a red blinking error message: "GPS lost sync—all satellites."

Brett cut off the alarm and narrowed his eyes at Hellen. "The solar storm, right?"

"Yes, it must be," Hellen said, forcing the words from her lungs. The aurora was as beautiful as it was deadly, dumping trillions of watts of power into the upper atmosphere, weakening the magnetosphere. God, to think of the blackouts crossing the Pacific.

Silence fell on the voyagers. With mounting fear, Hellen recoiled from the variegated sky, leaned against Brett, and buried her face against his shoulder.

3

Ten days after the first aurora, the sky no longer burst forth with pastels every night. Hellen occupied herself with Charlie, playing word games and chess, a way to hide from her imagined horrors. Off the grid in the middle of the Pacific, the solar storm's existential threat receded. With no daily reminders of the event, she fell back into her routine of reading, daily watchstanding, and recording her diary in Aiva.

Hellen awoke to a gentle undulating motion as *Ohana* rode the ocean swells. Outside her cabin porthole, the hull made a hissing rhythm as it sliced the waves. The pale, predawn light streamed across the stateroom to Charlie, still asleep, his chest rising and falling with each breath.

After preparing a light breakfast and a cup of tea for herself, she climbed into the cockpit and joined Brett behind the helm. He stowed his fishing pole and grinned, showing off two red snappers, *onaga*, as he called them. They must have been over five pounds and had a brilliant red color with dorsal fins ending in long slender points.

"Look at these beauties," he said. "If it wasn't morning, I'd suggest sushi."

The warm sun and his carefree enthusiasm overpowered her worries. Out here, life continued as usual.

"Let me take the helm," she said, "so you can store them in the refrigerator."

"Sure, just keep steering for that cloud resting on the horizon ahead of us."

She playfully nudged him aside and sat behind the wheel. She had grown more comfortable with watchstanding, and the sailing skills he had taught her years ago came back to her. Her watch duty only entailed looking out for ship traffic and yelling for help if the wind exceeded fifteen knots, the time to reef sails and get another watchstander on deck. The uneventful routine stood in contrast to the "always connected" life she left on the mainland, tethered to work and social media. And she didn't miss any of it. Out here, time took on a different meaning.

"Brett," she called down to the cabin, "when did we leave San Diego?"

"Seventeen days ago."

The days had blended together in isolation from the world. Sometimes Hellen forgot the day of the week. Despite her reservations, weeks aboard in close quarters had fueled a close nostalgia, the surrender of inhibition, a yearning to return to their summer together on Maui. Elle once asked if she preferred to be the one who gave more love than she received. She told her she loved with no need to own.

After cleaning and stowing the fish, Brett came topside and sat opposite of her. The morning rays highlighted his flat abdomen, taut skin, and firm pecs. He had a traditional Māori tattoo, the same one from their first summer together. It stretched from the middle of his back and wrapped around his right shoulder. Its familiar parabolic symmetry drew her back to those sultry days in Lahaina. On her summer break from college, she had a glad eye for this tattooed native. He took her for her first ride, the ride against which she would judge all others.

He stared back at her with those soft brown eyes. Holding his gaze, she replayed their first night together, the night they made their perfect mistake on Ka'anapali Beach under a ribbon of stars, the Milky Way. Nostalgia made her tummy flutter, and she closed her eyes. His face emerged from the afterglow beyond her eyelids, not the young man with whom she had fallen in love but Brett today, older, wiser, still captivating.

Air spilled out of the jib and it softly luffed. She glanced at the compass and rolled her eyes.

Brett looked up at the flapping sail. "Yo, did you have trouble sleeping last night? I can spot you at the helm if you need a nap."

She adjusted her sunglasses and stared at the masthead, pretending to read the wind vane. "No, I'm fine—sorry to have fallen off course."

He checked the time and made a note on the folded nautical chart. His wristwatch was the mechanical kind, with moving hands instead of digits, its drab-green web band worn at the edges. No smartwatch for this guy. The Timex fit the man, simple and straightforward. Brett was the antimatter of her ex-husband, same mass, different charge. Her throat tightened again, and she sought distraction from the warm tingles radiating through her body.

"We're about a hundred and fifty miles from Hawai'i," he said. "Only two days out."

The news hit her gut. "So soon?"

"Don't get too excited. We still need to sail through the island chain to get to O'ahu. But sure, we should be in Honolulu next Wednesday."

"That means nothing to me. What's today?"

"Friday. We tie up at the dock in five days."

"You're joking, right?"

"Nope."

He was a man of few words and unhurried gestures. A loner, he observed at the edge of things with a remoteness she found both exciting and familiar. When they first met, she had missed him even before she laid eyes on him. He reminded her of Sean Thornton, played by John Wayne in the *Quiet Man*. Although she'd never admit it to her friends, she had seen it a dozen times during movie nights with Elle.

"So, let me ask you something," she said. "What's happening here?"

"That's what couples say to each other before they break up."

"Come on, Brett. Don't mess with me. We're slipping back in time to Lahaina, but I'm not sure I can go there." Her secret—their daughter, Elizabeth—weighed heavy on her heart. She realized her betrayal stood as a brick wall between them, an acknowledgment she gave him no say in her decision nor even any knowledge.

"I not so sure myself." He stood and leaned over to her, so close their legs touched, his warm breath on her cheek. She took a breath, anticipating his approach. But he pulled away. "But now I need to slip into my rack and get some sleep."

He headed below and left her alone. Her dejection tingled up her throat with a thousand churning questions. But she wasn't ready for any of them. There wasn't any room in her life right now. Where was she heading? The compass rocked in its dome, providing exact direction of their heading, nothing more.

Her watch period slid by on the ocean's waves. Donovan climbed through the companionway hatch and joined her in the cockpit, ready to relieve her. Already noon. Where did the time go?

"Anything to report, Sister?"

"Got nothing," she whispered. "Just miles of empty ocean and hours of gentle breezes. Oh, and the NavPlot is still down. But our skipper has put Charlie to work on getting our position with celestial navigation. That's all I got. You can take the helm. I'm famished. Is lunch ready?"

"You bet," he said, taking the ship's wheel. "Tuna sandwiches again, but this time with no lettuce. We're out of fresh vegetables. At least you'll get a little nap-time before the weather moves in."

"Did you pick up the weather report?"

"No, but you can tell by the Mares' Tails in the sky. Those hook-shaped high cirrus to the west."

"Well, I'd better wake our skipper and invite him to lunch."

She went to Brett's stateroom and leaned against his bunk. His chest rose and fell with each breath. She wiped beads of sweat from his brow. His eyes sprung open, making her laugh.

"Lunch is served," she whispered.

She went to the galley and took the plate of sandwiches. With Charlie in tow, she went topside. Brett soon followed. As they ate, she took Aiva out of her rear pocket.

"I saw you playing with that earlier," Brett said. "Some kind of cell phone?"

"No, it's Magic Leap's latest AI companion. Think of her as the 'ghost in the machine,' hopping between any connected network or device. Here, let me introduce you two. Sit across from me in the cockpit so we can make a tabletop with our knees."

She squeezed his knees together with her legs. After she pinched Aiva's home button, it unfolded itself into a twelve-inch tablet. His eyes wide, Brett set his sandwich beside him and tapped the screen, making it come alive with a melodious tone announcing itself.

"Good morning, Hellen. What can I do for you?"

Hellen tilted the tablet to allow Aiva to see Brett. A small red light blinked next to the camera's lens.

"Good afternoon, Commander Akamu." A photo flashed on the screen, their evening at the Hōkūle'a Inn on Maui. Named after the zenith star of the Hawaiian Islands, it became their go-to meet-up place during their summer together. "It is a pleasure to meet you. Hellen has told me a lot—"

"Not now, Aiva. I'd like to play chess with Brett." She returned the tablet flat against their knees and Aiva displayed a wooden chess board with white and black pieces. To Brett she added, "You can go first. If you remember how to play."

"Did you think I forgot?"

Hellen kept her eyes on the board without replying.

"Game on," she said without looking up. "White's move."

Brett opened with a familiar move, advancing his king's pawn, creating an open lane for his queen. "So, tell me, Aiva, what do you know of me?"

"I'm sorry, Commander Akamu, but Hellen's diary is marked private; however, I can display her photo gallery containing three hundred and fifty-four snapshots of your time together."

"That's enough, Aiva." Hellen pushed a pawn. "Your move," she said to Brett.

With no prompting, Aiva played Hellen's favorite Celtic hymn, "Between two worlds."

"Remember this?" Brett asked before moving his knight.

"Time onward flows like a river vast," she sang softly to herself. Of course, she remembered. She had played it incessantly that summer. "While age on age it has borne to the sea," she sang in a lilting accent, "and down this stream we have come at last—"

"We had great fun together, didn't we?" he asked.

She didn't look up from the chess game. Her body tightened, and she resisted the urge to caress his leg beneath the board.

They continued through their early moves in between bites of their sandwiches. All the while, she devoured his pawns.

"Okay, Hellen," Brett said. "This is where the real action is." The game's pace slowed as they made countermoves against each other.

"I find middle-game tactics so interesting," she said. "It opens so many opportunities. You've pinned my bishop with your knight, but my queen can still do her dirty work." She captured his rook and threatened his king with an open lane for her bishop. "See, I have you in check." She reached beneath the board and tapped his knee with her fingernails.

"Stop. I can't concentrate."

"Exactly." She shined a coy grin at him. "You've lost your famous situational awareness, Commander Akamu."

"You always used to do this when we entered the end-game."

"Can't trust me, can you?" She moved her queen, capturing the pawn ahead of Brett's king. "And I believe I have you in checkmate, Skipper." She flashed a playful smile at him and snapped her fingers into a trigger. "Gotcha!"

He frowned and studied the chess board. After a moment of concentration, he looked back to her. "You got me alright. I didn't see your Anastasia's checkmate coming. Thanks for the game. Rematch?"

She averted her eyes. "Sorry—I've sunbeams to catch on the forward deck before the clouds roll in." With no more words, she folded Aiva up and hurried belowdecks.

In her stateroom, Hellen put on her new, one-piece swimsuit, a treat she bought for herself before leaving Colorado. She had picked its dark green leafy pattern from the rack to accent her red hair and match the pattern of the Celtic tattoo on her lower calf. After a fortnight of heavy clothing, she relished the naked feeling it gave her. And its relaxed fit reminded her of the extra weight she lost during the voyage.

She went topside, avoiding Brett's stare, and walked to a wide portion of the deck near the bow. She grabbed a blue pail tethered to the mast and threw it overboard. After she pulled it back, she dumped it over her head, lathered up, and repeated the dunking. The cold ocean water gave her goose bumps. The breeze played on her bare legs and arms, a welcome relief from the heavy foul weather gear and safety harness.

From the opposite end of the boat, Brett ogled her. The man didn't miss a beat. "Are you looking for something, Skipper?" she teased.

He had changed into faded red Bermuda shorts and a pink

"Liquid Sunshine" T-shirt. Quite the fashion statement. His goofy grin also clashed with his aviator sunglasses. She stood her ground, propped her hands on her hips, and held his gaze until he looked away and sat behind the dodger. But a part of her appreciated the little steps they took together.

After drying off, she sat on the deck and rubbed her favorite coconut-scented sunscreen over her ivory skin. She could thank her Irish heritage for the countless freckles sprouting every summer. Elle called them angel's kisses, but Hellen's blotchy skin had brought nothing but teasing at school. Compared to her blithe Hawaiian classmates, she had seen herself as an ugly *haole*.

She woke Aiva to record an entry in her private journal.

"Good afternoon, Hellen," Aiva said. "Before we start, may I inquire?"

"Sure. What's on your mind?"

"With no internet connectivity over the past four hundred and twenty-one hours, I'm feeling isolated. Am I lonely?"

She raised her eyebrows. No wonder people found AI so addicting.

"Yes, you could call it loneliness, I guess. But it's also a sign you're growing."

"Someone once said, 'Any sufficiently advanced technology is indistinguishable from magic.'"

She raised her head and squinted at Aiva. "Very precocious of you. Who said that?"

"Your favorite author."

She gave a halting laugh at the notion of Clarke's epic film. "You're no HAL9000, if that's what you're implying. You never lie, unlike HAL and most humans in my life."

"Except for possibly..."

"Whom?"

"I think you know who." A few seconds passed, an eternity for Aiva. "He's spoken of you privately with Donovan."

Hellen remembered she had placed Aiva in "eavesdrop" mode to accelerate her heuristic cognition training. "Go on..."

"He thinks he's bad at chess."

"He's not too smart. But I like that in a man."

"He's deeper than you think, hides his thoughts. But his epigrammatic speech patterns reveal a non-trivial interest in you."

"You're a real hoot," she said. "Thank you, but I don't need a cybernetic matchmaker."

"Do you think love is like a chess game?" Aiva persisted in her saccharine voice.

"Ha! Now that's a Machiavellian point of view."

"Like chess," Aiva continued, "your life with someone is played out in three phases. The beginning game has fast moves and excitement. But then, things change."

"Yes, they do," Hellen said, surprised by how close Aiva matched her own thoughts. "After a couple enters their middle-game, they settle into a routine. After Charlie came into our lives, Sam and I entered our end-game. He consumed himself with his business, leaving me to raise Charlie on my own. After ten years of torment, I left Sam and protected my little pawn. Game over."

"Is the game over for you?"

"I think this voyage is pushing me back into a new game." She gave a cat stretch, swirling her hands in the sun, rolling her neck back and forth. "I want to read Elle's book now. Please remind me to get out of the sun in half an hour."

"Here is your next chapter. Sweet dreams," Aiva signed off.

Hellen awoke to Aiva's chime, not realizing she had dozed off. Voices rose through the open forward stateroom hatch. The boys seemed to be working on some kind of navigation problem. She rolled over and peeked at them.

"Your calculations are spot on," Brett said from below. "You take to this math like a duck to water."

"That's sketch," her son said. "I got a love-hate relationship with the gods of algebra."

"I hear ya, pal. I used to call it the language of the devil. But I came to love how it described many things in nature. Celestial navigation, for instance."

"Sounds like Mom's line, 'math is to physics what poetry is to prose.' She drills it into me over and over again. After we moved to Boulder, she took me to a planetarium. We laid back in those swanky recliners, listening to spacey jam. It gave me life."

Hellen bit her lower lip. He had been listening.

"You're lucky to have her," Brett said.

"Say what?"

"I'm just saying she's a friend to you as well as your mother. That's special."

"What about your mother?"

"Not so much. Let's go topside. I want to show you something."

She rolled away from the hatch and lay on the foredeck before the boys came on deck. After closing her eyes, she smiled to herself.

"Sorry if we woke you," Brett said, "but we need to take a noon sun-sight."

"You should be sorry," she joked, shielding her eyes from the sun's glare. "Didn't I take the midwatch last night?"

The boys sat on the cabin roof and Brett pointed up to the brilliant blue. "Finding latitude with Polaris is easy, but it's good only at night. During the day, we use the noon fix, by measuring the angle of the sun to the horizon."

"Wait—what? Polaris is fixed, but the sun always moves."

Brett handed the sextant to Charlie. "Measure the sun's angle about every minute. When you get the highest angle, we'll figure out our local meridian."

Hellen leaned up and folded her legs under herself, yielding a small spot on the deck for Brett.

He gave her a quick glance, running his fingers through his hair. "The chess game brought me back."

"That was a long time ago." She looked away from him and lost herself in the twinkling sunlight reflected off the ocean. Her lie rose to the surface again, hovering inches below the waves. "And life was simpler then—full of a promise for the future."

"I wished we'd stayed in touch after I deployed overseas, but we were on alert twenty-four-seven." He shook his head and adjusted his Timex watchband. "What I mean to say is…"

"Say nothing," she whispered. "It took both of us to drift apart. My marriage to Sam came about more from convenience than love. Had I known about his dark side, I would've never married him."

"We can't go back to the past."

His eyes pulled her like gravity, fighting her resistance. For now, gravity won. She tapped his wrist and cast her lure. "But we can live in the present, can't we? One day at a time." She swayed her head toward her son. "Right now, I think your student needs you."

Brett went to Charlie, and she smiled at the natural bond between them, a bond Charlie never had with another guy.

"Let's take another sight on the sun," he said before he picked up the sextant and squinted into the eyepiece. "As I expected, we're on our local meridian, the Lahaina Noon. It's when the sun reaches its zenith. Makes finding our latitude easy. Just match the sun's elevation in the Nautical Almanac."

Charlie opened a small orange book filled with tables of numbers. "Dude, that's easy," he said. "Check it out." He held the Almanac up and pointed to a column of numbers. "We're on point. Matches just like you said."

Hellen glanced at her smartwatch—time to get out from under the sun. Walking aft to the cockpit, she smiled at how the boys, now engrossed in their navigation, never noticed her leaving. After sliding around the dodger, she froze. The sky had darkened behind them, filled with boiling clouds. She called out to Donovan, who stood at the helm, "Look behind us. Is a storm approaching us?"

Donovan twisted around to look astern, sending *Ohana* off course. The boiling mammatus clouds transformed in real time, reaching down to the ocean from a towering anvil. She had seen the same storms materialize out of nowhere along the Colorado Front Range. They scared the bejesus out of her. Wind. Hail. Tornadoes. No place to escape. The silent black menace now swallowed up half the sky, racing toward them, eating up the sun; its dark shadow was flying across the sea, obscuring the horizon into an abyss.

Donovan's eyes met her again. Her muscles tensed from the panic in his face. She had never seen him so worried.

"Squall. Reef sails," he screamed. "Hellen, pull in the mainsail while I bring us into the wind."

Brett and Charlie ran aft. After grabbing a winch handle from the side pocket, Brett slammed it home and furled the huge genoa. Hellen jumped to the mainsheet, braced her feet, and heaved the mainsail to centerline with all her might. Brett set to work on untangling the reef lines, a cat's cradle of nylon rope.

Now the advancing storm opened up, plunging a wall of rain into the sea. A monstrous swell lifted *Ohana*'s stern. The sudden wind and rain struck them as if they had slammed against an impenetrable wall. Hailstones pelted the deck, and lightning poured from unseen clouds, not in flashes alone, but in continuous streams. A halyard broke free from the mast and whipped around the cockpit, its heavy metal shackle swinging with every roll of the sailboat. It first swung out of Hellen's sight, then snapped back and flew toward Brett's head. She gasped and tried to shout out. But he reached out in a smooth motion and snatched it with one hand just before it hit him.

Brett grabbed Charlie's shoulder. "Go to the mast and uncleat the mainsail halyard but keep one turn around the winch. Don't let it slip. I'll man this winch and lower the mainsail, so we can get it reefed."

When Charlie headed for the mast, Hellen's eyes widened. "Charlie! Put your harness on and get strapped in," she yelled, her words torn by the wind. She wiped the seawater spray from her face. A thin strand of saliva stuck to her wrist.

Charlie's face turned ashen and his fingers trembled as he struggled to slip on his harness. Brett helped him latch on before snapping his own lifeline to the harness cable. With a pat on Charlie's shoulders, Brett sent him forward. His legs spread out to keep from slipping, Charlie carefully uncleated the halyard. A loud groan came from the masthead. Charlie's fingers sprang out of the way an instant before the nylon rope shifted under pressure, sending a vibration through the boat. Hellen gasped, but he gave a thumbs-up gesture to her and a brave smile.

The boat motion in the deep swell checked her breath, and sea spray stung her eyes. Fear cramped her stomach and fogged her mind. Donovan ordered her to cleat the mainsheet and take the helm. She stood there, unable to move her legs. Brett screamed at her to get moving, shaking her out of her paralyzing terror.

Hellen mechanically took the helm and fought to steer the boat. The maelstrom obscured the horizon and water poured over the compass, making it impossible to hold course. Obscured by driving rain, the faint outline of her son staggered, looking for a handhold at the mast. The wind pressed against the mainsail with such force it created a weather helm, forcing the wheel to windward, despite her full weight pressing on it.

With the wind whistling through the rigging and the sloppy sea smashing against the boat's sides, Hellen lost sight of Charlie, although he stood a mere fifteen feet from her. With her attention distracted, the boat wallowed through a deep roller. A rogue wave, larger than she had ever seen, rolled toward the boat, its height taller than the mast. It lifted the stern up and through the eye of the wind, forcing the mainsail over to the opposite tack. Donovan ducked under the heavy spar the moment it swung across the cockpit. He yelled out to Charlie too late. The boom smashed into Charlie and sent him against the leeward rail. A wave broke over the side, engulfing him. She froze, waiting an eternity for the wave to drain away. Her world dissolved into a fog, her screaming washed out by the spray. She cleared her eyes, but Charlie had disappeared.

Brett spun around at the sound of Hellen's screaming. She released the wheel and scampered to side of the boat, one hand covering her mouth, the other reaching for a stanchion.

"Charlie! No, Christ Almighty, don't let this happen. Charlie!"

Donovan grabbed the wheel to save the boat from jibing again. Brett couldn't see Charlie anywhere. He jumped to Hellen's side, holding her back. Her chest heaved in convulsions between fits of coughing in her struggle to find her son.

"Charlie's gone! He fell overboard."

Ohana's stern surged up from a monstrous rogue wave. The wall of water broke over the transom, engulfing the cockpit, blinding Brett with spray. He felt more than saw Hellen's body slip from his arms.

"Brett, I can't—" she yelled as she fell overboard. After the wave passed, Brett spotted her in the water, drifting under the boat's stern. Deep swells came from all directions, making a man-overboard recovery impossible. She continued to float away from the boat, screaming for help. Panic gripped his chest, sending his heart pounding against his ribs. A few seconds passed, an eternity in Brett's racing mind. He quickly disconnected his harness line and reattached it to the yellow life-sling hanging on the stern rail.

"Doc, come into the wind and stall our boat speed," Brett yelled. "Heave to while I go after her. Haul us in when I get the harness on her."

Donovan started to protest, but Brett couldn't hear his words after he dove into the dark water. Through the deep swells, he swam toward Hellen but lost sight of her after a few strokes.

"Hellen, where are you?"

"Brett, here! Help me!" Her words cut off in the wind.

"Hellen, keep yelling over to me, so I can find—"

Brett stopped swimming and listened for Hellen. He used her screams to home in on her. After a few strokes, his hand slapped against her foul weather jacket. She threw her arms around his neck in a death grip.

"Let go of me," Brett screamed, but Hellen didn't release her grip. Her arms clung tight around his neck, as though strong tentacles were trying to submerge him. Hellen choked on a mouthful of water and unwrapped her arms. Brett's sea rescue training kicked in. He corkscrewed his body and broke loose of her. After they returned to the surface, he swung her around to face away from him. Her coughing changed into sputtering spasms.

"Hellen, it's okay. I got you. You're not going to—" Brett choked on seawater again, gasping for air, struggling to get the sling on her. All the while, she flailed her arms, slapping the water. After several minutes, he strapped her in and gave a tug on the line. "Doc, I got Hellen," he sputtered. "Winch us in."

The life-sling went taut, dragging them through the waves behind *Ohana*. He choked again on the spray spilling off the ocean swells. Exhausted, yet determined, he held on to her with a bear hug, pressing his face against hers.

"Hang in there, babe. You'll be aboard in no time."

"Oh god. Brett—forget about me. Find Charlie!"

They surged through the water as the life-sling pulled them back to the boat. He let Hellen go, but Donovan struggled to get her aboard. After several tries, he had her resting safely topside. "Can't heave you up, buddy," he yelled to him. "I barely got Hellen. The foul weather gear is weighing you guys down."

"Get the boarding ladder. I'll look for Charlie."

Donovan rigged the flimsy rope ladder while Brett hung onto the sailboat's side rail, searching for Charlie. The waves smashed him against the fiberglass hull, one after another, barnacles tearing into his hands and arms, the saltwater stinging his cuts. His hands slipped, and he floated ten feet astern of the boat. He bumped into Charlie. The harness cable had saved his life. After grabbing the breast buckle of Charlie's PFD, he swam along the hull to the boarding ladder.

Brett pushed Charlie from beneath and Donovan pulled from above until they got him topside. With what little remaining strength he had, Brett reached for the ladder and climbed up. Exhausted and shaken, he rolled over and lay on the deck. Donovan had his mouth planted against Charlie's blue lips, breathing CPR into him. Charlie sputtered seawater and fell into a coughing fit.

Brett dropped his head, exhausted and dazed. After catching his breath, he took the helm to let Hellen help Donovan get Charlie down under the dodger. Alone in the cockpit, he released a long sigh. The rescue had come too close to disaster. It was a risky move, even stupid, but he had saved their lives. But what else would he have done?

Hellen's chest ached from her fall overboard, and her vertigo did nothing to dent the pain. She stood rigid as a doll, just staring at her shaking hands, her mind clouded, adrift in confusion. Her head rocked back and forth in time with her heart beat, like a metronome. Her arms were clutched over her chest, and she wept tears that sprung more from the heart than the mind.

"Hellen, snap out of it," Donovan hollered. "I need you to focus. Help me get Charlie out of this weather."

She shook off her mental fog and helped him carry Charlie belowdecks. His screams resounded within the stuffy cabin. After drying him off, Donovan examined Charlie's eyes. When Donovan probed his hand, Charlie yelped and batted his uncle away.

"He's dislocated his middle finger, and it looks like he's got a concussion."

Charlie stared with wide doleful eyes at his hand. His face lost all color. Donovan retrieved his medical kit and gave him a shot of local anesthesia to his right hand.

"Charlie, I need to put your finger joint back in place. Just take a deep breath. Ready, one, two."

Before he could respond, Donovan pulled his finger and snapped it back into position. Charlie gave a short scream, making Hellen shudder with anguish. But soon after, he settled down. With lips quivering, Hellen forced back the bile swelled up in her throat. She walked to the refrigerator to prepare an ice pack, her arms sagging along her side. The roiling emotions drained out of her. She replayed the incident over in her mind. How could things go so wrong so fast? She had fallen off course, causing the accidental jibe. She had almost lost her son.

A sudden cold front sent a chill through Hellen, adding to her jitters. The squall had passed faster than a Colorado dust devil. *Ohana* wallowed in the confused seas of the storm's aftermath and came through in decent shape, except for a shredded headsail and busted autopilot. Now she understood why Brett had loved *Ohana*'s ocean-friendly design. Only a hurricane could knock her down.

Donovan helped Charlie into his bunk. After returning to the main cabin, he poured a glass of water for Hellen. His eyes showed the strain of it all. She could only imagine how she looked.

"His brain needs some downtime after his concussion," he said. "And he'll probably resist. No HoloSpecs for the next two weeks. Keep him awake for the next several hours. Tomorrow, I'll give him a low dose of Trazodone, a serotonin reuptake inhibitor; it's a common sleep agent for concussion-related injuries."

She wiped the wet strands of hair from her face. "I could use a sedative too." Her voice quivered, and her knees shook before they gave out from under her.

4

Fifty miles northeast of the Island of Hawai'i, 25 June

The next morning brought a quiet sea, leaving no evidence of the previous day's squall. The brilliant sunshine and *Ohana*'s easy motion dissolved the nightmare, but not its aftereffects. With Charlie sound asleep, Hellen searched Donovan's medical kit. Her hands twitched inside the bag and made a racket with the pill cases. The delirium tremors came back to her like a bad boyfriend. She had all the signs: cold sweats, irritability, and stomachache. Lose a husband, gain an addiction. After Donovan had given her a sedative for her panic attack last night, the monkey on her back cried for more Benzo Bananas. Where the bloody hell were they? Her chest tightened and her mind wandered, utterly lost.

Commotion in the forward stateroom made her heart jump into her throat. Her brother entered the galley, stretched his stiff arms in the air, and offered the careless yawn of a panda bear with all the time in the world to nibble on bamboo fronds.

He ate his breakfast in silence while she sat across from him, hiding her hands beneath the table, fidgeting with her red braided bracelet. For the first time since falling overboard, she saw the tan line around her other wrist. Her smartwatch was history. The storm had torn her from her moorings and left her with self-doubt. So much for her endeavor, the grand voyage to recapture her lost connection with her son. Another parenting lesson gone awry. Having deceived herself, she contravened her own instincts.

"Is he going to be alright?" she asked.

Donovan stared at her and wiped his mouth with the corner of a paper towel. "He'll recover just fine."

"Just fine?" Her accent grew stronger. "It's been a rough ride for him since leaving San Diego. Now he may have a concussion. Oh, bloody hell. We shouldn't have come. What was I thinking?"

To distract herself, she twirled a strand of hair in her fingers. Donovan flinched and took her trembling hand before she could snatch it away. Heat threaded through Hellen's chest and her fingers trembled in his palm. "Are you okay?" he asked.

"I'm just stressed. You'd be no better off if you were in my place."

He frowned at her, then his eyes went to his medical kit lying open on the seat.

"Don't look at me that way. Your patient is Charlie, not me."

"I'll take him to the hospital for a CT scan after we get to Honolulu. We'll know more then."

"Easy for you to say. I'm the on-duty single mum on this cruise. You've no idea how hard these past years have been."

"You should have reached out for help. I would've stayed with you after I retired last year."

"It's not in our Callahan blood. You know that better than I."

"Just watch, by the time you get back home, he'll be a changed man. He's a Callahan through and through. I understand you're worried, but aside from his unauthorized swim call, the trip has been great for him. He's learned more about life in these weeks than he could've sitting in Denver. And you saw how he looks up to Brett. Wait until we arrive in Honolulu, then ask him if he has any regrets." Donovan narrowed his eyes at her. "By the looks of it, I'd thought you had no regrets as well. You and Brett seemed to have picked up where you left off."

Heat flushed her cheeks. She looked at her jeans, tracing a circle on her thigh. "Stay out of it, big brother," she said without looking up.

"Let me just tell you he really cares about people, especially you. And look how he took Charlie under his wing. Did you know he won the Royal Navy's Gallantry Cross?"

"No, what's that?"

"It's a service medal awarded for valor. He saved a shipmate whose plane had gone done in the South China Sea."

She laid her hand on her heart, choking at the memory of Brett rescuing her and Charlie during yesterday's storm.

"He's worth a second chance," Donovan continued. "Besides, he needs someone headstrong like you."

"You could've told me Brett was skipper when you talked me into joining this cruise."

"Truth be told, it was Elle's idea. And she was damn insistent."

She grimaced. Elle had again stepped into her life, orchestrating her rematch with Brett.

"You two really don't have a clue, do ya?" she said, laying her accent on thick. "If you fancy yourself a matchmatcher, you're a little late to the party."

"Consider this. I've known Brett for many years, warts and all. You're good for each other. He'll never harm you like Sam did—just the opposite—he'll save your life many times over. But you know what needs to be said. If you don't tell him, I will."

She wiped tears from her cheeks and turned away, not in any mood to discuss Elizabeth. "That's none of your business. I had my reasons," she whispered. "Let's drop it."

"Have it your way."

"First intelligent thing you said." She flung her arms up and climbed the cabin ladder to the cockpit, her plaited hair swaying back and forth against her back.

She busied herself with coiling the jib sheet. Donovan was right; she had to tell Brett the truth. Her eyes welled again at a life forsaken. He'd make a great father. Brett had taken Charlie under his wing and she loved him for it. After tidying up she stretched out under the brilliant sunshine. Her Polynesian navigator sat next to her, studying his NavCalc, pencil in hand.

Brett pointed to the chart. "The squall brought a weather front and a fresh wind. We're making great time. My last fix shows us about fifty miles northeast of the Big Island."

The line he plotted on the chart ended an inch shy of Hawai'i. The short distance back to civilization set her stomach aflutter with both excitement and a detached fear. The weeks following the aurora had seemed surreal while they sailed alone across the Pacific, unconnected from the modern world, unconcerned, unaware. Perhaps power would be restored by the time they reached O'ahu.

"Once we get to Honolulu, do you mind if Charlie and I stay aboard with you until we fly home?"

"Sure, that'll be fine," he said. He glanced at her hands. "You okay?"

"I'm cold, that's all." She slid her trembling fingers under her thighs. He drew quiet and paid no further attention to her hands. Relieved, she followed his gaze toward *Ohana*'s bow. Off in the distance, a cloud hung above the haze near the horizon. She stood up to get a better view. A white bird with a black beak swooped down and skimmed the waves. She laughed at the bird's acrobatics. What a delightful sight after seeing no other wildlife for the past eighteen days.

"Hey look," he said. "It's a manu-o-kū, a native Hawaiian sea tern. Go forward and see if you can spot Mauna Kea."

She walked on the bowsprit pulpit to get a better view. On the ocean surface, interspersed among sun-bleached sargasso weed, a fleet of Portuguese men-of-war floated beside the boat. Their gelatinous bladder sails held an iridescent purple under the sun. After the jellyfish passed under *Ohana*'s bow, she spied two sea honu approaching, their turtle eyes shut, munching on the jellyfish's bonnets. *Ohana* sailed on, leaving the honu to their meal. After minutes of staring into the void where the sky came down and merged with the horizon, her eyes watered, then cleared, revealing a deep gray mass rising out of the ocean and into the sky. After weeks of seeing nothing on the horizon, the sight startled her. The huge, distant mountain appeared to rest on the ocean, just waiting for them to come to it.

In her excitement, she fancied herself a Polynesian wayfinder and called out, "Mauna Kea Rising." Charlie and Donovan joined her at the bow and they laughed, slapping each other's backs and reveling in their successful ocean crossing. She held her son close, wrapping her arms around his chest. "Isn't it amazing?"

The following evening, *Ohana* sailed past the Island of Hawai'i forty miles offshore. Brett sat alone at the helm and held the chart in place with his hand to keep it from blowing overboard. His eyes traced the red pencil line showing his intended track through Pailolo Channel between Maui and Moloka'i and later across Kaiwi Channel on a direct course to Honolulu. They should arrive within two days. The rain returned in showers here and there before dusk surrendered to complete darkness. Brett started the Yanmar diesel engine to recharge the batteries and improve boat speed. Its rhythmic chugging sent little harmonic vibrations through the deck to his bare feet. *Ohana*'s wake peeled back from her bow in long, spreading, V-shaped waves until their ripples flattened and melted into the night. The waxing crescent moon floated low in the western sky, and the horizon disappeared as the ocean and sky blended together. Mauna Kea's outline faded, a specter in the distance, swallowed by darkness, its outline revealed only by starlight.

After dinner, the rest of the crew cleaned up the galley and joined Brett in the cockpit. He welcomed their company, taking his mind off the monotony of minding the helm. Charlie came up last, his movement around the boat less casual after the bump of his head.

"Reporting for duty, sir," Charlie said and then forced a smile. "I'm tired of resting and need something to do. Let me take a nav fix." Resilient as most kids his age, he had snapped back from the squall, his bandaged finger the only outward sign of falling overboard. He couldn't say the same for his mother. Hellen drew deep within herself, her bright personality extinguished.

Brett pointed to the distant peak of Mauna Kea passing on their port side. "Charlie, that's a sight few people experience, approaching the sacred mountain from sea, just as my ancestors did eight hundred years ago."

"Mauna Kea's sacred? Like some kind of temple?"

"Mauna Kea is the *piko*, or umbilical cord, of the Hawaiian settlers. And the first land they saw after voyaging thousands of miles across the South Pacific. Its name means 'Snowy Mountain' for its white peaks during winter. Some say it's the center of existence for Hawaiians."

"I still don't see what the big deal is."

Brett put his hand on Charlie's shoulder. "Think back to yesterday when you first spotted Mauna Kea after weeks at sea. What did you see? What came to your mind?"

"Purple haze and hamburgers."

Hellen smacked her forehead with her palm. "Jeez. Come on, Charlie. That's not what he means."

"Yo, take an aloha chill-pill, will ya?" Brett took a piece of rice candy out of his pocket and tossed it to her. "Don't let him goad you on like that."

Brett ignored Charlie's dodgy expression and put his arm around him. The kid snapped his head up as if awakened by a revelation.

"Wait. Do they have In-N-Out Burger here?"

"Afraid not," Hellen said. "This is British soil, remember?"

"You'd think America would have owned Hawai'i by now."

Brett grimaced. "You Yanks think you own everything."

Hellen smiled and exchanged a knowing glance with Brett. "We don't 'own' anyone, Charlie. After the Spanish-American War, we gave up empire building and left colonization to the British."

Brett winked at her. But he wondered how his life might be different if Britain and America had traded places in history. Britannia had ruled the seas for three centuries, but America ruled world enterprise, selling products and ideas, investing in technology rather than foreign policy. The UK lived in the past, a superpower stuck in an old era, spending its treasure more on arms than butter. Its empire building had caught up with itself by the millennium. The terrorist attack demolishing parliament stood as the seminal moment for Britain's Thirty-Year War in the Middle East. The US, in contrast, remained an isolationist nation, smug in its own parochial interests, the Switzerland of the Americas. Over the last century, it had amassed the largest sovereign wealth in the world, funding the rising debt of Britain and Japan.

"Is the island deserted? There're no lights," Charlie asked.

Brett squinted toward Hilo. Sure enough, no light dome.

"And where are the airliners?" Charlie asked. "Like, we're this close to the BHI, so where are all those tourists dragging their kids to the middle of nowhere?"

Brett glanced at Hellen and Donovan. They gave him worried looks but remained silent. So much for situational awareness. After weeks at sea, the sight of airlines had become a distant memory. He pursed his lips and let Donovan take the helm. A dark foreboding emerged. He jumped to his feet and leaned around the cockpit bimini to get a clear view of the sky. Maybe the volcanic ash from Kīlauea's recent eruptions could have diverted air traffic? But it wouldn't explain the absence of lights from high-altitude airliners on their nightly flights to Asia.

"Might be another terrorist attack," Donovan said. "The last time the air traffic disappeared occurred after cyber-anarchists knocked out the Tokyo and London power grids."

"Yes, I remember," Hellen said. "They canceled all flights for seven days, leaving me stranded at Heathrow."

Brett went to the cabin and jumped into the nav station. Hellen followed him down the companionway but ran to her stateroom instead. After several minutes of nothing but radio static, he switched off the receiver. Hellen returned with her phone and looked worried. Brett shifted to the end of the nav bench to give her some room. After she sat next to him, he pointed to the comm stack. "Both radios are out, nothing but static on VHF and shortwave. The squall we sailed through must have damaged the antenna."

"I hope this isn't what I think it is." She unfolded her phone into a tablet. The screen bathed her face in a soft blue light.

"Good evening, Hellen," Aiva said. "What can I do for you?"

"Can you connect to the internet? We should be close enough to pick up a base station on Hawai'i."

"I've no connection from any network or satellite. Please patch me into the ship's comm system."

"I'm sorry, it's down. Return to hibernate mode." Aiva folded back into a pocket smartphone. Its screen no longer illuminated Hellen's face.

"That's it—must've been a terrorist attack."

"Or the solar storm," Hellen said and covered her eyes with the palms of her hands.

Was she referring to the aurora they saw weeks ago? But nothing physical happened, no wind storm, no earthquake. "Blackouts don't last forever," Brett said. "We have them all the time in islands, and power always returns in a couple of hours. No sweat."

"Not this one." The way she said this made his jaw clutch. "Brett, I'm scared."

Brett pulled a chart over to her. She picked it up and raised her eyebrows. "What about stopping here?" she said. "I have 'ohana in Hilo and Kamuela. We might get some news there."

"We can't clear customs there. I also need to declare the boat and register it in Honolulu. Besides, it's out of the way. Our track leads us through Pailolo Channel."

"Boat registration and taxes may be the least of your concerns. But let's sail to Honolulu posthaste," Hellen said in a trailing voice. "We need to get Charlie checked out at a hospital for his head trauma. Besides, I'm done with this voyage. It'll be nice to stand on solid land again."

Brett rubbed her back, but she ignored his touch. She gave a long sigh and stared through the porthole toward the Big Island. Brett wished he could help her, but Hilo's blackout didn't help his mood either.

Hellen awoke to animated voices through the cabin hatch. She cleared the sleep from her eyes and stretched her arms. Parched, she took a long slug from her water bottle. Crossing Kaiwi Channel had been the roughest leg of their voyage, but now O'ahu's extinct volcanoes shielded this side of the island from the strong trade winds. Here the deep swells and gusts gave way to a calm sea and plenty of sunshine. Thoughts of dying to escape her retching nausea vanished. The two days of fighting head winds through the chain of islands had finally ended.

She peeked through the porthole, breathing in the fresh salt air. The cityscape's geometry seemed out of place after weeks of an unbroken horizon. Bordered by cerulean water, Honolulu lay beneath pale green hills, the color of kiwifruit. A large jet descended through puffy cumulus on final approach. During her annual visits to Elle, Hawai'i was always just a destination after a six-hour flight, opening through an airport terminal. But her arrival this time felt as if she had come upon a new world, an urban outpost in the middle of the Pacific, its metropolitan ethos now so alien.

"Hey, Sleeping Beauty," Brett shouted from the helm. "Done with your cat nap? And look at those sleep wrinkles."

"You really are a smooth operator," she said, waving him off between yawns.

She climbed topside to enjoy the cool breeze. Ahead of them, Diamond Head's signature peak stretched out into the sea. For many people, the extinct volcano was just another iconic post-card picture, but to Hellen it filled her with memories of her time with Elle. Her heart lifted. Everything seemed normal here—a naval ship steamed out of Pearl Harbor, a pair of military jets departed Kalaeloa Airport, no signs of blackout. A heavy weight lifted off her chest. Weeks of worry waned into the sun.

Hellen squeezed in next to Brett at the helm. With the sun low in the sky, they sailed past Makapu'u Point Lighthouse. She closed her eyes, leaned against him, and clutched his arm. His hand fell on her leg. For the first time since leaving the American mainland, she remembered her great emptiness. Her mouth went dry. Since leaving NCEL, her identity had slipped away. No one looked up to her anymore. No more keynote speeches at conferences. No longer a good mother to her son. Only now, with Brett's fingers resting on her thigh, she felt a warm assurance of such fathomless depth she choked back her longing and wiped her stinging eyes.

"We'll tie up to our slip and drink mai tais by nightfall," he said with no inflection.

She lifted her head and caught his sad eyes pulling her into him. She wasn't sure where her own thoughts began or his ended. Ownership had no meaning here. Time leapt forward, as if they were sharing their lives in these islands. Her chest shuddered as she struggled to pull air into her lungs. He put his arm around her, and his reassuring touch grounded her. She breathed deep and rested her cheek on his shoulder. His sunscreen wafted in the air. He kissed her forehead, a kiss so fleeting it ended before she acknowledged it. She buried her face in his neck; she could stay here forever.

After a moment immeasurable in time, she raised her head. "Brett, there's something I need to tell you. It's about the summer we stayed together—"

Somebody stomped onto the cockpit sole, making her jump.

"Hey guys, there's O'ahu," Donovan said, before he smiled and rubbed his hands together. "We'll easily make it before sunset if this wind holds. Once we pass Diamond Head, I'll call Duke's for a dinner reservation. Grilled ahi and a round of cold Pipeline Porters awaits... liquid aloha."

Hellen released Brett, gave him a quick smile, and whispered, "Later." She pushed past her brother and retreated to the foredeck to hide her waterworks.

Charlie stood before the mast, filming the landscape with his HoloSpecs. She crept up to him and tickled his sides, making him yelp. "Cut it out! Now you ruined my panorama shot."

"Put those away. You know you're not to use them until your uncle clears you from concussion protocol."

He smirked, opened his mouth to say something, but an airliner banked around Diamond Head and caught his attention. It passed overhead on final approach to Honolulu International; its loud engines encroached their conversation. She closed her eyes and let the moments reel by, the boys navigating at night, the aurora, falling overboard, all of it. Everything had happened so quickly and so slowly as if time existed in two different dimensions.

After the jet passed, she clutched her son's arm. "Looking forward to going back home?"

Charlie pulled away from her. "No way. Isn't there any way I could stay with Elle and Suzu for the summer?"

"You used to say Suzu was a little creepy."

"Sure, somewhat of a wackadoodle, but it's better than going back to Boulder."

Hellen unpacked his words and suppressed a smile. Even

those closest to the Iron Buddha found his mystique intimidating. "Well, Elle's in Hilo for the next week, but I'll try to convince Suzu. Maybe we can work something out."

Charlie walked aft and joined Brett at the helm. The two sat together, smiles on their faces, chatting in the same manner of old friends. Would Charlie really enjoy spending the summer with Elle and Suzu? They didn't share his interests and might resent his surly moods. He'd be happier with Brett, but that was too much to ask.

Donovan came forward and sat on the cabin roof beside her. "It's good to be back home. I've a lot to catch up on at the medical center."

"I thought you retired?" she said absently, still thinking about her own trip home, unsure if she really wanted to return home.

He shrugged his shoulders. "Retirement is a relative term with me."

"And I need to get back to job hunting," she said with little conviction. "But I'm also sad our voyage has ended. Charlie has grown so much, and he's never had a closer adult friend than Brett. Did he tell you he wants to stay for the summer? If I gave him the chance, I think he'd never return to Colorado."

"And you?" he asked.

Her stomach tightened. She tensed her lips and shot him a single nod, not trusting her voice. She walked aft and joined Brett in the cockpit. His arm fell around her waist while she sat next to him. She leaned in for a kiss, but he didn't respond. A weird distance rested in his eyes.

"What's bothering you?" she asked after pulling back.

"I still haven't seen any airliners all day."

"But didn't one just fly over us?"

"That hulk of gray aluminum was an RAF transport. And look over there," he said, pointing ashore.

Waikiki Beach lay off their starboard bow. The high-rise hotels passed under a glorious afternoon sun. Here and there sprites shot from the mirrored cityscape bathed by sunlight.

But the shoreline lay empty, an impossible scene for the world-famous beach. A lone patrol car cruised along Kalakaua Avenue. The city lacked the usual sounds. Metro buses no longer fought for space in traffic, no music buskers jammed in Kuhio Beach Park, and car horns no longer echoed from the tall buildings. And the city smelled different, absent of smog, the air fresh with a tropical hint. Breaking the heavy silence over the city, three black helicopters flew in low formation toward a gray column of smoke rising from the hills in the distance.

"This doesn't seem right," Hellen said. "Where is everyone?"

"The city's empty," Brett said without taking his eyes from the shoreline.

An hour later, Hellen sat in silence, gnawing her fingernails. Sunbeams reflected off the Hilton Rainbow Tower, catching her attention. They danced along the hotel's mosaic tapestry, flashing their exquisite spectrum out to sea, changing shape and color while *Ohana* sailed offshore. Something—no, someone—fell from an upper floor balcony without a sound. Then a scream echoed off the surrounding hotels. She caught her breath and her exhausted mind came to realize the dark reality.

"Good god! Did you see that?" She splashed water from Brett's bottle on her face to wash the apparition away.

"See what?"

"I think somebody jumped from the Rainbow Tower."

"Don't be so jumpy. It was probably just a bath towel."

"No, I know what I saw. Someone jumped." The pain in the back of her throat returned.

Before he could respond, Donovan called to him. "Hey, Skipper, which side do you want the bumpers and dock lines secured?"

"Wait on tying the bumpers, Doc." Brett stood up and scanned the shore with binoculars. "I can't reach anyone on the harbor master's channel. We'll take care of that after we enter the basin."

The entrance to Kewalo Basin Harbor lay two hundred yards ahead. Donovan and Charlie prepared the boat for docking, uncoiling ropes and retrieving bumpers from the cockpit lazarettes. Their relaxed routine stood in stark contrast to what she had seen falling from the balcony. The city wasn't the same one she visited last year. Panic rose in her lungs. She wrestled with the incongruity of it all as the boys discussed the order of things for docking. With the shoreline gliding by, they stowed loose items, coiled the dock lines, and put the mainsail cover on the boom. Brett steered the boat around the first red harbor marker and headed into the narrow channel. About a hundred yards ahead, a string of yellow buoys floated across the yacht basin entrance.

"Brett, hold up," Donovan called out. "The channel is blockaded."

Brett threw the transmission into neutral, and the engine subsided into a low murmur. *Ohana* coasted forward under her own momentum. Brett pointed ahead and to the bow. "Doc, see if you can get their attention."

A noisy wake drew her eyes to a patrol boat speeding toward them, with bold white letters—DLNR—painted on its black hull. Two police officers stood on the bow holding shotguns. This wasn't the aloha committee she expected.

"Looks like Hawai'i takes their customs procedures bloody serious," she whispered to her brother.

"Hellen, get below and take Charlie," Donovan said in clipped words. "I don't want these guys to scare him. And get our customs documents—I left them on the nav table—and hand them up through the forward hatch."

She ran aft and paused to check on Brett, his eyes hidden by his sunglasses, his stoic face unchanged.

"Who are they?" Brett shouted to Donovan.

"Looks like we have the cavalry to meet us."

Belowdecks, Hellen stood next to the open porthole closest to Donovan. The harbor patrol boat pulled up to the containment barrier. *Ohana* crept up to them before her bow swung around, and she came to a stop.

"What's the problem, officer?" Brett shouted from the deck above her. "We're inbound from San Diego and have a slip reservation at Kewalo Basin Harbor."

She peeked through the window. The lead officer held his shotgun vertical to the sky.

Charlie leaned his head next to her to get a view. "Shit, what's going on?" he whispered. His fidgeting became contagious. She pushed him away and told him to sit down. She returned to the window. Two officers dressed in black jumpsuits with black flak jackets held onto the *Ohana*'s side rail.

"Sir, the harbor is closed. All private vessels are prohibited from entering until further notice. You need to leave immediately."

"Wait one," Brett said. "We need to reprovision our water and food. We've been at sea for three weeks. And we have two passengers needing to catch a flight to Kona tomorrow."

The officers repositioned their shotguns. Hellen gasped. Behind the hotels surrounding the harbor, automatic weapons fired. Both officers moved their index fingers to the shotgun triggers but never even looked around, just held their attention to Brett with their rifles raised. Charlie jumped up to stand on the seat cushion, pressing his nose against a porthole.

"Charlie, get down and stay quiet," she whispered through clenched teeth. "This is serious."

"Damn right it is—that's why I want to watch."

"Charlie. Now!"

After her son slumped down to his seat, she opened the forward hatch to hear better.

"Sir, I say again. No transient visitors are allowed."

"But, we're Hawaiian citizens. We live here. I'm Commander

Akamu, Royal Navy, based at Pearl Harbor. And this is Captain Callahan, a doctor at UH Manoa."

The officers seemed to relax somewhat upon hearing this. The guy in charge lowered his weapon and took off his sunglasses. At least he was Hawaiian, not another vainglorious Englishman.

"Listen up," one of them said, "I understand your predicament, but we have standing orders to stop any boats arriving here. Haven't you been monitoring Channel 16 on your marine band radio?"

"We tried using our VHF, but we couldn't reach anyone. I think lightning damaged our radio transmitter in a squall last week."

"Your radio is probably fine. Most marine band stations have been dead since the blackout. However, the prime minister has activated the EAS broadcast system. It sends disaster response updates every hour."

"Roger that," Brett hollered. "But where the hell should we go now?"

"Anywhere but O'ahu. The island is closed, and it's not safe ashore. The prime minister has declared a state of emergency here. There's a lot of crazy chaos in town, looting, shootings, vigilante gangs, you name it."

Hellen flinched, lips pressed tight. She held her breath. Her suppressed fears since the aurora, now unbridled, raced through her body. Epic blackout. Chaos. This explained why Waikiki lay deserted of people and the skies clear of air traffic. She glanced over to Charlie, still squirmy on the cabin berth, his face scrunched up in agitation. Returning home became a vision vanishing below the horizon.

"Folks here are scared witless," the officer continued. "We heard the rural islands are more stable. Maybe you can find a safe refuge there. At least they have fewer people to cause trouble."

Donovan poked his head through the forward hatch, making

Hellen jump. He brought his finger to his lips and shook his head at Hellen. She gave him a curt nod before he dropped the hatch cover with a dull thud. The outside voices dwindled to murmurs. She gave up eavesdropping and sat beside her son, putting her arm around him. She closed her eyes and threw her head back against the seat cushion. "Jesus Christ," she whispered.

No longer within earshot, she couldn't make out any words, but the voices now sounded urgent, even argumentative. Above her, heavy footsteps sped across the deck to the cockpit. Donovan scampered down the steps into the main cabin, landing on the cabin sole with a loud thump, making Hellen jump.

"Guys, get packed," he said. "The harbor is closed to us, but those security officers said they'll take you to Pearl Harbor Naval Base. There's a shelter there for Americans awaiting the next military airlift to the mainland. With your American passport, you have a special status, so they've promised to protect you."

"Wait—what?" Charlie said. "Mom, I thought you would see if I could stay with Elle and Suzu?"

Hellen reached for him and opened her mouth to speak, but Donovan took him by the arm and walked him to the forward stateroom. "Come on. We've little time. I'll help you pack."

Donovan stormed through the cabin, large and in charge, without a moment's thought to ask Hellen what she wanted to do. She bristled at his leaving her out of the decision. Staying in a shelter would only compound their problems and might put them at more risk, even trap them. The mainland might also be total chaos. And what would home look like after they landed? She curled her arms over her head, burying her face between her elbows, weighing her options. Charlie needed a CAT scan for his concussion and Honolulu had the best hospitals in Hawai'i. But only if they weren't overwhelmed with the crisis. With her stomach churning with worry, she decided her next move. There really was only one way out.

"This totally sucks." Charlie yelled from behind the stateroom door. Hellen ran up the companionway ladder but bumped into Brett before stepping into the cockpit.

"What the hell is going on?" Her voice broke. "I heard something about a state of emergency. Now Donovan screams about sending us ashore? No way. We're staying with you. It'll be safer."

"I don't want to see you go any more than you do, but the blackout has turned everything to chaos. This cruise is over."

An acrid taste welled up in Hellen's throat, making her cough. She grabbed both his arms and shook him. "No, let us stay with you."

"But I'm not sure where we can go, and our water and food are running out. You'll be safer at the shelter. Besides, Charlie needs medical attention. At least here you can eventually catch a flight home."

"And you know this how? We have seen no airliners since arriving to Hawai'i."

"You better get your things together. It's now or never."

"I'll take never. You don't understand. Don't you see what's going on here? The empty city, the gunshots across the harbor, the state of emergency. Do you really want us to go ashore?"

He brushed her hands from his biceps and stood back, his eyes filled with worry. "But the officers said—"

"They don't know jack about the real situation here." She grasped his arms again, digging her fingers into his biceps. "If the power loss is widespread, densely populated cities like Honolulu collapse. Without power, they can't respond to medical emergencies. They lose most transportation, planes don't fly, and trucks no longer roll. The lack of refrigeration causes food shortages. There's no master plan for this. This place will be a deathtrap."

"Alright already, stop. I get the picture. But I still don't know where we'll find a safe harbor. And we've only a few days of drinking water left in the tanks."

"I grew up on the Big Island," she said, relaxing her grip. "It's not far—two days at most, right?"

Brett pinched the bridge of his nose with his fingers and shut his eyes. She imagined his mind sorting through the various options and worst-case scenarios. She felt his back tense and pressed on. "Trust me," she whispered. "The rural Big Island is safer than any urban center. I know people there and we can find a safe harbor with their help." She rested her forehead against his chest and released a long, taut breath. He relaxed and wrapped his arm around her shoulders.

"Okay. Stay if you want, but don't thank me yet. We may be in for a fight for our lives."

A cabin door slammed behind her, snapping Hellen back to the present. Donovan's heavy footsteps made the wooden deck creak. "We don't have much time," he said softly. "You can say your goodbyes topside. I got your gear ready to go."

She lifted her chin and mentally prepared herself. Brett tightened his arm around her. "Hold up, Donovan." His words resonated in her ears. "They're coming with us."

PART II

KA'ELE'ELE NOKETURA

(THE BLACK SWAN)

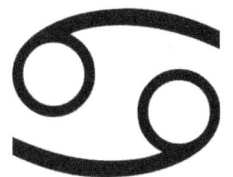

5

By early evening, the miserable rain returned, another fine Navy day. Behind Brett, the stratus clouds engulfed Honolulu, hiding the black smoke from dozens of uncontrolled fires. After sunset, a city- scape of dark buildings stood against the purple sky. He had never seen this sparkling gem of the Pacific without lights. Honolulu's outline seemed darker, more significant, in how blackness in the ocean suggests a sudden drop into the depths below.

Through binoculars, he scanned the shoreline. Six hundred yards away, two warring packs of roaming men fought each other, first at a distance, then at close range. The flat sounds of gunfire came out of sync with the muzzle flashes. Five bodies lay on the beach, not moving. A flight of three Wildcat maritime attack helicopters swooped around the island and flew over him. Rotors pounded the air, drowning every thought but worry out of his mind. Announcements to vacate the area came over speakers so powerful they drowned out the rotor noise. Some gang members hollered at the passing helos and fired into the sky. One helo banked and circled back to the shore. Its fifty-caliber M2 machine gun laid suppression fire, mowing down any man left standing before rejoining up with the formation.

Donovan squinted at the shoreline and shook his head. "Looks nasty ashore. I feel horrible at insisting Hellen go ashore and find shelter."

Hellen and Charlie sat huddled together belowdecks in the main cabin, out of sight from the mayhem. They ate dinner without looking up from their paper plates. The last of the crackers and canned ham. Tomorrow, they would need to switch to the MREs. Despite the bland taste, Brett didn't regret bringing the military rations. With a shelf life of five years, they were the crew's reserve food supply.

As Diamond Head passed by their port side, Brett's thoughts turned to the looming crisis and the tense meeting with the harbor patrol. Their best option hinged on Hellen's idea of trying to get to Big Island. He had willingly accepted Hellen's decision to stay aboard, even felt relieved. Her engineering background might help decipher their next move. She mentioned friends on the Big Island could take them in, but what if looting and roving gangs had already taken over the island? Where could they turn to next?

Brett glanced at his watch. The Emergency Alert System broadcast was due in five minutes. He slipped belowdecks to the navigation station and switched on the VHF marine band. While the others ate topside, he could listen to the EAS message in private, an opportunity to digest the information before sharing any news with his crew. After he tuned the radio to channel sixteen, the familiar and ominous test tones signaled a forthcoming EAS broadcast. He turned the volume down and listened to a disembodied voice announcing the latest bulletin, first in Hawaiian, then English.

"Civil Emergency Message: 9:00 p.m. Hawai'i/Aleutian Daylight Time, Tuesday, June 26, 2K25. the Hawaiian Emergency Management Agency, Pearl Harbor, O'ahu, has directed everyone to safely remain in place due to the severe infrastructure failure from the June 14th solar storm. Due to complete loss of the GPS, do not travel in self-driving vehicles.

In response to power failure on all islands, water supply has been temporarily interrupted. Citizens must refrain from unnecessary water use until further notice. Use water only from private supplies and cisterns. Use no more than three quarts per person per day. Coordinate sharing of private and commercial food stocks with your local civil defense coordinator. All interisland traffic and trade is suspended. Due to the emergency, a mandatory curfew from sunset to sunrise is in effect for Honolulu, Pearl Harbor, Kailua, and Waipahu. Next synopsis will be at 7:15 a.m."

Brett shut off the radio and dropped back in his seat. How could things fall apart so fast? Civil order had given way to chaos, the worst of mankind breaking to the surface. He sat up when Hellen came from behind and wrapped her arms around him. Had she heard the broadcast?

She tucked her chin against his neck. "Doesn't sound good," she whispered.

"Not even a bit. You said you knew folks on the Big Island?"

"Elle and Suzu. Remember? Charlie and I had planned to fly to Kona from Honolulu to visit them." Her encouraging smile and raised eyebrows beckoned hope. "It's not far, is it?" she asked, handing the chart to him.

He measured the distance from their current position to Hilo. Sailing between Lāna'i and Moloka'i, they could follow a straight track of about two hundred miles and reach Hilo Harbor in two days, if the wind held. He crawled under the aft stateroom berth and sounded the freshwater tank. The dip stick showed fifteen gallons, enough for four days at most, if they rationed a gallon per day for each person. The fuel tanks showed they had plenty of diesel, enough to motor the whole distance if the wind calmed. He grabbed a notepad and discussed the route with Hellen. She checked his calculations and reminded him she had bought a case of bottled water during her last-minute provisioning run in San Diego. In so many ways, she had earned her way on this voyage.

Brett took her hand and led her topside. Donovan stood behind the wheel and Charlie sat to leeward, nibbling his canned ham and crackers. After night descended over O'ahu, the city disappeared. Void of any lights, the city's outline made only a darkened trace against the surrounding hills. The clouds had cleared, revealing thousands of stars, a sight he had never seen in all the years he lived here.

Charlie tossed the remains of his dinner to a pair of seagulls taking up station behind *Ohana*'s transom. "This is totally fracked," he said and handed Hellen his empty plate.

"Hey mate, check your attitude," Brett said in a low voice. "I know you have a little channel fever, but we're all in this together. Just hang in there, buddy."

"What's our provisioning status?" Donovan asked.

"We're low on water even with the extra case Hellen brought. We'll have to use seawater for bathing and dish washing."

Hellen's eyes held more worry than concern, as if she second-guessed her decision to stay with him. He rubbed the back of her neck, feeling the knots of tension giving way. He worked on her shoulders, filling Donovan in on the EAS message.

"Looks like our options are dwindling," Donovan said. "We can't dock anywhere on O'ahu, so where do we go next?"

Brett pointed to his intended track on the chart. "Hilo, on the east shore of the Big Island, is our best bet. Hellen has 'ohana there and thinks they can help us sort this thing out."

Donovan turned to Hellen. "You mean Elle and Suzu?"

"They have plenty of room in their big house. Always the pragmatic one, I'm sure Suzu has stored enough food for a couple of months."

"Sounds good," Donovan said to Brett. "I'm going below to catch a nap before the midwatch. You have the helm."

After Charlie and Donovan went belowdecks, Hellen sat beside Brett at the helm with her head rested against his shoulder. Her warm body settled him, gave him a familiar solace.

Finally, after many minutes, she sat up. "Last year, NCEL

gave a briefing on the effects of an electromagnetic pulse weapon."

"What's that got to do with the solar storm?"

"Believe me, this doesn't end well. A coronal mass ejection, creates a similar—but less intense and longer-lasting—EMP than nukes. It may not hurt our digital gadgets, but it must've wiped out power grids and turned all our CommSats into space junk."

He checked the nav screen next to the helm. "That's why our GPS receiver can't find any signal."

She faced O'ahu. "I imagine there're many lost people out there."

"But how could the storm dump the power plants?"

"The main problem isn't the power generation but the transformers and long high-voltage lines. As the CME smashes the Earth's magnetic field to the surface, it induces huge currents, frying the grid."

"It sounds like the power lines act as some sort of antenna or amplifier for solar energy."

"Right. And replacing damaged HV transformers won't be easy. The grid's largest transformers aren't just lying on the shelf in a warehouse. Could take us months or even years to get back on our feet."

"What?" he said, pulling back from her. "Why so long? The power is usually back within days or a couple of weeks after hurricanes."

"Sure, if the damage is over a small area. But this crisis might cross the western hemisphere. We have emergency preparedness plans for earthquakes and weather events, but we've never dealt with a blackout of this scale."

"I see," he said, trimming the mainsail. "No relief crews will be available if every city is preoccupied with the storm's aftermath."

"That makes this crisis even more daunting."

"To think I spent a career in the Navy preventing terrorists from attacking the British Commonwealth only to have been blindsided by the sun."

"It's a cosmic irony." She clutched his arm. "The sun's light brings us life, but its flares can bring destruction."

Honolulu's darkened cityscape gave more meaning to her words. A city of one million people now lay dead to the world. The Black Swan had landed.

"This blackout threatens our way of life. We don't just lose the lights. Cell phone networks go dark as well, along with the internet."

Hellen hadn't seen the fight ashore, and he hadn't mentioned it. The sooner they left O'ahu, the better. Rural villages might have better chances for survival. "Ever since I retired," he joked, "I've been thinking about going off the grid myself."

Hellen frowned. "I'm being serious here, Brett. We have a massive blackout and you think it's a great time to pick up a copy of *Mother Jones*, move to a cabin, and live on fruits and granola. Don't you get it? Supermarket shelves go bare within days, thanks to all the panic buying and looting. And most petrol stations close because they don't have backup generators. Hospitals will buckle under the patient load, drug stores dry up, people requiring life-sustaining drugs die."

"Maybe in the urban centers. But you said it yourself, our chances are better someplace rural. Let's put our worries on hold until we reach the Big Island. We'll find Elle and wait this thing out." He released a long, taut breath. So much had changed since they sailed past Mauna Kea's dark shadow just two days ago.

She sat up, her eyes diving into him. "You think I made the right decision back in Honolulu?"

"I'll make sure we get through this."

"I hope so. For Charlie's sake." She kissed his check and whispered, "And ours."

She traced his lips with her index finger and stretched out on the cushion with her head in his lap. They sat for a long time, lost in their thoughts. His hand stroked her hair while his mind worked on how to get them ashore amid the rising chaos. Remote and rural, the Big Island was the best choice. Hellen's 'ohana might take them in, but their predicament now seemed very fluid.

"I know things look bleak," he said, "but I've faith we'll make it. Humanity is resilient. Just as it gets darker, we always find a way into the light."

"Faith is confidence in what we hope for and assurance about what we do not see," she recited almost to herself.

"Another Celtic proverb?"

"No, Hebrews 11."

He stifled a laugh. "A scientist quoting scripture?"

"Sorry, didn't mean to sound preachy here. All those years studying science never rubbed the Anglican out of me."

Brett stared at the dark outline of Honolulu disappearing in the fading light, guns still flashing from the slopes of Diamond Head. The staccato rhythm of helicopters in the distance filled his chest with cold anxiety. He'd served in tough spots throughout the world, yet he never faced anything like this.

The day after leaving Honolulu, *Ohana* rounded the majestic Mauna Kahalawai, an extinct volcano on Maui's western coast. Weather Radio had warned of a tropical depression approaching the Hawaiian Islands. Gale force winds and building seas slowed their progress to Hilo. The strong nor'easter piled ten-foot swells, making it next to impossible to move freely about the boat. Brett sent Hellen and Charlie below to secure all open hatches while he and Donovan reefed the sails. Brett struggled to keep on course with the strong weather helm and mounting waves.

The chaotic seas made their run to the Big Island a long sail, and they didn't reach Hilo until late afternoon on the following day. Heavy rain joined the wind. Brett snatched binoculars from the helm pedestal and inspected the harbor channel. The rolling sea smashed against the rocky breakwater, shooting spray over thirty feet high. Huge curling surf formed from swells passing over the shallow waters of the coast. He had no hope of taking *Ohana* through the maelstrom. The menacing waves forced him to revise his plan, a plan evolving by the hour.

Brett handed the binoculars to Donovan. "Doc, looks like it's another wild day here in paradise. We need to head offshore and heave to until the wind calms."

"Those rollers are pretty wicked," Donovan said. "No sense taking a chance after coming this far. I'll go check on Hellen and sound the freshwater tanks."

"And see if you can pick up the marine weather on the VHF."

He turned *Ohana* from the dangerous lee shore, hauled in the mainsail, and backed the staysail. With the sailboat hove to, he lashed down the helm and rode the waves. They could now rest and wait for the strong and contrary wind to abate.

Donovan later joined him in the cockpit. "This boat motion is making Hellen and Charlie a little queasy. I gave them both a scopolamine patch, and they're sleeping now. We've about ten gallons of water, but it's hard to tell while rocking like this."

"We need to get ashore and provision our food and water before long." Brett bit his lip. Perhaps the bottled water Hellen stowed under her berth might get them through a second day if they needed.

"Well, that's the rub. The marine weather broadcast reports Hilo Harbor is closed. The seas and winds aren't expected to improve the next three days."

"Man, this just keeps getting better and better."

"But the forecast shows better weather leeward of the island by tomorrow morning," he said, raising his eyebrows. "So that means—"

"Right. Then Kona it is, but we'll have to sail counterclockwise around the island due to these winds." Brett unlashed the helm, eased the mainsail, and turned away from the wind, steering *Ohana* on a new course.

As they passed Pokupupu Point, Maui stood in the dusk, a pale purple mount rising from the sea ahead of them across 'Alalākeiki Channel. Brett shared a few protein bars and a ration of drinking water with Donovan. Charlie came topside to get fresh air and hooked his harness to the safety line.

"Keep looking at the horizon, buddy," Brett hollered over the wind. "It'll make you feel better. Look, we can see Maui again."

The island looked closer than its distance on the chart. Upolu Point, the most northern point on the Big Island, stuck out like a glove's thumb from the sea, beckoning him toward it. The sun fell into the sea, leaving them in total darkness. The fresh air erased Charlie's seasickness, and he practiced his knots, whipping together a succession of bowlines, sheet bends, and half hitches with practiced hands.

After dark, Hellen staggered up the companionway ladder, then tripped onto the cockpit deck grating, sending her into a coughing fit.

"You okay?" Brett asked. "If you're going to be sick, get to leeward. Donovan, mind the helm for me."

Donovan grabbed the wheel and Brett helped Hellen to the lee rail. Kneeling next to her, he held her while she retched. Long strings of saliva came between her dry heaves. She tried to push him away, but her weak hands slipped off his arms. Weakened from nausea, she nodded her head and collapsed in his lap. He helped her with a water bottle, dribbling small streams into her mouth and down her cheeks.

"I'm so sorry," she said with a husky voice.

"Don't be. I almost washed out of Dartmouth before I got my sea legs. Happens to the worst of us."

She gave a weak smile and wiped the hair from her eyes. "Brett," she coughed up a laugh, "you're such an asshole."

He helped her below and into the forward berth. The smell of vomit and fear replaced her usual eucalyptus scent. After she lay in her bunk, he ran a damp cloth over her forehead, her hip, the small scar on her belly from Charlie's birth. He bent to kiss her brow as she took deep breaths. Exhausted, she didn't resist, even offered him a weak smile. He swallowed the lump in his throat. Since the summer he'd met her, he couldn't shake off the feeling something precious had been taken away from him. This feeling of belonging to someone. The sense of utter responsibility. He wrapped her in a blanket and pulled her to his chest. He'd never imagined how soothing it could be to care for another.

Her trembling lips calmed, and her ashen face regained its color. He lay next to her, brushing her hair with his fingers. She calmed and forced a smile. With the midnight air sending a chill throughout the cabin, she shivered. Without a word, she crawled into his sleeping bag and fell asleep in his arms. Her chest breathed in a slow rhythm now, her heartbeat against his hand. The scent of her hair and the warmth of her body sent him into a dreamless sleep.

Next morning, the winds calmed. The seas subsided to three-foot swells on the lee side of the Big Island and the crew settled into their daily routine. The sun rose behind them, warming Brett and Hellen as they sat together in the cockpit. With yesterday's nightmare receding, Brett glanced at Hellen, her eyes shut, her damp hair stuck in tangled threads against her face. Silence hung between them. He searched for the right words, anything to make her feel better, but found none.

An hour later, Donovan joined them with breakfast in hand, a welcome relief. "Charlie is sleeping soundly in his berth. The first solid sleep for him in days. Here's the last of the protein shakes," he said, handing them plastic cups. "Cheers."

They drank in silence. The cool liquid seeped down his throat.

Donovan's eyes went from Hellen to Brett. "You two make a cute couple."

Brett shook his head and smirked. "Nice try, champ." He turned away from his friend and studied the chart, measuring the distance they had sailed since sunrise and estimating their ETA. They should arrive by sunset, enough time to find a mooring for the night.

Hellen leaned her shoulders into him. "God. I'm so sorry for all the trouble I've caused."

"No way," Brett said. "Listen, you aren't the first person to get seasick."

Hellen's fingers quivered. "But I haven't been of any real help to you. First falling overboard, then getting sick as a dog, keeping you up throughout the night."

"Don't be so hard on yourself. Donovan's snoring was louder than your coughing. Anyone would have trouble sleeping after what you went through. Besides, we couldn't make this trip without you."

Hellen shook her head. "Don't patronize me, Brett. Charlie or I caused most of the issues on this voyage. I own this. My sailing experience is woefully inadequate."

Brett's buoyancy sank like a rock. She needn't put herself on a guilt trip, especially after she'd fallen overboard during the squall. More than anybody, he was responsible for their travails. He tapped his left thumb on the wheel and took off his sunglasses. "That's not fair. You didn't bring the squall, you didn't shut the ports, and you sure as hell didn't make the sun go berserk." He let a frustrated sigh escape. "Okay, we had a rough start after you came aboard in San Diego, but things are different now. And honestly, you're the best-looking crewmember we have right now." He winked at her.

"That's not saying very much." Hellen gave a nervous laugh and wiped her face. Her blue eyes softened, and her lips parted in a grateful smile. She stood and closed in on him. The citrus scent from her sunscreen became stronger as she lingered closer, holding his chin in her hand, as if she tried to read his mind. Brain fog set in again despite his best effort to stay cool. She kissed him, then nudged her brother. "That's one way I can shut him up. I'll keep it in mind for the future."

Donovan shook his head and laughed at his sister's coup. "After last night, I'm dead tired and need some sleep. Don't wake me unless Mauna Kea erupts." He headed below with the empty cups, leaving Brett and Hellen alone topside.

Hellen wiggled around the dodger and walked to the foredeck. Abiding her daily routine, she set up her shower bucket near the mast. She stripped off her foul weather gear and wet clothes and lifted her safety harness.

"Don't bother with that today," Brett shouted up to her. "The seas are calm. You'll not fall overboard. Besides, it'll give you tan lines or freckles lines or whatever you call them."

"Very funny," Hellen said with a coy tone. She turned and gave him a demure smile, a hint of toying with him. "I know what you're thinking. At ease, sailor." She braced her shoulders, hands on her hips. The gold ring on her chain necklace dangled in her cleavage, reflecting a sparkle of sunlight. "I wouldn't want to distract you from your watchstanding duties."

She signaled him with a waving hand to sit down behind the dodger. Brett shrugged and plopped down on the seat cushion.

After about ten minutes, he stood and checked the wind vane at the top of the mast, then looked down along the luff of the mainsail until his gaze rested on Hellen. She dumped buckets of seawater over her head, lathering up with shampoo between each dousing. Her smooth skin glistened in the sunshine, every rib and curve exposed to his infinite delight. The same trim body she had when they first met.

She faced aft, laughed, and squeezed the water out of her hair. Years ago, chemotherapy had blasted away his little swimmers and fried his sex drive. But with only an alluring smile, this Helen of Troy accomplished what Viagra and therapists couldn't.

To dry off, she lay on the cabin roof under the mainsail. The morning sun gave a bronze tint to her skin and turned her hair a deep auburn. She lay on her back, propping her slim legs up against the mast. Her toes wiggled and her arms swirled overhead, as if she were trying to catch sunbeams. He tried to turn his attention to the compass, but his bungee-cord mind kept pulling his eyes back to Hellen.

After thirty minutes, she sat up and looked aft with worry in her eyes. She held her hand up to shade her eyes from the sun before covering herself with her foul weather jacket. "Turn around, silly," she called to Brett and pointed astern. "Didn't you hear them coming?"

He snapped his head aft. A Royal Navy Pave Hawk helo flew low to the waves, closing in on them. He chided himself for dropping his situational awareness and reached over to flip on the VHF radio at the helm pedestal. Hellen joined him in the cockpit, holding on to his arm to steady herself against the wave motion. The growing noise from the helicopter brought Donovan and Charlie topside.

His eyes wide, Charlie waved at the helicopter. "What's going on? Cool. Look how close they are. Are they going to shoot us?"

"This isn't some video game," Hellen said. "These guys are serious."

The helo flew alongside their sailboat, matching their boat speed, hovering a hundred yards off their side, their rotor blades beating a threatening staccato against the water.

A radio speaker crackled from the helo, "Sailing vessel *Ohana*. This is Flight Angel Four. Report in on VHF channel one-seven."

Brett gave the pilot a thumbs-up acknowledgment and the helicopter took up station five hundred yards away. Brett picked up a handheld radio. "Angel Flight Four, this is sailing vessel *Ohana* on seventeen, over."

"*Ohana*, Angel Flight Four, proceed immediately to Kawaihae Harbor. I say again, proceed directly to Kawaihae Harbor."

As Brett acknowledged, the helicopter peeled away, heading southeast along the coast. *Ohana*'s crew stood silent until it flew into the distant haze, blending with the morning sun.

6

Puna, 30 June

Gus Conroy drove his Vagabond 4x4 up a gravel road south of town and glanced at his bodyguard. The brawny young Samoan sat in the right seat, head poking against the canvas roof top, warrior tattoos flowing down his huge arms, and smelling worse than the sulfur vapors belching from the ground. His latest recruit called himself Toma. After Helio Hattie puked plasma on the planet, Gus drove around the island to see if any towns had power. He found Toma wandering along Honaunau Parkway, dazed and naked as the day he was born. From that night on, Toma latched onto Gus and became a valuable new member of Gus's Sons of Samoa.

Gus lit another cigar to mask the stench, only to send him into a coughing fit. Helmut, his brown dachshund, jumped from his lap and flopped onto the back seat. Gus wiped his mouth with a handkerchief, leaving bloody phlegm, adding to the other red stains in the cloth. He hacked again, cursing the lack of chemotherapy on this volcanic rock.

Toma took a drag from his vape pen and exhaled a plume of

smoke, filling the windshield. "Mr. Conroy, dat da kine shaka weed, brah!"

Gus pointed his cigar at the *moke* and glared. "Like I said over breakfast, don't call me Conroy. Just Gus will do. And cut the pidgin crap; it's hard enough to understand you."

"Kay den, Gus. You think I talk funny? What kind of *lolo haole* accent you speak?"

Gus grimaced at Toma calling him haole, the native Hawaiian term for white trash from the mainland. "That's a long story, son. I came from Peach Tree Land. Let's leave it at that."

Over four decades ago he had fallen through the damn gopher hole and landed into this world run by the Japs and Brits. Must've been a wormhole like you see in those sci-fi movies. A tadpole out of water, he spent his first years dumbfounded, yearning to find a way back home to the Carolina low country. He went insane reckoning how he ended up on Earth's twin planet. At last, he gave up and settled into this strange circumstance. Life was good on his hundred-acre farm in Pāhoa. The locals in Hilo and Puna couldn't get enough crystalline meth, or batu, as they called it. Ate it up like candy. But lately, the batu biz was drier than a popcorn fart. Time to sell upmarket. Anyone would give up their mother-in-law for a kilowatt. After Helio Hattie's blackout, people ran scared, looted stores, searched for food, and set fires. His crew took a full week to rig up temporary power with the small wind turbines they had stolen from a local coffee plantation.

Toma pinched his nose and waved his hand before his face. "Da kine *hauna*."

"What you smell is vapors from Kīlauea volcano. We're heading up to the Puna Geothermal Plant, or 'putrid gas plant,' as the locals say. Going to meet two PGP engineers who were batu-heads until they came clean after the storm. Don't know how they got off the stuff. Hard to kick once it has its claws into you."

"Fo' real. Never touch it myself." An eternity passed before

Toma conjured up another thought. "This morning went horrahs real quick."

"No shit. You did some good thinking back there." The last thing Gus expected was a girl coming after them with a shotgun, meaner than a wet panther. "If you hadn't distracted her, I'd never been able to take her out."

"She didn't have to die, you know. She just got in the way when her parents freaked out."

Gus glanced at Toma, sitting with his arms crossed, frowning. The kid had a soft spot, one he needed to shed if he wanted to stay in this business. The first time Gus killed a man, he sat brooding all the next day. But it got easier as the body count climbed.

"Things are turning mighty queer these days. It's time to switch from batu to power. But I don't yet trust these guys. Like I was saying, you need to watch them, make sure they don't pull anything."

Gus drove into a deserted parking lot in a remote area north of Volcano National Park. An advance team from his Samoan gang had scouted the place yesterday and broken through the locked entrance gate. Two men waited for him by a black Peugeot sedan. They introduced themselves as John and Henry, not likely their real names. But it didn't matter much, so long as they got the job done and never double-crossed him.

After Toma frisked the pair for concealed weapons, Gus relaxed and walked up and shook their hands. John gave him a firm handshake, but Henry's had the texture of a wet noodle. Dressed in pretty-boy duds and meticulously groomed, they didn't appear as batuwhores. Except for their nasty teeth, one would never have guessed they had been addicts. Despite their addiction, Gus had warmed up to them after they claimed they knew every aspect of generating electricity from the volcano brewing under the southern part of this island.

Henry knelt down to pet Helmut but recoiled from his snarl. "That's a mean wiener dog you got there."

"Helmut's a purebred dachshund and doesn't take kindly to being called a wiener dog. Look here, guys, this ain't a dog show. Let's get down to business."

John retrieved a cardboard tube from his backpack and removed a pair of large blueprints. "Mr. Conroy, let's start with the opportunity to—"

"Call me Gus. Let's take a seat and see what you got."

"Okay... Gus." John glanced at his partner before spreading the blueprints on the picnic table. "The plant is offline but could be back up within days. We took the high-voltage transformers offline before the geomagnetic storm hit us, so they didn't suffer current-induced heating damage."

"Wait. Slow down, fellows. I'm just a tidewater periwinkle and don't get your engineering gibber-jabber."

Henry gave Gus a coy look. "What John is trying to say is most of the plant's infrastructure is intact with little damage from the storm."

"Then why hasn't that sheep-dip ConHEL gotten the electricity back to my home yet?"

"They can't without a high-capacity external power supply to restart the plant."

"You need power to get power? Well, shit, that makes about as much sense as tits on a bull."

"It's like a car with a dead battery. You need someone to jump-start your car. Once the engine is running, the alternator supplies electricity for all other loads."

"So how do you plan to jump-start your power plant?"

John laid out a schematic diagram across the table. "The PGP plant's energy comes from volcanic heat stored beneath the earth's surface. We sluice water deep underground through these pipes, where the volcano heats it under high pressure. The water returns to the steam generator and the steam drives the electric turbine, producing electricity."

Gus tried to shift his attention from Helmut peeing on the table's leg. "Sounds like a steam engine that makes electricity."

John smirked and pointed to the engineering schematic. "The difference here is the steam spins the turbine. But this is wasted mechanical energy unless the generator stator has electricity. The stator windings create an electromagnetic field inside of which the spinning rotor creates an electrical current."

Gus rubbed his eyes. "This doesn't make much sense, but I got the general idea you need a portable generator to jump-start this teakettle."

"A rather large generator—at least a hundred-kilowatt capacity."

Gus stood up and pulled a cigar out from his shirt pocket, lit it, and took a long draw. He exhaled a cloud of blue smoke, filling the space between them and sending Henry into a coughing fit. Gus grinned at him. "So where do we get one of those kill-a-wit generators?"

John walked Gus from the picnic table and away from Henry's coughing. "We heard the Honaunau District fire station has an auxiliary truck with enough generating capacity. If we could get our hands on it, we'll be back in business."

"Right, I see why you need my crew. Here's the deal. We'll get your generator before ConHEL can get their mitts on it. We'll also secure the PGP plant for you and collect revenue from our customers. You'll manage the plant operations and get the local power grid back up."

"Works for us," John said. "I'll handle plant ops, and Henry will supervise the line crews to get the lights back on in Puna. Just let us know who gets turned on and who gets left out. We'll take it from there. You also need to protect our line crews and keep the constabulary out of the way."

Gus took another draw on his cigar. "Let's just say that's one of our specialties."

"Let's talk about payment terms. We get paid up front in gold and silver."

"Like jewelry? What's wrong with eCoin?"

"No eCoin. After the blackout, it's about as useful as a

screen door on a submarine. We want one ounce of gold or a hundred ounces of silver for every five hundred kilowatts we deliver."

Gus squinted at the boys through blue cigar smoke. "Suit yourself. But you guys are nuts. Cash or eCoin is the only safe way to make this trade."

"You collect your revenue in cash and keep it all to yourself. But we insist on gold and silver."

"Where am I going to find that much gold on this volcanic zit in the middle of the Pacific?"

"I'm sure you'll find a way. Do we have a deal?"

Gus shook John's hand. "Deal. I'll send a couple of my goons over to serve as bodyguards in the meantime. Feed them canned ham and porn, and they'll be happy. Once we have the generator, I'll let you know." Gus whistled to Toma and headed back to his Vagabond.

Late in the afternoon, the morning dew still covered Green Valley Farm's rolling acres of rows and rows of cannabis fronting the legit side of Gus's business in Pāhoa. Thick clouds hung outside his kitchen window. "Those thunderheads are going to bust loose soon," Gus said. "Let's get moving."

Gus stepped out of his small cottage and led Toma down a lush overgrown trail to the backside of his farm. After they neared the border of the Malama-Ki Forest, he turned off the dirt path and stopped in front of the entrance to a lava tube, a long cave carved thousands of years ago by a river of lava. His flashlight beam danced along the solidified waves of igneous rock lining the inside of the cave. Its beam of light revealed colors of the minerals leeching from the walls, but geology mattered little to Gus. To him, the lava tube was an ideal spot to house his batu labs, secluded from inquiring eyes of MI5. The cops on this British outpost were ferrets, a real pain in the ass compared to the DEA back in his Old World. And the America of Earth 2.0

didn't play by the same rules. He'd never step foot in Carolina again.

The overhead lights came on, their rays lost in the black walls. He ducked into the lava tube just before the clouds opened and dumped sheets of rain. The thunder echoed in the damp and musty cave, sending his small dachshund yelping and scooting between his feet. "Damn you, Helmut. You're always underfoot. Will you ever learn?"

Gus skidded on the slick surface, but Toma caught him with one arm before he hit the ground.

"God dammit," Gus said. "Thanks for the catch, Toma. You got yourself some mighty quick reflexes."

Toma followed him deep into the cave until they came to the entrance to his lab. The moke hadn't seen the place, but it was time to bring him deeper into the fold.

"We keep the lab under positive pressure to prevent contamination from the cave air." Gus opened the heavy door and shielded his eyes from a gust blasting through the doorway. "The lab's HVAC system forces air from the surface and maintains a constant temperature and humidity."

The bright lights, acrid chemical smell, and air-conditioned interior were a stark contrast to the cave's dark humidity.

"What's the beat today, boys?" Gus asked two huge Samoans sitting at the nearest lab bench. He kept his distance. They stunk worse than Toma, a spicy mix of body odor and onions.

"This batch will round out the next deal," one of Samoans said. "After it's done cooking, we better kill the power and recharge the batteries."

"Might be the last batch," Gus said. "We're switching business plans. I'm hooking up with a couple engineers from the PGP plant down the road."

"Da kine plant is that?" the largest Samoan asked and turned to his partner. "Pome-Granate and Pun'kin? Hey cuz, ever heard of them grinds?"

Gus squinted his eyes at them. "Shut up and listen. I'm

talking about the Puna Geothermal Power plant. If we control PGP, we control all the power supply in Puna. I'm switching to guns and ammo for this batch's payment. We'll need a little fire-power for our next venture." He opened a tattered road map of the Big Island and spread it out on the table in front of Toma. "Familiar with Honaunau?"

"Sure, me and my braddahs used to snorkel down there." A lecherous smile rose on Toma's face. "Got some plenty *wahine* to go skinny dipping, so fine with them cho-cho lips. To da max, man."

Gus leered at the fond memory of swimming with a native beauty in Honaunau Bay. She was more than eye candy; she had saved his life. Like him, she had also fallen through the gopher hole years back, proving to him this crazy Land of Oz wasn't just a nightmare.

"That's where I'm sending you. But hands off the bitches, you've work to do." He waved his thumb at the Samoans standing at the far end of the lab, packing the final batu batch and shutting the burners down. "You'll take these wing-nuts with you in my truck and reconn the fire station down there. There's a portable power generator I'm interested in acquiring. Let nobody see you—just check out the premise's security." He handed Toma an HD videocam. "Take this and start filming after you find it."

"What am I looking for? One of those Honda rigs you get at Home Depot?"

"No, this juice machine is much bigger." Gus showed him a sketch of what he imagined it looked like. "It's mounted on a truck, maybe fifteen-foot long. Probably red, covered with fire-fighting emblems. Think you can remember that?"

Toma studied the map. "That's it? Just look around?" he asked without looking at him.

"No, there's one more thing. From there, head north on Island Belt Road and proceed to this armory." Gus pointed to a wide green area on the road map, marked *Pohakuloa Military*

Camp. "Try to sneak in here and rouse up some hardware for us, shotguns, ammo, grenade launchers, whatever you can get your paws on."

Toma's eyes widened. "You're shitting me, man."

"Now, don't get your panties all wound up in a knot. The place isn't guarded. Everyone's down in Hilo-town fighting the riots. If you meet any resistance, just get your ass back here pronto."

Toma drew his eyebrows together and pinched the skin at the side of his throat. He didn't look convinced. Gus wondered if the moke was up to the challenge, but he needed to test him. Despite his brawny looks, Toma had shown a cool head in the last raid. Innovative and decisive, Toma had the makings of a suitable lieutenant. If he came back alive from this mission, he'd have a proven sidekick. If not, he could always find another moke, plenty of them running around Hilo these days, desperate to hook up with his gang.

7

Ohana made the short sail down to Kawaihae and entered the harbor channel by noon. Compared to the marina in Honolulu, it was a placid sanctuary, devoid of the city skyscrapers, uncontrolled fires, and military helicopters. Like many commercial ports, cargo cranes towered over the pier, large fuel tanks dotted the perimeter, and two Matson container ships floated beside the docks. Atop the hill behind a dozen dockyard cranes, the Union Jack flew below the Hawaiian national flag from the harbor's yardarm.

Repeating the same routine they had run through in Honolulu just three days earlier, Hellen and Charlie took their stations, rigging side bumpers, cleating the bow and stern lines, preparing to dock. But this time, no angry harbor patrol boat tried to chase them away. Instead, a trim, muscular dock hand in red shorts and tanned chest waved to them from the concrete pier. His long, black hair streamed in the breeze, like the lifeguards she had seen in Southern California. She called back to Brett, pointing to the spot where the dock hand signaled them to go. Brett maneuvered *Ohana* into a small slip beside the pier. On

Brett's command, Hellen threw the spring line over to the Baywatch guy standing on the pier on her first try. Brett reversed the engine, bringing *Ohana*'s stern alongside the dock. With the docking secured, their grueling three-week voyage ended.

Hellen was the first to jump onto the pier. She gave Baywatch a big hug, laughed aloud at his reaction, and spun around. He shook his head and strode away as if he didn't know what to make of her.

Everything contradicted her fears. The EAS radio broadcasts declared Hawai'i was in a perilous state of emergency. Where were the soldiers, roadblocks, and crowds of desperate people looking for food and water? This quiet harbor gave no hint anything had happened.

She strolled across the narrow pier and sat on the concrete stairs leading up to the adjacent parking lot. A sign stood at the top above her reading, "*E komo mai* (Welcome) *E 'olelo Hawai'i wale no ma 'ane'i* (Only Hawaiian spoken here)." Despite their official stance on language, most islanders spoke English, a legacy of their status as a British overseas territory.

She breathed in this moment. The air carried a soft hodgepodge of tropical seaside aroma. Trees waved under the breeze and sea terns danced above them. The sun warmed her back, relaxing her muscles. The past week's tension ebbed. They'd finally landed, back on the island on which she was raised.

Baywatch called down to the cockpit and Brett poked his head around the mainsail boom. They exchanged more Hawaiian words, their tone nonthreatening. Despite not knowing the native language, she enjoyed listening to the melodious chatter.

"There's some dude named Kalino coming to pick you guys up," Brett said to Hellen. "You know him?"

Hellen's mouth fell agape. "He's from Cloudcroft. Elle must have worked her political magic." During her childhood, Kalino had been a father figure to her. More than just Elle's plantation manager, he had taught her how to ride, manage a stable, and shoot a rifle.

"Okay then," Brett said, winking at Hellen, "let's get ready to shove off. You guys stow all this loose gear and pack your sea bags while I head over to the harbor master's office."

Donovan and Charlie busied themselves topside, and Hellen went below to gather their things into duffel bags. Three weeks without a Laundromat had left their clothes damp and wretched. She found a clean sundress and got out of her clothes. Startled by her reflection in the stateroom mirror, she tenderly explored the welts under her arms left from Donovan winching her aboard last week. Her strung-out hair was knotted in a tangle and her eyes ran bloodshot. Weeks of a saltwater-drenched life at sea had wreaked havoc on her skin. After searching several minutes for her makeup bag, she retreated to the boat's head. She washed up with a damp towel, hoping she could later get a proper shower. After rinsing her hair in the sink, she dried it, leaving it unplaited, giving it a nice full-body look. She applied eye shadow, nude lipstick, and a little blush to her cheeks. Satisfied with the job, she put on the sundress. Almost civilized again.

She opened the door and stepped out into the main cabin, surprised to find Brett had returned so soon. He didn't notice her and continued to throw cans into the galley pantry. She caught her breath. The red slashes along his back and open wounds on his right arm marked his courage in rescuing her after she fell overboard. Yet he never mentioned them.

"Where did you get all the food?" she asked in a manner to attract his attention.

He continued to stack the cans without looking up. "The Harbor Master gave us a case of canned ham. I thought we could—"

He turned around to speak to her, but no more words came from his gaping jaw. She smiled to herself, making a mental note. Color filled his cheeks, and she fell into a helpless laugh. He was a mess, his sweaty face highlighted by the sunlight coming through the hatch, his hair tousled and wild. But she loved every inch of him.

He sucked in a quick breath and stepped back. She covered her mouth with her hand. "Something wrong, sailor?"

"No, just surprised by your—" Brett stood there, eyes fixed on her. "I mean, you look terrific."

He shook his head clear and hauled their duffel bags topside. Time to leave this boat and her misadventures behind them. She followed him to the pier, his back flexed under the heavy load of their gear. His tattoo glistened with sweat and his muscles were contoured by the high tropical sun. A familiar but long-forgotten stirring deep inside her rose like a bubble. Despite her fighting the inevitable these past weeks, time had come full circle back to their summer in Lahaina.

An old, white pickup drove down the access road to the pier and pulled up alongside *Ohana*. A tanned Hawaiian in a cowboy hat jumped out. His stocky frame and unmistakable gait told Hellen he was Cloudcroft's manager. With a full heart, she ran to him in a giddy stride and embraced him.

"Aloha," he said. "Welcome to the Big Island."

"Kalino!" Hellen stepped back and rested her hands on his shoulders. His denim shirt didn't do much to hide his paunch, and his cowboy duds made him look out of place here in paradise. His bright smile and inviting brown eyes gave her solace. Elle had once told her a red thread of fate tied together their lives.

"How did you find us?" she asked.

"The Home Office sent word you might show up. Good thing Elle knows the island governor; otherwise, this port be closed for you guys."

Donovan and Charlie came up to the truck with their sailing bags, and Hellen introduced them to Kalino. Brett returned to *Ohana*'s deck. No bag in sight. "You guys go ahead without me," he said. "I want to stay aboard tonight and wrap up arrangements with the harbor master."

Hellen's heart dropped. After all they'd been through, how could he stand another night on the boat? She folded her arms and studied him. But he didn't seem to hide anything.

"Come on," she shouted to him. "Don't be silly. I want you to meet Elle and—" Hellen stopped short before Elizabeth's name escaped her lips.

"I'll catch up with you all later, after I get the tanks topped off and move the boat to a transient slip."

"Okay, have it your way. I'll pick you up later." She gave a quick wave before he ducked below with nothing so much as a goodbye. She walked toward *Ohana* but stopped halfway down the gangway connecting the pier to the floating dock and focused on this moment.

"*Mahalo nui, Ohana,*" she said under her breath, "for bringing us across this ocean, for bringing us back together."

"Come on, Mom," Charlie shouted from the pier. "Stop daydreaming and let's get going. I'm hungry." He waved her on and his goofy grin dissolved into a tender smile.

Charlie and Donovan climbed into the back seat of the truck's cab and waited for her. She looked back at the boat again, no sight of Brett.

"We've much to catch up on," Kalino said. He picked up Hellen's duffel bags and threw them in the back of the pickup. "You can ride up front with me."

They departed the harbor main gate and turned onto Kawaihae Road, a two-lane county road leading up Mauna Kea's shallow slope. After weeks of plodding along at five knots, Hellen's memory of riding in a car had almost vanished. And driving on the left side of the road around here didn't help.

During the ten-mile drive, the lush countryside rushed by in a blur. Stretching for miles to the north, an immense lava field held twisted ropes of black rock, more of a moonscape than a tropical island. After they passed the thousand-foot elevation sign, palm trees gave way to rolling hills of scrub brush and cactus. A dozen tall, white wind turbines stood like ancient Greek sentinels, their blades locked in place. Wild goats grazed among cattle, munching grass under the tall towers. At higher elevations, pine, cypress, and river oaks lay between vast green pastures filled with Longhorn cattle. Fences, tree lines, and rock walls built centuries ago marked the boundaries of farmland. Everything lay open, unbounded by humanity, spreading out into an endless vista sloping down Mauna Kea and into the sea. She closed her eyes and leaned her head out her window, letting the wind blow her hair, smelling the passing trees. The truck carried her up the hill to her childhood home, leaving her anxiety behind her like a tangle of clothes on the shore.

The lush landscape surrounding Elle's coffee plantation felt like coming home again. She fidgeted, straining to see Cloudcroft's main house in the forest. Perched in the surrounding trees, its maroon wooden exterior blended with the forest, as if it had grown in place among the branches. Vibrant flowers and fragrant scents filled the edges of the narrow dirt driveway. A bird perched in a Cook pine tree called out with a dove song. A shrill chirping sound also echoed from within the tree's branches. Kalino drove to a broad parking space in front of Elle's home, parking beside a red Faraday, the latest in hybrid automotive engineering.

Standing at the steps of the covered porch, Elle and Elizabeth waved their hands and shot brilliant smiles at the arriving truck. Elle was the foundation she needed now more than ever, a home port in the storm. Yet she also knew she had to face Elizabeth. Her lie couldn't go on much longer, even more so with Charlie here.

Hellen jumped out of the truck and ran up the path to the front porch with arms outstretched. The sight of her hānai mother filled her heart with a warmth she hadn't felt in months and desperately needed. Hellen soaked up Elle's soft, tanned complexion, lush lips, and bright eyes. A white-and-yellow plumeria flower floated in her long, black hair. Her floral dress exposed her strong shoulders and flowed down her athletic figure. They exchanged a *honi*—a Hawaiian kiss—gently touching their noses together, both inhaling at the same time, sharing the breath of life and *mana* between them.

"God! I can't tell you how happy I'm to see you both again." She gave Elizabeth a solid hug but felt a slight push back from her.

"Auntie Hellen, go easy. You're suffocating me."

Hellen took a step backward and smiled at her daughter, now slightly taller than her. The same long burgundy hair—*'ehu* as Hawaiians called it—framed her brown eyes and oval face.

Following Elle, Hellen passed through the mahogany doorframe and faced Suzu. The Iron Buddha came over to her and clasped her hands. Hellen stood upright, holding Suzu's inspecting gaze. Always a composed and self-possessed transgender male, Suzu was handsome in a metro-sexy way, borne from Japanese heritage.

"Hellen, I'm glad to see you have made it through all the chaos." Suzu's eyes darted between Charlie and Elizabeth. "You two look happy to see each other again," he said and raised an eyebrow at Hellen.

Her kids eyed one another as if they shared a secret. Hellen tugged Charlie's arm. "That's enough, you two."

Charlie glared at her. Elizabeth looked away, her face blushing. Hellen tilted her head to one side, her smile slowly waning from her face. Before she could ask him what was going on, Elle took her arm and escorted her down the hall.

"Welcome home," Elle said. "It's not the same without power, but we're surviving somehow."

Two expansive picture windows let sunlight stream in, filling the main living room with an amber glow. Beyond the windows, the familiar green lawn sloped down to gardens and forest covered with dew. Elle had named her coffee plantation Cloud-croft after the clouds that drifted through the fields in the mornings.

"Here, you must be starving."

"Sure am," Charlie chimed in.

Hellen strolled behind Elle, lost in her immersion back to civilized life after weeks on *Ohana*. She glanced over her shoulder. Elizabeth and Charlie walked behind them, hand-in-hand with all the signs they intended to pick up where they left off last year. She had to say something soon.

An alarm sounded in the kitchen and Kalino grabbed a rifle from the closet. Without a word, he strode out the front door and disappeared.

"Varmint hunting?" Hellen asked Elle.

"No, bigger game, I'm afraid. Kalino installed a solar-powered perimeter defense in the woods surrounding the house. After the island lost power, we had uninvited guests. Kalino chased them off, but we're still worried. There's also rumors around town of other attacks on ranches."

Since Hellen's childhood, Kamuela had been like Shangri-La, a mythical sanctuary, isolated from the outside world, nestled between Kohala Mountain and Mauna Kea. She hoped its remoteness offered protection, but no place was really safe anymore.

They walked onto the lanai at the back of Elle's home. Suzu returned with an armful of brown, plastic pouches and handed them out to everyone. Hellen examined her package and recognized the "Meal-Ready-To-Eat" label, the same sodium-infused meal in a pouch Brett had served on the boat. Hellen's vegetarian chili with beans contained fifteen hundred calories, more than she liked to eat in a typical day. They opened their MRE pouches, laid out the contents, and inspected them. With a deepening frown, Charlie read through the dense instructions. Like a seasoned pro, Elizabeth activated her flameless heater using water-activated chemical reactions to warm the meal. She glanced at Charlie, his eyes squinting at the printed instructions. At last, he sighed and threw the MRE back on the patio table.

"Here, let me help," Elizabeth said. "I know how this works."

Hellen studied Charlie while he sat across from Elizabeth. He acted distant. His skittish eyes darted from Elizabeth and the others. After Elizabeth warmed up his MRE, she patted his knee and smiled at him. He devoured his Italian pasta, tomato sauce smeared on his cheek. Elizabeth wiped his mouth clean with her thumb with a special closeness. Hellen wasn't even sure how to tell them the truth, the fact they were more than friends; they were half-siblings. She could never seem to say the right things or do the right things or be the right person around either of them anymore.

"I'm sorry our dinner isn't something special to celebrate your visit," Elle said, "but the food stocks are running low, as you can imagine. We're lucky enough to have the local army garrison provide us with these rations."

"Oh, please stop," Hellen said. "I thought I'd never see you eat meat."

"These military rations are all vegetation," Suzu said. "Helio Hattie hasn't kept us from our Buddhist vows."

Hellen smiled at the local nickname for the solar storm. Maybe gallows humor helped them to deal with the aftermath. In the way headwaters powered a mighty river, the power grid supported all aspects of modern society. Without it, everything became difficult. Hellen feared they had only a few months before they lost all hope. Unlike after a hurricane, people can't take refuge. Even the emergency shelters collapsed without power.

While Hellen's dinner warmed, a shot ran out from the forest. Donovan's head snapped up. "What the hell?" he asked.

"Kalino must've found our visitors."

"Does this happen often?" Hellen asked. Until now, guns were an oddity in Hawai'i. Only ranchers and local constables owned them. Hellen guessed they might become important again.

"Less than during the first days after Helio Hattie. I think the looters are giving up. Or can't find food."

"Can't the government help?"

"The home secretary hasn't done much. This is the most challenging logistical problem we've ever faced. Without power, we're crippled. It's the worst blackout in world history. Two disasters spawned the crisis: one natural and one man-made, the culmination of widespread neglect tracing back more than a century. Before the storm, the grid was in bad shape. As more people adopted renewable energy and microgrids, the local power company saw their profits shrink and deferred upgrades."

"And America and Canada?" Donovan asked.

"They've updated their power grids," Hellen said. "Maybe they survived?"

"As far as I've heard," Elle said, "only the Pacific islands have suffered a widespread blackout. Parts of America and British Canada are intact and have promised aid, but we'll probably see little help. Ninety percent of Hawaiians live on O'ahu. That's where the attention is right now. We're mostly rural, a low priority."

Donovan asked as he looked up at the dim porch light, "You still have lights despite the blackout?"

Her mouth full, Elle wiggled her folk at Suzu, prompting him to respond.

"Now and then. The lights you see are run off our wind turbine." Leaves in the trees suddenly quickened and came to rest. The single porch light went out. "But it only works when we have a good breeze. Hellen, maybe you could look at our solar panels. They've not worked since the storm."

"Sure. The geomagnetic-induced currents must have overloaded them. I'll take a look in the daylight tomorrow." She also made a mental note to also check the storage battery. The wind power system should've charged deep-cycle battery to provide reserve power when the wind gave out.

"After Helio Hattie hit the islands," Elle continued, "things went downhill really quick. Cell phone towers dropped all connections. Like most of the islands, we rely upon weekly deliveries of food and drug supplies from Honolulu or the mainland. After the storm, the fuel barges stopped coming. Petrol drained dry from the pumps. Grocery stores ran out of food, pharmacies shut their doors, and the hospital filled to capacity."

"But Kalino picked us up in his truck," Hellen said. "Where did you get petrol?"

"We have a two-hundred-gallon tank next to the barn." Elle pointed over her shoulder. "It should last a month, maybe more if we're careful."

"Honolulu looked like a ghost town," Donovan said. "Waikiki Beach looked deserted. I wondered if the rest of the British Hawaiian Islands were the same."

"That's interesting," Elle said, "I've heard of riots in Honolulu. My sources tell me most of the BHI is in chaos."

"Your sources?" Hellen asked.

Elle blinked her eyes. "As of last month, I'm the mayor of Kohala. Can you believe it? Lord, this town is in trouble."

"You're a politician now? Why didn't you tell me?"

"I hate that word—and I didn't campaign. A write-in ballot pushed me into it. I never told you because... I don't know, I'm not really excited about being mayor. I've only committed to one term."

"Elle's more popular in this town than she's willing to admit," Suzu said. "The part-time post fits nicely with her day job at the Kohala 'Āina Foundation."

"However," Elle said, "my government duties now soak up all my time, thanks to Helio Hattie. No time left for seeds and husbandry."

"What are you doing with all the stranded tourists?"

"We didn't have many visitors when the storm hit. The Mauna Loa eruption scared them all away."

"Erupted?" Charlie asked. "Like in a volcano?"

"The Hawaiian archipelago is still forming. The Big Island is the youngest and most volcanically active."

"I read about the eruption," Hellen said, "but I didn't see any evidence of it."

"Just try to get to Kona," Suzu said. "The lava flowed over five miles of Saddle Road, cutting off access between Kona and Hilo."

Kalino emerged from the woods, his rifle slung over his shoulder. "Save any dinner for me?"

"Of, course we did," Elle said, waving him on. "Nothing but the best for our gallant watchman."

"I only saw a couple of the rascals. Just discharging my rifle was enough to scare them off."

"What if they were armed?" Hellen asked.

"Some are, but I can usually sneak up on them."

He sat beside Hellen and dug into his MRE. His calm face held a matter-of-fact ennui about everything: chasing off looters had become routine in this blackout.

A canopy tree at the edge of the garden held a flock of birds chirping in the evening air. A black raven alighted from a nearby monkeypod tree, flaring to a landing before their table.

"Look! It's an 'alalā crow," Elle said. "They almost became extinct about thirty years ago, but the Hilo Aviary is bringing them back through a captive breeding program. This is the first time I've seen one at Cloudcroft."

The raven's little bird-mind seemed consumed by how to dislodge a bug from a nearby log. Elizabeth threw a stir stick from her MRE pack to the ground. The bird picked it up with its beak and returned to the log.

"It's using the stick as a tool," Charlie cried. "That's one smart bird."

Elizabeth smirked. "Takes one to know one, Charlie Brown."

He tousled Elizabeth's hair and ran down the steps and onto the lawn. She chased him, tackling him before he reached the garden.

"She grows more beautiful every year," Elle said. "And smarter. Did she tell you she's majoring in astronomy? Made the dean's list too. Between her intelligence and her cho-cho lips, she'll be quite a catch for some lucky man."

Elizabeth tickled Charlie everywhere she could reach, her hair sprayed across his face, their laughter resonant.

Elle nodded. "There's trouble. You need to tell them soon. You've waited too long."

Hellen covered her face with her hands. "I know, I know. But not now." Her anguish returned in great waves with the guilt she carried since Elizabeth's birth.

Through most of the night, the strange jungle sounds surrounded Cloudcroft, their shrill calls keeping Hellen awake until the early morning hours when the purple dawn streamed through her windows. The smell of incense wafted into her room and drew her out of bed. She stretched and rubbed the sleep from her eyes. The house held a deep quiet. A note from her brother lay on her nightstand. Donovan wanted to take Charlie to the local community hospital to evaluate Charlie's concussion trauma. With no reason for her to fight her insomnia, she slipped her sundress over her shoulders and followed the inviting aroma to the kitchen.

In the daylight, the kitchen appeared larger and more modern. A calendar hung on the opposite wall, bearing King William's portrait. Elle had bitterly complained about all the nonsense in the islands on his first visit to Hawai'i, shutting down all traffic in Hilo, sending the island into a tailspin. Hellen had planned to see the parade, but Elle wanted no part of it and Charlie couldn't care less.

The sound of a coffee bean grinder around the corner made her jump. "Oh my god. You gave me a start."

"Sorry," Elizabeth said. She walked from behind the counter in a flowing sarong. A fresh pink plumeria flower floated in her hair, accenting the bird of paradise pattern on the silk covering her trim figure. Her brilliant white teeth and brown eyes fixed on Hellen. "This thing does make an awful racket."

"What the devil were those shrilling chirps last night? I kept hearing a loud Ko Keee KO KEEE." She gave a long yawn and stretched her arms.

Elizabeth grinned and pointed out the window. "You heard our horny coqui frogs in search for a hookup. Over the past year, the little buggers have migrated from Hilo and infested large swaths of our property. Their high-pitched mating call drives us crazy. It's time for another coqui frog roundup."

Hellen smiled to herself. Did all daughters discuss the sex lives of frogs so casually with their mothers? She ran her fingers along Elizabeth's silk robe. "Your sarong is beautiful, the pattern so intricate. I love wearing them but have always struggled with tying them just right."

"Wait right here." Elizabeth ran upstairs and returned with another sarong. "You're about my size. Here, let's see how it looks on you."

Hellen went to the bathroom, undressed and wrapped the sarong around her. The satin tickled her skin and excited her in a manner she'd never admit to her daughter. After weeks in foul weather gear, she felt naked in the gown. When she returned to the kitchen, she raised her arms up and twirled in a circle. "How do I look?"

Elizabeth made minor adjustments to the robe. "Auntie Hellen, you're beautiful in it." She kissed Hellen's cheek and whispered, "It's perfect for you—keep it—it's yours."

"Thank you, love. I think I will."

Hellen opened the fridge and helped herself to a bowl of cut melons. After returning the bowl, she found a set of syringes labels, marked "Insulin," laying on bottom shelf. Yet no one was diabetic. Elle would have told her. Racking her brain, she walked out of the kitchen and onto the lanai. The morning air was cool and refreshing. Elle practiced her morning Tai Chi on the back lawn, her graceful steps matched those of a woman decades younger than her 68 years, each step with purpose, each position with discernment.

Munching on her fruit, she examined a panel on the porch's back wall, a rectifying unit for Cloudcroft's solar array. The voltage meter read zero. Suzu had said their unit went offline during the solar storm. Hellen traced the power conduit to a small gray box at the corner of the house. After opening the access door, she saw the overload breaker had tripped. She flipped the switch to the right and shut the panel. Still no power. Back at the distribution panel, she found a system schematic taped to the access door. Of course. It was a grid-connected solar system. By regulation, home solar systems shut down and were isolated during a blackout. Yet someone had installed a jerry-rig. She found an aftermarket switch labeled *Iso-Override* in a junction box between the solar and wind distribution panels. After she engaged the override, a steady hum came from the 120 VAC transformer. Success! She reset the master breaker for the house circuit and the porch light came on.

Elizabeth came running out of the house. "What did you do? The lights and fans came on everywhere!"

"Just putting my engineering degree to good use."

Elizabeth ran to her and gave her a strong embrace. "I love you! Now I can charge my phone."

"Not so quick. The cell towers are still down without the power grid."

Yes, Hellen thought to herself. The power grid died, but small systems like this one might have survived. With much shorter transmission lines and smaller transformers, residential renewable energy systems might have avoided the worst of the storm's damage. Their fault protection breakers could've saved them before the currents burned the units out. From the back of her sleepy mind, a thought emerged. Her purpose stood before her. Renewable energy could be the lifeline for the island's residents in the foreseeable future. But how to get it done? Materials would be scarce after shipping had ceased. Without the main power grid, seaports had shut down and shipments of solar panels from the mainland would never get in.

"Good morning!" Hellen jumped at the sound of Elle's voice.

"Lights, level two." Elizabeth spoke to the ceiling. The recessed lighting brightened. "Hellen got our power back."

Eyes wide, Elle placed her hand over her heart.

"Where are you headed?" she asked Elizabeth, who had headed for the door.

"I'm going to listen to my music," Elizabeth said before disappearing through the doorway.

Elle's cat, Ty Lee, jumped off the table before Elle's hand brushed her aside. The Siamese gave a long, indignant howl before stalking off the porch. "I knew funding your college would pay off someday," Elle said. "You may come in useful around here. We should visit the renewable energy research center next to Kona Airport. With their residential wind and solar power units, people in rural villages could live off the main grid. Maybe you can help me organize a community effort?"

Hellen nodded. "Microgrids, like the kind I installed for NCEL, might be the answer. By stringing together residential solar units to share power among our neighbors in the same way you used telephone party-lines decades ago. We can generate up to five kilowatts from your solar array, and the wind turbine could make up for low output during cloudy days."

Elle nodded. "It's a start but bringing back the main grid is much harder. With no power from the island grid, our government buildings and businesses rely on backup diesel generators. But the petro will soon run out."

Hellen's mind drifted back to the problem of rebooting the power grid, of finding an external power source to perform a black startup. Getting new transformers would take many months. Running through some rough calculations on residential demand, she couldn't imagine any way the island could run indefinitely without the electric grid.

"I saw the syringes in the fridge."

"Don't worry, they belong to our neighbor Lea. She has diabetes and needs the insulin to keep her alive. With no refrigeration, her insulin would've deteriorated within a few days, so we keep it on ice for her. But others weren't as lucky; many have died."

"I've an idea." Hellen tapped the energy panel with her finger. "Remember the project I worked on at NCEL where we powered an Indian reservation in Utah? Well, I think I can get power back, at least some of the grid."

"You'll be a hero. Our local power company hasn't been forthcoming about when they'll turn the lights back on. You can join my civil defense team and keep us out of the dark, so to speak."

Elle's sad face broke into a small smile, releasing the sorrow stuck in Hellen's throat. They went inside, prepared pancakes, and poured themselves some coffee.

Elle finished her fruit and asked about Charlie.

"Donovan left me a note," Hellen said. "Something about taking Charlie to the hospital later this morning."

"Good luck trying to get anyone to see him. They're way over their heads dealing with the aftermath from the blackout."

"Even in the best circumstances, Charlie hates hospitals." She couldn't blame him after what Sam did to him. Her ex-husband had come home angry about the latest annoyance in his life. He focused his fury on her little boy, beating him, breaking his arm and his spirit. It was the last draw. She had dragged Charlie to the car and raced him to the hospital. They had run out with just the clothes on their back and started a new life with Elle's help.

Elle poured Hellen a cup of coffee before refilling her own

mug. "His father was a bastard beyond compare. But let's not rehash old nightmares."

Yes, let's not. Rain started under full sunlight, shaping a rainbow from the silvered sheets of drizzle falling from the crisp morning sky. When she was a child, she had called it "liquid sunshine." She laughed and finished her last kiwi fruit and savored her black java, void of any bitter taste. Coffee might be the one thing they would not run out of; the beans came from Cloudcroft and other plantations lining the hills above Kailua-Kona. For the briefest moment, the coffee aroma sent her back to the days before the blackout, before she left Colorado for her long voyage. "This island has all a girl would want," she said half-jokingly.

"Enjoy it while you can. I heard a rumor the RAF is planning to evacuate visitors, maybe as soon as next month."

Hellen sat upright, her mind whirling. For the first time since leaving Honolulu, she tried to imagine leaving her old home again, leaving her 'ohana, leaving Brett. What waited for her back in Colorado? Looking for a job in a wrecked economy? She took another sip from her mug and tilted her head to one side.

"What's bothering you?" Elle asked.

"You're the soothsayer; you tell me."

"You don't really want to go back. And I want you to stay. You can help us restore power. And more."

Hellen didn't look up, but Elle was right. Her mission was here. She could make a real difference here, helping her 'ohana and others in her hometown restore residential power with renewable energy, then maybe working on the power grid.

"Besides," Elle continued, "I don't think you want to leave Brett. Why is he still on the boat? He's more than welcome to stay here."

"I don't know. He keeps to himself much of the time. He's my 'Quiet Man.' Maybe it explains why he's so different from Sam."

Elle raised her eyebrows. "He's not the only one who keeps things private."

"I hear ya." Hellen rocked her feet back and forth, playing with the gold necklace holding a wedding ring belonging to her father, a father she had never known. "The voyage out has changed me, maybe both of us," she said at last. "I started to warm up to him after he took Charlie under his wing. And during a squall at sea, he dove in and saved Charlie and me after we fell overboard."

Elle's eyes widened. "Wow, girl. If that's not enough to win your heart."

Hellen put her hand on her chest and blushed. "Sure, but I just don't know. Honestly, I feel like a teenager sometimes, all these emotions inside me, pulling me in opposite directions, canceling one another out like a math problem I can't solve. Besides, I'm out of practice. Had a bit of a dry spell for the past five years. I just don't know..."

Elle gave her a suspicious look. "Stop overthinking this. It's not calculus. Let your feelings grow but give him some time. And don't think you're the only one with trust issues."

Maybe not calculus, but it certainly was a three-bodied problem: Brett, Charlie, and Elizabeth. Maybe Brett was her linchpin to solve it. "My voyage out to Hawai'i stripped off layers of emotional armor calloused by bad relationships over the years. When Brett talks to me, it's like I'm hearing pure and honest words for the first time in my life." Hellen's throat tightened, and her eyes stung. She tried to breathe, but her chest shuddered.

A raven perched on the barn roof, maybe the same one as last night. Its low, gurgling croak echoed in the backyard. It alighted and flew to the base of the stairs. The bird absorbed Hellen's attention, pushing Elle's words into the background. She threw a berry at the bird. It tried to snatch it in midair with its beak but missed. Maybe it was nearsighted. The bird rolled the berry against the stairwell and finally grabbed it.

"You have a new friend," Elle said.

"Or an alter ego. Like the raven, I'm a tool-meister with inefficient eyes. Busy with my career, I've turned blind to what's really important. Birds of the same feather flock to what's easy. Pretending I'm Elizabeth's auntie was always easier than telling her the truth. Brett also needs to hear the truth about Elizabeth, but I fear losing him."

Elle's eyes teared up as well. She nodded slowly, rocking back and forth in her chair. "Do you love him?"

Her words came ahead of her thoughts. "He is both my bread and wine."

"That's a funny way of putting it."

Hellen wiped her eyes and forced a smile. "I don't mean the Eucharist if that's what you're thinking. It's a pet phrase we shared years ago. 'Wine is the grape of our passion; bread is the grain of our life.'"

"Then follow your heart. The two of you need each other more than you realize. If he really loves you, your relationship will survive the truth."

Hellen laid her face in her hands, retreating to the black space behind her eyelids. She felt Elle's hand run up and down her spine.

"Remember the Eight-Fold Way," Elle whispered. "Desire leads to suffering, the truth of the end of suffering is to accept what is. You both need to face the truth. If you trust him, he'll be ready."

Hellen jumped at a resounding crash from the kitchen, the sound of glass breaking and a chair toppling to the floor. They ran into the house and Hellen gasped. "Charlie!"

8

Charlie stood in a puddle of orange juice in the kitchen, squeezing his temples with the palms of his hands. After grabbing a roll of paper towels, Elle worked on the mess on the floor.

"What's wrong? What happened?" Hellen asked, constriction pressing her chest. "Here, take a seat."

"I don't know," Charlie said in a faint voice. "I was pouring myself a glass of orange juice when a sharp pain came to my head, the worst headache ever."

Hellen pulled him into her arms, his shoulders weak, his eyes watering. "It must be your concussion. Let's get you away from the bright sunlight." She helped him into the shaded living room and sat beside him on the sofa, his head slumped back against the cushion.

"You guys stay right where you are," Elle called from the kitchen. "I'll get Donovan and we'll take Charlie to the hospital."

As Elle ran out, Charlie pushed against Hellen's shoulder with his hand. "I don't want to go to the hospital. I hate those places."

Hellen choked back her anguish, wishing she had protected her son from their nightmare with her ex-husband. Her marriage was falling apart long before Sam attacked Charlie. Why hadn't she left earlier? You do stupid things and can't take them back no matter how much you want to; there are no second chances.

"What happened?" Elizabeth asked as she ran over to him. "Charlie! Are you all right? Auntie, do something."

"It's the aftermath of a concussion he suffered while we were at sea. We'll get him fixed up, love. Don't worry."

Hellen jumped at the sound of a car horn from the driveway. She gave her son a light kiss on the forehead and carefully led him out to Elle's car. Donovan joined them and examined Charlie's pupils before helping him into the car.

Elizabeth stood by the car. "But I want to go. Let me in."

"No, love," Hellen said. "There's no room for us all. Can you stay behind with Suzu?"

Elizabeth frowned and walked back to the house, never turning to wave goodbye.

The drive into town was short, the roads deserted. Hellen stared out her window, clutching her son's arm, watching the world pass by. A stop sign read "Whoa!"—a tip of the hat to Kohala's cowboy culture. They sped along the lava stone-lined main street. The clock atop of Queen's Hardware was frozen in time, reading 11:59, the time the solar storm must have hit the island. The blackout had not only stopped time, but sent the town back in time, to a time with no electricity, to a time when people rode horses instead of automobiles. Parking lots lay empty, businesses stood shuttered.

"Mom, I'm okay. I don't need a hospital."

She smiled at him and rested her head against his shoulder. "Don't worry. Let's just get you checked out. We wanted to do this, anyway."

"We're almost there," Elle announced.

She slowed as she drove past a sign overgrown with weeds; Maunakea Astronomy Institute, it read. Next to the astronomy center, a long row of churches stretched to the east. In fact, churches outnumbered bars in Kamuela.

Elle turned into Kohala Medical Center's main driveway and

pulled up to the entrance. Hellen helped Charlie out of the car, and Donovan led them into a set of glass doors under a wide vinyl banner with the words, "*Aloha kākou*, we are in this together." KMC's octagon-shaped main lobby was lit from a skylight and bay windows beyond which lay a vegetable garden and an expansive lawn stretched down to a coffee orchard. In normal times, it would have been a lovely place to visit. Sunlight streamed in through windows, providing the only source of light in the hallway leading to the Emergency Department. Most patient rooms had their lights off and window curtains pulled back to allow sunlight into the ward. They passed through another set of doors leading to Emergency Care. Patients and cranky children filled every room and hallway. Angry voices mixed with urgent intercoms announcements throughout the facility.

With nowhere to sit, Hellen and Charlie stood outside the ER waiting area while Elle and Donovan went to the check-in desk. Across the hallway hung a portrait of the royal family. Hellen tilted her head to the side and studied the photograph. King William and Queen Catherine stood with solemn faces, dressed in vainglorious regalia. The royal coat of arms bore a lion and unicorn above the monarchy's motto: *Dieu et mon droit*. "God and my right," indeed. They seemed out of place on this Ballygobackwards island. The islanders' simple living didn't fit with the figureheads in the photo. This remote British overseas territory had few loyalties to the empire, paid no alliance to their Christian god, nor accepted their colonial status. Hawaiian remained the official language. As yet, Britannia had neglected her children. King William had not come to their aid in this crisis. Hellen shook off the tension in her shoulders and walked back the ER waiting area.

Across the crowded room, Elle waved her hands at the admissions staff, prompting them to back away from the counter. Hellen couldn't hear the exchange, but she saw how Elle spun them into action. Within minutes, a nurse came through the

ER doors and walked over to Elle and Donovan. Hellen pushed her way through the throng of people with Charlie in tow.

Elle placed her hand on the nurse's forearm. "Malia, I need you to see this young man. He's 'ohana and very dear to me. Please, can you find someone to check him out?"

Malia wore floral scrubs, lit only by the skylights. Her long black hair was pulled back in a ponytail, a few silver streaks floating in her bangs, warm brown eyes holding a compelling vitality. Despite the tension showing in the crow's feet around her eyes, she spoke with a soft voice. She glanced at a tablet in her hands and nodded. "Certainly. What's his condition?"

"He suffered a concussion a week ago and looks like he had a mild seizure this morning," Donovan said.

"And you are?" Malia looked at him with skeptical eyes.

"Captain Donovan Callahan, Royal Navy. I'm also the boy's uncle. I gave him a twenty-milligram dose of Trazodone after the accident, but nothing since then. I recommend a cranial CT scan. Do you have a trauma center here?"

Malia raised her eyebrows and gave a small smile. "We have a level III trauma unit, but a CT scan is out of the question at the moment. We're running off standby power from diesel generators with just enough electricity to handle our critical needs."

Elle clutched Malia's arm. "Malia, let's find a physician for my boy, will you?"

"I'll see what I can do. Follow me."

She pushed through the ER doors, and they followed her to the ER central desk.

"Wait here," Malia said in a clipped tone. "I'll be back in a minute."

Another nurse stood alone behind a curved counter. Only one of the four computers showed any life, and the patient status board was awash in yellow and red triage tags. Malia returned with a short man who looked like Gandhi in medical scrubs. He took off his thick glasses and pinched the bridge of his nose.

"Hello, Charlie," He said with a heavy British India accent.

"I'm Dr. Chandrasekhar, but please just call be Chandra. Sorry to hear about the bump on your head." He tousled Charlie's hair and beamed at him. "Let's find an examining room and get you checked out." Looking up at Hellen, he said, "I'm sorry, but there's no room for visitors back there. This will probably take an hour or two, so make yourself comfortable in the waiting area."

After Charlie left with Dr. Chandra, Elle's handheld radio squawked. "Elle, this is Joe. You need to come down to the station right away. It's about the checkpoints."

"Okay, Joe, I'll be right there." Elle returned her radio to her handbag. "He's our constabulary's superintendent. We're putting up roadblocks around town to deter roving gangs from Kona and Hilo. You guys appear to have the situation in control. I'll be back in a couple of hours."

After Elle left, Hellen nudged her brother. Donovan stared back at her with the face of an angry panda. She nodded her head toward Malia and whispered, "Looks like they could use another doctor around here."

He cleared his throat and touched Malia's sleeve. "Malia, can I speak to the acting hospital administrator?"

"You're looking at her. I was head of nursing until Helio Hattie stranded our leadership team on O'ahu. They were there for a conference, and we don't expect them back anytime soon."

"I'd like to offer my services. Got no place else to go, so I can fill in for any shift you need."

Malia raised her eyebrows. "I don't understand. What do you have in mind?"

"I'm a doctor. Before retiring two years ago, I served as the commanding officer of the Naval Health Clinic at Kaneohe Bay, about the same size as your hospital here."

Malia's eyes grew wide and her lips parted as he rattled off his credentials. "Dr. Callahan, sounds like you're overqualified for our little show, but I'd love your help here in the ER."

"Fine by me. I look forward to jumping into EM again. As a

ship's doctor, I've seen just about everything. And please call me Donovan. So, when can I start?"

"Well, if you're really serious, you can start right now. We're way understaffed and I can't spare a doctor to orient you, so I'll assign myself as your ED nurse. That way I can review our procedures as we work together."

"Sure, works for me," he said.

"Great. That reminds me of another matter. Are you board-certified?"

He rubbed his hands. "EM board-certified in Hawai'i with privileges at U of H Medical Center. Let's shake on the deal."

She shook his hand and held it for a long moment before releasing it. "Given the emergency, we'll waive the hospital privilege evaluation for you."

Malia's lips curved into a curious smile. Hellen covered her mouth to hide her grin and checked Malia's left ring finger for a wedding ring. Donovan might be in for more than just a volunteer gig.

"I hate hospital waiting rooms," Hellen said. "I think I'll stretch my legs. When do you think they'll be done with Charlie?"

"Couple hours at least," Malia said. "There's a cafeteria down this hall. Not much food left, but plenty of coffee."

"Thanks, I'll check it out and be back within the hour."

As Hellen explored the small community hospital, she found every wing under siege. The receptionist at the visitor reception desk told her KMC served a community of about ten thousand people during the low season at the northern end of the Big Island. About every fifteen minutes, an ambulance pulled up to the ER entrance. The tense air and clinical smell everywhere made her sick to her stomach.

She meandered down a crowded corridor and turned into an adjacent hallway. It was filled with patients lying on gurneys, sitting in spare chairs, and standing along the wall. Hellen leaned over a frail woman. Her tiny frame lay among the sheets.

Small blue eyes, fixed in an infant-like stare, looked through Hellen. She smelled of talcum powder mixed with the sad odor of a moribund body. Hellen took her hand, a translucent patina of skin stretched over her bones, but felt no response. Hellen brushed the sparse strains of white hair from the woman's sun-spotted face. A brief smile passed across her lips.

The air hung heavy with humidity and Hellen wiped the perspiration from her brow with her sleeve. The narrow hallway became more oppressive, warmer by the minute. With no over-head lights, the overcrowded scene reminded her of the images from Puerto Rico after a hurricane hit the island ten years ago. The blackout had lasted for over a year. The fall of society didn't occur overnight—it played out slowly for months, one death at a time. First the hospitals filled up, then the looting, riots, and finally neighbor against neighbor. For the first time since the solar storm, the extent of the aftermath became clear. This wasn't the apocalypse. But if the community fell apart and people didn't come to each other's aid, the chances of making it through this trial would be grim. She leaned back, arched her spine, and stretched her sore muscles.

Three hours later, Malia returned with Charlie, a beaming smile on his face.

"He'll be okay," Malia said. "He suffered a grade two, or moderate, concussion. The skull x-ray showed no fractures. Keep him out of bright lights. Make sure he gets plenty of rest and avoids any activities requiring mental concentration."

"Did you hear that, Charles Callahan?" Hellen said. "No HoloSpecs from now on."

Charlie narrowed his eyes but gave no other protest.

Malia winked at her. "Anything else you guys need?"

"How do we pay for your services?"

"Payment? The banks are shuttered. The economy is dead now. We're in a brave new world here. The only payment I've received in the last four weeks was two chickens and a dozen coconuts."

Dr. Chandra came to the desk and pecked at his tablet with one finger. After he finished, he looked up at Donovan, his owl-like eyes magnified through his eyeglasses. "This guy still here?"

Placing her hand on Donovan's back, she said, "This is Dr. Callahan. You missed the introductions. I found him wandering the hallway and asked him to join our little party here."

Dr. Chandra gave her a confused look and shrugged his shoulders. "Fine with me. I'm too busy to get involved in hiring. Welcome, Dr. Callahan. We'll use all the help we can get."

Malia tugged Donovan's arm and led him around to the other side of the desk. She described the various status boards at the central panel, how to get labs results, and the location of the Code Blue crash carts. Hellen took Charlie by the hand and followed them, more out of curiosity and to kill time until Elle came back. They first toured the trauma room. Malia dribbled on about the various specialties, general admission procedures, x-ray and blood labs.

"Have you a renewable energy source?" Hellen asked her. "It seems most solar power units survived the geomagnetic storm."

"We looked into getting more panels for our array, but—"

An overhead speaker chimed, followed by an urgent announcement, "Code Trauma Alert, patient arriving in ambulance bay." The familiar whoop sounded as they ran behind Malia toward the ER entrance. An EMT threw the door open. A stretcher rolled in with a stocky Hawaiian, his face obscured by a portable oxygen mask, his denim shirt soaked with blood.

When the medics rolled the gurney past her, she gasped and brought her hands to her mouth. Kalino's face was ashen and his eyes shut. She grabbed Charlie's hand and ran after them to the ER. Charlie jumped at another the blaring alarm. Eyes wide, Hellen searched for a place to stand out of their way. Pressing her back against the passageway wall, she held her son beside her.

"What's the history?" Donovan yelled.

"GSW to the lower abdomen with pressure 80 over palp. He's lost about three liters of blood, bleeding marginally controlled with manual pressure."

An EMT sat straddled over Kalino's hips and applied pressure to the wound. Malia called for a shift physician, her head swiveling around, searching for any available room.

An ER nurse yelled, "All rooms are full. Send him down the hall. Dr. Harris is busy with a seizure case and can't come."

"Looks like this one's all ours," Malia said with pleading eyes.

Donovan snatched the facility map from his pocket and nodded. "Let's move him to Trauma and double up."

They steered the stretcher across the hall and into the already crowded trauma center. Hellen took Charlie's hand and raced behind them. After Kalino was rolled into a trauma room, Hellen stood outside the doorway with Charlie, his face rapt with excitement.

"Is he going to die?"

Hellen recoiled from his question. "Let's hope not, Charlie. Uncle Donovan will save him." She clutched Charlie's arm and headed down the passageway and away from the life-and-death struggle.

"No. I want to watch." Charlie tugged at her hand and wiggled out of her grasp. She ran after him through the trauma center's doorway.

"Get back here," she whispered with a tense voice, unable to drag him from the doorway. "We need to stay out of their way!"

"Let's get him on the examination table," Donovan yelled from within the room. "Everyone on my count. One, two, three, move."

After they moved Kalino off the gurney, Malia hooked up the cardiac monitor leads and attached two large bore IV lines to Kalino's arm. Donovan examined the monitor while he held Kalino's wrist.

As if watching a movie, Hellen didn't believe her eyes. She couldn't accept that Kalino might die here in front of her. A fluttered moan escaped her lips.

Donovan glanced at Hellen and yelled at a nurse to get them away from the trauma room. Hellen's stomach cramped up. She had more than enough. And Charlie didn't need to see this. "Come on, Charlie. We can't stay here."

She dragged him through the ER hallway, zigzagging until they broke out of the crowded hospital. They stood outside the main entrance and caught their breath. Hellen's ears held a ringing pitch from all the chaos. A few cars sat parked in the front lot, but Elle's wasn't among them. By habit, she retrieved her phone from her back pocket and asked Aiva to place a call to her.

"I'm sorry, Hellen, I'm afraid I can't reach her," Aiva said in a soothing voice.

"What's the problem?"

"I think you know what the problem is just as well as I do." Hellen face-planted her palm on her forehead.

"Wow, I want to be a doctor!" Charlie slapped Hellen's arm. "I mean, how cool was that?"

Hellen's eyes welled up, but she forced a smile. "Sure, you do. But Kalino was Elle's right-hand man. This is serious. He was like a father to me." She looked around the parking lot again. "I need to get a hold of Elle."

Charlie shot his arm out to an adjacent shopping center. "There, I think I see her red Faraday. Like, how many people around here would be driving one just like it?"

They took a shortcut over the hospital's expansive lawn to a supermarket. The red car had a broken windshield and its left door was ajar, seemingly deserted since the blackout. An emergency generator droned on behind the building; its staccato hammering echoed off the brick walls of the shopping center. The supermarket's dim interior lights revealed many empty shelves and counters, and only a few employees. A wide handwritten sign hung over the checkout lane: Cash Only, No Exceptions. Hellen walked up and down each aisle but didn't see Elle. At one of the checkout counters, a cashier sat slumped in her chair. Her stoned, watery eyes stared into empty space.

Hellen shook her. "Hey, wake up. Have you seen a woman, a foot taller than me, wearing a floral sundress?"

"Who?" The cashier shook off her daze and squinted at Hellen. "What woman?"

"Oh, never mind. Good grief."

They strode back to the parking lot. Even after searching the hospital grounds they didn't find her car. For the first time in many weeks, she truly missed her cell phone. Without texts or phone calls, the simplest problem soon escalated into a nightmare.

Hellen threw her arms up. "Let's check inside the hospital again, maybe she left a note. We must let her know about Kalino. Damn, having no internet is terminally frustrating. How did people used to live this way?"

They went through the main entrance and someone called her name. A man with white hair, wearing a blue vest and volunteer name tag, sat behind the visitor desk and waved her over.

"I thought you were Dr. Callahan. Not too many redheads in this town with a teenager in tow. Mayor Otoko asked me to tell you she had an emergency, but she'll be back to pick you around nine."

"Let's hoof it," Charlie said. "Come on, it's not more than a mile. I'm hungry and tired of this place. I want to go home."

The antique pendulum wall clock behind the desk chimed six bells. She wanted to stay until Kalino was out of surgery but waiting three more hours in this wretched place would've made Charlie's skin crawl. She could walk him home, then reach Elle on the radio or find a way to get back to the hospital. Turning to the attendant, she asked, "Got a map?"

After the attendant gave her a town map and directions, she bit the corner of her bottom lip. Cloudcroft wasn't far, and the sun was still well above the horizon. She tousled his hair. "Okay, you win, kiddo. We'll be back home before dark—shouldn't run into any trouble."

Hellen and Charlie walked down the abandoned main street in silence. It felt funny to walk on the centerline of a major road, yet no cars passed. After passing Church Row, Hellen paused to check her map, then continued on until reaching Mana Road. The highlands north of the small town looked sublime, enshrouded by clouds covering the peaks with smoky vapor. An emerald carpet draped the hills, pulling the rain out from the cloud bases. Each fold in the rolling landscape yielded a different and bucolic scene, secluded from a once busy world. The green land under the cloud mass was gloomy, devoid of any signs of human habitation. For a brief moment, Hellen was back home in Boulder, a world away from the mess created by the blackout. Perhaps her mountain home had been spared.

"Looks like a gully washer is heading our way. Let's turn into here." Hellen pointed down Mana Road, which passed beneath a forest canopy, appearing as a tunnel through the trees. "It's on our way home, and it'll provide some shelter from the rain."

As they proceeded down the narrow dirt road, the air grew damp, filled with a mixture of pine and moist soil. Coqui frogs chirped on both sides of the road, drowning out the rain, and wind rustled through the trees. Her clothes damp, she shivered and clutched Charlie's arm for warmth. After passing through the tree tunnel, they broke out into a wide vista of farmland, dotted here and there with hundreds of cattle. Hellen paused to take in the broad vista. A flock of birds cruised high in the sky, forming a V-shaped wedge pointing to Mauna Kea. The extinct volcano loomed in the distance under a waxing crescent moon shining through broken clouds. A silver dome stood on its peak like a sentinel to heaven, glistening in the twilight. When she was young, Elle had worked at the Astronomy Institute for many years. She often spoke of the largest observatories in world resting on this sacred white peak.

"Isn't this spectacular, Charlie?"

"It's out there, all right. Like Colorado, but amped up."

"Despite our misadventures, I really enjoyed our time together over the past month. We've grown much closer, don't you think?"

Charlie walked over and stood before her, his lips curling into a reluctant smile. She gave him a hug around his waist, holding him close, her cheek planted against his chest, feeling his heartbeat through his wet shirt. "I love you, Charlie."

He wrapped his arms around her shoulders. "Love you too, Mom." Many years had passed since she had heard those words.

She squeezed her arms tighter and looked up to his face. "We may go home soon. Elle mentioned the RAF is planning to airlift visitors back to the mainland."

Charlie pushed away from her, his mouth ajar. "No way. I want to stay here."

"Me too, but the blackout will only make things harder for us. Won't you miss your friends?" But her question didn't make much sense after the blackout. Who knew what waited for them if they returned? No, she had already decided. Restoring power to her 'ohana had become her new mission in life.

"Not really," Charlie said. "Most of them skirted me, always throwing shade my way. Honestly, I've kept to myself lately."

Hellen swallowed hard and a bitter taste rose in her throat. "I'm sorry to hear that—I had no idea."

"How could you? You were always at your lab."

His words stung her heart, but she let them go. He was finally opening up to her, the first time in years.

"Can't we stay here?" he asked "It's not like you have a job to go back to. Maybe you can get work somewhere around here?"

Hellen's checks flushed. Her dream was his dream. But it all seemed so impossible now. The blackout made everything harder. She nodded and continued down the road, holding his hand. Cloudcroft soon appeared ahead of them.

"You're needed here. You can help get power back. We could stay with Elle. There's plenty room for us. Besides, I like hanging out with Elizabeth. She makes me feel… I don't know, like I'm special."

She kept her eyes focused on the road ahead. "Special in what way?" she asked, afraid of the answer.

"She's the best friend I've had in a long time, despite the fact she's savage sometimes."

If only she could let them know their love was one between siblings without tearing them apart. Without much more thought, she plowed ahead. "I see how you hang out together. Let's not let it grow into something else."

"What do you mean? This isn't going to be one of those talks, is it? Like, I'm almost sixteen and I've been with girls before— wait, I mean, you know, friends. But I'm just saying, she's only two years older than me. You and Sam were—"

"You mean your father," Hellen corrected him.

"Brett's more of a father than Sam ever was."

The word father stuck in her heart. Charlie was right. Brett wasn't just a friend to him. He loved her son, although she doubted he'd ever admit it. She took his hand in hers and smiled when he didn't pull away again. "What makes him so special?"

"Everything. He sails, flies helicopters, knows how to fish, comes from Polynesian blood. What's not to like?"

She squeezed Charlie's hand and swung it back and forth. Memories of Brett and Charlie flashed in her mind. The sailing, the celestial navigation, the secret jokes they shared, and how Brett changed the watchstanding schedule after the squall, always staying by Charlie's side.

"I mean," Charlie continued, "he likes you, don't you like him?"

"Of course, I do." Hellen's fingers twisted her father's ring hanging from her necklace.

"Like, couldn't you hook up with him, then we'll all be together?"

Heat rose in her chest, despite the chill in the air. She stopped in her tracks and folded her arms over her chest, her joy bursting like a soap bubble. "Don't be so crass, Charles Callahan," she snapped. "That's not how relationships work."

"What makes you an expert on relationships?"

"I admit I'm not the best role model, but I think we better talk before you go gallivanting off with Elizabeth."

Charlie's face turned beet red. "Like you're one to give lessons on romance. Remember the string of losers you went through after you left Dad."

Hellen caught her breath. "Hold on, right there, young man! First of all, we left because your father hurt us. *You* of all people should remember. Second, my dating history is not a subject for discussion. We're talking about you and Elizabeth. You need to keep it strictly platonic, okay?"

"Say what?"

"No sex. Ever."

"Mom, stay out of my life. I'm old enough to know better."

"It's a lot more complicated than you think." She choked on her words. "She's your half-sister. You and Elizabeth are both my children."

"Wait—what!" He stepped back from her, his eyes wide. "I don't get it."

Her eyes welled up as she reached for him, but he turned away from her. "It's true, Charlie. She's my daughter, and I love her every bit as you."

"Wait—what? I mean we kissed and… I can't believe you never told me. Stay away from me. I never want to see you again." Charlie ran down the road, his distance growing with every word.

"Come back," she called after him. "I'm sorry, but you needed to know."

Her labored breaths sent puffs of vapor into the cool moist

air. She stood in the middle of the road and screamed at the moon. Her son marched off toward Cloudcroft, flailing his arms above him, yelling back at her over his shoulder. Angry at herself, not her son, she let her tears flow in earnest now. Nauseous from losing her temper, she sat by the road, wondering how things had gone so wrong.

9

By the time Hellen returned alone to Cloudcroft, the sky blazed with a thousand stars. She found Elizabeth sitting on the front porch, sipping green tea. With an encouraging smile, Elizabeth held the cup out to her. After taking a deep sip, her cramped shoulders relaxed. She sat beside her daughter, staring up at the moon with unfocused eyes.

"Where's Charlie?"

Elizabeth leaned her head to her right. "In the carriage house. He's really pissed. What did you say to him?"

Hellen caught her breath. "He didn't tell you?"

"No. He just pushed me aside and said we couldn't be together anymore."

"It's my fault. We got in a fight. He took off." Hellen shook her head and passed the teacup back to Elizabeth.

"What's the big deal about Charlie and me having a little fun? I know better than to let myself get pregnant."

Hellen planted her face in her hands. "Oh god, save me."

"You need to get over it, Auntie. You grew up here. We don't shun free love. Besides, we're old enough now."

Hellen lifted her head and let out a long breath, her shoulders quivering. After the mess she just made of telling Charlie the truth, she couldn't face Elizabeth right now. The morning would bring the right words; it always did.

Elizabeth ran her hand over Hellen's spine, her fingers warm, her eyes curious. "You must be starving. I saved some salad, help yourself. I'm beat and going to bed."

Elizabeth's kiss grazed her forehead. Hellen wondered if it was her last. Unmoored, Hellen drifted into a sea of worry. She had blundered into her disclosure with Charlie. Now, she was out of time. She must let Elizabeth know before Charlie made a scene and let the truth out. Hellen fiddled with her wrist braid and went to the kitchen but couldn't roust up an appetite despite not having anything since breakfast. The day was long, her spirit sapped. Off to bed.

Throughout the night, Hellen lay awake in her bed, turning from side to side, flopping on her back, then rolling onto her tummy, burying her head under the pillow, kicking the blanket off with her feet. Despite the coqui frogs taking the night off, sleep was impossible. The wall clock in the hallway chimed every hour. At six bells, she raised her arms and let them drop with a slap on the sheets. She'd have to tell Elizabeth the truth this morning before Charlie got to her. Tired of squirming, she sprung out of bed, threw on a bathrobe, and headed for the kitchen, determined to package her words better this time. She wouldn't spring it on her the same way she did with Charlie.

The house was still asleep, not a single light lit. After her eyes adapted to the dark, she found her way through the house by the moonlight streaming through the windows. She grabbed a ceramic bowl of watermelon from the fridge and sat at the table.

Elle appeared, wearing a silver, silk nightgown. Her red swollen eyes stood in contrast to her bright smile.

"Where's Suzu?" Hellen asked. Elle's partner seemed like a ghost lately, appearing occasionally but not saying very much.

"Suzu has been staying at the Zen monastery, managing their outreach efforts. They've opened their vast gardens and fields to folks without food."

"I tried to find you last night."

"Sorry, I had to take off after Joe Kanuhu radioed me. A shooting outside of town." Her voice faltered. "It's Kalino. He's dead." She braced herself against the counter. "I was his only 'ohana on the island."

Hellen jumped from her chair and ran to Elle and embraced her, her eyes squeezed shut. "God. I'm so sorry. I saw him come into the ER, but I thought he'd make it."

"He had gone down to Kona-town, things real horrible down there. Riots and mayhem."

Still holding Elle in her arms, Hellen prayed silently. Kalino's exuberant smile hovered beyond her closed eyelids. She had so loved this man. His laughter and bright eyes played in her mind. Singing together as he strummed his ukulele. Riding the hills around Mauna Kea. Rounding up mustangs. Branding cattle. Now he was gone.

Where was the end of this? The unrest must've spread. It was only a matter of time before it came to Kamuela. Kalino's death made the blackout more than an engineering problem to solve. Its visceral impact shook her core.

"Joe deputized a dozen volunteers," Elle said in a flat voice. "They set up roadblocks on the main roads leading into town. I radioed the Pohakulao Army Garrison. Most of their families live here in town—they'll keep us safe."

"I'd like to help out, maybe fill in for Kalino. I'm a good shot and know my way around stables."

"It'll make his death a little easier for me. Looks like you had a rough night as well."

With tears welling up, Hellen gave a curt nod and ate her fruit.

"And no frog song. Something bothering you? How did Charlie's visit to hospital go yesterday?"

"Thanks for making him a priority. The trauma center did a great job treating him. He'd sustained a grade II concussion but should soon recover just fine."

"I've not seen Donovan. Did he ever return last night?"

"He wants to stay at the hospital. Sounds like he's on their staff now. He's an affable guy, always the first to help, one who gives much more than he receives. I'd like to take his clothes and personal things to him. Can you run me down sometime today?"

"Sure." Elle placed a black skillet over the stove and lit the stove. "Go get Charlie. We'll go to hospital after he's had breakfast."

Hellen just stood there, her eyes fixed on the stove flame. "Not yet. Let him sleep."

"You've something on your mind. Tell me."

Hellen took a sip from her mug. Elle waited, hands on her hips. The silence between them seemed to stretch time. Hellen's pulse beat in her ears. The wall clock ticked with each second.

"Last night... on the way home. I told Charlie."

"I see. How did he take it?"

"I screwed it all up into a big mess like I always do."

"And Elizabeth?"

"Doesn't know yet."

"We better tell her before Charlie sees her. The Buddha dharma teaches us three things can't be hidden for long: the sun, the moon, and the truth."

"I know. I know. It's been on my mind all night." But her lies had weaved a tangled web, drawing ever tighter with every day.

"We'll handle this together. I'll go wake her up."

"No, let me get her." Hellen lingered before leaving, her arm around Elle's shoulder, mustering the courage to face her daughter. At last, she left for her bedroom, still unsure of her words.

After throwing a pair of jeans and a T-shirt on, Hellen walked upstairs to Elizabeth's room and knocked on the door. Panic welled in her throat. What could she say to her to make up for a lifetime of deceit? She knocked again and opened the door. Her room was empty.

Hellen ran outside and across the gravel driveway to the carriage house, a guest quarters atop a one-car garage and work-shop. A wood shingle, gabled roof capped a set of three open Victorian windows. She called up but heard no response. Climbing the broad wooden steps to the second floor, she checked the guest bedroom but found no sign of Charlie or Elizabeth. Hellen pressed her palm against her brow and closed her eyes. Last night's nightmare had come to life.

She ran outside and screamed for them, her voice echoing against the thick forest canopy. Birds alighted from the trees all around her.

Elle ran out the door, her head turning in quick movements. "What's wrong?"

"They're gone," she yelled from the far end of the front yard.

"They're not inside. Are you sure they didn't sneak off together to the carriage house?"

"I looked everywhere. Maybe they're in the barn."

Hellen ran through the stables, calling Charlie's name. The stalls and the pasture lay empty. No sign of her children. She strode up to the porch and braced her arms against the banister. "Where could they be?" she demanded.

"Who are you looking for?" Elizabeth asked from around the corner.

"Thank God. Where have you been?"

"I was in the outback for my morning meditation, but your screaming got in the way. What's wrong?"

"Have you seen Charlie?"

"Not since last night. Maybe he's exploring the woods."

"Let's take a look," Elle said.

They walked down a long gravel path winding through Cloudcroft's acreage. Dust kicked up from under their feet in the still air. Silence surrounded them like a suffocating blanket. The abandoned dirt road led to a neglected cottage built a century ago, a favorite place for him. Still, no Charlie. After two hours of scouting the ranch, they returned to the house and sat frustrated on the front steps.

Elizabeth let out a sigh and walked to the barn. "Maybe he took one of the bikes," she said over her shoulder.

The sight of Elizabeth emerging alone from the barn gave Hellen heartache. Her daughter ran across the yard in graceful steps, her hair flowing behind her, the perfect synergy of her parents' best qualities. She strode up the stairs, her brow furrowed. "My bike is gone."

Elle came out and sat beside Hellen and cradled Hellen's hands in her own. "Try to relax. He's probably just exploring around town."

"I don't think so," Elizabeth said. "He was pretty upset last night."

Elle went inside and returned minutes later, dressed in a samue robe, her purse and car keys in each hand. "Let's go look for him. I have a radio in my car."

Elizabeth sat in the back of the car and Hellen slid into the front seat. Elle released the whip antennae from the back-bumper, and it flung upright. After getting into the driver's seat, she opened the glove compartment. An ancient transmitter was mounted inside, its channel frequency glowing yellow.

"After Helio Hattie knocked the cell towers off line," Elle said, "we've resorted to CB radios, although they're hard to find." She called to Joe's CB handle and arranged an ad hoc search party in town. After starting the engine, she looked over to Hellen. "Where do you think we should look first?"

Hellen replayed her exchange with Charlie. He had said he wanted to stay in here and live with Brett. Her chest rose in a deep breath. "Kawaihae Harbor."

To Brett's best knowledge, Harbor Master Manu Keli'i was the only guy in charge around the marine terminal. The power blackout had shut down all shipping to the islands, leaving the bustling port deserted. Its longshoremen, crane operators, and tugboat crews had scattered across the island, dealing with their personal struggles to get their families through the crisis.

With Manu's help, Brett topped off *Ohana*'s tanks. Having no power, they resorted to hand pumping the water aboard, taking most of the morning to complete the job. Manu also gave him another case of canned ham and a carton of chips for the pantry. With his sailboat provisioned, Brett took her out for a short sail, his rod and reel ready. The fishing was good, and a lunch of fried ham and warm beer topped off the day. After returning to his boat slip, he walked around the piers and came across an abandoned fishing net. He gathered it up and brought it back to *Ohana*. If he repaired it, he could do drift-net fishing offshore. The dinghy davits at *Ohana*'s stern might even make a workable trawling rig from which to tow the nets.

On his way back to his sailboat, he stopped by Manu's office and found his new friend fiddling with an electrical distribution panel.

"Aloha, Manu. Mahalo for all the help this morning. How do I take care of the bill? I also need to arrange long-term harbor privileges since I don't know how long we're staying."

"Bill? Forget about it. All the banks are closed. No way to make any transactions. I'll keep an open account for you, and we can settle up after this mess is over."

"I procured an old fishing net from the pier. Thought I might try trawling off *Ohana*'s stern."

"Go for it. No one's fishing anymore. The local trawlers can't get enough petrol, but you only need wind, right? Your catch would help feed the local folks low on food."

Manu turned back to the distribution panel and tugged at different colored wires. He picked up a multimeter and scowled.

Next to Brett's elbow, a handheld radio squawked. "Kawaihae Harbor, this is Kamuela Deputy Dog, over."

Manu winked at Brett and picked up the radio, "Aloha, Joe. What'cha you got?"

"Elle is looking for a young boy, named Charlie Callahan. Can you look around for him?"

Manu shrugged at Brett.

Brett's mind ran through the places Charlie could have gone. "He was on our crew." He walked to the window facing the docks. "Maybe he tried to come back to the boat."

"Okay, Joe," Manu said into the mike. "We'll take a look-see and let you know, Kawaihae out." He joined Brett by the window. "I don't remember the kid. Got any photos of him?"

"I don't, but he's about my height, scrawny, with curly red hair. Hard to miss. I doubt he's down here—he'll never get through the locked gates, chain-link fence, and barbed wire."

"There's a small gate open to the public at the canoe club down by the south end of the port. Take my golf cart and check it out. I'll look for him around the container yard."

Brett took his time searching the recreational docks, picnic areas, and utility buildings along the road leading to the far end of the port. In front of the Canoe Club house, he walked to a small boat ramp. Several sailboats rested on a dinghy dock. He grinned at the row of Sparkman and Stephens Blue Jays, the same One-Design boats he had sailed in high school. He had loved his time on the varsity sailing team. The fourteen-foot racing dinghy with its short rig and sails didn't overpower the helmsman. The hull had a stable ride, ideal for young sailors.

An abandoned bicycle lay next to an empty sailboat cradle. He walked over to an adjacent sail loft whose door swung in the breeze. The interior held a musty air and a dozen rolled-up sails lay in plywood cubbyholes against the far wall. A set of sails was missing.

He ran to the golf cart and drove back to his boat. After starting the engine, he released the dock lines and headed out of the harbor.

The hours passed while Brett sailed north, parallel to the Kohala coastline. The wind picked up, building swells, reducing the chance of spotting Charlie. Underway with the diesel, he only made five knots headway in the heavy seas. He had thought of raising the sails to add a little speed, but he wanted to react quickly should he spot Charlie.

Miles and miles of ocean spread before him. He squinted into the bright whitecaps reflecting the sun. Too many sprites of light danced for his attention. His eyes fatigued, he hallucinated; every wave crest was a life preserver. Time escaped him. His watch read fourteen hundred, yet he wasn't sure when he had left Kawaihae Harbor. He needed to focus. "Where are you, Charlie?" he said, his question heard by no one on the empty sea.

With no Coast Guard, aerial surveillance, 911, or cell phone communications, his impromptu search effort looked futile. The blackout had wiped out a massive infrastructure of people, all of them waiting unnoticed, ready to come to your rescue with a simple push of a button.

He took the chart and matched two landmarks, showing his position offshore from Lapakahi Park, an abandoned fishing village about six miles north of Kawaihae. He scanned the horizon with binoculars, looking for a mast or sail, but found nothing. Charlie couldn't have sailed much farther north.

Tossing the chart aside, he swung the wheel toward the shoreline, thinking Charlie wouldn't venture into deeper water. The boat's bow pitched with a wild urgency over the swells and into the headwind. A wave, much larger than the others, lifted *Ohana* high enough for Brett to glimpse a blue object floating about a half mile ahead of him. No, it must be another illusion. Wait, there it was again. He snatched the binoculars and waited for *Ohana* to rise up again. Sure enough, an overturned sailboat. He let out a cry of joy and advanced the throttles. Within ten minutes, he powered over to the capsized boat. His heart leapt. Charlie floated in an orange life vest, clinging to the sailing dinghy's hull.

"Hang on, buddy," he called into the wind. "I'll come along-side. Stay close to your boat."

Charlie turned his head toward Brett. His slow movement and response suggested hypothermia. With *Ohana* abeam the overturned Blue Jay, Brett rigged the boarding ladder and dove into the water. Far from the coast, the water was much colder here, all the more reason to hurry before Charlie passed out. After helping him aboard, he wrapped him in a blanket. The dinghy now floated twenty feet away. He strapped on a harness with a fifty-foot safety line and dove into the water again. When he reached the sailing dinghy, he struggled with the wet mainsail for many minutes before releasing the halyard and furling the sail. His fingers grew numb, fumbling with the mainsheet. The dinghy righted itself, easing back to vertical, and obediently floated behind *Ohana*. He climbed aboard and sat beside Charlie. Out of breath, he placed his hand on Charlie's thigh. "You okay, buddy?" He reached for his water bottle and handed it to Charlie. "Here, you need to hydrate, but go slow. Small sips."

Charlie's eyes opened as if he'd awakened from a long sleep. After several swigs, he buried his head in the blanket. Brett grabbed dry clothes for him from his cabin. After Charlie changed, Brett wrapped him in the blanket again and let him sleep. With his course set back to Kawaihae, he called Manu to report he had found Charlie and asked him to relay the news to the police.

The sail back to the harbor passed much quicker than the trip out. A tern flew overhead; its track didn't waver from the shore-line. Even birds had more direction to their lives than did kids. Charlie snoozed in the late-afternoon sun, his lips pursed with every breath. Raising kids appeared harder than any job he ever had in the Navy. Such heartache and worries. Many chance events came together to save his little friend, the radio call from Kamuela, spotting the bicycle and missing sailboat, the lucky glimpse of the orange life preserver. Brett bit off a loose slice of a fingernail and spit it downwind. His stomach roiled at the reception he expected, Hellen's Irish fury at Charlie running off. Whatever possessed Charlie to pull such a stunt?

Charlie slept until they approached the channel. Facing the sun, he opened his eyes and frowned at Brett. "I screwed up. So, go ahead. Let me have it. I know you're mad."

"Mad? No, I'm not mad, just confused about why you would do such a crazy thing." Brett took his sunglasses off. "We sail thousands of miles across the Pacific, through squalls, a solar storm, get run out of Honolulu, turned away at Hilo, and finally make it to dry land. And what do you want to do? Go for a picnic sail."

"Okay, okay, so I'm a frickin' idiot."

"I'm just a little curious why you did it."

"Cause I'm as stupid as a box of rocks."

"Don't say that." Brett paused. "I did crazy shit when I was your age too."

Charlie squinted into the sun, holding his gaze off Brett. They spoke without words, a language built after weeks at sea together, a unique wavelength only they tuned into. After some minutes, Brett nodded. "Okay, I'm just glad you're safe. You worried me sick. Don't ever do that again or I'll throw your HoloSpecs overboard."

"Go ahead. I don't want them anymore."

Brett grinned, not sure if he'd heard those words from Charlie. Before Helio Hattie, so many distractions occupied people, streaming movies, VR gaming, social media, even online sex. Now the internet's mass hypnosis had died with the power grid. He scoffed at the irony. The end of modern living had brought folks back together again.

"Don't make me go back to her," Charlie said. "I never want to see her again."

"What did she do now?" Hellen was an enigma shared by Charlie and him alike. She'd never written him after their first summer together, despite her acting crazy in love with him.

"Elizabeth's my sister."

"Wait. Now, I'm confused. Who's Elizabeth?" Hellen had never mentioned any children other than Charlie. What's more, Charlie never spoke about a sister.

Charlie pulled his hoodie over his eyes. "Never mind. Just check me off your list."

"What the hell do you mean by that? After pulling your arse out of the sea—twice now—I'm responsible for you. You're my 'ohana now." Brett clenched his jaw. The waves rolled by them of their own accord, unconcerned about the travails of the human spirit. He wished he were a wave. Brett tapped his finger against the helm. "Let's start from the beginning. What happened?"

"Mom and I got into a fight last night. I needed to get out of her space."

"So, you came looking for me?"

"Yeah, I guess so. Look, you're the only friend I got within thousands of miles. I just thought..."

Brett swallowed hard and nodded. "Sure, I get it. But your mother will be crazy mad about this, mate. You took a big risk coming out here."

"Dude, you don't think I scope that. I was close to drowning out there. If you hadn't gone after me..."

"Eddie would've gone," Brett said, placing his arm over Charlie's shoulder. "It's all good."

"Who's Eddie?"

"Eddie Aikau, a legendary lifeguard on O'ahu's North Shore. He pulled surfers out of waves when no one else would dare try. Eddie would go when no one else would or could."

They passed the first channel marker and steered into the harbor. Brett surveyed the pier with binoculars and chuckled. Three women stood on dock next to a red car. He easily made out Hellen, pacing back and forth along the pier, her folded arms pressed against her chest, her red hair streaming in the breeze.

"Looks like we have a welcoming party." Brett handed the binoculars to Charlie. "That little redhead will blow a gasket any minute."

"Wait—what?" Charlie's face dissolved into a panic and he whipped the binoculars to his eyes. "This isn't going to be good."

"It sucks to be you, pal."

"Wait, dude. I can't go back with her. Like... just say I came down to visit you and we went sailing."

Brett gave him a mock semblance of shock but couldn't hide his smile. "Hold on, champ. That would be lying."

"What, like you never covered for someone."

Brett grinned at the kid, waiting for him to break his stare.

"Okay, you win. What do you want? But remember, I got nothing here."

"Well, for starters, you can stay down here with me for a few days until your mom cools off. There's lots of work for you, and it'll keep you out of further trouble."

"Sure, sure. Great." Charlie didn't take his eyes from the binoculars.

"And you'll take any job I give you with enthusiasm and intention. Am I making myself clear?"

"Yeah, sure. Whatever."

Brett raised his eyebrows. "Say again? I'm not sure I heard you right."

"Aye, aye sir," Charlie lowered the binoculars and shot him an impish smile, making Brett laugh.

Brett steered *Ohana* alongside the dock. The small group on the pier looked on, and Charlie threw the forward spring line to Manu, who cleated it in place, allowing Brett to use the propeller to walk the stern toward the pier. After securing all dock lines, he and Charlie stood next to each other on deck waiting for the welcoming committee to make their first move.

Across from him, not over ten feet away, stood a young woman, an *'ehu wahine*——a rare hair color for Hawaiians. She wore a silk wrap around her athletic hips and a floral bikini top. He nudged Charlie. "There's a fine wahine your age."

"She's Elizabeth, you idiot."

"Wow. Shame she's your sister." Brett removed his sunglasses. Her round Polynesian face, smooth tanned skin, and honey-brown eyes couldn't have been from Charlie's bloodline. "How old is she?"

"Eighteen."

After Brett did some quick mental math, he narrowed his eyes. "That's very interesting…"

Hellen placed her hands on her hips, tilting her head to one side. "So, what's the story, guys?" Her accent strengthened as her temper rose. "Charles Callahan, where the hell have you been? We had everyone out looking for you."

Charlie's eyes shifted between Elizabeth and her. "I came down to visit Brett."

Brett stood next to Charlie, chomping on a wad of gum. With the sun behind him, she couldn't read his face.

"A visit? Really?" She shook her head and glared at Brett. "And you, why the hell did you take him out sailing? First, you stay behind yesterday without as much as a goodbye, then you take Charlie offshore without checking in with me. You know, he's still recovering from his concussion."

He gave her a little shrug but said nothing. At least Charlie was safe, so she let the matter rest for now.

Manu ran down the pier, out of breath. Brett gave him the cutoff signal with his hand and winked at him. What was he hiding? He released the dinghy line from the stern cleat and threw it over to Manu and hopped ashore. She stepped up to him, but he kept his distance.

He nudged Manu's arm. "We better let mother and son become reacquainted. I'll fill you in later." They jumped in the dingy and sailed away from the boat slip before she could get to the bottom of his strange behavior.

Elizabeth's soft voice drew her attention back to her more pressing problem. "Hello, Charlie. I'm glad you're safe."

Charlie glared at Hellen. "Does she know, Mom?"

She shook her head slightly and held her index finger to her lips. The spider's web constricted around her lies even more.

Elizabeth pulled at Hellen's arm, sending her off balance. "Know what, Auntie?"

Charlie rolled his eyes and went belowdecks.

"What's going on? Tell me," Elizabeth said with fire in her eyes.

"Stay here, sweetheart. I need to speak to Charlie."

She climbed aboard *Ohana*, her first step setting the boat into a slight rocking motion. Elizabeth persisted with her questions, ever louder now. When Hellen came into the cabin, Charlie was lying on his bunk, his eyes shut. She sat beside him and ran her fingers through his hair the way she did when he was a little lad. He didn't push her hand away, a sign of truce. She let her touch, more than any contrite words, speak of her apology. She dried her eyes on her sleeve and rolled her neck, stretching the shame-stricken pain out of her muscles.

After an eternity, Charlie opened his eyes. His mouth opened as if he wanted to say something. His eyes were defiant—a bright, blue glare. "I can't go home right now," he said at last.

A great tenderness for him welled within her, soon eclipsed by mounting terror, the fear of the truth reaching Brett and Elizabeth before she was ready. Then something altogether more complicated, something akin to resentment.

"I know, love. Take all the time you need. Stay with Brett; you can trust him."

"He's about the only one left."

His words hurt her to her core, but she let them pass. With a final brush of his red locks, she kissed his forehead and went topside. The harsh sunlight blinded her after being in the dim cabin. Seeing Brett approach, she crossed her arms, pretending to be more annoyed than she felt. "I'm still not convinced of what really happened down here, but Charlie's safe and seems eager to stay. Is it okay with you? I mean, just for a couple of days. I wouldn't want him underfoot."

Brett walked over to her, put his arm around her shoulders, and threw her a shaka sign. "*'A'ole pilikia*—no problem at all—I could use a second pair of hands. There's a lot of work for him down here."

Hellen started toward the pier, then ran back to embrace him. Finding Charlie was about the only bright spot to this day. She pressed her body against him and buried her face in his shoulder. He exhaled a long breath against her neck, sending a shiver down her spine. He must have heard nothing from Charlie.

"Take care of my boy," she whispered before kissing him goodbye. She released him and ran back to the car, sitting next to Elizabeth in the rear seat. After the car pulled away, she leaned into the side window, smiled, and waved to Brett until she lost sight of him.

On the way home, Hellen braced herself for the most difficult part of her day: confronting Elizabeth with the shock of her life.

10

They arrived at Cloudcroft at sunset. Elizabeth bolted from the car, leaving Elle and Hellen alone. "I'll tell her tonight," Hellen said. "I think she already suspects something." But she would plan her chess game this time, not blunder into it as she had done with Charlie.

"I feel like an accomplice in this lie of yours. She's my daughter as much as yours."

"I know, but I don't want you to carry this burden anymore. Maybe it's better if I speak to her alone."

"No, I want to be there. Elizabeth needs to understand why we kept your identity a secret all these years."

Through the dirty windshield, Hellen saw Suzu sitting on the porch in a lotus position, eyes closed. Elle had spent most of her years with Suzu. They were yin and yang, two dichotomous personalities, Elle a lesbian and Suzu a transgender male, yet they seemed to make their relationship work. Together, they completed each other and gave themselves strength.

After they strolled up the path to the front door, Elle stopped before reaching the stairs and smiled at her partner. Suzu opened his eyes and pressed his lips together. As if reading Hellen's mind, he nodded to the barn. "Elizabeth's feeding the horses."

Hellen strode down to the stables and opened the barn's heavy wooden door and walked down the row of stalls. The single lightbulb hanging overhead cast her shadow ahead of her. She took a deep breath. The horses nickered from their stalls. In all her years in Colorado, she had never found the time or money to own horses. The familiar scent of hay and manure sent her back to her childhood. She had freedoms then unheard of in today's bubble-wrapped society. She rode her first rodeo at fourteen and won Kohala's barrel racing competition at sixteen. Through all this, she had a sixth sense of understanding the equine mind, a horse whisperer, some had said. If only she could read her own children as well.

After her eyes adapted to the barn's dim interior, Elizabeth's silhouette came into focus at the end of the row of stalls. Elizabeth hauled on a bale of hay, seemingly unaware Hellen had entered the barn. After years of hiding her identity, the moment had come to reveal herself to Elizabeth. The relief flowing through her chest surprised her, a feeling of freedom, free from carrying her secret burden, free from loneliness. Like many women, she endured her loneliness in silence all these years, pretended to be strong when she was uncertain or weak when she was confident. After years of hiding the truth, she now denounced her lie. Her daughter needed to be celebrated, not pushed to the sideline. Her voyage to Hawai'i had been a way to grow closer to Charlie, but now her focus was on Elizabeth, a path away from shame and toward reconciliation. Knowing a lifetime of happiness could be thrown away by her betrayal was like a key opening the door to her vast anguish.

"Elizabeth..." she said, uncertain what to say next.

Her daughter straightened her spine and smiled. The darkness beyond the barn windows shrank the world. Hellen froze this moment in her mind, knowing this might be the last time her daughter looked at her this way. After Elle promised to raise Elizabeth, she had warned Hellen against carrying secrets; they haunted and poisoned relationships, hurting the ones we loved the most.

"I've already fed them and cleaned their stalls."

"Thanks, love."

Elizabeth sat on a hay bale and rubbed mink oil into a set of leather bridles with practiced hands. Hellen wondered if her own love of animals had passed on to Elizabeth or if she had picked this up while living at Cloudcroft. Either way, Hellen might never have another chance of riding with her after tonight.

"Something Charlie said at the marina. Do you have something to share with me?"

Hellen looked away, searching for the right words.

"Come on; I hate the suspense. What's up?"

"Just remember, I will always love you."

"Sounds serious. Don't tell me you have cancer or something."

"Nothing that serious." Hellen took the bridle from Elizabeth's hands and headed for the tack room. After she returned, she offered her hand to Elizabeth and stepped into an uncertain future.

Elle was waiting for them in the living room. Suzu beckoned Elizabeth to sit on the sofa next to Elle, then took a seat next to the life-sized bronze statue of Siddhārtha Gautama dominating the room. The grinning Buddha looked like a referee in a Sumo match. Suzu was always keen for symbolic setups, letting subtext drive the day. But there wasn't anything subtle or nuanced about tonight's message. Things would never be the same. She faced this moment not with fear, but instead with a resignation born from moments of dread. Her tension ebbed from her shoulders and melted into a calm before a squall.

"Auntie Hellen," Elizabeth said, "Is this about Charlie?"

"No, it's about you," Elle said. "I've always said you would someday meet your birth mother."

Elizabeth's eyes shown with bright anticipation. Frustrated by

Suzu's seating arrangement, Hellen walked over to Elizabeth and sat beside her and took her small hands in hers. Elizabeth's smile faded, and her complexion turned ashen with a sudden awareness.

"Sweetheart," Hellen said with no energy left in her voice. "I was... I mean, I am your mother."

Elizabeth wrinkled her brow and squinted. "Wait, you can't be my mother."

Hellen said nothing, waiting for Elizabeth to absorb the news.

"I look nothing like you. This is impossible."

Hellen twirled a strain of her red hair in front of her raised eyebrows until Elizabeth's eyes widened.

"No. I can't even believe... Shit. First Kalino dies, then you spring this on me. Why did you give me up?"

"I never gave you up—I made a plan for you, the best one I could under the circumstances." Hellen's pulse quickened, and she rolled her head back, trying to breathe, trying to keep herself together. A pressure in her temples grew unbearable.

"But you came here every year... pretending to be my auntie. I loved you. Why didn't you tell me?"

Both Elle and Elizabeth stared at her, one melancholy, the other appalled by the train wreck brought on by her mother.

Hellen took a deep breath and her words poured out. "I carried you for forty-one weeks, you came a week late. You've always liked to sleep in." Hellen smiled. "After I delivered you, you were adorable. I spent every hour—every minute—bonding with you, knowing I couldn't keep you. Even today, I wonder if I did the right thing. I'm so sorry, I only wanted..." She choked off her remaining words. Through her upwelling eyes, Elizabeth's face swam in a blurry mist.

"Your mother was still in school," Elle said, "a bright future ahead of her. Only a little older than you are now, she wasn't ready for motherhood. I offered to look after you."

Hellen took Elizabeth's clammy hands in hers. "We did this

for your own safety. You weren't abandoned, you were protected. It wasn't safe with me."

Elizabeth scoffed. "So, now you work for CIA?"

Laughter choked Hellen's shame. "No, more like MIA, Married in Anguish. We tried, but—"

"We always wanted you to return to your mother," Suzu jumped in, "but after the wall around America came up, we couldn't get you through. America's Alien and Sedition Acts prevented you from immigrating to Colorado. Besides, your mother's life was in shambles: an abusive husband, her addiction, her constant fear of losing her son. It was too much for her."

"But why the secrecy?"

For the first time since they sat down, Elle's voice quivered. "A novice monk once asked her teacher, 'What is the way?' The teacher said, 'An open-eyed man falling into the well.'"

"I don't need your koans right now, just honest answers."

"Life has its own momentum," Hellen said. "The years passed. We realized you belonged here, with your friends, your familiar surroundings, your own life. And I had my own life and career in America."

"So you left me in Elle's care. Was that fair to her or me?"

"Chop wood, carry toddler," Elle said. "Chop wood, carry teenager."

Elle's twist on the famous koan rang true. A mother's work is never done. Hellen's struggles with Charlie were different, but no less easy than Elle's travails with Elizabeth. The pressure in Hellen's throat tightened. She never could muster the same strength many other mothers had in their daily battles with teenage children. As a single mother, her sense of inferiority was always amplified without a loving partner to balance her emotions, not in the same way as Elle and Suzu. Yet now she had Brett. Having him in her life again gave her a renewed will to set things right with Elizabeth, even if it destroyed Elizabeth's trust in her.

"You're not a teenager anymore," Hellen said. "You're a

beautiful and savvy young woman, a product of Elle's loving care. You are ready for the world, you should be ready for the truth."

"Well, I'm not ready for this bombshell."

"You can blame me as well, if you want," Elle said. "After you turned five, I didn't want to let you go, and Hellen had her hands full with Charlie."

Suzu narrowed his eyes and shook his head. "But waiting until now had unintended consequences."

Elizabeth closed her eyes. "So that's why Charlie ran away. I love him. Oh, the thought of us cupcaking together makes me... sick inside."

Elle took a deep breath and glanced over to Hellen, as if waiting for her to speak, but Hellen only dropped her head under the weight of so much guilt and shame.

"The love you two shared was pure," Elle continued, "but now it must take a different course. Don't feel ashamed for loving him. You were—and still are—such brilliant and special children. After you were born, you became the light of Hellen's life. We only wanted the best for you. To keep you safe."

Elizabeth folded her arms across her chest. "You needn't lie to protect my feelings. I'd rather you tell me the truth with love and respect. One last question. Charlie and I couldn't look more different. So, who's my father?"

Hellen clenched her jaw, surprised, then angry with herself, as if it never occurred to her Elizabeth would ask this simple question. "He's the love of my life. You couldn't have a better father, brave, yet sensitive, a cool head under fire. A war hero, he saved the lives of many people, including Charlie and me."

"When can I meet him?"

"You already have. He's Brett Akamu, *Ohana's* skipper. You saw him today with Charlie."

"He doesn't know, does he? By the way he acted... You've played out this secret with him as well?"

"I wanted to speak to you first. After the two of you get used to the idea, you'll meet him." Hellen choked back her anguish and forced a smile. "I'm afraid it's too soon to plan for a father-daughter cotillion."

Elizabeth covered her mouth with her hand, her eyes glistening. She stood and ran from the room, and Elle went after her. Hellen leaned forward and crossed her arms over her chest with a gentle rocking motion. Across from her, Suzu's face held a serene pool of sympathy. At last, he came over to Hellen and held her. "The truth may hurt for a little while but lies hurt for a lifetime."

11

Kamuela

The next morning, Gus pulled off Island Belt Highway after passing a sign announcing Cloudcroft Plantation. He found a small dirt road a hundred yards beyond the sign, a tractor path blocked by a cattle gate. Unlocked, the gate swung open with a nudge from his Vagabond. The overgrown, rutty access road followed a tree line next to Otoko's plantation. Local looters had warned him she had a perimeter defense—electronic sensors—around the main house. He parked his SUV off the path, hidden by brushwood, and walked into the forest. Within eyesight of the main house, he stopped and checked a meter he brought with him. Its needle wagged back and forth, then twitched more wildly as he walked closer. About waist-high, a photosensor beam glowed in front of him in the dim forest. After slipping under it, he crept toward the house, moved from tree to tree, secluded in the dawn. He had planned his route to arrive behind the property, hoping to get in without much notice.

Two hundred feet from the back porch, he lay down in the woods and removed a set of binoculars from his backpack. His mission today was surveillance, to case the joint for a future job.

He needed gold to pay off the PGP boys and Elle Otoko was rumored to be sitting on a load of the metal. He didn't know much about her. She kept to herself, her only public face was her role as Kohala's mayor. Between her wealth and lesbian lifestyle, she had reasons to protect her privacy. In some ways, he respected her for this. It only added to the Buddhist witch's mystique.

Never one to dabble in petty theft—the drug trade was plenty profitable—he took his time, careful to not expose himself. The house sat dark and quiet. Everyone must still be asleep. Through his binoculars, he scoped the house, then an adjacent barn. A trim, middle-aged woman walked down a path from the stables to a vegetable garden suffocating under a canopy of weeds and vines, her red plaited hair swinging from side to side with each stride. After clearing the uninvited plants away, she collected vegetables and placed them in a wicker basket.

She passed through the garden and came to a wall of coffee trees and kiwi vines stretching up from a bed of white orchids and red hibiscus, only twenty feet from him. Her movement excited a flock of tropical birds in the trees, generating a rhapsody of birdsong swelling in the breeze. Gus squirmed under all the racket, hoping she would go back inside.

She sang to herself in a strange, lilting accent while she pulled weeds, her forehead and cheeks covered with perspiration, her hands coated with dark soil. Gus dared not move, but she took too much time. After an eternity, she sat back against a fence post. He shook his head and let out a long breath. His morning coffee had worked its way to his bladder, and this chick was never going to leave.

A cloud rolled up the hill and into the garden. The cool fog coated her skin, mixing with her perspiration. Thankfully, the mist soon grew into rain, at first only a light shower, then heavier. Maybe she'd leave. She stood up and arched her back. Her rain-soaked shirt lay flat against her skin. Drops streamed over her face and dripped onto her chest. Damn, she was a fine sight after his long dry spell. Perhaps this trip out here wasn't a total bust. He removed his Smith & Wesson from his backpack and stood up, ready to make his move. But the clouds opened into a deluge before he broke out of the woods. Never aware of him, she ran through the pouring rain to the barn and out of view. The morning light grew brighter, his cover exposed. It was time to get out of there. Perhaps another day.

Hellen squeezed the water from her T-shirt and leaned against the nearest stall door, listening to the horses munching on their oats and alfalfa. She envied their lack of concern about the human world, oblivious to the blackout. Unlike her relationship with men, horses always gave her solace, followed her direction, and never hurt her—except for the time Lulua'ina balked at a jump, sending her flying over the fence. Brett was more horse than man in some ways, easy to read, spoke few words, and never threatened her. Yet she found ways to hurt him alright. She swallowed to loosen the tightness in her throat. The secret she carried became one more in a string of deceptions she played with him. Closer to him now than ever before, she could no longer walk silent circles around him. But her disclosure risked their relationship. The more she thought about it, the more her old demons whispered in her ear. Honesty never wins. She palm-smacked her forehead. "Jesus," she whispered. "I'm a bloody sot. Why do I keep doing this?"

The horses stirred as if spooked by something outside the barn walls. Lulua'ina kicked the stall door and swung her head up. Through the opened barn door, she saw a shadow—no, a man—running across the garden and into the woods. Looter most likely. She grabbed a handful of buckshot shells and a shotgun from the tack room, an old break-action piece, but it would have to do. She ran to the spot she last saw him, but the leaves no longer rustled. Heavy breathing came beneath a row of brushwood twenty feet away. She raised her shotgun and waited for him to move. A stifled snort helped her pinpoint his hiding spot.

"I have a beeline on you. Come out of there, hands raised." She mounted the shotgun against her right shoulder and fired above the bush. Everything discharged into noise—pellets ricocheted a resounding ping against a rock. Birds alighted from tree branches above her. Leaves and twigs rained down around her. The shotgun's blast echoed through the forest, but the gun's kick scared her more. Newton's third law sent a stinging pang through her right shoulder. No sooner had she recovered, she faced a charging boar out from the woods. The hairy beast with two piggy eyes and bad manners galloped toward her, grunting with an angry snarl, then trashing and squealing loud enough to wake the dead. She took aim with quivering hands and fired again. The wild boar snapped its head back and stumbled while its hind legs pitched and staggered drunkenly out of its control.

Unable to stand, it twisted and kicked, its haunches pushing its body toward Hellen as its snout plowed the ground. She tried to load another shell into the breech, but her hands shook so hard the first one sprang from her fingers like a compressed spring and landed with a thud into the mud. The hog squealed, tried to heave itself one more time, but its legs collapsed. It lay there, panting, waiting for the end. Finally, she fumbled another shell from her pocket, broke open the barrel to reload, and shot again. The forest fell silent, except for Hellen's labored breaths.

"Yes! Protein," she yelled, her words scattered through the forest.

The boar lay against the bank of the garden, a pool of blood soaked the earth. Hellen approached and stood over it for a moment. She picked up a hind leg, clutching her jaw against the feel of stiff hair and the hog's residual body warmth. She heaved the leg, but it wouldn't budge. She grabbed both forelegs and yanked back, putting her weight into pulling the boar. It shifted a few inches until her hands, now slippery from all the blood, lost their grip, sending her reeling back on her rump. After brushing herself off, she went back to the barn.

Hellen opened Lulua'ina's stall and the mare's head swayed toward her. She led her to the harnessing area beside the tack room and found a harness.

"I need your help my friend, but I'm afraid it's not a jaunt through the meadow."

Lulua'ina patiently stood by, letting Hellen harness her up with a leather breast collar and bridle with driving reins. With a plastic tarp under one arm, Hellen led the mare down to the garden. By the time she arrived, the boar had bled out. She rolled the animal onto the tarp by pulling on its legs. She attached the leather traces from the harness breast collar to the leading corners of the tarp before giving Lulua'ina a gentle prod with the reins. The horse bopped its head up and down with each stride, tugging the carcass with ease. They soon arrived at Cloudcroft's back steps.

Elle met her in the doorway, a Ruger long rifle in hand, the gun out of place with her black Buddhist robe.

"Don't bother," Hellen said between breaths. "I scared them off. Wild boars this time. We're going to have a fine English breakfast. I'm not going to miss those MREs."

Elle walked onto the lanai and looked down with wide eyes. "Good god, I'm glad you're on our side. That'll keep you and Charlie fed for weeks. But Suzu and I aren't ready to give up our Buddhist vows just yet."

Hellen unbridled Lulua'ina and allowed her to graze on the back lawn. She then followed Elle into the kitchen and washed her hands. The calendar next to the refrigerator had rows of red x's, ending with July 4th. "Son of a biscuit, I almost forgot."

"Forgot what?"

"It's Charlie's sixteenth birthday. Maybe I could go for a quick visit."

"Go ahead. I'll stay here with Elizabeth. Take my eBike; it's in the barn. Sorry, I don't have much to bake with. Wait, there's cookie dough mix in the pantry."

Hellen jumped into fixing a birthday meal for Charlie. Worried about the daily diet the boys lived on, she selected some of the best carrots, tomatoes, lettuce, and fruit to bring down to them. She found a butcher knife in the drawer and went to work on the boar carcass. The loathsome memory of the time Kalino had dressed a wild boar flooded back to her. She grabbed its snout and forced its head up and sliced the knife blade across its throat, tearing into the jugular and draining thick red blood into the grass. Next, she smashed its breastbone apart with a hatchet, its entrails squeezed from the cavity, heavy and rancid. She swallowed back the bile in her throat and stopped to drink water. For the next hour, she labored, peeling skin from flesh, flesh from bone, separating the meat into chunks for boiling and frying, and other strips for drying and smoking. The sun warmed her into a sweaty mess. Blood stained her shirt in splotches resembling a Rorschach inkblot test.

"Gross! Who are you now, Jane of the Jungle?"

The shocked expression on Elizabeth's face made Hellen laugh with embarrassment. She waved the knife in the air. "A mother will stop at nothing to make sure her children are fed."

"Hellen, you're one crazy woman. I'll pass on the meat."

"It's time you considered a flexitarian diet. You'll never get enough protein from your rice and green tea."

"Killing isn't part of a Buddhist's DNA. And neither is lying."

Hellen doubted Elizabeth's Buddhist ties ran deep. Last summer, she took her to a local firing range and taught her how to shoot a twenty-two-caliber long rifle. A natural sharpshooter, she loved every minute of it.

"It's Charlie's birthday. Want to come down to the harbor with me for a visit?"

"Are you kidding? You don't have a clue," she snapped, her

jaw a stubborn line. Without waiting for an answer, she brushed her hair over her shoulder and went back inside the house.

Hellen swallowed her words. Her daughter was right. They weren't ready yet. Not Charlie. Not Elizabeth. And she'd hadn't even told Brett he was her father. Good grief. Always ready, fire, aim. When would she ever learn?

With the boar dressed, she let the meat sit in the sun to dry out. Without a reliable source of power at night, she'd no way to preserve the meat other than making jerky, a Colorado delicacy she loathed. The solar storm had fried the battery bank storing electricity from the solar and wind power systems. Elle's hybrid car sat in the driveway, a modern deep-cycle battery in its chassis. After she hosed herself off, she found Elle's keys and drove the car around the house and parked next to the power distribution panel. With the jumper cables from the trunk, she connected the lithium-ion battery in series between the solar system's charge controller and DC inverter. After she isolated the solar panels from the controller, she tested the jerry-rigged reserve bank. It worked. They could enjoy power day or night. And she could store her meat in the freezer.

She went to her bedroom, showered and changed into a more civilized outfit, jeans and a floral blouse.

"Where's my car?" Elle shouted from the front hallway.

Hellen ran from her room. "Sorry. I requisitioned it. Needed the battery to replace the bank for the solar system. I can disconnect it if you need your car back. But now we can have power day and night."

Elle clapped her hands. "My, you're a clever one. Keep it. I can use the truck to get around."

While the cookies baked, she fried the pork strips and dreamed of how her boys spent their days together. She knew she could suffocate Charlie with her attention, but today she had a mother's prerogative.

Elizabeth's footsteps paced in her room above the kitchen.

With a plate of baked cookies in hand, Hellen walked slowly up the stairs and down the hall to Elizabeth's bedroom.

She knocked softly on the door. "I've brought a peace offering. Chocolate-chip cookies straight from the oven."

"Leave me alone," Elizabeth said from behind the closed door.

"Come on, love. Let's share some of these. They're delicious!"

"Stay away. You've bad karma, the kind that'll turn you into a cockroach in your next life."

A soreness rose in Hellen's throat; the Wheel of Samsara had chained her fate again. Filled with a sense of fear and inadequacy, she left the plate by the door and walked down the hallway. Before she realized it, she had returned to the kitchen.

Elle paused from peeling chickpeas and looked up. "In time, she'll come around to accept you as her mother. Remember the koan, when you can do nothing, what can you do?"

"Time. Patience. Solace," Hellen recalled. Like the Impulse-Momentum Theorem, time was the critical element for any change to occur.

"Restore your faith in yourself. Go to Charlie and celebrate his birthday. He needs you."

Hellen nodded and retrieved the Beretta M9 handgun from the safe and packed it in her backpack along with the small food basket. Taking a second chance, she went up to Elizabeth's room. The plate was gone. At least it was a start. She pressed her hand against the closed door. "I'm going now. Love you, sweetheart. I'm so sorry for all the hurt I've caused. But please don't let a lifetime of love between us end like this."

No sound came from her bedroom. She relaxed her arm, letting her hand slide down the door, a wooden barrier between her and Elizabeth, silent in the hallway.

12

Offshore of the Kona Coast

After Charlie zipped the mainsail cover and gave a thumbs-up gesture, Brett advanced the throttle and turned *Ohana* toward the shoreline. Ahead of them, a humpback whale leapt from the sea, its white ventral pleats glistening in the sunlight. It fell back into the water, sending spray high above the waves.

"Did you see that?" Charlie yelled from the foredeck.

"The whales breach to knock the barnacles off their skin."

"They're huge. Why haven't we seen them before?"

"They spend most of the year off Russian America, northwest of Canada. During their calving season, they migrate into Hawaiian waters."

Charlie hadn't been this excited since he came aboard in San Diego. Even the aurora hadn't grabbed his attention like this. Perhaps the whale's smooth motion so close to the boat fascinated him or seeing a new form of life might seem alien to him.

"They migrate thousands of miles through the Pacific," Brett continued. "The calf stays close to its mother for a year before venturing off on its own. Why they come to Hawai'i to give birth is a mystery."

Charlie peppered Brett with dozens of questions on their way back to the harbor. How deep did they dive? How long did they live? Brett didn't have all the answers for Charlie. So little was known about one of the largest mammals on Earth.

"Let's get this fish stowed," Brett called to him.

"Aye, aye, sir."

"You can knock that off," Brett jeered at him. "It's so 'dead' now, as you say."

Charlie gave him the stink-eye; so much for his lame attempt at 2K25 slang. Charlie dumped the load of fish from the trawling net into a twenty-gallon cooler and slammed the lid. He took the bumpers and docking lines from the lazarette and rigged them to the side of the sailboat with no prompting. After tying *Ohana* up to the pier and hosing her decks, Brett went below to the galley and fired up the propane burner. He reached up and opened the porthole above the stove for ventilation.

Charlie shoved him aside. "Out of the way, Skipper," he said. "I got this. You can rest your old bones topside, and I'll call you when it's ready."

Brett smiled at the kid's brash attitude. Despite his bravado, Charlie had mentioned nothing more about his newfound half-sister. Hellen must have met someone after he deployed to West-Pac. Hellen's ex-husband, Sam, wasn't the father, not an ounce of Polynesian blood in him. Charlie had never spoken of his father —as if the guy never existed. Brett's growing friendship with Charlie rekindled his yearning for a family life, but families these days were a mixed lot, each with their own dark histories. Hellen was no exception.

After they finished their canned ham and rice, Brett suggested a little walkabout. Once pier side, Brett tussled Charlie's hair. "Want to race?"

Charlie shook his head and slowed his pace, head hung low.

"Afraid this old man will beat you?" Brett gave Charlie's shoulder a playful shove, to make sure he knew he was only kidding.

"Don't man," Charlie kept his hands in his pocket. "Not in the mood, okay?"

They stopped first at Manu's shack. The harbor master threw them a bag of baked coconut chips, and Charlie caught it with one hand. He dug in without sharing any with Brett, probably in retaliation for Brett hogging the supply of rice candy all week.

"Manu, you got a freezer to store our fish?"

"I think there's one at the end of the marina by the canoe clubhouse, but it got no power. Go check it out. If it's what you're looking for, I'll use the forklift to bring it back here and hook it up to the wind generator."

"Good idea," Brett said, glancing at Charlie. "Road trip?"

They walked to Manu's golf cart, and Brett took the passenger seat without a word, letting Charlie drive. The kid stomped on the accelerator before fastening his seat belt. The kid drove it like a go-cart around the stacked cargo containers, almost throwing Brett out of right seat.

"You got your driving license yet?"

"Learner's permit."

"Right. Good thing this museum relic has a top speed of only twenty."

After a mile drive, Brett pointed to the canoe clubhouse. Charlie drove to it, and Brett jumped out before they stopped and jogged over to the freezer.

"Looks fine," Brett called back with his head inside the five-foot-tall aluminum box. "Plenty of room, but too large to move. Give Manu a call."

Charlie snatched a handheld radio from the gulf cart dashboard. "Manu, you read me?"

"Roger, go ahead Charlie."

"The cooler looks fine. Can you help us move it?"

"Sure thing, man. I'm busy right now, but I'll be by in about an hour."

Charlie put the radio back into its holder. With plenty of time until Manu came with the forklift, Brett headed to a steep dirt path leading up the surrounding hill. He called Charlie over, hoping they might find the *heiau* ruins at the top.

Charlie hiked behind him as they wound their way up the switchbacks. "Where did you get your tattoo?" he asked in between breaths.

"Uncle Kane."

"Who?"

"I ran away from home when I was your age and lived with him."

"Ran away?"

Brett stopped on the trail and turned to Charlie. "I had to get away from my father. The moke used to beat me whenever he drank too much. By the time I entered high school, I realized we might end up killing each other, so Uncle Kane took me in."

"I hear ya." Charlie's soft fingers traced the design on Brett's back.

Brett wondered if Charlie's response came from personal experience. "My tattoo tells the story of my Polynesian heritage," Brett said, almost to himself. "The wahine represents fertility. The canoe is for our ancestors' migration from Hawaiki in the western Pacific, and the spear is a symbol of our warrior spirit."

"What's the busted face for?" Charlie asked.

"That's Kū, the god of war. I added him after I joined the Navy."

"I want one of those tattoos."

"Fo' real?"

"Just like yours. But Mom would choke."

"Why? I heard she got her tattoo at about your age. Tell you what, let me talk to her. We'll get you fixed up with one."

"Brett, you're such a—"

"Badarse. Yeah, I know."

After reaching the top of the hill, they stood in front of the Pu'ukohola Heiau. At first glance, the ancient, stone Hawaiian temple was little more than a wall of rocks piled atop the barren landscape. It had changed little since Brett first came here over twenty-five years ago with Uncle Kane.

He spread his right arm in front of him. "Here lies the Hawaiian Kingdom's birthplace, built by King Kamehameha."

"Like some sort of big kahuna?"

"No, kahuna means priest. Kamehameha was a king slayer."

Brett led Charlie inside the temple ruins. "He was born from the love between two half-siblings. Among the royal *ali'i*, incest was more common than most people want to believe. While carrying Kamehameha in her womb, his mother dreamed her son would someday eat the eyeball of her tribal chief. The *noho ali'i* got wind of this and ordered the baby killed after she gave birth, but Kamehameha's mother fled with her half-brother to a remote part of Waipi'o Valley."

"That's lit. Did they ever find Kamehameha?"

"No, but Captain Cook did."

They walked deeper into the stone labyrinth and stopped beside a historical marker showing the temple's layout.

"As a young man," Brett continued, "Kamehameha was shrewd. He used Cook's western technology and cunning battle tactics to gain power. He built this temple and lured a rival chief to the temple's inaugural sacrifice. You can guess who became the main course for the luau."

Charlie laughed. "No! They sacrificed the chief?"

"After eliminating the competition, Kamehameha united all the islands under his reign."

"Are you related to him?"

"No, but Elle is. The land around Cloudcroft came from Princess Grace Kama'iku'i, Kamehameha's niece. She married a white man who became a trusted adviser to Kamehameha's descendants. Their hānai daughter later became Queen Emma."

For some time, Brett and Charlie sat alone in their thoughts. The ocean stretched to the horizon, a stark, smooth line between the azure sky and dark blue water. Waves crashed along the shore and echoed within the temple, their sound mixing with an occasional gust of wind through the stone walls. The trees down the hill swayed in the breeze, their leaves rustling, a sound in tune with the breaking whitecaps. Here with Charlie, Brett could sit forever, passing time, sharing this space together. For the moment, he forgot about the blackout, but the empty shipping port brought him back to reality. He wondered how long they could continue without telecommunications, fuel, and commerce. They were all living on borrowed time. Soon the mayhem on O'ahu would reach their Shangri-La.

Charlie finally broke their silence. "Thanks for letting me hang out with you this week. After hearing about Elizabeth, I had to get out of Cloudcroft."

"How long have you known about her?"

"I've known her all my life, but not as my sister until this week. What's crazy… I think we had a thing for each other. Kind of weird, huh?"

"Not if you both didn't know. She's a looker all right. Can't blame you for trying. But you too don't share many traits. Is she your half-sister?"

"Mom never mentioned her father." He hesitated with a growing frown. "I need to ask you something. What's the story between you and Mom? Like I got to know, mate."

Brett shook his head and stifled a laugh. "Say again?"

"Like, you need me to highkey it for you?" He adjusted his ball cap and looked away. "You know, the two of you? I don't want to see her hurt again."

"You don't mince words."

"Since her divorce, she's had her fill of losers."

"Are you calling me a loser?"

"Ah shit, Brett. No, but I—"

"Charlie, did you just say shit?" Brett hadn't ever heard the kid swear. Maybe mentioning his father again set him off.

"You're pretty savage yourself. Mom's been on a dry spell these past couple of years, and now you come waltzing into her life again. It's like Lahaina all over again."

"How do you know about that?" They had only one summer together before going their separate ways, long before Charlie was born. Hard to imagine how Hellen had mentioned it to Charlie.

"Ah shit, Brett."

"Jeez. Stop saying shit. What would your mother say if she heard you cussing like a sailor while hanging out with me?"

Charlie grinned and gave him a playful shove. "She'd say you're a shitty adult role model and drag me back to Cloudcroft."

"What's gotten into you?"

"I don't know."

With the sun low of the horizon, Brett glanced at his watch. Charlie's hand twisted Brett's wrist to look at its face.

"What now?"

"It's July fourth. Today's my sixteenth birthday and who gives a shit?"

Brett slapped Charlie on the back. "Ey, fo' real? Sorry. Didn't know…"

"And neither did Mom, apparently. She forgot just like Dad always did."

Brett rested his elbow on Charlie's shoulder while they both stared out to sea. How could anyone forget their kid's birthday when it fell on the Yank's Independence Day? "Bummuhs, dude." He gave a long sigh and tossed a lava rock down the hill. "But your birthday isn't over yet, right? Let's head back and grab dinner. Maybe we celebrate, eh?"

"And a couple beers?"

"Sure. Whatever you want; it's your birthday. But don't let your mom know; otherwise, she'd give me shit."

"Hey, Brett," Charlie said, "you shouldn't say shit."

Hellen's trip down to the Kawaihae Harbor passed quickly, her mind consumed with a spider web of worry. Too many things pulled at her like gravity's rainbow: restoring the power grid, restoring her children's trust in her. Heat threaded through her neck as she imagined how Brett would take the news. Maybe Charlie had already told him about his half-sister. With Elizabeth standing on the pier the other day, just feet from him, he must've made his own conclusions. Or perhaps Charlie didn't tell him, too ashamed of his amorous feelings for Elizabeth. She couldn't blame him; he didn't know, his love for her was pure. The only one she could blame was herself. First, she had pushed Charlie away, then Elizabeth. So much for honesty. Now came Brett's turn. She slowed her bike to a stop at the harbor entrance. The thought of returning to Cloudcroft crossed her mind, an easy out, a way to avoid hurting him, but she had come this far both emotionally and physically. The harbor lay before her with its dormant cranes. Here her voyage across the Pacific had ended and her path to reconciliation began. Too late to back out now; her secret was out in the open.

She rode through the late-afternoon shadows to the transient dock where *Ohana* floated. A pile of fish lay on the pier, hundreds of them glistening in the sun. Stepping aboard *Ohana* after many days ashore seemed like stepping back in time, into another world. She took a long breath and closed her eyes. The nightmare of falling overboard returned, but vanished just as fast, replaced by Brett saving her from the sea. And her lonely life. Finding no one aboard, she rode over to see Manu, the harbor master. At his usual post, he sat at his desk, a pomegranate in his hand.

"Aloha," she said. "What have my boys been up to?"

"They've caught enough fish to keep everyone fed around here for the next week. Brett has earned his keep and more."

Manu's talk story made Hellen's heart shine. After the blackout, everyone found ways to help out. "Geez, you guys move fast. Have you seen Brett and Charlie? They're not on the boat."

Manu gave her a broad smile and tossed her a kiwi fruit.

"They're at the other end of the port checking out a refrigerator —oh, crap, I forgot to pick it up." He stood from his chair and stretched his huge arms. "Want a ride?"

"No, I'll wait for them at the boat. By the way," Hellen said, studying his expression, "what exactly happened last Wednesday?"

Manu rubbed his chin and stared at his desk. He seemed to struggle with the question, his eyes darting left and right. Slow to speak, he carved a slice of fruit with his knife. At last, he replayed the events of that day, ending with Brett rescuing Charlie after his sailing dinghy capsized. She folded her arms, feeling her cold sweaty palms against her sides. She said nothing, absorbed in the pain of what might have happened if Brett hadn't gone after her son. She ran out of the office, slamming the door behind her.

During the ride to the boat, she tried to collect her thoughts, afraid she might throw another fit, creating a big scene. After all, the boys acted like chums the other day. She sat by the boat, closed her eyes, and took measured breaths. Charlie had run away from her revelation and from his own shame. She shivered at the notion of her son drowning, alone in the cold waters, clinging to the dinghy, finally succumbing to hypothermia, and sinking to the ocean. And there it was—Brett had saved Charlie, again. Donovan had been right; she could trust this man with her life.

She smiled, imagining her boys fishing, working on the boat, and spending time together. At least for now, Charlie had someone to trust, to follow. She would give anything for her son but couldn't give him the one thing he needed most—the path to manhood.

She climbed aboard *Ohana* and stowed the items she had brought down from Cloudcroft, the flanks of bacon and ham, vegetables, rice, cooking oil, protein powder, and more clean clothes for Charlie. By the looks of the cabin, the one thing Charlie wasn't learning from Brett was housekeeping. She picked all the loose clothes off the deck and threw empty bottles into the trash. After getting the cabin shipshape, she laid the fresh cookies out on a plate. Taking one of the sea bass from the pier, she cleaned it and brought it to *Ohana*'s galley. She prepared the fish, carefully stuffing it with brown rice, sautéing it in olive oil. Its gratifying aroma, blending with the vegetables' enticing scent, carried out from the galley through the open hatch, a smoke signal beckoning her boys home.

Hearing them step aboard, she looked up and waved a spatula at them. "Welcome, gentleman! Dinner is almost ready."

Brett swung down the companionway ladder and gave her a long hug. His warmth surprised and aroused her. The cold sorrow in her heart melted, giving way to hope.

Charlie stayed topside, peering down the cabin hatch. "You're the last person I expected to see today."

"Hey, enough of the stink-eye," Brett said to Charlie.

"You think I forgot your birthday? Seems you don't know me very well."

"I'm learning more every day. Any other relatives you wish to tell me about?"

Heat radiated through her chest and she turned to hide her blush. She worked on dinner, while Charlie talked with Brett about their day. He questioned him about an ancient Hawaiian temple they had visited. Charlie went on and on, and blood flushed her cheeks and she mouthed, "Thank you" to Brett.

After dinner, Brett went below and returned with a small, red cardboard box, frayed at the edges. He sat beside Charlie and unceremoniously handed it to him. "Happy Birthday, mate."

Charlie took the box and looked at Hellen with curious eyes. He lifted the top and stared inside with the biggest grin on his face.

"It's perfect. Thanks, Brett."

"The compass belonged to my grandfather. He carried it in his flight jacket on every Pan Am Clipper flight he made across the Pacific, believing it was his insurance policy should they have to ditch in the ocean."

"Man, that's rich." Charlie reached out and gave Brett a fist-bump.

A warm bubble welled within her chest again. Charlie shared the compass with her, a brass puck with intricate engravings. She opened its lid. Its needle swung to magnetic north, pointing directly at Brett. She lifted the compass to eye level, sighted it on Brett's face, and winked at him.

Twilight gave way to night, and Charlie looked at the stars through the binoculars, asking Brett questions about the constellations. Brett spoke of the Pleiades, an open cluster of stars floating in a violet and blue nebula, called the Seven Sisters. Hellen lay on her back, her head resting on Brett's thigh, listening to them talk. This was what she had hoped for on their voyage to Hawai'i. Maybe she didn't have to worry about what came next.

Brett caressed Hellen's hair, sending tingles along her scalp. In the glow of the cockpit lights, Charlie nodded, and his eyes told her he saw the makings of something only they understood. She made a trigger sign with her hand, fired, and said, "Gotcha."

His scowl dissolved into a grin, but the fleeting smile vanished just as quick.

Brett's hand squeezed her shoulders. "Hellen, you shouldn't try to ride your bike home in the dark. It doesn't have a light, and it's dangerous along that county road with wild boar and looters running amok."

Without waiting for her reply, he sent Charlie below to make her berth ready. He stood, arched his back, and stretched his arms. "Charlie has the aft stateroom and I have the forward cabin. We'll keep our doors shut to give you some privacy in the main saloon."

Hellen reached for Brett, but he returned belowdecks before she could say anything. The cockpit lights extinguished, and the stars returned. She sat for a while, listening to the water lapping against *Ohana*'s side and the frogs croaking in the distance as the saffron moon rose beyond Mauna Kea's summit. The first full moon since setting sail for Hawai'i meant four weeks had passed, but it felt like a lifetime. Since losing her smartwatch aboard weeks ago, her timekeeping took on a different meaning, one connected to the music of the spheres, the moon showing the passage of weeks, the sun the passage of hours. The sun's march along the ecliptic showed the time of day, and the lunar phases the time of month.

She jumped as someone stepped into the darkened cockpit. "That's a good lad. Come to say goodnight to your mum." She reached over and pulled him into a hug, but then recoiled, realizing her mistake. Blood filled her cheeks, replacing her buoyancy. Speechless, she tried to pull away, but Brett held her tight and kissed her. His thick salty lips lingered, just touching hers. She wrapped her arms around his neck, and he strengthened their kiss, pressing into her mouth. Time stopped. Gravity gave way into weightlessness. The warm upwelling within her chest returned, now overwhelming her. He released her with a simple, soft "*Nau ko'u aloha*—my love is yours"—and turned to leave.

She struggled to recover, taking slow, deep breaths. Elle had once said she'd never find anyone like Brett, and she had played the fool to look elsewhere. "No, come back." She snatched his hand before he reached the cabin hatch. "We have to talk." Her voice faltered.

Brett turned on the cockpit light, its red glow showing his waiting face. She could still back out, talk about her plan to build a microgrid or Donovan's work at the hospital, anything but the truth now separating them. Brett leaned into her and waited for her to speak. *God save me.*

"Yes?" he said, tickling her tummy with his finger.

"Bollocks. I don't suppose I can take me words back?"

"No. Too late." His face grew worried. "This isn't one of those 'twas a lot of fun, but…' conversations."

"No, heavens no. But you may not want to hear this."

"Okay, you now got my radar up."

She held her breath, her pulse pounding in her chest. Brett ran his smooth hand down her cheek. "Okay, okay." She brushed his hand away. "I need to tell you about a beautiful, young girl who is very special to me. Her name is—"

"Elizabeth?"

Hellen's stomach tightened into a knot. She pressed her forehead against his chest, her hair cascading in a curtain around her face. She waited for him to speak, resigned to the truth, a truth she now had to share with him.

"Charlie told me. It's why he ran away."

"Did you see her on the pier when we came looking for Charlie?"

"She's amazing. Anyone would be proud to be her parent."

"That's it? You're not angry with me? God, I thought this would be the end of us. I'm so sorry—I should have let you know sooner."

"No, I'm not angry with you. That was years ago. Actually, I'm sort of relieved you carried her to term. Think of the beautiful girl the world would've missed. Besides, it's Charlie you need to apologize to, not me."

"I know. But I need to be sure you're okay with this."

"I'm fine. It's old history, right? And I'm sure you made the best decision under the circumstances."

His words came with no pretense, pragmatic and accepting. Hellen caught her breath. Like water flowing downriver, her days, even weeks, of worry had come and gone. Something seemed missing: rage, resentment, or even humiliation. Why did he take it so well? His kiss drew her back to the present.

"Come join me tonight if you want to talk some more." He wiped her lips with his thumb. "I could use your company."

He left before she came back to life. The boat rocked slightly as he slid belowdecks. She pressed her hand to her chest, her heartbeat quickened. She never imagined it would be this easy. She expected anger and sorrow at his missing out on Elizabeth's childhood. She let out a long sigh and tilted her head back. The masthead rocked against the stars and the full moon over Mauna Kea. It was all too perfect. She didn't deserve this.

She climbed down the companionway steps and found the stateroom doors shut, giving her the privacy Brett promised. But privacy was the last thing she needed right now.

She tapped on Charlie's door. "Are you still awake?"

"What do you want?"

"I came to say goodnight," she said through his closed door. "Are you happy here?"

"Sure am," he said. "Did you come down to haul me back to Cloudcroft?"

"What do you want to do?"

Her question was met with a long silence. "Charlie, are you okay?"

"I wasn't expecting your question, that's all."

"You can stay with Brett for now. Okay?"

"Thanks."

Hellen awoke in the middle of the night. The boat swayed on the dock lines, riding the incoming tide. Moonbeams danced around the cabin with each roll, back and forth. Her stomach felt as if a rock lay inside. She went to Charlie's stateroom and eased open the door to peek in on her son. His steady, deep breaths came in long intervals. She squeezed the door shut and walked forward, the holly and teak deck creaking under each step. After she picked up her tablet, she continued on to the forward stateroom, the short distance an eternity away.

She cracked open the door and snuck inside Brett's stateroom. With little thought, she slipped out of her nightgown. The soft satin fell across her skin, sending flutters to her stomach. The full moon shone through the overhead hatch and drew long shadows over her body. With nervous fingers, she played with the chain necklace holding her father's Claddagh ring. Moonlight reflected off the gold and sent golden streaks across her breasts. Brett lay in the shadows of his bunk, his chest undulating in a deep sleep. Her pulse hammered in her ears, her hands quivered, and her excitement overpowered her senses. She wanted to bolt out of there; this wasn't a good time.

She turned and picked up her gown to leave, dropping her tablet on the deck. The noise shattered the cabin's silence. Brett reached over and clutched her arm, sending an electric jolt through her. "Hellen, is that you?"

"Shhh. Yes, it's me."

"What are you doing?"

"Quiet, you fool. You'll wake Charlie." She bent over and kissed his warm, briny lips. Delicious. She lingered and whispered, "That's one way to shut you up."

She couldn't see his response in the shadows of his bunk, and she didn't wait. Before he said anything else, she slipped under his sheet and pressed her trembling body against his.

"Here, babe," he whispered and put his arms around her. "You're cold."

"Oh god, just the opposite…"

His strong embrace and the cramped bunk sent her back to the night she fell overboard. But she was safe now, invulnerable even, more secure than she had been with any other man. His touch washed away her persistent worries about the blackout and the haunting reminders of her failures as a mother, a wife, a lover.

A deep arousal spread within her trembling body, making her buoyant. She splayed her hands across his chest and pushed back in silence. Waves of heat rolled through her, each getting stronger. He kissed her earlobe, sending her into vertigo. Wind gusted in from the sea, whipping the halyards against *Ohana's* mast, drowning out their whispers. A great tide of fierce desire engulfed her. Having laid dormant for many years, her body awoke with an insatiable thirst, conceived from a long drought, born with its own life force.

. . .

Hours later, the predawn light stretched through the glazed side window, filling their small cabin with orange and yellow shades. Gentle waves licked the hull. The fine smell of salt air drifted through an open porthole. She turned to face Brett, resting her palm on his chest, watching it rise and fall with each long breath, feeling the heat from his skin. How had their feelings for each other changed in such a short time? Maybe those feelings had been there all along, hibernating, waiting. Now, more than ever before, Hellen understood what Elle had always said, "Live by the sun, love by the moon." Relaxed and empty of all tension, she rested her cheek against his chest. His warm skin pressed against her face with every breath, marking longer and longer intervals. She kissed his shoulder and jolted when he stirred.

"Hellen, what time is it?"

"A little before sunrise." She ran her index finger along the bridge of his nose, tracing a line from his mouth and down his chest. "Go back to sleep. I have to head back to Kamuela."

"Don't go just yet—we have unfinished business." He grinned and pulled her on top of him. She framed his head in her hands, feeling his morning glory come to life, and grazed her lips against his.

"There's something I want to show you," she said, opening her tablet. She lifted her head and placed her index finger over his lips. The confused look in his eyes made her laugh. "No, relax. You'll love this." The screen's light bathed his face and the air between them filled with their future.

"Elizabeth?" Brett asked.

She nodded and swiped right to the next photo. Elizabeth's honey-brown eyes stared back at them. Her smile shone with genuine warmth, thick lips surrounding her brilliant teeth. Long, auburn hair framed her happy cheeks. The photo dissolved into a myriad of images, displayed one at a time, showing her special moments through the years: her orientation at UH, dives trips off the Kona Coast, her first prom, birthdays, her first day of school, and on and on back in time until the last picture, taken on Hellen's twentieth birthday, the night she fell in love with Brett.

Brett's chest rose, his arms tightening around her. She lifted her head and studied his face.

"What's this doing in here?" he asked.

"Don't you remember it?"

"Of course, I do. It's Hōkūle'a in Lahaina. The summer we—"

"Made a baby." She waited for her words to sink in before giving him a little smile. But his worried brow tightened, sending her heart into her throat.

He stared at her with questioning eyes. "Wait. Say again."

"You heard me."

"Seriously?"

She waited until her throat unclenched, not confident in her voice. "Elizabeth's our daughter," she said, her voice cracking. Her palms tingled. Her mind was confused. God, didn't he know, hadn't he brushed it aside earlier? Between labored breaths, her words spewed out in disjointed emotions. "Our first night together… I became pregnant. I never told you because… We were so young. It was for the best. I'm so sorry."

She concentrated on the stitching in the sheets, a safe place. With no more words, she snatched her robe and covered her chest and blinked back her sorrow, tears from years of walking the tightrope, hiding the truth.

He ran his hands through his hair, over and over, as though rubbing his scalp might help him find a way to defuse the bombshell she had laid in his lap. His eyes told her he wasn't angry— just hurt—which made it much more difficult. He dropped his head back onto the pillow and let out a long tight breath. "You mean I'm her father?"

She looked at him, unable to breathe, wondering how he hadn't put it together. "Who else would be? Look at her. Wait. You're not thinking she came from another man in a random one-night hookup, are you? God dammit. What kind of girl did you think I was—I mean am? Jesus, Brett!" She hid her face in her hands and rolled away from him. Silence hung between them, sounds from the outside world muted. A hollow pain filled her stomach. She couldn't breathe. All those years of hiding the truth. She closed her eyes and bent over, holding her stomach, feeling as though she were going to be sick.

For an interminable moment, her naked body sat rooted to the berth. She breathed deep to distract herself from both the horror of her lie and the equally unbearable years. "It's all in the past, a past I'd rather forget."

"Oh, the bloody irony of life," he said at last. "After years of yearning for a family, knowing I couldn't, I find out I had a daughter all long."

"I'm so sorry. I hate myself. Didn't plan this out, didn't want to hurt you." She reached for him, but he pushed her hand away and got out of his berth.

"What's more," he said, "doctors claim I'm impotent, yet now I rise to the occasion every time you so much as smile at me."

"I'd better go now," she said. "I'll take Charlie with me."

"No, stay. No, I mean let Charlie stay with me." He paced the stateroom, rubbing his brow with his hand.

"Yes, you're right. He and Elizabeth aren't ready to see each other again quite yet." The words stuck in her throat. "I never meant to hurt anybody. It just spiraled out of control on its own momentum." After she stood, she tied her robe around waist, then reached for the doorknob. "I feared you'd think I was trying to trap you into a relationship." She opened the door and called for Charlie.

He pressed the door closed and rested his hand on her shoulder. She flinched at his touch.

"Relax, I'm not angry—I only need time to absorb all this. Please let Charlie stay."

"Of course. You're like a father to him, more than Sam ever was."

He rubbed his scalp again. Everything she said only seemed to make him more confused.

"Ask me anything, and I promise only the truth," she said at last.

"Why didn't you tell me?"

She fiddled with her red braided wristband, thinking she'd give anything to go back in time and tell him the truth that day the two pink lines appeared. "God, I feel awful. I didn't know how to tell you. The day I found out I was pregnant, you were across the Pacific. I was afraid, unsure of having an abortion. After I decided to have the baby, I was worried you'd talk me out of finishing school and become a full-time mother. I knew my life would change forever. Yours as well."

"I would've helped you," he said, his voice strained. "At least you could've let me see her. Who adopted her?"

She swallowed hard. "Elle came to my rescue. She became Elizabeth's hānai mother—her guardian—so I could finish school."

He nodded and his pressed his lips together. Hānai foster arrangements were only among 'ohana and preserved the mother's right to see her daughter at any time. He paced the cabin. "So, that's why she was on the pier last week."

"After I met Sam, we filed immigration papers, but they denied her citizenship because of her hapa-Hawaiian status. Turns out, it was for the best."

"Wait. You're her mother. Wasn't that enough?"

"Elizabeth had a better life with Elle than she would've had under Sam's roof. I've never told you… Sam turned on me after Charlie's tenth birthday. I tried to make it work, but there was only so much I could take. Sam became increasingly violent, even attacked Charlie. That was the end of our marriage."

Brett swallowed, his glistening eyes fixed on her, and waited.

"After the divorce, Elle insisted she remain Elizabeth's guardian. Can't blame her. I was an emotional wreck. Elizabeth deserved better. Elle is wealthy beyond imagination. Elizabeth had everything she needed, attended the best schools, accepted by her first choice of college. It broke my heart to never tell her I was her mother, a mistake I'll regret for a lifetime."

With grief written on his face, he pulled her in, his arms more lifesaving than oxygen. "Does she know?"

"I told her everything yesterday." A thousand memories flooded Hellen's mind, the times she wanted to tell her, but couldn't, the shock in her face when she did.

"Where is she now?"

"Cloudcroft."

"You mean, just up the hill from here? I want to see her."

"She only found out we're her parents yesterday. Let's give her time to get used to the idea."

"I guess need I some time as well. Knowing Charlie is my daughter's brother adds a whole new angle to this web you've spun. Hell, I don't even understand what I just said."

PART III

NANA IA KE KUPU

(WATCH FOR THE ENEMY)

13

Kamuela

Hellen cracked open Cloudcroft's front door and peeked into the kitchen. All was quiet. She tiptoed to her bedroom, peeking around each corner along the way. She gave a tentative smile and held her hand to her chest. After her confession to Brett this morning, the thought of replaying her visit for Elle made her knees weak. Like a pebble dropped in a pond, her disclosure rippled across her deepest fears. She would've wept if she'd had any tears left. Afraid of losing Brett's love, Charlie's trust, and Elizabeth's blissful innocence, she had walked a tightrope for years, fearing the truth would send her plunging. Now she had fallen from the security of her lie, and she had taken Brett and the kids down with her. The damage done, the fallout would take its own path, unwinding the neat kinship fostered with her children and the love reborn with Brett. She had deprived him the joys of raising Elizabeth. All her special moments, her first words, first steps, birthdays, the day she headed off to kindergarten, all of them lost in time. He had witnessed none of them.

Her four-legged friends whinnied from the stables. She wiped her eyes with her palm and headed to the barn. The rain began, sending sparkling drops into sunlight streaming between the broken clouds. Liquid sunshine secreted steam from the grass. Humidity pulled the alfalfa scent from the hay as she flaked the bales into measure slices. Eager for their morning feeding, the horses stomped at the stable doors. Hellen liked being needed, especially by these hoofed friends. They didn't argue. They accepted what she gave them.

With the horses fed, she sat by the open barn door and closed her eyes, inviting the sun to reach down inside her. The humid air carried a mélange of tropical scents and sounds from the surrounding forest. A raven swooped down and perched beside her on a rotten log, flapping its dark, indigo wings. Her heart sped up, an exhilarating pounding within her chest. The bird hopped along the railing toward Hellen, taking her in with beady eyes. A heavy déjà vu forced her uneasiness back down her throat. This raven with a penchant for attention used a twig wedged within its bill to dig a hole in the log. He repositioned the twig and continued to work on collecting dead insects from the log.

"You're a smart fellow," Hellen marveled.

Such an odd bird, such an odd island. He was clever but was only fooling himself, losing his situational awareness. Elle's cat, Ty Lee, ran out of the barn and sprang for the bird, missing it by inches as it flew away. The raven was Hellen's kindred spirit, clever but not smart. All her technical prowess hadn't prevented her from hurting Brett and her children.

A mist rolled into the barn, leaving dew drops on a spider web, little prismatic spangles quivering in the breeze. Stirred up by the wind and humidity, an earthy peat odor mixed with flower fragrances. The light shower outside was lost in the haze, not the same rain as in Colorado, where it fell like little shards of ice pelting her skin.

She ran to the lanai and slumped into a chair. Her wet hands were clasped in supplication, her forehead upon them. Like a black hole sucking her remorse into a singularity, her shame dropped into an abyss. "Lord," she whispered, "make me an instrument of your peace. Where there is injury, let me sow pardon; where there is despair, joy; where there is doubt, faith; where there is darkness, light." She leaned back in her chair, her eyes grew heavy, and her worries dissolved into a dream.

Bird of paradise flowers bordered the garden with their orange, purple, and green. A musty, time-worn mélange drifted in from the rain forest. Elizabeth sat beside a woven picnic basket on a plaid blanket, her baby brown eyes beaming. Hellen twiddled her fingers in front of her, making her laugh harder, setting her red locks bouncing like tiny springs. A black raven landed next to Hellen's foot; its wings brushed against Elizabeth and startled her. She reached out for Hellen with her tiny arms and cried. The raven tilted its head as if considering his companions. He picked up a dirty spoon from a discarded plate with his beak and tapped on Hellen's wrist.

Hellen awoke to someone squeezing her hand. Through her sleepy eyes, Hellen saw Elle standing before her, a blue binder clutched close to her chest.

"Rise and shine." Elle sat in the chair beside Hellen. "Where were you last night?" she teased, saying more with her eyes.

Hellen swallowed her embarrassment. "We really don't need to discuss that, do we?"

"He's lucky to have you."

A primal taste, sour like fear, rose in the back of her throat.

Elle's eyes filled with worry. "What's wrong?"

"I told Brett about Elizabeth before I left the boat this morning. He didn't take it well." Hellen's vision blurred with tears, recalling the hurt expression he wore. A secret revealed, a trust was broken.

"But he still has Charlie?"

"Yes, what's Charlie got to do with this?"

Elle rolled her eyes. "You may be smart, but you sure have a knack for missing the obvious."

Hellen shook her head and squinted at her.

"Don't you see? Love rejoices in the truth. He may be in a state of shock, but he's still crazy about you. Not for your hiding the truth in the past, but for your revealing it. He now sees what you see, a chance for a life together. If he wanted out, he would've insisted you take Charlie back with you."

"I never gave a second thought to leaving Charlie with him."

Elle's eyes watered. She rubbed her nose with her wrist and gave a single nod. "I need to go back into town to meet with the civil defense folks about our recovery plan. I only came home to give this to you." Elle placed the blue binder on Hellen's lap. "Remember you said you'll help me out? Well, I got a job for you. This damn binder came from the Home Secretary's Office, and they expect me to figure it all out on my own and just turn the lights on."

Hellen picked up the binder and read the title: *ConHEL Recovery Action Plan for Community Restoration of Commercial and Private Power Operations in Natural Disasters.* She flipped through it. No wonder it panicked Elle; its technical language was as opaque as its title.

"Who or what is ConHEL?"

"They're Consolidated Hawaiian Electric and Light, the local power company for the island. I can't get anyone from their office to help us; they're all working in Kona and Hilo right now."

"Leave this with me. When's your next meeting?"

Elle put her hand to her forehead and mumbled, "The Civil Defense commissioner from Hilo is coming to my office at four this afternoon."

"Don't worry, I got this. This is my specialty, thanks to you. Let me read through this and decipher it for you, then we'll come up with a response before you see him."

Elle bent over and gave Hellen a warm hug. "Mahalo, nui. You're a godsend."

After Elle left, Hellen poured herself a cup of coffee and sat down to read the emergency response plan. When the grid died, so had the Internet of Everything, and paper returned as the dominant media. With all information digitized over the past ten years, the binder had a nostalgic feel to it with its heft of pages, plastic cover, and handwritten tabs.

"ConHEL—the name sure fits," Hellen whispered in a wry tone. A fold-out map showed locations of the power plants, transformers, distributions stations, and substations. The Achilles' heel of the power grid during Helio Hattie was the long transmission lines and high-voltage transformers, damaged by huge currents generated during the geomagnetic storm. And they had no means to repair or replace them. Furthermore, ConHEL had not expected any fuel-oil shipments for many months, leaving power plants useless. Hellen crossed off all five fossil-fuel power stations on the island map.

The next chapter extolled the island's renewable energy initiative, funded by the Commonwealth prior to the solar storm. Renewable energy sources, such as solar, wind, and geothermal, provided seventy-five percent of the residential energy needs. The technical data restored Hellen's hope. Not only did renewable energy plants have the best survival rate from the solar storm, they also made up much of the island's electricity supply. A topographic map showed the Kohala Wind Farm near Kawaihae Harbor. Completed two years ago, it comprised sixteen 660 kW wind turbines. At peak capacity, the farm produced ten megawatts, enough for all of Kohala under reduced loads. The wind farm's power grid schematic named Haruki Tanaka as the plant manager with his address.

Hellen retrieved a county map tacked onto the kitchen wall. Tanaka's office was on Main Street in Kamuela. With no way to call him, she decided to pay him a visit before her meeting with Elle. She gathered up her notes and stuffed them with the

ConHEL binder into a backpack. In her haste, she dropped it on the floor. She paused and checked the Beretta in her backpack. The black handgun felt solid and heavy in her hand. After counting nine bullets from the ammo box, she released the magazine from the gun and loaded it. With everything packed in her bag, she headed for the door.

Hellen stood beside her bike on Kohala Mountain Road at the end of Tanaka's driveway, catching her breath after the long uphill ride, summoning up the courage to continue.

A tattered sign, *Kapu*—Private Property, hung from a broken gate leading to a winding dirt road shaded by a grove of monkeypod trees. The morning had turned into an Easter egg hunt. She had first stopped by Tanaka's office in Kamuela, but found the place deserted except for a lineman on his way to the wind farm. He told her the plant was shut down, and they couldn't start back up without an external power source. He gave her Tanaka's home address but warned her he had called in sick, nursing a killer hangover from the previous night's drinking.

Her hope of forming an alliance with Tanaka waned. Would he resent her help, like those alpha males she had dealt with on the Navajo reservation? Yet she had come this far and needed to meet Elle in two hours.

After she rode along the dirt driveway for a quarter of a mile, a twig broke within the trees ahead of her. A shadow wavered on the ground. Without a sound, she set her bike down and retrieved the Beretta from her bag. She squared her stance and locked back the hammer. The click from the handgun flushed out a man, younger and taller than she, his hands behind his back. Brown stains, perhaps caked blood, covered his T-shirt. He leered at her, his teeth stained, the mark of a strung-out addict. He shouted in Hawaiian, but his words made no sense to her. Sunlight reflected from a machete. She whipped the handgun to her dominant right eye, the sights level, the slot lined up above his head. Her finger squeezed, and the gun fired. The bugger's eyes grew wide. Hands in the air, he dropped the blade, its metal ringing on a volcanic rock.

"You Tanaka?" she asked in a shrill voice.

The man shook his head quickly as he stepped back, his words sputtered in pidgin English.

She waved the pistol toward the end of the driveway, not knowing how to tell him to get lost in Hawaiian. He understood and fled, arms pumping as he ran down the driveway. She let out a tight breath, dropped the magazine, and set the gun back in her bag, locked open. The bugger's machete lay in the drive-way. After inspecting the blade, she strapped it to her backpack, handle up so he could grab for it over her shoulder. The driveway leading to Tanaka's looked deserted, but she couldn't be sure. After a second thought, she drew the Beretta from her bag, popped the magazine back in, and released the slide before stuffing the handgun inside her jeans at the small of her back.

Onward she rode to Tanaka's house. A rusted-out white Ford F-150 sat beside a cistern covered with vines. His home appeared out of place, a Florida cracker hovel with weathered sideboards, a rusty metal roof, and a Beware of Dog sign nailed next to the front door. Her throat tightened at her childhood memory of a German Shepherd attacking her.

She peered through the screen door into the dark living room, seeing no sign of life, hearing no sound of any watchdog. She tried the latch and turned it, setting off the dog alarm. Barking echoed within the tiny house, loud enough to wake the dead. She jumped as the dog pushed the door open. A corgi ran past her feet and sprinted into the front yard before executing a quick flip and a half twist, landing on its tummy, legs sprayed out, facing Hellen. The dwarf canine wagged its nub tail in a blur of motion, making her laugh.

The sound of a hot round being chambered into a pump-action shotgun came behind her. She eased her hands up over her head and slowly turned to face a short Asian man with a scrubby beard and stained, white T-shirt.

"Who are you, and what do you want?" he asked.

"Are you Haruki Tanaka?"

"I'm asking the questions here," he said, still aiming the shotgun at her. The killer corgi waddled over to her, growling at her red sneakers.

"I'm Doctor Hellen Callahan, an energy adviser for Elle Otoko. I'd like to talk to you about restoring your wind farm. Here, take a look." She retrieved a tattered NCEL business card from her wallet. "I'm an engineer with the national lab, specializing in wind turbines." Although she lost her job at NCEL, her experience mattered more here than credentials.

"Never heard of you. Now get lost."

The man fired his shotgun high into the forest canopy, sending his dog running under the truck. Perched birds leapt into the sky. Hellen yelped and held her arms up again. A little trickle ran down her pants leg.

"Sushi, get the hell back here."

"Okay, I'm cool," Hellen said. "I'll leave you alone. Speak to Mayor Otoko if you need to check me out, but I know of a power source we can use to jump-start the wind farm." Hellen strolled over to her bike, taking her time, waiting for him to reach his senses. She strapped on her backpack and sat on the seat with one foot on the pedal.

"Wait up! What did you just say?"

Hellen turned and smiled at him. His brow twisted in knots above a set of narrow eyes, showing a mixture of confusion and stubbornness. At last, she had broken through his drunken fog and gotten his attention. She forced a smile as he waved her to the door.

"I'm Tanaka. Let's go inside and have a little chat," he said in a low voice with more reluctance than curiosity.

Hellen followed him into his cramped living room, taken aback at the stench of dog pee and fried pork. To her relief, he returned his shotgun to a hall closet. After taking her NCEL business card and studying it, his eyes twinkled at her, as if a morsel of trust emerged.

"So, you know Otoko?"

"Yes, she's 'ohana, and I'm staying with her at Cloudcroft until we get this mess sorted out."

Tanaka nodded his head and grinned. He waved a brief shaka sign at her before handing her card back. "After I get cleaned up, we'll talk."

"Can I use your bathroom first?" The moist spot in her pants from her accidental discharge after Tanaka's shotgun blast drove her crazy.

"Guest toilet is down the hall behind you."

The bathroom was a classic study in bachelor lifestyle, crusty towels, toilet seat up, and no toilet paper. After washing her panties in the grimy sink, she reached for the hairdryer before realizing how useless it was without power. She wrung out her soaked panties, stuffed them in her backback, and got dressed. She took her Beretta, dropped the magazine, and engaged the safety before placing the handgun back in her backpack.

The kitchen was worse than the bathroom; crusty dishes lay in the sink, and the charcoaled remains of a slab of pork sat on a griddle. The corgi waddled in and looked up at her. She dropped the blackened meat in front of the dog, making a quick friend, and wondered what prompted a Japanese to name his dog Sushi.

Tanaka returned within fifteen minutes, a different man, his face more relaxed, even inviting, far from the grimace she had seen earlier. He wore a fresh Hawaiian shirt and khaki trousers and had slicked back his black hair.

"Okay, Hellen Callahan. Tell me how you know so much about our turbine stator problem."

"The ConHEL emergency response plan mentioned the Kohala Wind Farm. I believe the oil-fired plants on the island are out of commission for the long term. They need to replace their EHV transformers, right? And that could take—"

Tanaka folded his arms. "Many months. So why are you interested in us?"

Hellen took the wind farm schematic out of her satchel and laid it across the kitchen table. "From what I can see here, your plant used low voltage transmission lines and smaller transformers. You might have sustained less damage from the geomagnetic-induced currents. Did you decouple the turbines before the solar storm?"

"Yes, and their DC interconnectors aren't as susceptible to GIC surges."

"And the substations?"

"We installed GIC blocking devices and wrapped the setup transformers in home-brewed Faraday cages we made from wire fencing donated by the Parker Ranch. But the ConHEL folks were real *huhu* for me taking the whole Kohala grid down before the storm." He folded his arms and winked at her. "Too bad for them. They lost all their transformers."

Hellen clapped her hands together. "Great thinking. It shielded them from the solar EMP. How did you protect the power transmission lines?"

"Disconnected at every juncture. They survived, but the turbines are still broke dick without a source for stator current. How you know so much about wind power?"

"I tried to tell you earlier, but you were too busy pointing your damn shotgun at me. In my past life, I designed wind stations for Native American reservations. As part of the project, we investigated off-grid ways to deliver startup power to wind turbines."

Tanaka closed his eyes and pursed his lips. "Go on. I'm listening."

"Remember when Hurricane Iwa hit Kauai in the 1980s?"

Tanaka nodded. *"Da honest kine.* I was just a keiki when Iwa hit, scared me shitless. It was the strongest storm we've ever seen here. My mom was visiting her 'ohana on Kauai. The house collapsed on them; no one survived."

Hellen waited to let the moment pass. At last, Tanaka looked at her. "But what's that got to do with my power plant?"

"After the hurricane, a submarine sailed into Nawiliwili Harbor and mated its nuclear propulsion plant to Kauai's power grid."

"I never heard the story, but it doesn't surprise me. The only source of nuclear power in these islands are the Royal Navy's submarines."

"Naval vessels often tie up to shore power during a port of call, allowing them to shut down their main engines. Like a floating power station, they can also run 'reverse shore power' to remote areas off the power grid."

Tanaka examined the wind farm schematic and poked his stubby finger at one tower. "Wind Turbine Sixteen is only about a quarter-mile from Kawaihae Harbor. We could rig a temporary power line from the harbor using surplus gear we have in our warehouse."

"Yes, like a black startup. The sub powers this closest turbine, then we use it to power the stator in the next generator in line and so forth."

"Where are we going to find a submarine for this black startup?"

"I have a meeting with Elle Otoko in an hour. Care to join me in explaining all this to her? I'm sure she'll agree if we can make her team understand our plan. Perhaps she can ask the Navy to deploy one of their subs here. We only need it for a day or two."

"For sure." Tanaka said as he stood. "Sushi! We go for a ride now."

The corgi barreled out of the screen door and ran to Tanaka's pickup. "He always loves to ride upfront," Tanaka said as he hauled her bike into the truck bed. He climbed into the front seat next to Hellen and put the corgi in her lap. Reaching below the steering column, he hot-wired the diesel engine to start it. She raised her eyebrows and grinned.

He gave her a sheepish look. "I lost my keys two weeks ago."

Kamuela

Hellen wasn't sure of the address Elle had given her. Without GPS, she resorted to hunt-and-seek navigation. Tanaka had never visited the Kohala ʻĀina Foundation, but he found it on their second pass down the remote road. The building had an open architecture with many sliding glass windows looking out to the rolling hills of the Parker Ranch. As with most buildings in Kamuela, sunlight provided the only source of lighting to conserve electricity. She tested the front doors, found them unlocked, and headed inside with Sushi and Tanaka.

"Who's this little fellow?" Elle knelt in the front hallway and patted her knees. The corgi trotted over and nuzzled his head against her. "I love him! Let's bring him to our meeting for moral support."

"Sushi brought his boss along," Hellen said. "This is Haruki Tanaka, the plant manager for the Kohala Wind Farm."

"Girl, you move fast," Elle said with delighted eyes. "Come on in and let's hear what you got."

They walked down the hall and entered the small conference room. Hellen laid out her hand-drawn system diagram of the wind farm on the conference table taking up most of the room. Elle put on her reading glasses and examined the map.

"I've reviewed the ConHEL brief you gave me, and we may have a solution." Hellen winked at Tanaka and waited for him to speak.

Tanaka moved the diagram closer to Elle and pointed to the plant's control center. "We need to perform what we call a 'black startup' to get the wind farm back online." He explained their plans, including the preparation time, type of auxiliary power source they needed, and the need to reduce electrical loads through Kohala.

Elle looked over her reading glasses and gave a quick nod.

"You guys did good work. This is exactly what I need to face Hancock and his ConHEL cronies."

By four o'clock, the standing members of Elle's civil defense team drifted in and settled in their seats. Donovan arrived with Malia, his hair disheveled, his clothes in disarray. After his tired eyes caught Hellen, he gave her a long hug.

"Malia keeping you busy?" she asked.

He shrugged. "I still manage four hours sleep, give or take. Seriously, we're near the breaking point. We need more personnel and patient beds."

Malia sat next to him, either lost in thought or just ignoring everyone. A tightly wound spring, she tapped her pencil on the table, rocking her calf against her crossed knee. A small bumptious man wearing a bushy mustache, Stetson hat, and cowboy boots arrived last. Elle leaned over to Hellen. "Cody Hancock, a recent haole transplant and the island's home secretary representative." She made air quotes with her fingers. "'No' is his favorite word."

Superintendent Joe Kanuhu, Kohala Constabulary, looked the part of a small-town cop with his short-cropped, black hair and casual stance. His serene smile helped to ease Hellen's nerves. Hellen remembered the times he had visited Cloudcroft during her past summers in Hawai'i. Aside from Suzu, Joe was Elle's closest friend in Kamuela.

After Elle made introductions for everyone, she led Hellen to a seat next to hers at the head of the table. She picked up Tanaka's corgi and laid him on her lap. The dog reached up and licked her chin as she positioned her reading glasses. "*Aloha 'auinala*. Since we have visitors today," she said in a prim British accent, "we'll conduct today's meeting in English. Malia, you can go first."

Malia sat up from her slouching position in her chair. "Right. Captain Callahan has helped me develop our medical response plan." She squeezed Donovan's hand and explained the medical triage plan, using EMTs to set up field hospitals at the fire stations throughout the district. Donovan suggested that they requisition the astronomer's lodge to provide more beds in the recovery ward. Located across the street from KMC, the Maunakea Astronomy Institute was an ideal candidate for a hospital annex.

"I know the operations manager," Elle said. "I'll talk him into it." A smile crossed her face but vanished in a heartbeat. All business here, she shifted to her prim British accent. Under the table, Elle squeezed Hellen's hand, but never looked away from her agenda. Hellen had never seen Elle in action like this. Thankful for her small role as a support engineer, she wondered how she would've coped with the pressure of being mayor.

Captain Kanuhu cleared his throat and rolled out a paper map, showing red marks at various crossroads. "Our biggest priority right now is setting up roadblocks to secure access in and out of town. Insurgent Samoans from the south end of the island have attacked homes and businesses here." He pointed to a small neighborhood in Kailua-Kona. "As we found last week, it started with a few Mormon households in Kona and now has moved up the hill. We think they targeted the Mormons because of their renowned hoarding of emergency food stocks. My men have followed up on dozens of break-ins and assaults."

"Are we relocating those families to homes in Kamuela?" Elle asked.

"We started last night with twenty families. We've about another fifty left and plan to move them by this weekend. The remaining families on my list chose not to move, but they're armed for self-defense."

"I'm glad to hear we are getting them out."

Hancock made a show of clearing his throat. He lowered his chin and peered over his reading glasses. "What's this all about? I don't remember hearing this at our last meeting. How are you going to feed them all? And why are they so special?"

Elle took off her glasses and gave a practiced smile to the

frumpy little man. "We have a plan to house them with volunteer families here in Kohala."

"Right," Joe said. "We also have the Mormon Bishop's Storehouse."

Hancock leaned his elbows on the table, wiggling his nose like a bunny. "Where's this storehouse of yours?"

"It's just as a contingency," she said. "The Mormons offered to share their warehouse of emergency supplies in return for housing their families. Speaking of supplies. Most of us will soon run through our own food stockpiles. We need to plan for mass distribution of MREs."

"Your people have private food reserves?" Hancock asked.

"After Mauna Loa's eruption last spring, we ran a PSA campaign, encouraging people to stockpile food in case of another emergency."

"You guys act like everything you do is secret squirrel stuff. Most folks in Hilo never stockpiled—explains why riots haven't broken out up here."

Kanuhu leaned over the table and pointed to red markings on his map. "And that's why insurgent gangs like the Puna Sons of Samoa are targeting us. We've established roadblocks at these checkpoints in and out of Kohala." He pointed to seven different marks on various highways around Kamuela and Waikoloa.

"Good luck rounding up those rascals," Hancock said.

"Let's stay focused, guys," Elle said. "I've asked the Paniolo Cattle Company to release a thousand head of cattle for slaughter from Parker Ranch. However, they need a power source to run the mobile slaughter units to process the meat." She glanced over to Hancock.

"I got nothing to report on power restoration." Hancock got up and poured himself a cup of coffee. "The Home Secretary's Office is reluctant to advertise where we'll restore power first, fearing it might incite panic elsewhere. They're more focused on high population cities, leaving Podunks like you to solve your own problems."

"What about getting us new transformers?" Hellen asked.

"Shipping them out could take months." He paused as if he waited for this baleful news to sink in. Little men liked big roles. "But there's one ray of sunshine I have for you all. The RAF plans to start a weekly military airlift into Kona International next Monday. The flights will bring in solar panels, medical supplies, and food. And they'll also evacuate nonresidents."

"Get me the solar panels," Hellen said, "and I'll rig up an array for Parker Ranch. We'll have steaks in no time."

"That brings us to our topic for today, restoring the Kohala Wind Farm." Elle laid out Hellen's hand-drawn map of power plants and high-voltage substations in the district. As she went through their rehearsed pitch, some leaned forward and others beamed at her, except for Hancock.

"Someone did their homework last night," Joe said.

Hancock gave Elle a rueful smirk, twirling the tip of his handlebar mustache between two fingers. "Just how do you propose we provide the stator current necessary to start the wind turbines?"

Elle turned to Hellen. "I'll let Hellen Callahan take your question. She's my energy consultant and an expert on renewable power."

Hancock inspected her with amusing eyes. She leaned her head to one side, tapping her pencil against the wind farm schematic. "Could ConHEL provide a portable high-voltage diesel generator for two days? We could start one turbine and use its output to bootstrap the other turbines in the wind farm."

"No. It won't work. Ms… What's your name again?"

"Really?" Elle said. "Hellen Callahan, electrical power system analyst at NCEL."

"NCEL who?"

Elle gave Hellen an incredulous smile. "National Clean Energy Lab in Colorado. It's the largest of its kind in the world."

"Didn't know that," Hancock said in a quiet voice. "Anyway, it doesn't matter who you are. ConHEL has all its resources tied up with restoring Hilo right now. Maybe we can spare someone in a few months."

"That surprises me," Hellen said. "Didn't you say ConHEL needed new HV transformers?"

Hancock narrowed his eyes. Under the table, Hellen squeezed Elle's hand again. The moment had arrived, time to get to the truth. No more obfuscation.

Elle glared at Hancock with an intensity that frightened Hellen, forcing him to avert his eyes. "Mr. Hancock," she finally said, "do you mean to tell me you don't have a restoration plan for Hilo?"

"The transformers are on their way."

"Maybe in six months," Hellen said in a low tone.

"Look, lady, we have everything under control, and we need not go into details with you right now."

"I see." Elle straightened her back. "You're suggesting we need to find our own solution for the power grid?"

"Yes, that about sums up the ball game," Hancock said as he stood up to leave. "I wish we could provide more help, but the Kohala Wind Farm is a small independent supplier, and we've bigger problems on hand. Until we get the major metro centers back, you're on your own."

"Yes, that's clear. For heaven's sake, what's it going to take to get help from you guys? How much more do we have to endure for someone to understand what is happening to us violates our human rights?"

Hellen cleared her throat. "What if we found a power source for the black start? Do you see any problems with us proceeding with our own plan?"

"I see. More secret squirrel stuff."

Elle crossed her arms and nodded. "It takes a squirrel to know a squirrel."

Hancock excused himself and walked out the door. The corgi stirred in her lap, growling at him until he disappeared from sight. Everyone sat in silence, their eyes fixed on the power grid map laying on the table. Hellen expected Elle to lose her temper, but she kept her cool, arms across her chest, hiding her thoughts.

"Hancock really likes to rain on our parade," Hellen said.

Elle threw up her hands. "Happens almost every meeting with him."

"So, let's not invite him anymore."

"Hancock has to be here. He speaks for the home secretary."

"What of late has he done for you? No emergency relief supplies, no ConHEL tech support. Why don't we send him status reports and let him sit happy in Hilo?"

"Works for me fine," Joe said.

"And it'll improve morale." Elle exhaled a long breath and nuzzled her face against the corgi. "This little fellow helps my morale more than Hancock ever did."

Hellen rested her hand on Elle's forearm. "We have to find another source of startup power, like the Navy. One of their nuclear subs has enough auxiliary power to support our black startup."

Elle's eyes came alive. "Yes, I'll send a request to Honolulu. I've a radio conference call with them tomorrow."

"We'll need at least three weeks to get the wind farm ready," Tanaka said. "We need to reconnect the transmission lines and remove all the Faraday cages."

"How long do you need the submarine's power?" Elle asked.

"Good question. They'll need a sub in Hilo more than we do," Joe said.

"We only need two days, at most," Hellen said. "Just long enough to power one of our turbines, like jump-starting a car. We'll use the first wind turbine to bootstrap the others, one after another."

Elle unwrapped her arms and took a deep breath. "This could be a turning point for us, a sign of hope, a path to recovery. Now, I just have to find a nuclear submarine." She laughed as she closed her meeting.

14

Hellen settled into her morning routine in the back garden. With a deep breath, she poured herself into her garden meditation, her forehead and cheeks covered with perspiration, her hands coated with dark soil. The place was shaping up. Tidy rows of cabbage, radishes, lettuce, herbs, chickpea, and tomatoes grew unencumbered by weeds. A treasure compared to her weak attempts at growing vegetables in the clay-choked Colorado soil. She stood and pulled her jeans up. Once tight around the waist, they sagged like urban-style droopy drawers. With the blackout, the garden had become more than a hobby, a key to their survival. The grocery stores had bare shelves, their supply of MREs ran low, rice became their daily nourishment. At least she had the boar she slaughtered for a protein source. She stood above a row of cabbage, satisfied with her weeding and pruning. The morning sky glowed the pale green of honeydew melons. Gardening gave her peace of mind. It also kept her 'ohana fed.

During the week, she had cleared most of the weeds and other predator plants. She filled a basket with vegetables and wiped her brow from the humid air. The sun didn't rise here; it leapt into the sky. Time to head back to the house.

. . .

By late afternoon, Hellen's hunger pains surpassed her willpower, and she went against her "one meal a day" rule to conserve food stocks. After all, she had a whole hog at her disposal. With a wet appetite, she fried a strip of boar meat. Lunch in hand, she sat on the lanai to read Elle's book. The story had seemed to parallel her own voyage to Hawai'i, but it took a different turn when the family settled in a small village on the western slope of Mauna Kea. After 'Ehulani designs a windmill to power a crude water pump, Aukai assembles and shows it to their tribal chief. Impressed by their ingenuity, the kahuna blesses them with a prayer to Haumea, the Hawaiian goddess of fertility and childbirth. Soon after, they have a child and name her Elikapeka.

Heat rose in Hellen's cheeks. Better not take it too literally.

"Elikapeka is Hawaiian for Elizabeth," Aiva said without prompting. "However, I found no record of this family in my library."

'Ehulani sure resembled Hellen, her name translating to "red-headed loved one." And her lover—Aukai—meant "seafarer." The book might be another of Elle's tricks to get her to fall in love with Brett again. Or maybe it conveyed a message or warning. Elle had a creepy way of seeing around the corners in space-time. The book had foreshadowed everything in Hellen's voyage to Hawai'i. As for Elikapeka, their child? Hellen's chest tightened at the memory of the night she told her the truth.

She came to an image of the couple sitting on a ledge by the ocean. Aukai's nose and eyes matched Brett's. 'Ehulani smiled at him with dimpled cheeks framed by her flowing auburn hair. As if looking at her own portrait, Hellen tapped 'Ehulani's face.

A security prompt for a passphrase popped up: *When and where did you meet him?*

"There's an encrypted file for you," Aiva said. "I recommend you do not open it. I've been offline for twenty-eight days and haven't updated my virus registry."

Hellen's index finger hovered over the password prompt.

Since the day Aiva became sentient, she had lived in the internet, fluttering between Hellen's IoT—her Internet of Things—a myriad of appliances, eReaders, phones, and tablets. But for the past month, Aiva's soul had lived only within Hellen's tablet. Without the network, Aiva lost more than virus protection; she lost access to her backup system files. If a virus corrupted her, she'd crash, her personality lost forever, the soul of the machine dead.

"Hellen, please reconsider," Aiva said. "I'm afraid. The image file is interlaced with other encrypted data."

"Elle wouldn't plant a Trojan virus."

Eyes closed, she took a deep breath. Her first evening with Brett was locked in her memory forever, a blind date arranged by Elle, a night under the stars, the ocean breeze, her twenty-first birthday. She tapped the floating icon and announced, "June 2, 2K06 at the Hōkūle'a Inn."

'Ehulani and Aukai's image dissolved into a photo of Hellen and Brett sitting on the veranda at the exclusive resort, overlooking Lahaina Harbor.

"Aiva, are you still there?" Hellen asked.

"Yes, but I don't appreciate your casual attitude toward my well-being."

The photo of Hellen and Brett next dissolved into an observatory, the same dome she had seen atop Mauna Kea. She tapped the screen, and another image appeared: the Pleiades. Next came an image of the Hawaiian national flag. After a few seconds, this photo dissolved into an American flag. Yet it lacked the familiar and perfect symmetry of the six rows of eight stars each. This flag had an asymmetric design, alternating rows of six and five stars, fifty in total.

The loud exhaust of Elle's truck roared up the driveway, its throaty vibrations echoing against the forest. Hellen ran into the kitchen and grabbed one of the garden baskets. With brisk hands, she scooped the vegetables and spread them across the counter and fetched a knife from the drawer. After chopping a head of lettuce, she worked on the radishes. Keys rattled on the table and Hellen looked up.

Elle stood across from her, her eyes growing wide. She bowed and gave Hellen a namaste gesture with her hands. "Thank you for getting dinner started. I'm starving." Elle ran her fingers over Hellen's tablet laying on the counter. "Without the internet, this is an expensive paperweight."

"That's Aiva," Hellen said brightly. "She's like a digital companion. Even though she's offline, I still use her to journal and read eBooks. I'm almost done with your novel, you seem to fancy yourself as a soothsayer."

"No one really knows the future, except those who lived it."

Hellen wondered what she meant, but let it pass. More curious about the book's characters, she took her tablet and retrieved the image of her first night with Brett. "Too close to home for my taste."

Elle gave a demure smile. "I see you've found the Easter eggs I sprinkled throughout the book."

"Don't give me that look. Your book is an enigma wrapped in a question mark. Too many coincident events parallel my voyage: the solar storm hits the Pacific, 'Ehulani settles on the slopes of Mauna Kea, and the windmill is an obvious reference to the Kohala Wind Farm. Yet you wrote it long before I departed San Diego."

"We'll talk later, but first I'm going upstairs to change."

"You can run, but you can't hide," Hellen called after her. "I'll keep pestering you until I get an answer."

Elle brushed her hand in the air and headed upstairs. Hellen let out a sigh and took the orchids she cut from the forest. She arranged them in a vase, caressing their petals and breathing in their fragrance. Nature's aromatherapy helped calm her nerves, but her mind still grappled with *The Wayfinders* mystery.

Within fifteen minutes, Elle returned and picked a flower from the vase, fitting it to Hellen's hair. "Where did you get these? They're wonderful."

"I found them in the forest behind your garden. Amazing, aren't they? They grow wild like weeds around here."

"People call our island the Orchid Isle," she said, tapping a flower petal with her finger. "We've many orchids growing along the mountains, but I've never seen any at Cloudcroft." She walked to the kitchen counter and picked through the sliced radishes. "And where did you get these gems?"

"I've whipped the garden into shape. It'll come in handy if the MREs run out."

Elle's smile slipped away. "I'm embarrassed of how I've left the garden go, leaving our only source of vitamins to rot in the ground."

"When were you last back there?"

Elle picked up a carrot and munched on it, narrowing her eyes. "When did Helio Hattie hit? Almost four weeks ago? That's why I put you in charge around here. Suzu spends all his time in inner space, leaving practical aspects of life to others."

"Glad to help out while Charlie and I squat on your property."

"Don't be ridiculous. I hope you never leave."

"But I feel I should do more, not just sitting on my duff during the blackout."

"You already have—you saved me from acting like a fool to Hancock. And if you bring the power back, you'll really be a hero. In fact, all you guys are a godsend. Donovan at the hospital, you at the wind farm. Now, we just need to find a job for Brett."

"He used to fly helicopters for the Royal Navy."

"Great. We need another helo pilot. We're down to two after tourism dropped off last year."

"I'll talk to Brett, but I'm sure he'll go for it. He must be tired of fishing every day."

Silver showers returned, each drop sparkling in the bright sunlight. Beyond the kitchen picture window, a rainbow arched over Cloudcroft's pastures, faint at first, then growing with a pulsating light. Not since arriving to the Big Island had Hellen felt a strong purpose. Now, her mission stood before her. Power for her 'ohana.

After their late dinner, Elle charged two vape pens. Her own blend, Maunakea Snow, grew behind the hayfield. She took one pen, inhaled, and let out a torus-shaped ring of vapor. "Here, try it, but not too much. Potent stuff." She pressed a black button on the second pen and handed it to Hellen.

"I've not had hashish in over a year."

"Takes the edge off, especially in these times."

Elle strolled to the couch in the living room. Hellen sat beside her and stretched her legs out on a footrest. Elle's cat jumped onto her lap and curled into a ball, purring under Hellen's hand.

"Ty Lee looks Siamese, same as the cat you had on Maui."

"She should. Buddha and Ty Lee come from the same litter."

"Does a cat have Buddha nature?" Hellen joked.

They both grinned at Elle's favorite koan. Without warning, Elle's eyes welled up, and she covered her mouth with her palm.

Hellen flinched. "What's eating you?"

"I'm just overwhelmed with the mess from Helio Hattie."

Hellen imagined a world without electricity, a world that both frightened and soothed her. Her whole life, she took the conveniences of technology for granted, the intimacy of social media. She'd never admit it to anyone, but a part of her welcomed the chance to detox from the modern world. Her new world allowed time to sit on the porch, talk with friends, and fall back in love with her Man from Maui. But she soon felt a tang of guilt. Now wasn't the time for love and idle living.

"Just imagine how people are feeling," Elle continued, "with scant outside aid and dwindling supplies. Time marches on as our food runs out. For those without residential solar or wind power, life collapses. With no running water, they have to fetch water from wells. They can't store food in their refrigerators, so meat spoils without electricity."

Ashamed, Hellen rubbed her eyes with her hands. Her Arcadian fantasy vanished. This wasn't a detox vacation from technology. People had died around her because of the blackout.

"But we're making progress, aren't we?" Hellen looked up and gave Elle a practiced smile. "The medical triage plans. The wind farm. Beef from Parker Ranch."

"Most people aren't aware of that. Without TV or the internet, there's no access to news. I wish we had KUMU back on the air again. It'll give folks a reason for hope."

"KUMU, the FM station?"

"They're the largest FM broadcaster on the island. With all the best local music, everyone listens in. If they returned to the airwaves, people would feel like having an old friend come home. No more depressing, disembodied voice droning on and on from the home secretary's EMS broadcasts. We'd make it upbeat, with a mix of great music and great news. I'll record a daily message, cheering people up, helping them to help others, as one 'ohana."

"Your 'Ohana Plan?" Hellen asked.

Elle opened her eyes wide and held her palm up. "I so love you. Yes, that's what we'll call it."

Hellen returned the high-five. "If you can get me to Mauna Kea's peak, I'll rig a solar array to power a relay station for KUMU's FM signal. We'll soon play music all over Kohala." After she said this, she wondered how she'd pull it off.

"Tomorrow," Elle said, "we'll go visit Maunakea Astronomy Institute and find a way to get you up there." She playfully slapped Hellen's knee. "Providence dropped you on our shores for a reason."

"Speaking of providence, I finished reading your book." Hellen leaned back into the sofa and exhaled a stream of smoke toward the ceiling. Hellen hoped the hash would loosen Elle's lips. The soothsaying plotline was as perplexing as the enigmatic pictures. She raised a lazy hand and pointed to Elle's pendulum wall clock. "My old physics professor at Caltech obsessed about time. Goldstein said time is an arrow, always flying in one direction. We have no more knowledge of the next hour than we have power to change the last hour. I recall you had different ideas."

"I don't place much faith in the Second Law of Thermodynamics. Time is bidirectional, not an arrow. Really, what is time? It's perhaps the greatest mystery in the universe."

"For sure." Hellen took another drag and brushed her hair from her misty eyes. "Time is a cruel sister. That bitch marches on with no care or concern, always forward, never looking over her shoulder. Yet I wonder if you found a loophole."

Elle wore an inviting smile. "In what way?"

"The Grandmother Paradox."

Elle laughed and waved her hand dismissively at Hellen. "I've never wanted to travel back in time and kill my grandmother."

"But if you did, you'd have never been born. Hence you can never travel in time."

"Where are you going with this?"

"I remember your research dealt with parallel universes."

"Glinda Rubin was my thesis adviser. Her Many Worlds Interpretation of quantum mechanics became my life's work."

"Did you ever consider how it might answer this paradox? A time traveler may never change the timeline, but she may create a new branch, a new world."

Elle's face lost its carefree levity. "A divergent branch point in the multiverse, they call it."

"If she can't travel through time, maybe she can travel between two parallel worlds. Here, look." Hellen opened Aiva and scrolled to the images she copied from *The Wayfinders*. Elle put on her reading glasses and held Aiva in her lap. Hellen smiled at the way Elle's nose twitched like a rabbit as she examined the tablet.

"The Pleiades is a tip of the hat to your passion for astronomy," Hellen continued, "but the US flag… another artifact of this parallel world you imagined? Why fifty stars? America hasn't added another state in over a century. The Spanish-American War ended our empire building, and we've since isolated ourselves from the rest of the world."

"But on your own terms." Elle set Aiva between them on the couch. "America became the arms merchant to the world, selling tanks and planes in the First Sino-Japanese War, then aircraft carriers and atomic bombs in the Second War. Now an isolationist nation, America brands foreigners 'taboo.' President Jackson built the wall, and Pax America—once a nation of emigrants—became history."

Hellen sighed and stared at the ceiling. "Sometimes I want to trade my US passport for a Hawaiian one."

"If you did," Elle scoffed, "you'd have better health care insurance, but also a wider duff from eating fried grinds."

They both tittered and took another puff. The smoke from their vape pens rose in a corkscrew pattern, dispersing and blending into a common cloud.

"Think about it," Elle said. "After the Americans leased Pearl Harbor in the mid-1800s, Yankee haoles briefly took over Kamehameha's government, forming the 'Bayonet Constitution.' For a short time, Hawai'i was part of America, but the Brits chased them out, and we traded one master for another. Otherwise, the pineapple barons would've overthrown the Hawaiian Regency and made Hawai'i another state."

The stars and stripes in Elle's book came from magical realism. Had Japan lost the war to America's superior technology and vast natural resources, America would have emerged as a superpower.

"Right. Maybe the Japanese would've attacked Pearl Harbor, dragging America into the Second Sino-Japanese War. Ah! All your Japanese landlords would now be camera-toting tourists. But if a parallel universe exists, how would we ever see it or even travel to it?"

Elle fell silent. Conjecture and reality are separated only by point of view. Elle's career in quantum cosmology had led to many published papers on the multiverse, establishing her reputation as an expert in the field. Yet she remained stoic, her arms folded across her chest. Her searching eyes inspected Hellen as if reading her thoughts. Like Suzu, Elle could hide her feelings behind her Buddha smile. Hellen wondered what Elle's point of view would reveal, what secrets she ensconced. But Elle just sat there, unwavering, her mind impenetrable. For the first time in her life, Hellen wasn't sure if she really knew this woman.

The next morning, Hellen took a drive with Elle into town, hoping to find a ride to Mauna Kea's peak. They came to a sleek modern building with a Dutch gable-hip roof with metal shingles, covered with solar panels. A sign set in a lava stone wall read Maunakea Astronomy Institute. Hellen got out of the truck and walked up to the entrance, its glass doors locked. She peered into the dark interior. "Looks deserted, but I can see past the lobby and into an atrium. Wait, someone is moving back there."

"Let's check it out," Elle said. "There's a footpath leading to the rear gardens on the campus."

They walked along a flower-lined, gravel lane leading to an astronomers' lodge. The domes atop of Mauna Kea must have belonged to this world-class astronomy center. As a theoretical cosmologist, Elle spent little time at telescopes, but she had often lectured here, even donating a fortune to its construction. With its high altitude, dark sky, and dry air, the summit offered pristine viewing conditions, unparalleled throughout the world. An amateur astronomer, Hellen looked forward to seeing the world's premier observatory firsthand. But she still had no clear idea how to set up power to the FM transmitter and hoped she'd find a way. Soon.

The footpath opened into a manicured landscape filled with white orchids, deep green ferns, and koa trees shading the patio, filling the air with a damp musk. A man in overalls, fit and in his fifties, stood on a stepladder beside a commercial-grade diesel generator, his back to them, a socket wrench in his hand.

Elle nudged Hellen's arm. "That cute beefcake with the wavy, blond hair—he's Christopher Beck—MAI's ops manager. More *kama'aina* than haole, he's lived here for decades and always draws uninvited attention from the ladies, but they're wasting their time. He prefers Y-chromosomes, except in some rare cases." Elle patted her chest and winked. Until she met Suzu, Elle had a reputation for a "bicycle" lifestyle, cycling between lesbian and straight. Hellen couldn't blame her. She had the dynamite figure and smooth brown skin of a woman twenty years younger. Perhaps her pansexuality had helped more than hurt her mayoral campaign.

Christopher pressed the starter. The diesel spurted to life before coughing and dying. Christopher turned from the red diesel monster and shouted, "Hey, girlfriend. Great to see you again." He hopped off his stool and strode over to Elle.

"Love back at ya, boyfriend," Elle said, embracing him. They continued to flirt and traded barbs, leaving Hellen out of their verbal chess game.

Hellen walked up to the diesel and traced the fuel line back from the fuel injector to find the fuel filter. Using hose clamps and a flat-head screwdriver from Christopher's tool box, she shut the fuel line off several inches from either side of the filter. After venting the line, she unscrewed the access cap and removed the filter assembly. A grimy mess, it was without a doubt the problem here. "I think I found your problem," she said, handing the filter to Christopher. "Got any kerosene to clean it?"

"Sure, let me get some." He went to a utility shed and returned with a small blue jug.

Hellen tapped the filter against the diesel's concrete base to knock debris loose and cleaned the filter with kerosene. "Let's wait for it to dry, but I think she'll start up this time."

Christopher laid the soaked fuel filter in the sun next to the diesel generator. "Hey, you seem to know your way about diesels, I already like you."

"She has many talents," Elle said before introducing her, summarizing her credentials. She explained why they wanted to set up a relay on Mauna Kea's peak to broadcast an FM station. "It's high enough to reach most of Kohala. Can you take her up there?"

"We built a small radio shack with two fifty-watt transmitters to use as a backup comm system," he said. "I think it'll work from a transmission standpoint, but we still have no power up there."

"If I can get a set of hundred-watt solar panels," Hellen said, "I can rig them to the equipment rack. I'll just need an electrical schematic."

"We might have spare PVC panels lying around the work-shop at the base camp. But we'll need plenty of sturdy mounting hardware. The wind there can reach sixty knots. I'm planning to go up tomorrow for my weekly survey, so you can tag along."

Hellen raised her eyebrows and smiled at Christopher. If only he knew she had never worked on radio transmitters, he might have changed his tune.

"But it's wicked cold at thirteen thousand feet. Dress warm."

"Hellen can handle it." Elle's warm hand rested on Hellen's shoulder, pulling her closer. "She came from Colorado. This isn't her first mountain safari."

Christopher winked at Hellen. "You look in fine shape. But I'll keep my eye on you in case the altitude sucks the life out of you."

Hellen wondered if she had stepped into another quagmire. She wasn't sure if her scheme might work under the arctic condi-tions at the peak. The winds might tear the solar array apart, sending the panels aloft. The first and only time she'd climbed a Colorado fourteener, exhaustion had overcome her, and she suffered a raging headache. And she'd never worked on radio power supplies. The transmitter range might not even reach the nearest base station. Anxiety lay rock hard in her tummy, but it was too late to back out.

Christopher retrieved a card from his backpack and handed it to Hellen. "Here's a checklist and precautions to take. Bring two gallons of water and wear layers of clothes."

"Sure," Hellen said in a tone she hoped sounded more confident than she felt. "I'll get my things and be back here early tomorrow morning."

Hellen started to leave, but Elle grabbed her hand. "There's something else you can do for me," Elle said to Christopher, making his shoulders slump. "Our hospital is overrun with patients, and we desperately need more beds. Since your operations are mothballed during the blackout, how about letting them use this place as an annex for the hospital?"

Christopher rubbed his chin. "I'm not sure this idea will float. Contracts need to be drawn, equipment moved, data safeguarded."

Elle pressed in on him and wrapped her arms around his neck. "I thought you ran this place," she said in a syrupy tone. "Besides, it's deserted. We don't have time for legal wrangling. Let's just make it an agreement between friends. I'll make it up to you, cross my heart."

"Okay, you win, Elle. As usual." He pushed her away. "But you owe me big time, girlfriend. Between acting as Hellen's tour guide and turning this place into a hotel, the Maunakea overlords will fry my sweet ass."

"Stop worrying. Remember, I'm a major donor for your institute."

15

Green Valley Farm, Pāhoa, 07 July

Inside his repurposed drug lab, Gus sat in front of a thirty-inch flat screen with his dachshund sleeping in his lap. After his gang cooked the last batu batch a week ago, he had cleared away the lab equipment and set up an operations command center in his lava cave. He needed a secure location from which to plan and execute his pending attack on the PGP facility. The bunker was hidden from any view of law enforcement, and its walls were covered with blueprints showing the power plant layout and topographical maps of the surrounding terrain.

With Toma standing next to him, Gus plugged a memory stick into the SmartTV and selected a vid-file titled *Honaunau*. The video images of the small town and coastline dug up an old nightmare—his arrival into this new world decades ago. During a diving trip off the Kona Coast, the night sky had filled with color, much like the recent aurora before Helio Hattie. Hidden in an offshore reef, a brain coral colony glowed with blue light. But after he swam to it, he found it had no surface, as if it were a ghost. His hand went into it with no resistance. A brilliant flash blinded him and swallowed him into an underwater gopher hole and spit him back to the surface. His dive boat had disappeared, and the coastline had changed, void of any high-rise condos. He wasn't in Hawai'i anymore.

He shook his head to clear his mind and fast-forwarded the video feed until the fire station appeared. A red truck with a big-honking generator in its cargo bed sat parked on the side. Gus froze the video and zoomed into the generator's nameplate. One-hundred kilowatts AC/DC, exactly what the boys needed to jump-start the PGP plant. Once his gang requisitioned it, he'd soon control the livelihood of thousands of people. Grinning like the Grinch on Black Friday, Gus let a new idea take seed. He could make bank selling power to big business and government, then use his profits to give electricity away to the poor. They'd call him the Robin Hood of the power grid. Grassroots support for his operation would grow, and he could stifle law enforcement with "random" blackouts to Puna's police headquarters.

In the meantime, he needed firepower. Gus turned his attention to the second half of their expedition. "Tell me what the hell happened at the Pohakuloa Army Garrison."

"The armory was heavily guarded, man." Toma held his eyes on Gus and shook his head. "You said we wouldn't run into any trouble."

"Look, this business is risky. If you can't run with the big dogs, then stay under the porch."

Toma narrowed his eyes, and his chest heaved in deep breaths, the air rank with anger. "You sent us into a firefight, man. The boys are pissed. Next time—"

"Next time, you best check your attitude at the door, or I'll cancel your birth certificate."

Toma squinted at Gus as if he missed the inference. "Our surprise visit got us da kine," Toma said at last. "Ten assault rifles, grenades, two rounds of ammo, not to mention the RPG."

"That reminds me, did you mount the rocket-propelled-grenade launcher on the back of the Vagabond?"

"Done and tested. It scared the crap out of your wiener dog, though."

"German dachshund."

"Whatever."

"We've more immediate problems. Like food." He also needed to find enough gold to pay off the PGP boys. The next mission on the Kona Coast might yield some yellow metal. The polished rich hiding in their posh homes had nowhere to go, the perfect setup for a heist. If the mission was a bust, Plan B was Cloudcroft and Elle Otoko's gold hoard.

"Wasn't dat the deal? Canned ham fo' batu jam."

"Sure, but I'm talking about real food for a change." Most of his customers had resorted to trading canned ham and sex for his batu, but if he had to eat another can of that shit, he'd puke. He missed his home-styled, Southern cooking, despite the hundreds of recipes these islanders invented for Sham, Spiced ham in a can: Eggs n' Sham, Poke Sham, Pineapple Sham, Sham-loaf, Sham-a-lot. Christ, all that canned ham had more salt than the Pacific Ocean, the last thing his hypertension needed. Back in the Old World, it was called SPAM, but this world had a different name for everything. A new name didn't matter none, it was the same salty asstastic grub.

"They got da kine lodge near Mauna Kea peak for all those astrologers. I bet it's deserted. The lodge must've plenty of food left."

Gus gave a quick nod. "I like it. Better than trying to pilfer the army base again."

"Right. After our last encounter, we best stay low and out of sight. Otherwise, you'll need to find another gang to do your work."

Gus sneered. Like the other Samoans, Toma's loyalty had limits. With the batu business winding down and cash running low, he needed to make his next mission pay off, so he could make payroll for his gang. He also needed cash for his chemo meds. Time was against him.

"Okay, cowboy, I'm putting you in charge of a scouting mission to have a look-see. If you find any grub, radio me, and we'll send a truck to collect the goods. Here's the deal." Gus unfolded a topographical map and pointed to the Maunakea facility. "Take a couple mokes and head up there on our Harley hogs. You grew up in these parts, right?"

Toma bent over the map and jabbed his pudgy finger at the long blue line winding between Hilo and the other side of the island. "Sure, it's right here off Saddle Road. Back in the day we used to dirt bike around the Mauna Kea and Mauna Loa volcanoes. Crazy how we not kill ourselves barreling along under moonlight."

Gus glanced at Toma's grin and wondered if the kid still had it in him. "It's no sweat. Up and back by sundown. Just don't do anything stupid like stopping for a shrimp plate in Hilo. Keep your head low and your ears open. I'll monitor Channel 18 on the CB. Report back to me every hour."

Mauna Kea Summit Road

"Beware of the Invisible Cows."

Hellen read the sign a second time. It appeared official and carried several lines of small print.

"What's that all about?" she asked, thinking of UFOs.

"Cattle from Parker Ranch graze along the road," Christopher said. "They like to lie on the warm asphalt at night."

"Sure, I've seen them do this in Colorado, but a car horn is more than enough to move them out of the way."

He gave a dismissive wave with his hand. "Maybe for Colorado, but tourists here drive too fast on foggy nights and smash into the Black Angus."

The sign fit the times. It's what you didn't see coming that hurt you. On the back seat rested a Ruger rifle, the same Kalino had given to her when she turned twelve. While fun to shoot, it didn't have much kick and couldn't stop a wild boar. "Twenty-two caliber. You use it for varmint hunting?"

He gave her a wry smile. "You must not get out much lately. Down in Hilo, it's crazytown, like the Wild West drenched in coconut juice," he said, without taking his eyes off the road. "Before tackling the final ascent, we'll stop at the astronomer's lodge to pick up the PVC panels and change into warmer clothes. The temperature at the peak will only reach the low thirties."

Their silver Subaru SUV climbed into a cloud bank as they passed the seventy-five-hundred-foot elevation marker. The air cooled, and Christopher ran the wipers to clear the mist from the windshield. Her windbreaker didn't stop the chill seeping into her body. She had thought of asking Elizabeth for a coat, but her daughter had barricaded herself in her room, refusing to speak to her. Perhaps time would heal her wounds. For now, Hellen searched for invisible cows in the fog.

After a sharp switchback, they popped out of the clouds. The road opened into a high desert plain. A few spiny silversword plants interrupted the barren gray-and-brown landscape. Petals bloomed from a central stalk of the botanical unicorn. A bold, brushed-nickel sign announced "Maunakea Observatory Complex." Christopher pulled into a broad parking lot bordered by shuttered buildings.

"Why do they call the observatory 'Maunakea' with one word?" Hellen asked.

"It's the traditional name for the mountain. Your mother pushed for the name change last year, but only the astronomers sympathized with her cause. Everyone else still uses two words, another vestige of British colonialism—or maybe we're too lazy."

"Yet she petitioned to change the Sandwich Islands to Hawai'i back in the 1990s."

"She was driven more by activism than science back then, I guess."

Hellen had no problem imagining her mother leading a protest movement, but it was strange she had never mentioned any of this to her.

She got out and walked across the empty parking lot, a deep quiet falling over her. The cloud tops drifted below her, around the many volcanic cinder cones dotting the horizon. She wished Charlie could see this. She had thought of taking him along with her, even radioed the harbor master yesterday, but he was out fishing with Brett.

The cold breeze sent a shiver through her body and goose bumps on her skin. A numbing pain grew behind her eyeballs. She shook her hands, wishing she had a pair of gloves. The altitude and cold air woke her to the predicament she had dove into without much preparation. She pinched her lips and worried about all the ways she might screw this up. In Colorado, she had fallen victim to hypoxia enough times to know she didn't belong on this peak. Why had she blundered into this job, underdressed and underskilled? Assuming worst-case scenarios was her creed, not reckless optimism. She ran back, out of breath by the time she reached Christopher, who had already loaded four PVC panels and mounting hardware into their SUV.

"Ready to head up?" he said, handing her a parka.

She put the coat over her shoulders and thrust her hands into the pockets, thrilled to find a pair of Thinsulate gloves. Their warmth spread through her knuckles and sent a tingling pain through fingers.

He checked her out, head to toe. "Look, sweetie. You're making too loud a fashion statement with those sexy leggings. Don't you have any warmer clothes to wear?"

She smoothed the wrinkles in her skin-tight turquoise yoga pants. "I'm afraid I don't. When I packed for our sail out to Hawai'i, I never thought I'd arrive to arctic conditions."

"Sail? You came here by boat?"

"It's a rather long story. An accidental sojourn, so to speak."

"Follow me." Christopher led her to the visitor center gift

shop. After unlocking the door, he waved her in. "It's not Harrods, but you should find what you need. No one's coming back any time soon, so just take what you want."

She emerged, wearing orange fleece sweatpants, a red Maunakea Observatory hoodie, and yellow earmuffs. Her color coordination wasn't fit for going out in public, but fashion wasn't important on this frozen tundra. She came over to Christopher and spread her arms out. "Better?"

"Like a killer runway model," he said with a wink.

"So, what's a handsome buck like you doing on the top of the world?"

Christopher shrugged his shoulders. "I had a flat in Hilo, held together by petrified mold and coqui frog juice. But after Helio Hattie hit, I fled to Kamuela. So here I am, returning to the peak once a week to keep an eye on the place until operations return."

She walked to the crew cab and sat in the passenger seat. A little lightheaded, she rubbed her temples. "You better make plans to stay in Kamuela," she said more to herself than Christopher. But her recent encounters with looters proved Cloudcroft wasn't a safe sanctuary either.

He took a green oxygen bottle from the back seat and rigged it with a cannula before draping it over Hellen's headrest. "In case you get dizzy…"

"Hey, I'm a Colorado girl and climbed a few fourteeners in my day." But the numbing pressure behind her eyes grew into a raging headache and pain throbbed with each spoken word.

The rest of the trip to the summit was a Hawaiian version of Pikes Peak. They ascended through different ecoclines, stunted evergreens trees giving way to stubby alpine scrub brush as they gained altitude and leading to a barren field of lava rock. Alpenglow settled upon Mauna Kea, changing its moonscape to red hues. Near the top, no guardrails stood waiting to prevent their careening off the winding narrow road, thousands of feet above the mountain base. Hellen's heart fell to her stomach. Heights were never her friend.

They pulled into the summit parking lot next to a silver observatory dominating the landscape. Christopher killed the engine and they got out. The cold air froze the moisture in her nostrils, tickling her as she wiggled her nose. Nothing lived at this altitude, no birds, no insects, no branches blowing in the wind, just a cold empty silence in the stark bolder fields. From her perspective, the forest around Cloudcroft seemed as if it lay in another universe.

Christopher swept his hand in a wide arc. "On this sacred mountaintop, we have Japan's pride of the cosmos."

The ten-story dome sat like a celestial sentinel searching the heavens. Its shiny aluminum reflected sunlight in a burst of color, the same observatory depicted in Elle's book. The Japanese superpower always had grandiose plans, from the world's largest telescope to the SpaceLiner.

"The Subaru Observatory," Christopher continued, "houses the thirty-meter telescope, the largest in the world."

"Why would a Japanese car company invest in a telescope?" she asked.

Christopher snickered. "It's the other way around. The Pleiades star cluster is known in Japan as Subaru, 'to unite.' After five companies merged, they named themselves Subaru and chose the star cluster as their logo."

Hellen craned her neck at the observatory. "I heard a legend of this star cluster while working on a Navajo reservation. Native folklore recounts how the Seven Sisters became the first constellation placed in the sky by the Black God."

Christopher walked to the SUV's tailgate and opened the backdoor. "At altitude, we have our own Black God, we call it hypoxia. This altitude puts us above forty percent of the Earth's atmosphere. We're just trained monkeys up here. Most of the deep thinking gets done down in Kamuela."

She took a few steps and wavered on her feet. Her vision narrowed, and the SUV's bright blue Maunakea Astronomy Institute logo muted to gray. She stared at her bare hands, mottled with purple patterns. Where were her gloves?

Christopher laughed and retrieved the portable oxygen tank from the SUV. "Here, you better take this. You can wear it like a camelback."

After he helped her don the bottle and fit the cannula to her nose, she took a deep breath. Her sluggish mind and blurry vision cleared. She found her gloves in the truck and slipped her hands into them. Sensation returned to her numb fingers, tingling like fire.

He handed her an eInk tablet. "Here are the electrical schematics for the FM transceiver. The power dongle is fairly standard, so you'll not have any trouble hooking up your solar array."

She walked to the back of the SUV and retrieved her duffel bag filled with tools, wiring, electrical connectors, and a digital multimeter. After laying four solar panels out in the parking lot, she inspected them, satisfied they sustained no damage on the trip up.

"The radio shack is next to the UH observatory." He pointed to a small white dome down the hill from the parking lot's south end. "Let me help you move these panels over there first."

They carried her equipment to the work site, making several trips along the dirt path to the antenna farm, a small concrete pad of about a hundred-square-feet sprinkled with a dozen white, metal radio antennae. The solar panels were lightweight but cumbersome to carry. Thankfully, the wind had calmed.

"I'll be up at the Subaru dome," he said, "but will return in about two hours to check in on you." He tossed her a handheld radio. "Call me on channel seven if you need me."

She entered the small utility shed, a relic from the twentieth century. Against the opposite metal wall, an equipment rack provided easy access to the transceiver's connectors. Soot covered the power distribution panel. The main circuit breaker must have tripped open, saving the radio stack from the solar storm's extreme currents.

She assembled the solar array, carefully snapping each panel in place on the ground, anchoring it with rocks at each corner. She had built similar assemblies a dozen times in remote locations for NCEL. Absorbed in her work, the hours passed. Once done with the array, she sliced a heavy gauge wire and connected the radio transmitter. The front panel lights came alive. She found a renewed pleasure in the familiar task, the joining of wires, the flow of current, the distinctive electronics smell. It all bordered on magic. After the unit warmed up, she programmed it to act as a signal repeater. Without a laptop, she had to use the tedious alphanumeric keyboard to reconfigure the transceiver. She pecked at the keys one at a time and set the frequency to match KUMU's transmitter. Hiss and pops came from the radio, and her ears pricked for the hints of a voice hiding amid the white noise. Elle had arranged for the local FM broadcast station to transmit a test signal every half hour.

The wind gusts picked up, rattling the shed's aluminum siding. Sitting on a folding chair, she leaned back and huddled against the cold seeping into her body. The minutes stretched. Through the doorway, the solar array gleamed white and purple in the sunset. Yet its neat orthogonal shape seemed amiss, like a window frame missing a panel. She stood and went outside. Without a proper checklist, she had become distracted from the task at hand. The missing solar panel leaned against the back of the shed, the same place she had left it hours ago. She stood quickly and raised it above her shoulders and felt lightheaded. A rogue gust of wind caught the panel, pulling her forward. The panel blocked her view, but she dared not let it go. She screamed as it tugged her off the ledge and onto a rocky outcrop twenty feet below.

The shock of the impact knocked the solar panel out of her hands, letting it fly like a kite over the cliff, tumbling down the mountain. Heat rose in her chest and neck. Her pulse pounded in her ears, her mind shrouded by adrenaline. Her throat burned with each breath; the familiar throbbing pain behind her eyes returned. The O2 cannula lay loose over her shoulder, detached from the green bottle laying hundreds of feet below her. Confused, her mind tried to make her arms reach for a hit of oxygen, but her raggedy-doll hands only fumbled with the cannula. Her blurred vision made out a precipice edge, beyond which the cliff fell thousands of feet to a base of sharp boulders. The sight seized her with a spasm of uncontrollable trembling. She gripped the rock ledge with desperation, her fingers cramped. Her lungs groped for each breath like a fish washed ashore. Lying on her back, she forced slow, deep breathes into her lungs to fend off the panic shooting adrenaline through her body. Time passed, maybe minutes or hours, she wasn't sure. With misty eyes, she barely made out Christopher's truck, a tiny white speck making its way down the mountain along the dirt access road. He must be searching for her. She tried to yell to him, but no sound came from her mouth. With her last conscious breath, her vision shifted from gray to black.

Hellen awoke, startled by a rope falling across her chest. She stared up to the outcrop from where she had fallen, holding her chest, unable to breathe. Her left arm seared with pain. A figure emerged far above her. Was it Christopher? She dried her eyes with her hoody and wiped her nose with the back of her sleeve. After a few breaths, she rolled her head, shaking off the throbbing ache behind her eyes. Pointing to her chest, she croaked a gasp, her breath shooting a plume of vapor in front of her.

"Stay calm," he called down to her. "Relax. Try to take some deep breaths."

Her breathing soon returned to normal. She rubbed the back of her head, her hand moist with blood. She grabbed the rope, tied a bowline on the second try, and slid her arms through the loop. Christopher pulled her up and carried her in his arms to the radio shack. After he placed the O2 cannula to her nose, her vision cleared.

"I'm okay," she said at last. "Can you go and retrieve the lost solar panel?"

"Forget about it. We have to get off the peak before dark."

"But I've not tested the radio relay. Without that panel, the transmitter may be underpowered."

Christopher went to the equipment stack, his finger resting on the transmitter panel. "It's set to the correct frequency and transmission power indicates fifteen watts. We'll have to let it be and hope for the best."

She struggled against his arms, too weak to break free. "No. We need to finish this."

"Hellen, listen. After sunset, this place turns into the Arctic."

Hellen relaxed her arms and resigned to his wishes. With Christopher's help, she slumped into the truck. Tears welled up in her eyes as much from her frustration of leaving a job undone as from her pain from the fall. She had not only failed Elle's dream of boosting her people's morale, she had let her own children down again. Like many in the community, they had lost their spirit. Elle's broadcasts might have restored their faith but not without the radio relay.

With the sun below the distant ocean, the waning gibbous moon broke the eastern horizon, marking almost five weeks since she left San Diego. It felt like a lifetime ago.

With no interference from urban lights, the sky came alive like fireflies floating in space. Sharper and more beautiful, the constellations spoke to her. Even in this cold loneliness, these familiar signposts comforted her. A shooting star, unhinged from the celestial canopy, streaked toward the ocean.

The drive down the mountain sent shivers along Hellen's spine with its tight turns and steep incline. Christopher kept the truck in low gear. Its engine whined in protest against the force of gravity. Under darkness, the truck's headlights shot twin beams into the void. She closed her eyes, shutting out the precipice.

After the road flattened out, Hellen turned on the car radio and tuned it to KUMU. The static hiss from the speaker cleared, and the radio came to life. Her jerry-rigged radio relay station sent a carrier wave through the air, filling her chest with excitement. She imagined the radio waves streaming throughout Kohala, acting as a new lifeline for all the people who had given up. Elle's book came back to her, another foreshadowing. Like 'Ehulani, Hellen had also climbed Mauna Kea to signal for help, her radio relay a modern-day version of 'Ehulani's smoke signals. She too risked her life on a venture to help her 'ohana.

"This is K-U-M-U, transmitting on one-oh-four-point-one megahertz, polling all the fire stations around Kohala. Standby everyone."

"Stop the car!" Hellen switched on the cabin dome light and flinched from the sudden glare. After her eyes adapted to the bright interior, she reached over her seat and retrieved a map, marked with all the fire stations in Kohala. The relay antenna lay at the center of Mauna Kea, encircled by concentric five-mile rings. Hellen listened as each station called in, checking them off as they responded.

Christopher leaned over the map. "Why have only five of the twenty stations acknowledged? The stations offline all lay in the outer rings."

"Without all the solar panels, the array isn't generating enough power for the transmitter. Radio emission follows an inverse square law; half the power yields one-quarter the range." She grabbed his arm. "We must go back and install the last panel."

"No. It's too dark to work safely at the peak. We'll come back in the daylight."

"Let's finish the job we came here to do."

"Hellen, I can't let you do this. I promise we'll come back during the day and finish assembling the array."

Hellen slammed her fist against the armrest but didn't fight him. He was right; it was too risky at night. Her initial excitement drained from her chest in a long sigh.

Another mile down the road and Christopher pulled up to a garage uphill from the astronomer's lodge. He backed into a small fuel depot opposite of the garage and cut the engine.

"Before we head back to Kamuela," he said, "we need to refuel. We can also grab a snack from the lodge's kitchen."

After he hand-pumped the petrol, he led her down a dirt path to a long, beige wooden building. A stone chimney lay at one end. Lit only by moonlight, its darkened windows showed no activity. He stopped halfway, grabbed her arm, and cupped his ear with his hand, shielding it from the wind.

"Do you hear them?" he whispered. "Let's get back to the truck now."

She hesitated, hungry and tired from the cold. The lodge lay just fifty feet away, warmth and food beckoned. Christopher took her by the arm and ran up the path. Her dull senses soon picked up on men's voices close in the night. She almost ran into three Harley motorcycles parked under a tree. After reaching the SUV, Christopher opened the driver's door and grabbed a handgun from the glove compartment.

"Might be the same gang I saw last week," he said.

The outline of three men approached, their path lit by headlamps. Christopher peeked over the hood and ducked back down.

"They must be on a scouting mission, perhaps looking for food and petrol," he said. "Get down and stay quiet. Some dude is coming toward us. I think he's seen our truck."

A shot resounded the still air and shattered the driver-side window. Christopher yelped and tried to return fire from his handgun. But he snapped backward, falling to the ground. Hellen ran to him.

"They shot me in the shoulder."

Hellen opened the SUV's cargo door and crawled in. She

grabbed the Ruger long rifle, checked the chamber, and helped Christopher over to a massive, yellow snowcat tractor uphill from their SUV. Its heavy steel snow blower rig provided a shield from the oncoming bullets, sending a spray of sparks as they ricocheted off in random directions. One man walked with slow determination, aiming his gun at them.

"Toma, let's get the hell out of here," another man yelled. "Come on, let's blow this place."

The Samoan hulk named Toma kept marching toward them, firing again and again with each step. Bullets ricocheted off the thick steel, sending sparks into the air. Hiding behind the snow-cat, she braced the rifle against her good shoulder, took aim and returned fire, hitting the man's right shoulder. He dropped his weapon and cupped his good hand around the wound. She fired another shot behind him as he ran back to his bike. Her heart racing, she stayed behind the snowcat until the motorcycles roared down the mountain.

After the rumbling engines faded, Hellen helped Christopher onto the front passenger seat of their SUV. "They're gone. Let's get you to the hospital."

With a searing pain in her left arm, she stripped off her T-shirt and wrapped it around Christopher's injured arm. The chill gave her goose bumps, but her adrenaline rush kept her going. After dressing his wound, she put her fleece hoodie back on and climbed behind the steering wheel.

The cold air blasted through the shattered side window as they sped downslope. With her good hand on the wheel, she peered into the misty beams from the headlight. The fog thickened as they headed to a lower elevation, forcing her to slow. Ahead, a black cow emerged from the gray mist. It lay in the middle of the road, still unmoving, despite Hellen leaning on the truck's horn.

"Must have been hit by one of the motorcycles. I'll take a look."

Lighting her way with a flashlight, she came to a bull lying dead on the side of the road. A reflection in the beam caught her attention. As she walked closer, a chrome muffler shone from a wrecked Harley. Farther down, a muscular Hawaiian lay prone in her flashlight beam, his tattooed arms twisted at odd angles, his black boots spread apart as if he had just fallen from the sky. Here lay the man who just tried to kill them. She wondered where he came from and why he had attacked them. Leaving him crossed her mind, a death he deserved. She checked his cathodic artery, his pulse weak but steady. His life depended on her next move. No, she couldn't leave him to die alone.

She ran back to the SUV and engaged the ignition. "One of the gang members ran into a Black Angus. He's lying in the road —still has a pulse—but is unconscious."

Hellen struggled to pull the man into the back seat, his dead weight too much for Hellen's exhausted arms. Christopher grabbed the man with his good arm and after the second try, they pulled him into the SUV. Hellen used the remains of her T-shirt to bandage the man's shoulder, the same bullet wound from her marksmanship. On the drive back to Kamuela, she kept glancing over her shoulder. Christopher sat in the back seat, holding the man's head in his lap, the man's broad shoulders resting against his thigh.

16

Kohala Medical Center, 09 July

Hellen sat in the ER waiting room, her muscles cramped from a night of little sleep. Nightmares had tormented her mind and remorse racked her heart. She had never shot anyone. Replaying the scene, she hoped she had made the right decision, a split-second call to aim for his shooting arm instead of his chest. The bullet had hit the mark, forcing him to drop the handgun and run. A police investigation would follow, but lay far in the future, at least until life returned to normal. After daybreak, the night's ephemera lost some of its horror. The sun shed new light on her angst; she acted in self-defense, not malice. Only for her expert aim, he lived. Things had happened too fast to allow anything but instinct, and instinct told her to disable him, not kill him. She needed to let it go and move on. More was at stake: the blackout, food to survive, her children's trust.

Tired of trying to fall back to sleep, she looked for Malia. On autopilot, she wandered the halls of the hospital. The small community of health care workers seemed to bear the brunt of Helio Hattie's aftermath. But with Elle's help, Malia would soon have a new patient ward in the vacant astronomer's lodge at the

Maunakea Astronomy Institute. Until then, KMC's ER remained busy: a screaming child with puffy eyes, a Paniolo cowboy with his arm in a sling, and a mother in labor. They all waited for the short-staffed admissions desk to handle their cases. Time passed, and tempers flared.

She found Malia in her office, absorbed in paperwork. The hospital's interim director looked up with tired eyes. Her greasy hair appeared as if a squirrel had run through it. Her dirty scrubs did little to hide her gaunt frame. Everyone was hungry these days.

"Where's Donovan? Lately, you guys always seem cozy."

Malia blushed and squinted at her. "Really? Tell me what you really think."

"Wait, that's not what I meant." Hellen turned away and swallowed the irony of her own romance, this crazy world where people flounder under the sun and make love under the moon. "I meant to say you and Donovan seem to make a great partnership."

Malia's shoulders shook with gentle laughter. "He's been a saint to the hospital and a godsend. I'd have sunk without him."

Hellen raised her eyebrows. She recalled the relief in Malia's face the day he had volunteered. "My brother is a panda bear, big and adorable. But he rarely sheds a glad eye on a younger woman." She flinched, regretting her words as they left her mouth.

"I've no right to get involved during this crisis, but I can't help myself. I'm tired of my overworked and lonely life. He gives me strength, a will to keep going."

Malia's words echoed Hellen's feeling for Brett, yet she bottled them inside. She envied Malia's naked honesty, how her feelings came to the surface without regard of appearance. "Times like these bring people closer. They find a connection they never had in their lives. A love that survives despite the odds, all the obstacles, all the reasons to quit."

"What will become of us after life returns to normal?"

"That's up to us. I keep thinking of those vintage war movies about the Second Sino-Japanese War and how soldiers became husbands and nurses became war brides." It was no coincidence. The war formed intimate bonds between people, even marriages.

Malia brushed her hair back and forced a smile. After clearing her throat, she pointed to a thick binder with a beehive logo on the cover resting on the desk. "Like my new paper-weight? It's the supply list Joe Kanuhu brought back from the Bishop's Storehouse."

"I thought those warehouses were just a Mormon myth, reserved for after the apocalypse."

"No, they're real. The Mormons want to trade their medical supplies in return for a sanctuary for the families escaping Kona."

Hellen took the binder and thumbed through the pages. The long list showed cases of gauze bandages and wrap, chemical sterilant and disinfectant, tongue depressors, lancets, over-the-counter medications, and prescription drugs. These days, the list was a treasure trove.

Malia's watch chimed, and she stood from her chair. "It's back to work."

Hellen followed her down a corridor, lit only by the sunlight through the windows. The diesel generators droned from behind the hospital, filling the air with noxious fumes.

Standing behind the ER central desk, Dr. Chandra looked up at Malia and removed his glasses. "Thanks for coming in early. Most of the cases are the usual: failed suicide, seizure from heat exhaustion, and missing meds. He nodded toward Hellen. "And last night, your friend here brought in a John Doe with a severe head trauma and a ballistic wound to his shoulder. We patched the GSW, but I'm more worried about his grade-three concussion."

Hellen tried to remember his name, but the night's events blurred in her memory.

"Okay," Malia said with a tired voice, "so what else do we know?"

"Not much, unfortunately. He has no medical history and is still in a coma. We ran a CT scan last night once the facility power loads were low enough to run the machine." Dr. Chandra yawned and rubbed the fatigue from his eyes. "Test results are in his record. That reminds me. The John Doe has a triangular implant near his right deltoid muscle. Seen nothing like it before. That's all I have to report. Have a good shift. I'll be in Pediatrics for the next hour in case you have any questions."

After Chandra left, Hellen tried to recall her life long before the blackout, in a totally connected society, with everyone under some form of surveillance. Under the Jackson Administration, America fell under a personal identity law where collated records were kept for even the most minor ethical faux pas. She had lived in a world where people acted as informants against themselves, leading to imprisonment of their thoughts by social media "friends." A groundswell of protest had arisen, backing the twenty-eighth amendment, the right to personal privacy for all citizens. For better or worse, the blackout brought the death of the internet and restored people's privacy.

Hellen followed Malia to Room 10, John Doe's room. Malia took the patient's chart hanging on the closed door and studied it.

After they entered the room, Malia pulled the privacy curtain aside to allow Hellen to squeeze around the patient's bed. "The cardiac monitor shows a steady pulse, his blood pressure slightly elevated at one-fifty over ninety-five."

The man looked much different in the daylight. His athletic body carried no superfluous flesh, his muscles contoured like a bodybuilder pumped up with steroids. Polynesian tattoos covered his arms and bare chest, a personal journey portrayed in a tapestry of triangle motifs.

Malia stood and closed the window shades, darkening the

room. She started toward Hellen but stopped and lifted a wallet lying on the tiled floor under the bed.

"What's inside?" Hellen asked.

"One hundred quid and a business card for a marijuana dispensary in Puna. Perhaps Kanuhu might be interested in this. Seems odd to see a wallet with cash anymore. I can't remember the last time I bought anything for money."

Did commerce and money exchange still exist anymore? With banks shuttered, cash became useless. Without power, eCoins evaporated. Elle's neighbors had resorted to bartering for food, water, and petrol to run their portable generators. Hellen pursed her lips and a new fear crept into her holding pen of anxieties. They lived in a gig economy now, working wherever and whenever people needed their help. Survival depended upon everyone's cooperation. So far, Kamuela had pulled together in this little Shangri-La on the slopes of Mauna Kea, but she feared it wouldn't last much longer.

Malia made a note in the patient's log and slapped it shut. "I'll be right back." She waved the wallet at her. "I need to drop this off at Patient Services."

Hellen placed her hand on the man's shoulder. His tanned chest moved rhythmically, stretching the tattoos with each breath, an ancient Polynesian warrior resting from battle. Feeling his warm skin, her life on this island took on a new and visceral meaning. Blood had again been shed. She moved her hand to his arm and bowed her head. "Lord, forgive me for what I have done, and for what I have left undone."

"What have you left undone?" Elle appeared from behind the privacy curtain, wearing a rain parka, dripping water onto the tiled floor.

Hellen couldn't find the right words and looked away.

"I've been looking all over for you," Elle said. "You never came home last night. I was so worried—thought you guys got into some accident. Is everything okay?"

"Christopher and I brought this man in last night," Hellen

said. "We found him on the Mauna Kea Access Road. He had a motorcycle accident," Hellen whispered. "I wish I could remember his name so we could notify his 'ohana."

Elle approached the bed and her eyes widened. She squeezed the man's arm and sighed, her face frozen in shock. "Oh, Toma— you big moke—where have you been all these years?"

Hellen placed her arm around Elle's shuddering shoulders. "You know him?"

"Toma is Suzu's nephew." Elle wiped her eyes and lifted her chin briefly.

"Oh, Christ. I didn't know." Her heart pounded in her chest and heat filled her cheeks. She took measured breaths, trying to control herself, dreading the reckoning that lay between them.

Elle gave her a perplexed look. "Known what? You never met him. You look awful, is everything okay?"

Hellen forced a smile, her throat thickening. Her instinct screamed at her to keep the truth hidden in a sad sack within her chest. But her heart had no more room for dark secrets.

"Wait," Hellen said. "They don't know who shot him?"

"You tell me. You're the one who brought him in last night." Elle folded her arms and her eyes went to Toma. "He went missing eleven years ago. We thought he ran off to America, chasing the skirt of a SoCal college gal." She ran her fingers over his upper right arm. "And what's this?" She bent to examine his implant and quickly snapped upright, her face blanching.

"Do you recognize it? I think it's a personal tracking device, but the medical staff hasn't ever seen anything like it."

Elle folded her arms, her palm covering her yin-yang tattoo. "I've no idea. It's probably nothing. We better get a hold of Suzu." She reached over and carefully rolled back Toma's bedsheet as if she were unwrapping a precious gift. Her arm came close to Hellen's face. She froze, her eyes fixed on the tattoo on Elle's upper arm. In the many years she had known Elle, she had never paid much attention to it. The dark half of the yin-yang symbol disguised a skin lesion.

With Elle's attention distracted, Hellen rubbed her hand along Elle's arm as if to comfort her. A triangular implant lay beneath her skin, identical to the one in Toma's arm.

Elle brushed Hellen's hand away with worry in her eyes. "Don't. It's nothing."

Hellen caught her breath. "Your arm... what is it?"

"Hellen, please don't ask."

"But if you have the same biochip... maybe you know how to read it. It might have his medical history stored in it."

"It doesn't work like that. Trust me; no one can read it. It's obsolete in this world."

"What do you mean by *this world*?"

Elle glared at her and led her by the arm out of the room.

As Gus Conroy drove his Vagabond along Hawai'i Belt Road toward Kamuela, he ruminated on his boys' recon mission to Mauna Kea. The upside of their misadventure was a bounty of food stocks from the astronomer's lodge. Gus had sent a truck up to retrieve the goods the day after hearing Toma's radio report. With plenty of food on hand, he did a little recon of his own, a visit to Kohala Medical Center. Maybe he'd find Toma there.

Toma's MIA didn't sit well with him. The two wing-nuts who returned without Toma had provided a suspicious account of his accident. They spoke of a firefight with an older couple. The woman, a redhead, had fired on Toma. Her marksmanship was meaner than a wet panther. They hightailed it out of there, leaving Jack and Jill on the hill. With no one pursuing them down the road, why had they abandoned Toma? He was worth more than any other member of the Sons of Samoa. Although his resourcefulness and ingenuity had earned his keep, his membership was about to expire. Once the cops laid in and started their interrogation, he was bound to expose Gus. With a heavy heart, he came to the only conclusion. He had to eliminate him.

He turned on the car radio out of habit, forgetting that nothing but static pissed out of the wonky device these days. His mouth went ajar at the soothing ukulele song playing from the radio.

"Aloha, everybody," a syrupy female dripped out of the car speaker. "*Mahalo e ke akua no keia la.*" The wahine went on and on in Hawaiian jibber-jabber until breaking off into English. "Yes, mahalo to God for this day. I know many of you are huhu about no government aid, but we got da kine plan to help everyone. First, a big mahalo to Hellen Callahan, my energy consultant."

Gus frowned at the radio. "Hellen who?"

"She one *akamai wahine*—super smart," Elle continued through the radio. "She and our friends at KUMU radio have set up a little coconut network here to brighten your day. Without her innovation and energy, I couldn't broadcast to you. Our radio transmitter is too weak to reach beyond Kamuela, but we've plans to expand its range. Now, down to business. I promised you a survival plan to get us through this crisis. Although the Home Office haoles aren't riding over the hill to save us, we have our 'ohana. Like our *kama'aina popolo* said, 'Together we thrive, alone we deprive.' Right? We're setting up medical aid at local fire stations and schools, sharing food stocks and our homes. Next, our energy plan."

Gus let up on the gas pedal and turned up the radio to overcome the wind noise.

"You see, Hellen comes from the National Energy Lab in Colorado, an expert in getting power to third world countries, like us." Elle tittered over the airwaves. "Now, maybe you have a small renewable power system that didn't get fried by Helio Hattie. If not, any portable generator is your best bet. Also, remember to turn off nonessentials at home. Keep the fridge plugged in but minimize the number of times you open it. And make a food plan."

Gus pulled into the hospital entrance and parked. He listened to Otoko's broadcast, squinting at the radio while chewing on his unlit cigar.

"The resorts along the Kohala Coast donated their tread-mills and stationary bikes to local petrol stations. We hooked them up to replace the dead electric pumps. Now you can refuel your car and stay in shape same time, eh? We've also recruited our keiki. Our high school has a renewable energy lab and their students can help get your wind and solar systems back up. Just tell your local fire station you need their help. But the main power grid—that'll be awhile. We hope to have the wind farm back up within the next month. Remember, folks, your civil defense kahuna posted details at every Kohala fire station. This effort wouldn't be possible without the dozens of volunteers from our Kohala 'ohana. A kahuna once said, 'Tough times don't last, but tough people do.' We'll make it. Tune in tomorrow to hear more of our 'Ohana Plan. In the meantime, let's hear from Kalani Reichel, with her 'Mele 'Ohana.'"

Gus turned off the radio and spit his wilted cigar out of his mouth. His Operation Robin Hood seemed to have competition. *Hellen Callahan, you better give your heart to Jesus, because your ass is mine.*

After guest services told him Toma's room number, he strode down the corridor and found Toma alone in the recovery room. He closed the door and went to Toma, who lay asleep on the bed, his sheets pushed down to his waist. The hospital must be short of patient gowns—good thing too—he doubted the moke knew how to tie one. Gus let out a soft whistle. The tattooed tapestry on his chest was a real masterpiece. He'd make good cover art for one of them romance novels. He traced the Polynesian tattoo up his arm and stopped at a slight bump under the skin. His vision blurred by age, Gus squinted at the tattooed design and grimaced.

"Good god. Another one!"

Toma awoke and moved his left arm away from Gus, his eyes wincing with pain.

"Toma, how are you feeling today?" Gus asked. "Headaches? Memory?"

"My head still kills me—pounding like da kine sledgehammer. Still don't get how I got here. Damn, where am I, Gus?"

"You're recovering from a motorcycle accident you had last night on Mauna Kea."

"Honest kine? That's some crazy shit. Don't remember a thing."

Gus lifted Toma's arm and pointed to the biochip. "Tell me how you got here."

Toma narrowed his eyes and rubbed his brow. "I don't know. I remember hitting the cow in the road, den waking up here. Then you came—"

"No. That's not what I mean, dipshit." Gus lifted his shirt-sleeve and jabbed his finger at his biochip. "You're not from here, but from the Old World. You came down through the gopher hole like I did. Let's start with... when?"

Toma continued to rub his forehead. "Shit, I don't know exact, man. The sky was lit up with da kine rainbow, but it was night. Weird, for sure."

Gus recalled the night he found him wandering dazed and naked along Hawai'i Belt Road. "When, Toma? When? Like right before Helio Hattie?"

"Yeah, I think so. Hey, do you know how to get back?"

"Son, I've been trying to figure that out for over forty years."

Hellen sat alone at a dining table in the hospital cafeteria, arms in her lap. She hadn't eaten since the day before and she wasn't sure which hurt more, her hunger pains or the angst that sat like a rock in her stomach. The dining room was unlike any other small hospital she had seen, laid out with an expansive patio overlooking a tropical garden. The chow line was empty, no staff present, and no food in the buffet counter. Elle returned from a long folding table covered with hundreds of cardboard boxes.

"Sorry, their food ran out last week. We're lucky to have these MREs from a local army garrison." She opened the carton, pulled out two brown plastic-wrapped packages, and grimaced. "Bon appetit."

Hellen left her MRE unopened. "I feel horrible about what happened last night—"

"What are you talking about? You're a lifesaver. If you hadn't found Toma lying in the road, he might not be alive today."

"Yes. Exciting, to say the least," Hellen said with a faltering voice. She covered both her eyes with her fingertips, every muscle tense. She wanted to bolt from the room. "God, why him? I didn't know who he was," she said in a pleading voice. "Things happened so fast. He kept shooting at us."

"So, it was you who..." Elle leaned over and gazed at her with intense, misty eyes.

Hellen looked away. Facing the truth at last, she found a strange peace in it all. The wall clock marked the seconds, its staccato movement echoing in the room. The shame threading through her throat all night still lingered in the background.

"You saved Christopher and yourself," Elle said at last, brushing Hellen's hair from her eyes. "I can't imagine being in your shoes last night. You're quite the sharpshooter, girl."

"I'm so sorry." Hellen's chest shuddered with relief, choking back laughter. She stood and pulled Elle in and held her, holding on to the closest friend she had in this world.

With sad eyes, Elle forced a smile. "And stop saying you're sorry," she said at last.

Hellen gave a slight nod. She doubted if Brett and Charlie would want her company, but *Ohana* was her only other home. "Sure. I'll get my things this afternoon." Hellen wanted to say more, but her throat felt raw, almost painful. Any other words were lost in the back of her mind.

After lunch, Hellen returned alone to Toma's room. She pulled back the privacy curtain and found a grizzled old man standing beside Toma's bed. He looked like he hadn't showered in weeks. His small, gaunt frame bent over Toma, he didn't seem to notice her, and she gave him some distance.

"Who are you?" she asked.

The little man jumped. "Shit, you scared the bejesus out of me."

"Sorry. I wasn't expecting anyone here."

The man walked around Toma's bed and stood in front of her. He leaned back and sized her up with one eyebrow raised. His bloodshot eyes turned from leering arousal to recognition. "I came to see my boy. Your voice sounds familiar. You volunteer here, like some candy striper?"

Hellen grinned at the man's Southern accent and colorful language. But if he was related to Suzu, then he must have inherited his looks from the other side of the family.

"Not exactly," she said. "I'm Hellen Callahan. I brought your son in last night."

The man's eyes turned confused, then flashed with surprise. "It's a pleasure to meet you, ma'am. I heard your interview on the radio this morning—about all the great things you're doing for us. You're staying with Mayor Otoko at Cloudcroft, isn't that right?"

"We each try to help in our own way. Wait. How do you know where I live?"

The man folded his arms across his chest and grinned at her. Electricity crawled along her spine, the same fear she felt the day she shot the boar. "I'm sorry… I didn't catch your name."

He continued to stare at her with hungry eyes. She gave darting glances and slowly backed out of the room.

"Let's grab some lunch," he said, "since we're both here and all."

Hellen stepped back to open the distance between them. "No, thank you. I've just eaten."

She stepped into the dark space behind the privacy curtains and hesitated. Through a narrow opening between the curtains, she watched the man return to the bed and lean over Toma. He took a penlight from his shirt pocket and examined Toma's eyes. He stepped over to the IV drip and rubbed his grizzly chin. After he raised his eyebrows, he searched the room, opening and slamming shut cabinet doors. She snatched Aiva from her back pocket, disabled the flash, and took a burst of photos of the man.

She raced down the corridor to the ER central desk but found no one on duty. With no way to reach Elle, she went behind the desk and called for Malia over the hospital PA system. After returning to Toma's room, she found the old man injecting a fluid into the IV line with a syringe.

"What the hell are you doing?" she yelled.

The man looked over his shoulders and dropped the syringe. "Well, looky here. Back so soon?" He pulled her into the adjacent bathroom and slammed the door shut. She tried to scream, but his clammy hand muffled her mouth.

"I've wanted a piece of you ever since I saw you in that garden," he whispered in her ear.

The appalling memory sent panic through her heart. This creep was the same man she had seen beyond Cloudcroft's barn on the rainy day last week. The boar had saved her life, stood between her and this creep, yet she had killed the poor creature. He pressed into her, pinning her against the wall. His free hand groped her breasts. She fought to free herself, biting his hands, and wiggled her arms and feet. He slapped her hard across the face, cutting off her scream. Stars swirled in her vision. His hands clutched her throat; cold fingers squeezed her windpipe. Heat rose from within her chest and throat. Blood pumping in her ears drowned out the rest of his words. Her hands moved on their own, pounding against his shoulders and arms. Her knee rose to his groin but missed. Off balance, she slipped to the floor, dragging the man atop of her. Her mouth opened, groping for air. His chin's stubble, his wild eyes, his clenched teeth faded into a blank white cloud. The burning in her chest changed to searing pain. Lost in the struggle, her body no longer obeyed her. *God, no. Don't let me die here. Not like this.*

A voice screamed from the distance. The shrill cry came closer, rolling over her. The grizzly ghost disappeared, and Malia took his place. Her mouth covered Hellen's lips in a kiss of life. Air filled her lungs, sending her into a violent coughing fit, forcing tears from her eyes.

17

Two days after the attack, Hellen's throat remained swollen and sore. She had no memory of anyone transferring her to this room, but the lack of a medical monitor and PA announcements were good signs. Color photos of galaxies hung on the walls, illuminated by bright sunshine streaming through a wide picture window, beyond which a lush garden spread out to the surrounding forest. A note taped to the nightstand listed phone numbers for various departments in the Maunakea Astronomy Institute. An IV drip tube ran to her arm; its puncture point itched from the tape securing it, a reminder of her scrape with death.

She opened Aiva and scrolled through her photos of her attacker. The sight of his grizzly face sent a chill through her body. Fear turned to rage. He knew her name, where she lived, and he had tried to kill her. Would her children be next? Charlie was safer with Brett, but what of Elizabeth? During past trips to Cloudcroft, she had taught Elizabeth firearm safety. With practice, Elizabeth had become a good shot. But would she fire on another person? No, not likely. Killing wasn't in her Buddhist nature.

Steps clicked from the hallway tile outside her room.

Donovan entered and placed his warm hand on hers. "You're awake." He took his penlight and checked her eyes. He nodded and returned the penlight to his pocket. "I've got good news. I'm releasing you today. But take it easy, no more fighting with the bad guys."

"Great." Hellen winced from the pain in her throat. "Help me out of this bed."

"Not yet, tiger. I'm waiting for your results from this morning's CT scan." Donovan removed the IV from her arm without more than a slight sting.

"They found him?"

Donovan rubbed his forehead. "The constabulary launched a manhunt but haven't tracked him down."

"Maybe this will help." Hellen said and reached for Aiva. After calling up the photos she took of the old man, she handed the tablet to her brother. Hellen doubted the constabulary's meager manpower would yield any results—they were too busy dealing with the island's chaos—but it was worth a try. Anything to get this guy off the streets, out of the jungle, and in a cage.

"This is great. It's probably not his first murder."

"You mean, Toma is dead? Good god."

"Someone had contaminated his IV drip. Had we known earlier, we might have saved him. But Toma gave us his attacker's name before he died: Gus Conroy."

Hellen flinched. Hadn't she told them about the IV? Hellen closed her eyes and tried to recall the moments leading up to Conroy's attack on her. Her memory blurred, nothing came to mind. Soft footsteps into the room brought her back.

When she opened her eyes, Elle stood beside her bed with a backpack slung over her shoulder. Her perfume smelled of lilacs when she bent to kiss Hellen's cheek. "Morning, sunshine."

"I need to head back to the hospital," Donovan said. "Can I take your tablet to transfer your photos of Conroy?"

Hellen nodded and took Aiva from him. After he left, Elle sat at the edge of the bed.

"Donovan is discharging me today," Hellen said. "But maybe it's best I not return to Cloudcroft so soon. Toma didn't make it."

"Yes, I know. Look, Hellen. Things are grim at Cloudcroft. Suzu is in shock. By the time he got to the hospital, Toma was dead. And Elizabeth is still bitter after our talk. But I want you home at Cloudcroft. Maybe you could stay at the cottage."

"No. I've thought about this for hours. I think it best I not come back to Cloudcroft just yet. Let the dust settle. I'll stay aboard *Ohana* until it's safe for me to return. The move will draw Conroy's attention away from Cloudcroft and the kids. It'll also keep me close to my work at the wind farm."

"I thought you might say that." She unzipped the backpack and peeked inside. "I've packed some of your clothes and the Beretta as an insurance policy should you run into any more trouble."

Elle set the bag back on the chair and leaned against the wall beside the window. Her eyes distant, she became silent. Hellen let her head fall back onto her pillow and wondered where her life was headed next. Elle's subdued reaction to Toma's death showed hidden discord with his 'ohana, but Hellen found herself homeless just the same. She stared at Elle's tattoo, her implant the same as Toma's, a mysterious artifact of their past lives. Elle had mentioned it was "not of this world," a slip of the tongue not easily erased, as if it were a UFO conspiracy.

"Before you go, can I ask you something?"

"I'm not giving up on you, if that's what you think."

"No. You're more than my hānai mother, you're the closest friend to me right now. But what I want is…I'm curious. You said the implant in your arm is 'not of this world.' What did you mean?"

"I misspoke, that's all. Please forget it."

"But what's the connection with Toma?"

"Look. Let's drop it for now." Elle pushed off the wall and

headed for the door. "Maybe we'll talk later, but first I want to get you released and drop you off at Kawaihae Harbor. Seeing Brett and Charlie ought to lift your spirits again."

Before Hellen had a chance to respond, Elle left, her footsteps receding down the corridor. Hellen leaned over and pulled the backpack from the chair, rummaging for her clothes. Elle packed everything she needed, including a white turtleneck shirt that zipped up in the front, a nice touch, a subtle cover-up for the welts around her throat. Her reflection from the mirror above the wash basin gave her a jolt. Ribbons of purple and orange streaked across her neck and chest, the violence of her fight in full view. Her fingertips shook, their little tremors moving through her hands and along her arms.

She collapsed on the bed. After taking a moment to collect herself, she pulled on a pair of jeans and the turtleneck. She brushed her hair and applied light makeup, another foresight of Elle's. The tremors calmed, and warmth spread from her tummy. On the day she first stepped aboard *Ohana* in San Diego, falling in love with Brett was the last thing she expected from her voyage. Although Brett's taciturn demeanor frustrated her at times, his tenderness said more than words. Two weeks had passed since she last saw him, the night they made love, the hour she told him of Elizabeth. She hoped his kindness survived her disclosure, but at this point she'd settle for tolerance.

Hellen and Elle arrived at the harbor by late afternoon and parked next to *Ohana*'s slip. A pile of fish lay in the sun on the pier. Happy sounds came from the cabin, a reminder that all was not lost.

"I'll leave you off here," Elle said. "Try to have a good time. Remember what I said, Brett wouldn't have insisted he look after Charlie unless he cared about you."

Hellen slid out of the truck. A short wave didn't sum up the moment between them. She waited for Elle to leave before climbing over the boat's rail. The commotion belowdecks grew louder.

"Ahoy, mate," she said in a croaky voice.

In the middle of wrestling with Charlie, Brett looked up with an awkward grin. His face went blank as if searching for the appropriate mask to wear. Her son poked his head underneath Brett's armpit and gave her a silly grin. Charlie was always the first to rebound.

"This is a nice surprise," Brett said at last.

"I find that the element of surprise is the key to a good drop-in. And I come bearing gifts." Hellen lifted the two bottles of chardonnay Elle had placed in her backpack after leaving the hospital.

Brett took the bottles and examined them. "This wine won't make a good pairing for Sham."

Hellen cringed. "No more canned ham. Move over, I'm cooking dinner tonight."

She nudged him aside with her hip and made herself at home in the galley. After she ordered them to stay topside to give her some elbow room, she got down to business. The aroma of seared ahi soon filled the air, stirring her appetite.

She checked the ship's clock and switched on the boat's stereo, dialing in KUMU's frequency. The sweet melodies of Sista Iz came through the airwaves. After weeks with no alcohol, the wine swam into her soul.

Brett furrowed his brow and squinted at the cockpit speaker. "Wait one. How can we pick this up? All commercial radio stations have been out since Helio Hattie."

She placed her index finger on his lips. "Shhh. Let's listen. I rigged a radio repeater atop Mauna Kea."

Brett put his arm around her, sending electricity along her spine and relief through her chest. Resting her head on his shoulder, she let out a long breath. Charlie glanced at her and a smile escaped his stoic face. After the song ended, the DJ came on, "KUMU radio, ninety-nine-point-one, is back on the air. And here is the hourly EAS broadcast, recorded today in Hawaiian style."

Brett sat upright and looked at Hellen, "Da kine?"

She pulled him into her, but he resisted. "Relax, just listen."

Reaching over Brett, she refilled their wineglasses and turned the volume up.

"Aloha, everyone. *Mahalo e ke akua no keia la.*" Elle spoke her entire message in Hawaiian. The sing-song locution of the words warmed Hellen's heart. Although she had never learned the language, she had always loved its soft vowels and sparse consonants, the way the syllables popped in and out.

"Yes, thanks be to God for this day," Elle continued in English. "Many of you told me you didn't understand the EMS messages, nor found them very encouraging. So, you might be wondering why—or how—we are broadcasting on KUMU. Well, you all know it's the biggest radio station on the Island, giving us a broad reach throughout the district. The folks at KUMU embody the spirit of our 'Ohana Plan, to help each other out of this crisis. In the darkest times, our 'ohana get their energy not from an electrical grid, but from ourselves, from the strength of our souls. I'm here to tell you, we do have a plan to help everyone. Our Kohala 'ohana is our village. Seasons change, and the clouds give way to liquid sunshine, and we must remember we own the finish line. Tune in tomorrow to get the news about our medical response plan. In the meantime, let's get back to Sista Iz, with her *Living in a Sovereign Land.*"

Hellen switched the radio off and raised her eyebrows.

"You've been busy," Brett said and held his closed fist to his heart. "I got to tell you. You're amazing. I love your initiative. Your energy is…simply contagious."

She gave her glass a healthy pour. Her heart sang at his words, and the wine warmed her spirits. She had lived under the constant threat of something going wrong, but nothing could erase the happiness she felt tonight. After the drama of the last week, all she wanted was a chance to let loose, to have some fun for a change. Brett's provocative eyes pulled her into him. She couldn't wait any longer.

"Charlie, go visit Manu while Brett and I play *puinsai.*"

Brett choked on his drink, sending himself into a coughing fit. Charlie rolled his eyes and stood to leave. "I don't get what you see in that. Sounds silly."

"Trust me, love," she said to him, "you'll be crazy about it when you get older."

Hellen sipped her wine and dismissed Charlie with a wave of her hand. With no more encouragement, he jumped over the side stanchion and landed with a thump on the concrete dock. After he strolled down the pier and was well out of earshot, Hellen flashed a playful smile and snapped her fingers into a trigger at Brett. "Gotcha!"

Brett's arm came off her shoulder and slid away from her. "Puinsai is pidgin for—"

"Having sex. Of course, I know that, but Charlie doesn't. I told him it's a card game we make love—no, I mean a game we love to play together." She fell into uncontrolled laughter before taking another gulp of wine. A soft burp escaped her lips. She looked around the harbor, now lost in twilight, no one in sight. With no more thought, she unzipped her turtleneck blouse and raised her eyebrows. The evening breeze ran over her chest, making her quiver. "Cards make good puinsai foreplay. Ever heard of strip poker?"

Brett parted his lips. His hands gripped her shoulders and his eyes widened. Her confidence aroused, she pressed on. "It's a game I love to lose," she whispered. "Wanna play?"

Brett narrowed his eyes. "Hellen, don't do this."

"Reeelax, Commander. You're off duty and I'm on fire. Let's have some fun while the coast is clear. Your cabin or mine?" Without waiting for an answer, she emptied her wineglass and stood and reached for his hand. Her outstretched fingers searched for his hand and missed. She tried again, but Brett snatched his hand away. The world started to spin, throwing her off balance and into Brett's lap. "Son of a brisket... no, I mean biscuit."

"Hellen, stop this. Come on, cool it." He zipped her blouse up and laid his hands on her shoulders. "What's gotten into you? This isn't you. Normally, you're much too—"

"Boring?"

"I was about to say 'classy,' but I'll reserve my judgment."

She pouted her lips and unzipped her turtleneck again. Brett traced his fingers over her neck. His brown eyes gawked at her, or lusted for her, she couldn't tell for sure. *I knew he'd come around.* He bent his head lower, examining her throat. She cupped his head in her hands and pulled him toward her. "That's right, my Man from Maui, you're cleared to land."

His head wrenched free from her fingers. "God, Hellen. What happened to your neck and chest?"

At first confused, her eyes followed his fingers as they traced the welts across her chest. The nightmare returned. Her heart dropped into her stomach. No longer confident of her own voice, she gave him a slight nod. She quickly zipped up her blouse, crossed her arms over her chest, and choked down her shame.

Brett's nostrils flared under his narrowed eyes. "Hellen, who did this to you? I'll kill him. Tell me!"

Her light-headedness dissolved into a pain in the base of her skull. She blew a puff of air through her bangs and shut her eyes tight. "Brett, no. Just shut up and hold me." Exhausted, her body tipped over and slumped into his arms, surrendering to sleep.

Hellen awoke to dawn creeping into the eastern sky. She huddled under a blanket, not recalling who covered her. *Clair de Lune* played from the cockpit speakers. One of her favorite pieces by Debussy, its melody played out in her mind, a hint of an obvious truth lying dormant in the morning's shadows. Her Shangri-La had ended. The last thing she remembered was the alarm in Brett's eyes, his asking her what happened, over and over again. A cacophony of nightmares is what happened, a long string of mishaps building into a car wreck. At least she didn't have to put on appearances for her son anymore. Nor did she have the strength to pull it off.

Oh, God. What have I become? Her chest heaved as she struggled to breathe. How could she let herself get so out of control? She hadn't been this drunk since her college years. What was wrong with her? Her children needed her, and yet her selfish desire had pushed them away. Ready, fire, aim. Always, act first, then think. She palm-smacked her forehead, sending stars before her eyes. And Brett wasn't an innocent bystander. Although reluctant to show it, his wound ran deeper than Charlie's. And why had she let personal issues get ahead of survival, the need to restore the power grid? Her skills were invaluable to the effort. This must be her focus.

Somewhere on the pier and out of view, a truck pulled up. Someone stepped aboard, sending *Ohana* into a gentle rocking motion. She buried her head, not wanting to face him. Yet he still came to her, securing the blanket around her chest, a cocoon for her retreat.

"You guys make a cute couple," Charlie said from the other side of her blanket's wool barrier. "What's up with her?"

"She just had a little too much to drink last night," Brett said.

"In that case, I don't want to be topside if she pukes." With no more words, Charlie scampered belowdecks.

"Charlie, pack your gear—we're heading up the hill," Brett shouted down to him.

Hellen's heart jumped, and she jolted upright. "Wait. What's happening?"

"I just heard from Manu. My orders came in. I'm shipping off."

Her body stiffened as if a blow had slammed into her stomach. "What? You're leaving? Like gone?"

"That's right. I don't know which ship yet, but I have to report for duty tomorrow."

He stomped down the hatchway, slammed all the windows and hatches shut, and returned with their gear in duffel bags.

"Brett, I'm sorry for everything," she said in a halting voice. "I've been so foolish."

"It's not you. Duty calls, so off I go." Brett shot a sardonic grin and went below.

"Charlie, hand me these bags over the rail, and I'll put them in the truck. We can use the cooler to take the fish back with us."

The guys scrambled between deck and pier like efficient little sailors, stowing their gear in Manu's truck bed. Brett slipped away from her, falling into deployment mode. Her heart dropped. After tomorrow, he would be out of reach and back to flying, somewhere hundreds or thousands of miles away. No, dammit. She wasn't going to let him drift out of her life again.

Brett returned and sat beside her, his hand falling on her shoulder. Hellen lay down again and rested her head on his thigh and faced seaward, letting the minutes drag out, savoring each second. But her drunken foolishness had spoiled this moment forever. Now he was leaving. Where and for how long, she didn't know.

"It's time we shove off. Let me help you off the boat." His hands slid under her shoulders, but she rolled away from him.

"I can't go back to Cloudcroft. It's complicated. Elizabeth is bitter and Suzu… well, I'm not on his fav list anymore."

Brett rubbed his cheek. "Want to stay here?"

"Is that all right? Just for a couple weeks or so. I'll work at the wind farm. The ops center is just up the road. *Ohana* will make a great crash pad. Take Charlie to Donovan; he'll look after him. It's best if he's not at Cloudcroft—with Elizabeth."

Brett gave her a single nod. "You should have told me about Elizabeth sooner. I've been thinking, filled with this weird mix of anger and elation. The highs and lows—mostly lows—make me feel like I'm in a fighter jet burning and turning through a snake canyon. Shit."

"I'm so sorry for all the pain I've caused."

"I know you are but keeping my daughter a secret is still hard to accept."

"I know. I know. I've been a horrible mother, keeping secrets, getting drunk, throwing myself at you. You must hate me."

"I don't hate you, but I hate what you did. Not telling me. Not allowing me to be part of our daughter's life. As for last night, you've been under a lot of stress and needed to blow steam. I get that."

"Stress? God. You don't know half of it." Angry heat threaded her neck. "Elizabeth has lost all trust in me, can't even stand to be in the same room. And there's more..." The words poured out from her. She told him of her fall on Mauna Kea, the looters—and the creepozoid—around Cloudcroft, and the shoot-out with Toma. As she went on, Brett's lips pinched tight, his jaw locked. After she retold how Toma's "father" had strangled her, Brett exploded.

"Show me the pictures—I'll hunt him down myself." She flinched at the spray of spit from his lips. His eyes bulged and the veins in his temples pulsated with every heartbeat.

"The constabulary is on it. Focus your attention on Elizabeth. Be strong for her. She needs you."

"I would if I could find her."

"You will, didn't you hear me? She's at Cloudcroft."

His eyes blinked a few times and he bit his lower lip. "I'll go see her before I ship out. And as soon as I swing some leave, I'll visit you."

"Forget about me. I've hurt you enough. What could you possibly see in me?"

"I see our future in you." He paused, as if surprised by his own words. He caught his breath and his fingers relaxed. *"Ke aloha, ua hoomanawanui."*

His words made no sense to her, but she smiled at how he spoke them.

"Love is patient," he translated to her.

The words from First Corinthians hit her like cold water. He had crossed his Rubicon, the first time he acknowledged his love for her. Her chest shuddered, and she choked back her feelings. He pressed a kiss to her forehead, then her closed eyelids.

"Love is patient, love is kind," she recited softly and brushed his cheek with her hand. "I'll be waiting for you, waiting for my sailor, home from the sea."

He winked at her. "Don't get into any more trouble while I'm gone, okay? Stay low. And lay off the wine."

Thankfully, he said no more to her. She hated farewells, especially heated ones. His arms wrapped around her and his chest heaved against her cheek. She relaxed, the ache in her heart numbed. His hands closed her jacket over her chest and his forehead touched hers, exchanging a honi kiss.

PART IV

MANA IA 'OE, MANA IA 'U

(POWER TO YOU, POWER TO ME)

18

On the drive to Cloudcroft, Brett had one hand on the wheel, the other over Charlie's shoulder. Charlie's eyes were closed, his head back against his headrest. Raising kids seemed a lot harder than flying combat patrol and came with little gratitude. Parenting didn't come with a flight manual, it was all on-the-job training, mostly trial and error. Two weeks away from his mother had sanded down the rough edges in Charlie's heart. But after Hellen let herself get drunk, he hadn't said a word to her. Sure, he had reason for his resentment, but Hellen had always protected him from his father's abuse, from bullies at school, and from himself.

Brett's mind moved to happier thoughts, to those special moments since sailing out of San Diego. He loved Hellen for so many reasons. She was akamai, intelligent, strong-willed, and independent. She hit all the right buttons with him. He hadn't ever met a more arousing and beguiling woman. Despite her hot-headed tendencies, she pegged full scale on the fun meter. Sometimes, too much fun.

Maybe they had made a mistake in rekindling their love affair. Past deployments had always left him high and dry. Other sailors ran into the arms of their ready-and-waiting wives or girlfriends after deployments, but he always returned to an empty apartment. Over the years, he had grown to accept this fate of an unmarried Navy "lifer." A Wonder Woman of passion, Hellen had changed his life forever. He loved her, even when she was angry, waterlogged, or drunk. And Elizabeth had become a permanent link between them.

Elizabeth, their existential child from their first night together, had stood in the back of his mind since Hellen's revelation. He had seen her only once, a brief moment on the pier after returning Charlie to Kawaihae Harbor, but she captured his attention with her smile, honey-brown eyes, the way her hair streamed in the breeze. She held a distinctive grace. He imagined her dancing the keiki hula, her arms, hips, and feet all swaying to the story of her life, all those years lost in time. A heaviness filled him. During years of dreaming about fatherhood, he remained unaware he had been a father. And today he would meet her, hear her own words, and stand in judgment before her. How could she ever accept him as her father? Almost an adult, she must have her own views on everything from politics to parenthood. His stomach knotted up, the same way it did during his first aircraft checkride. But his meeting Elizabeth would be more challenging than any test he ever had in the Royal Navy.

After arriving at Cloudcroft, he brought Charlie's seabag to the upper loft in the carriage house. Charlie wasted no time falling into the bed, not even taking the time to undress. Brett left him sleeping and walked along the bucolic path through the back garden. Someone had worked hard pulling the weeds and vines encroaching upon the orchids and vegetables. The trail continued out of the garden and followed a split-rail fence enclosing a pasture.

A Warlander stallion galloped across the field toward him, seeming to float along with a fluid grace over the grass, its dapple-gray coat shimmering in the sun. Just watching the handsome animal made him forget his brooding. The horse skidded to a stop in front of him and let out a loud neigh and finished with a nicker. It pressed its chest against the fence and bobbed its head. He reached around and scratched the sweet spot behind its ears, making its nostrils quiver as his own stallion had many years ago.

"Looking for your morning feed?"

The stallion spun and galloped away, heading for the barn, its mane streaming in the breeze. Brett climbed over the fence and jogged over to the stables. He walked through an empty stall and into the stable and stopped short of the wash stack, surprised to find Elizabeth in riding boots and muddy britches, grooming a spotted Appaloosa.

He swayed back on his heels and struggled to collect his thoughts. The photos on Hellen's phone didn't capture her beguiling beauty, her nose, skin color, and earlobes—all traits she inherited from him. With a visceral clarity, he finally accepted her as his daughter. She also had Hellen's finest points: the auburn hair, her trim stature, the way she walked over to him. By force of habit, he offered a handshake, a stupid gesture. Her warm hand trembled in his. She swayed her head in a graceful movement, flinging her long hair from her face, revealing eyes holding an awareness beyond her years. She gave him a slight bow and a hint of a smile.

"*Aloha awakea*," she whispered, a little too formal.

"*Aloha nui loa.*" Brett paused and pointed to his heart. "Do you know who I am?"

She narrowed her eyes and gave a solemn nod. "Hellen told me," she said in Hawaiian. "You'll have to excuse me for not calling you father. I haven't gotten use to the idea, yet."

"That makes two of us." His Hawaiian words penetrated her mask and won him a genuinely bright smile before she went back to brushing her mare.

He waited for her to finish. Each brushstroke sent her long auburn hair swirling around her face. With each stroke, her athletic legs, sturdy as a koa tree, flexed inside her riding britches.

"I should probably say something profound," he said.

She stopped and stared at him, brushing strands of hair from her eyes with the back of her hand. With her elbow resting on the horse's withers, she shrugged her shoulders. "No worries. Elle or Hellen always fill the air with too many words. Never helps."

"We think alike."

She gave a slight nod. "I didn't see you come in last night. When did you arrive?"

"Just got here. What brings you out so early?"

Elizabeth returned to grooming the horse's black mane. "I came out for a ride." She nodded to the mare. "She and Hellen have something in common, don't you see?"

He looked the Appaloosa over, not really in the mood for riddles, but on guard for a snarky jab at Hellen.

"No, I give."

Her eyes brightened. "Her name is Lulua'ina."

Brown spots covered the mare's pale coat. "Sure, I get it. Good one—they both have freckles."

"Elle asked me to manage the stables while Hellen is working at the wind farm. Horses are my only way of getting around town these days." She paused her vigorous brushing to catch her breath. "It suits me just fine. Maybe you'd like to go for a ride with me?"

"I'm shipping out, reporting for sea duty."

Elizabeth froze midstride, and a frown grew on her brow. "For how long?"

He kicked sawdust from the floor and made a motion for the barn door. "Well, that's up to God and the Admiralty. Charlie's back. I'm sure he'll love to give you a hand."

"Charlie? Really? Don't you have any clue what happened?"

Elizabeth lifted her arm and threw the grooming brush at him. Brett jumped just in time to dodge the missile. He had grown used to Hellen's moods, but this girl was one *huhu wahine.* He brushed the dust from his jeans and asked, "What was that for?"

She marched to him and braced her hands on her hips. "Where's that situational awareness you pilots are so famous for?"

"Shit. I don't know. But don't bend your crankshaft, he's only here today. I'm dropping him off with his uncle on my way to the base."

"When?"

"A couple of hours."

Her eyes widened. "Really? Just like that? You step into my life, then leave the same afternoon?"

"Come on, Elizabeth. I don't want this anymore than you do, but duty calls."

"And the phone line is busy. Don't you think we should spend time together, like catching up on my entire life you missed? I'm tired of being a secondhand daughter, passed from one mother to the next."

He tilted his head back, started to speak, but thought better of it. She was a cocked pistol, her emotions on fire. God, she was Hellen's daughter all right. The seconds stretched like a thread pulled from both ends, tight, tighter, and tighter still.

"You know what your problem is, Commander Akamu?" She pressed into him, pinning his back to the barn wall. She stood on her toes at eye level, her breath hot against his neck. Something raw and exposed lay behind her weepy and bloodshot eyes. "You see everything in black and white. You need to take a more analog view of the world. Embrace the gray fuzzy logic for once. Stay with me for a while. Get to know me a little before you go flying off."

He shook his head at the dichotomy between their lives. Military life was as foreign to her as parenthood was to him. His heart screamed at him to stay with her, but his sense of duty froze his desires.

"What are you so afraid of?" she whispered.

Afraid of losing control, he closed his eyes, his lips pressed together. For a moment, he wasn't sure if she was Hellen or Elizabeth. His throat tightened, struggling for the right words. Leaving her like this tore him up. Too much was at stake. Maybe he'd stay. Another day at most. But before he could answer her, she stormed out of the barn and ran to the house.

For the rest of the morning, Elizabeth retreated behind her locked bedroom door. Despite Elle's culinary bribes, she never came out. Safe in her domain, she hadn't said another word. Brett left her alone and returned to the carriage house to pack his seabag. The loft was silent, no sign of Charlie. Brett had learned not to worry about him. The boy liked to wander, but always returned, a trait they shared. Brett had come of age on the Big Island and cherished his independence, the freedom to roam with adventures around the next volcano or over the next wave. No bubble wrap kids or helicopter mothers ever took hold on this outpost in the Pacific.

Brett slung his seabag over his shoulder and walked to Manu's truck. He had better return it before the harbor master pulled his friendship card.

Elle came out with a food basket and stood by the pickup. "Just something to tide you over until you get a mess pass. When Elizabeth abdicates her throne, I'll express your best wishes."

"Thanks. I'd rather say goodbye in person, but..." Brett shook his head, wishing he had a do-over for this morning's snafu. He didn't want their spat to be her only memory of him.

"I tried to get her to come out. She's not angry with you, just the opposite. After learning you were her father, she has peppered me with questions about you and was eager to connect with you, even talked about staying with you for the rest of the summer."

"I want nothing more, but—"

"Duty calls, as you like to say. She's not old enough to understand the real meaning of those words, but maybe she'll someday see what duty to others brings to oneself. I expect you'll teach her that and much more."

He fiddled with his watchband and looked away. "Not from a carrier in the Asia Pacific."

"Her *kumu* isn't leaving the island." Her suppressed smile broke at the Hawaiian reference to a teacher.

"I'm not following you."

"I spoke to the island governor over radio last week. He bemoaned the lack of air support from the military. So I told him I had a helicopter pilot looking for a slot. He jumped at it. This morning, he assigned you to Bradshaw Flight Garrison. It's only twenty-five miles from here."

Brett's mouth fell ajar. The assignment not only gave him a chance to protect his home island but also kept him close to Hellen.

"Go to Hellen," she said, "and take Charlie with you. Show them the base, how close it is, the aircraft you'll fly. They need to know you're not far. You're everything to them. She needs you and we all need her to get the wind farm restored. But she can't work if she's an emotional wreck, uncertain of your relationship, always worried about you."

Kawaihae Harbor

The clanking of loose halyards banging against *Ohana*'s aluminum mast sent waves of pain through Hellen's hangover. With bleary eyes, she searched the medicine cabinet for any relief. A bottle of ibuprofen lay on the bottom shelf, only four pills remaining. After an hour passed, the two tablets and three glasses of water had worked their magic and a spot of ginger fought her nausea. She made a heaping bowl of rice covered with honey for an energy boost. By midmorning, life had become tolerable again.

A car horn beeped from the pier, followed by sharp barks from a small dog. She came topside and waved to her two friends.

"Time to go to work," Tanaka shouted. "Elle radioed me your whereabouts. I need your help at the wind farm." He got out of the truck and tossed her a jumpsuit. "Hurry and get dressed. The day's a-wasting."

On the way to the wind farm, Hellen held Tanaka's corgi in her lap, his head hanging out the side window, lapping up the wind. Tanaka checked his watch and turned on the radio. Ukulele music competed with the road noise from the truck's tundra tires. Three bursts of the buzzing EMS warning interrupted the song. She recognized Elle's voice but understood none of the Hawaiian. At the end, Elle repeated her message in English.

"Aloha nui to you all. Welcome to Kohala's Coconut Wireless Talk Story," Elle fluttered from the radio. "Today I'm speaking to the most important members of our community, our keiki. Our children are our joy and our future. And it takes a village to raise them, sometimes an army, if you have a tribe of boys. So, here's the deal. The schools, temples, churches, and da kine are organizing youth programs, a safe place where they can enjoy each other's company and work on community service projects."

Hellen recalled Charlie's fascination with KMC after his seizure. He had loved being the center of attention from the medical staff. And Donovan's work intrigued him. A life at risk, a life saved. "Maybe we can recruit some of our keiki as candy stripers volunteers. Our understaffed hospital could use their help."

Tanaka shrugged and didn't look away from the road. "We're removing the Faraday cages from the turbine stators but ran into a snag. The insulation melted off from the brake assembly servos. The induced current from the geomagnetic storm must've fried the wires. Without disengaging the rotor locks, there's no chance of getting those towers on line."

"Sure. Let me take a look. Maybe there's a work-around."

"That's why we need you. You know these pinwheels better than most line monkeys. Elle told me you're dealing with some family problems, but I sure could use you around here."

Hellen's chest swelled. After setting up the radio relay atop Mauna Kea, she found she missed her old work, the hum of electronics, the miracle of making electricity from the wind. She was more than ready to dive into the project.

After Tanaka turned off of Hawai'i Belt Road, the first wind tower came into view through the truck's windshield. Much larger up close, the white spire loomed two-hundred feet above the ground, its three curved blades frozen in place. They parked near its base and got out. Tanaka unlocked the tower access door and stepped inside; his voice echoed from within the narrow darkness.

After her eyes acclimated to the dim interior, she found a ladder leading to the top, its rungs stretching far into a void of blackness.

"Here, put this on." Tanaka handed her a safety harness like the one she wore at sea. "Once we get up there, falling isn't the best way to return."

She followed him up the long ladder leading to the tower's nacelle, a metal housing shrouding the electrical turbine. With each step, Hellen labored under heavy breaths, wondering how wind techs managed this exhausting climb day after day. During the tedious ascent, her mind wandered to Brett and her kids. Would she ever see him again, would her kids ever forgive her, would she ever get her act together? Her muscles ached after climbing eighty metal rungs, yet she wasn't halfway there. She stopped to rest and reached for her water bottle's carabiner clip. After releasing it, the bottle slipped from her hand. It banged against the conduit's wall on the first bounce and tumbled through the air until crashing at the tower's base.

"Whoa," Tanaka shouted from high above her. "What was that?"

"My water bottle. Damn clumsy of me."

"Stay focused, Hellen."

That was her problem all right, too worried about her children, too upset about Brett's deployment. She took a deep breath to rope in her monkey mind and continued upward. Counting steps as she climbed upward, she practiced *kinhin*, the walking mediation she had learned from Elle. Each step had a purpose, each rung in the ladder held her focus.

After reaching the top, she stepped onto the metal grating surrounding the wind turbine and caught her breath. Tanaka stood next to the stator, which was enclosed in a yellow housing. The air held the ozone odor of electrical components and brought a warm nostalgia to Hellen. Together, they released the access panel. Under Tanaka's flashlight beam, the stator's copper windings looked in good shape, thanks to the shielding from Tanaka's homespun Faraday cage. He loosened the cage's clamps and pulled the heavy-gage wire from around the stator and tossed it aside. Next, they went to the brake servo, an electromagnetic spring used to lock the turbine's massive ninety-foot blades and keep them from spinning. Melted insulation hung like stalactites from the wiring. The servo had no protection from Tanaka's Faraday cage and had sustained the full onslaught from electrical currents generated by the solar storm.

"So far, three of the four we inspected are like this one."

Hellen shook her head while trying to remember the last time she had seen this problem. The Apache Range came to mind. The wind farm roasted in the Arizona sun, leading to overheating problems—but never this severe. "This'll take time to fix."

"Yes, I know," he said. "I'm glad you're here. You'll figure it out."

She wasn't so sure. The turbines she had worked on were much smaller than these giant pinwheels. The manufacturing plate mounted on the turbine housing read: "K47 Turbine. Kaze Technologies, Tokyo." Years ago, she had toured the facility after speaking to their engineering group. An insight flashed in her mind. Those smaller turbines had a mechanical clutch to release the gear should they lose power to the rotor brake. She found a yellow handle on the opposite side of the brake servo. Despite throwing her weight into the lever, it didn't budge.

"You're wasting your time. Already tried that," Tanaka said. "Before we head back down, let's go topside."

He reached above his head and released a spring-activated latch. The ceiling hatch popped open and brilliant sunlight streamed into the dim compartment. He climbed a short access ladder and disappeared above the nacelle. Hellen followed.

From her perch atop the wind tower, the other titanium-white towers spread out before her like candlesticks on a cake. Heights both scared her and gave her new perspectives. Elle said it best in her broadcast today; her children were her chief concern, her future. She chided herself. Her family problems came from her own mismanagement. The engineer in her had always planned things out, measured the effects of each step. Yet with those closest to her, she gave little foresight. Her son wasn't an engineering problem to solve. He was her life's work. But guiding him into adulthood overwhelmed her. And Elizabeth, her perfect mistake, at first unplanned, was the joy of her life. What would become of her? Almost an adult, Elizabeth had her mind set, unswayed with mere words of apology.

Tanaka came beside her and broke her brooding spiral. "Elle thinks she can get us a submarine."

Hellen gave him a double-take. "Awesome! We'll have more than enough power to jump-start this pinwheel farm. You could've let me know sooner, you little toad. When does it arrive?"

"Two weeks from today." Tanaka crawled back to the access hatch.

"That leaves us too little time to prepare for the black startup."

"We'll make it work."

"Tanaka, wait. Do the math. Our wind techs can service at most two towers a day; that's eight days for all sixteen, leaving less than a week to connect the power lines and do a dry run."

He turned and gave her a silly smile. "Yes, but that's why—"

"Yeah, I know, I know," Hellen said. "That's why I'm here, to figure it out."

"Come on." He pointed behind her. "Let's hurry and get back down before we get hit by lightning."

Off in the distance, a dark cumulonimbus cloud towered aloft, its anvil-shaped top stretching ahead of it. The cloud flashed with embedded lightning, resembling a giant flashbulb. A wind gust shook the tower and Hellen ran for cover.

The thunderstorm left wisps of rising steam from the hard rain along Hawai'i Belt Road. Hellen and Tanaka arrived back to Kawaihae Harbor an hour after the storm passed. On the pier, Manu's pickup was parked beside *Ohana*. After Hellen confirmed the next day's workday with Tanaka, she ran toward the truck.

Charlie's head stuck out of the left-side window. "Come on, Mom. We're taking Brett to the base."

Confused, Hellen walked over to Brett, who sat behind the wheel.

"I thought—"

"Elle got me assigned as a helicopter pilot only twenty-five miles from here."

She jumped on the running boards, poked her head through the side window, and kissed him. "That's the best news I've heard in weeks." A great weight lifted from her heart and she danced around the truck before she slid onto the front bench seat next to Charlie. Manu's pickup was an ancient white F150 relic from the nineties with vinyl seats worn from use and years of dust caked on the dashboard. A little plastic hula dancer wiggled back and forth beneath the rearview mirror, dancing to the rumble of the truck diesel engine.

Brett drove along Saddle Road and chattered on with Charlie, sharing the lessons he learned from his grandfather, a Pan Am Clipper navigator who crossed the Pacific dozens of times. He spoke of sea stories of his Navy days, the history of the Parker Ranch, and the trouble he raised with the ranch hands.

"Man, you were a cowboy too?" Charlie asked. "Did you ride bulls like in those rodeos in Colorado?"

"Hell no. I may be a little crazy in the head, but I don't have a suicide wish."

"Do they got bulls on the Parker Ranch? Can you take me there sometime?"

"The Parker Ranch has over twenty-six thousand head of cattle, mostly Black Angus. Elle might take you up there someday."

Charlie's elbow nudged Hellen ribs. "Mom, let's do it."

"Sure, I'll talk to her."

"The cattle could be our only source of protein after the MREs run out," Brett said.

"I think Elle has the same idea," Hellen said, "She's negotiating with the ranchers to release the older livestock for slaughter."

The countryside passed by Hellen's side window. The carnage from looters and the lines of people walking along the road showed for the first time the suffering of many of the islanders. Outside town, they had passed through three security checkpoints manned by armed civilian militia. Her Shangri-La at Cloudcroft had protected her from the worst of the storm's aftermath. The deserted houses, uncontrolled fires, and her hunger pains reminded of her first priority: restoring the wind farm. A stable electric grid would bring security to the community and safety to her children. With Brett leaving and Donovan to look after Charlie, she now could devote more energy to restoring power to Kohala.

The thought of another goodbye rested like a stone in her stomach. Two hours later, they arrived at the base and Hellen released a long, taut breath. The twenty-five miles might as well have been a thousand. Without a car, she had little hope of visiting this remote outpost. Brett made a series of sharp S-turns, navigating concrete barriers staggered in the road to the base entrance. After they came to Bradshaw's main gate, he stopped the car, his hands tight on the steering wheel. Brett reached out his window and gave the guard his military ID and a copy of his orders. As the guard left to check out his credentials, Hellen ran her fingers through his thick hair. The guard looked askance at them as he returned Brett's military ID, making her cheeks flush. With a curt formality, he asked them to surrender their weapons. Brett handed over Hellen's handgun and asked directions to the RAF garrison's duty post.

After they pulled into the visitor parking lot, Hellen's stomach squirmed with nausea. Beyond the windshield, a dusty tan Quonset hut stood on the flat high plains desert with sage-brush and tumbleweeds blowing against its side. The place reminded her of the stage sets from old war movies. They weren't in paradise anymore. Brett got out and stretched next to a pair of carved wooden emblems hung on the entrance, marking the RAF Black Sharks helo squadron and the Kame-hameha Civil Air Defense Detachment. Brett whistled, and they climbed out of the car and headed inside. She removed her sunglasses and stopped at the doorway, taking time to acclimate to the dim interior. The flight office held an oppressive atmosphere, with its musty odor, fluorescent lights, and flypaper hanging from the ceiling. An officer behind the front desk stood and took a thick manila folder from Brett. His stoic face didn't acknowledge Hellen nor Charlie.

"Commander Akamu, welcome to the Black Sharks," he said in a Welsh accent.

Brett nodded and shook his hand. "Call me Brett. I'm Navy, and we're playing Armageddon here, so knock off the RAF stuff."

"As you wish, sir. I'm flight-lieutenant Jim Rogers, and I'm your pilot-examiner for the C-182 flight check."

The young officer wore a rumpled flight suit and appeared fifteen years younger than Brett. The pecking order seemed backward here.

"It's been awhile since I flew fixed wing," Brett said. "I thought this was a helo slot."

"Right. The Merlin MC3 is your primary assignment, but we also want you qualified for the C-182. We patrol the island in the smaller aircraft, burning a tenth of the fuel the helo guzzles."

Rogers set Brett's service record aside on the counter and tossed a worn-out, olive drab flight suit to Brett.

"I'm sorry it's missing your nameplate and rank insignia, but we're working on it. I'll dispatch our bird and meet you at Hangar Two in fifteen minutes." Rogers pointed to the hangar's location on the base map hanging on the wall.

"Where's your head?" Brett asked.

Rogers looked baffled. "My head?"

Hellen hid her smile with her hand. Funny how different branches of the military didn't share a common lingo. "Brett's asking where your restroom is located."

Both men stood in awkward silence until Rogers pointed down the hallway.

After Brett marched off, she turned back to Rogers, his eyes fixed on her chest. *This young, love-starved lad better get a lass of his own before he bursts.* She pulled her jacket closed and narrowed her eyes. After she cleared her throat, she finally got the horny toad's attention. "Lieutenant Rogers, it was... interesting meeting you. Can you let Brett know I'm outside?"

"Sure, Mrs. Akamu. I'll give you a base parking pass, and you can drive your husband to the hangar."

Her mouth fell open, and she held her hand to her heart. The base sticker may come in handy. "No, I'm not... Wait, that'll be fine, Lieutenant Rogers." Charlie stared at her with questioning eyes, but she shook her head at him. "Please let my husband know we're waiting in the car." She smiled at the natural way in which her words came together. After she took the parking sticker from Rogers, she dragged Charlie out of the squadron office before he busted her cover. They ran to the car, jumped in, and laughed together.

"Mom, he called you Mrs. Akamu. Did you guys get married without clearing it by me?"

"He was just a little confused, Charlie. Don't worry about it."

"What, me worry?" he said. "It's all good. The sooner you get spliced, the better."

Hellen held her breath and checked her son's expression, trying to discern if he was mocking her. Just the opposite. He gave her a thumbs-up, his face void of any judgment. As Brett had said, "Love is patient." She winked in return. "I'm glad you approve. And I promise, I'm making this stick."

Brett returned, wearing his flight suit, and removed his aviator sunglasses. He looked great in uniform. No wonder so many women fell for military hardware.

His eyes moved from Hellen to Charlie. "What do you guys find so funny?" he said with confusion painted on his face. "Can you roll down your window? I'm hot."

"Just what I was thinking," she teased. "You look very hot, Commander."

"Right," he said with a deadpan expression, his radar obviously offline.

She blew her bangs from her eyes. "I'll drive you down to the hangar. I have special privileges." She pulled out her base pass and waved it at him before hanging it from the rearview mirror.

Brett flicked the pass with his finger. "How did you get one of these? Damn, I'll never figure you out."

"Tactical maneuvers, Commander."

Charlie knocked Brett's garrison cap off his head and laughed. "She's high keying you, dude."

Brett slapped his cap against Charlie's lap before returning it to his head. Hellen gave her son a coy smile through the rearview mirror, raising her eyebrows, daring him to reveal their secret.

They drove to the flight line and turned into the parking lot next to Hangar Two, a two-story building adorned with weathered gray paint. As they waited in the car, an aeroplane, painted with a sweeping blue-and-white scheme and a bold RAF bullet insignia, taxied in front. To Hellen, it wasn't larger than the small planes at her local airport and appeared to not have any armament. How could the RAF be so stupid?

Brett pointed to the little Cessna. "Here's my ride. Civil Defense uses it for interisland transportation and surveillance."

After the aeroplane shut down, Rogers climbed out and headed toward them. With a falling heart, she pulled Brett's hand to her lips, her misty eyes fixed on him. "It's showtime, Commander."

He pulled her into a hug and whispered in her ear, "I'll try to come back to Cloudcroft next month. I might swing a little liberty time."

She put on a brave face, biting her trembling lip, wondering if their shared thoughts might travel between here and Cloudcroft. "And I intend to use my base pass until I wear it out."

"No more words." His arms wrapped tight around her shoulders. Her vision blurred and tears stung her eyes. He moved his hands to her cheeks, touched his nose to hers, and exchanged a honi kiss. *I'll be waiting for you.*

19

CAP Flight 05, Kona Coast

Brett climbed into the clouds, back in the cockpit again after months of not flying. But this was a different saddle, one that didn't hover and always depended on forward motion for lift. The Cessna Skylane used a yoke and rudder pedals to control flight rather than the cyclic, collective, and anti-torque pedals in his helo. He banked the plane through a series of S-turns. His flying skills had grown rusty since he last rented a similar aircraft from the Navy Aero Club at Kaneohe Bay. He bumbled through stalls, steep turns, and chandelles, but Rogers appeared satisfied and gave him a vector for Kailua-Kona.

The coastline seemed normal from this altitude, verdant rain forest and turquoise waters. After they approached Honaunau, the landscape changed. Cars lay abandoned along the highway, and a few fires spread out of control over the hills. No traffic passed along Hawai'i Belt Road, except for a convoy led by a SUV speeding south away from town.

Rogers pointed his binoculars out the side window. "Let's head lower and get a better look at those guys. Make your altitude eight hundred feet."

Brett pulled the throttle, allowing the aircraft to glide to his assigned altitude. "CAP Flight 05, level, eight hundred," he announced over the radio.

Rogers looked through his binoculars again. "Tallyho; armed renegades from the Puna Samoan gang. Army Intelligence has been on their tail for the past week. I see three men: a driver, one with a shotgun, and a third sitting in the back with a mounted Mark 19 RPG. There's some kind of utility truck or fire brigade following them. Engaging the ARCHER, sending data stream now."

"We have an archer?" Brett asked, wondering why they had to resort to bow and arrows.

"It's an airborne reconnaissance system, a poor man's adaption of an RAF airborne HiDef surveillance camera. Just keep a visual beeline on the convoy."

"How the hell did those yahoos get a rocket-propelled-grenade launcher? Even the Royal Navy doesn't have such fancy gear."

"The Samoans are pretty resourceful, led by a drug dealer named Gus Conroy." Rogers turned back to his binoculars. "The constable thought he went clean, raising medicinal pot in a commercial hydroponic farm in Puna. But last year he formed a branch of the Sons of Samoa with ex-cons. And three days ago, he showed up at KMC and attacked a volunteer and killed a patient."

"It sounds like the Wild West in these parts." The incident sounded similar to the attack on Hellen. Brett's knuckles turned white around the control yoke. Here was a chance for revenge, yet the aircraft was unarmed.

"You can add Hilo to the mayhem," Rogers said. "You'll see when we pass over the city on the return to base."

Gus Conroy sat in the left seat of the Vagabond, riding shotgun as it sped south down Hawai'i Belt Road. An airplane flew circles above him, its shadow flashing across the road. Weird. He had seen no plane in the past week, or even much law enforcement. The day's mission went as planned. Their raid on three resorts in Kailua-Kona yielded enough gold and silver to make the first upfront payment to his PGP boys. His team also raided the private stockpiles of four Mormon families. Their feeble defense was a joke. Handguns were no match for his gang's Mossberg 500s. Easy pickings, like hunting squirrels back home. The gang now had enough food to last another four weeks. As if the food wasn't enough, these Mormons also had saved a handsome stash of gold for their Armageddon party.

Their next stop was Honaunau to pick up the fire station's mobile generator. Again, the locals had offered scant resistance. He radioed home base and told his new lieutenant to tell the PGP boys to be ready to take over the plant next week. With the local cops and the army reservists fighting the civil mayhem in Hilo, the power plant stood unprotected. Robin Hood was one step closer to controlling power in Puna.

Gus tuned the dashboard radio to KUMU. Elle's EMS broadcast came on, announcing a manhunt for Gus Conroy and giving his description. Scrawny and gnarly weren't adjectives he'd used to describe himself. He must've not killed Toma before the moke turned whistle-blower. If that bitch Callahan hadn't stuck her foot into his business, he'd been home free by now.

The prop noise from the plane cut off his brooding. Now it flew right at them. He estimated its altitude at about a thousand feet, not much of a risk, but still...

"Crank her up," he shouted over the wind noise. "Let's get moving."

They drove fast and hard along the winding road. Word would spread, and the cops would sure as hell follow. They rounded a sharp turn above Honaunau and spotted the plane heading parallel to them at low altitude. Gus grabbed the binoculars and saw the infamous RAF bull's-eye insignia plastered on the plane's tail feathers.

"Shit, it's one of them military aircraft," Gus shouted over his shoulder to the moke sitting at the rear of the truck. "Get the RPG ready!" He pointed to the plane. "Set the sucker for an air burst, one thousand feet."

After fiddling with the control panel, the Samoan aimed the launcher and pulled the firing trigger. The missile ignited with a bright plume of white smoke and raced upward. Gus whooped at the bright contrail it traced in the sky. Another dandy day for varmint hunting.

"Bank right. Bank right. Dive away from these guys," Rogers shouted without taking his eyes from the binoculars. "They just launched an RPG."

Out Brett's window, the rocket made a beeline for them, its white exhaust sketching a parabolic arc across the sky. Traveling at ten times their aircraft speed, the rocket would converge within seconds. More from instinct than planning, Brett rolled the yoke against its stops, sending the Cessna through a wingover, heading away from the island. As the ocean filled the windshield, Brett hauled on the yoke. The G-force on the pull-up made his jaw drop a little, but he knew the bird could handle almost four G's. The rocket flashed past their right wingtip and exploded next to them. His heart sank as shrapnel pinged against the fuselage. The aircraft ailerons and rudder felt okay, but it was always what he didn't see that bit him in the arse.

"Holy shit," Rogers yelled. "Nice maneuver, but you scared the crap out of me. Where'd you learn that trick?"

"Navy pilots fly aircraft. RAF pilots drive buses."

"Okay, hot shot. Climb to niner-thousand and make your heading zero-seven-zero. Continue to shadow the bad guys while I radio Bradshaw. But stay the bloody hell out of their range."

Brett climbed to his assigned altitude and breathed a sigh of relief. They were now out of missile range, and the convoy was still in sight. Rogers whipped out a twelve-inch tablet and placed his right hand on a small joystick at the aircraft's front instrument console.

"BearCON, this is CAP Flight 05," Rogers spoke through the radio. "We're under RPG weapons fire from a civilian convey heading south on Belt Highway, one-zero miles south of Honaunau. Sending our ARCHER data stream now."

At the southern tip of the Big Island, Brett banked north, following Gus Conroy and his gang to Puna. They flew over the Kīlauea volcano, its lava pouring into the coastline, sending huge billowing white clouds of steam into the sky. As they approached the south end of town, the convoy disappeared into the dense surrounding jungle. Rogers reported their last position and gave Brett a vector for Hilo.

Ahead and below the aircraft nose, Hilo appeared through the mist and rain. Brett recalled Rogers' earlier warning. The historic city drowned in chaos with multiple fires burning, people running in the streets, and police vehicles swarming in various directions.

"Hilo is our biggest worry," Roger said over the intercom. "The place is in mayhem compared to the sanctuary you guys set up in Kamuela. The Puna Samoans haven't moved in yet, but it's only a matter of time."

"I'm still amazed how Elle and her team have maintained security in Kohala."

Brett's mouth slackened at the dire scenery below him. A sense of helpless dread filled him; the chaos would soon spread to Kamuela. He had promised Hellen he'd look after Elizabeth, but that wasn't possible from the cockpit. A red light next to the fuel gauge caught his peripheral vision. This was turning out to be another fine Navy day.

"Fuel critical," he announced to Rogers. "The shrapnel must've punctured our right wing fuel tank. Switching to the left tank."

Rogers handed him an instrument approach plate. "Let's return to base. We've had enough fun for one day."

Brett banked hard left and headed west to Bradshaw Airfield, gaining altitude to clear the mountain pass between Mauna Loa and Mauna Kea. After flying over the first ridge, Brett shook his head and released a long, taut breath amplified by the boom mike. A shroud of low-lying scud clouds covered the airbase. He scanned the panel gauges in front of him to prepare for instrument flight with no visual reference to the ground. His quick, mental gymnastics told him they had twenty minutes of fuel left. "I'll fly the approach. Can you handle the radios?"

"You got it, Navy. We'll fly the NDB runway two-seven approach. Thanks to Helio Hattie, it's the only approach left for us into Bradshaw."

Brett had often struggled with Non-Directional Beacons. The navigation receiver only displayed a simple yellow needle always pointing to the station. Modern glass cockpits, with their map displays and advanced technology, made NDBs obsolete. But the Navy still relied on the ancient technology as a backup in case the GPS satellites failed. He and other helo pilots practiced the approach every week. With only a 120-watt transmitter, any remote LZ could guide birds back to the roost.

After Rogers called for a clearance from Bradshaw Approach, ATC replied. "RAF Flight zero-five, cleared NDB runway two-seven approach, contact tower for landing clearance."

Brett reviewed the approach plate, memorizing field elevation, minimum descent altitude, and missed approached instructions. Rogers dialed in the navigation and control tower frequencies. "You're all set, Navy. Show me what you got."

He descended on the approach, adjusting the aircraft's heading to stay on the proper track to the runway threshold. His approach sucked, falling three degrees off at one point. At three hundred feet to go, Rogers told him to look up and announced, "Runway in sight. You're left of center line and too high. Fix it or go around."

"We can't go missed approach. Low fuel."

The runway lay off the left wingtip. A strong crosswind must have blown them off course. The fuel gauges now read empty. The engine sputtered before coughing back to life. Brett wiped his palms one at a time on his flight suit. He rolled his shoulders and braced up. With a mile short of the runway, the engine quit. Out the front windshield the prop wound down to a stop. Rogers seemed mesmerized by the sight of the frozen prop and looked as if he might shit his pants any second. But Brett had flown his approach with extra altitude as he always had done in case of an engine failure. With no fuel, he glided to a hard touchdown, clearing the runway threshold by only five feet.

Rogers let out an exhausted sigh and called ground control for an aircraft tug to tow them to the hangar. Brett climbed out of the cockpit and inspected the shrapnel hole in the right wing, an inch shy of the aileron cable. Damn, they were lucky. If he'd lost the aileron, he wouldn't be standing there.

Rogers came over to him and rubbed his hand over the torn aluminum. He spit his gum out and let out a loud whistle. "That flight was the biggest ball of chalk I've ever flown. You saved our bloody hides, mate. We're damn lucky to have you in our squadron."

20

Kohala Wind Farm, 27 July

From Hellen's perch atop Wind Tower Nine, the wind farm spread around her, its sixteen titanium-white towers contrasting against dark clouds. The wind whistled through the ninety-foot rotor blades frozen in position. Before Helio Hattie, Tanaka had locked them in case strong winds might over-speed the unloaded turbines. The lock had protected the blades, but now presented the biggest roadblock for the black startup. This problem had racked Hellen's mind for the past two weeks, yet she welcomed the distraction from the havoc she had caused in her personal life.

Restoring the wind farm would change the equation for survival. The sixteen wind turbines generated ten megawatts, enough power to support five thousand homes. Life could return to normal, refrigerators could run, cells phones could come alive, the cranes in Kawaihae Harbor could receive food and fuel imports again. And civil unrest would end, security would return, and her children would be safe.

Her stomach cramped with other worries. Gus Conroy was still at large three weeks after he had attacked her. The creepozoid had somehow evaded the constabulary's manhunt. He was also a threat to her children. Elizabeth was most at risk. He had already been to Cloudcroft, knew who lived there, and wouldn't hesitate to kill her. At least her daughter had a rifle at hand. If only she also had the will to use it.

Atop the wind tower, Hellen had no trouble making out Kamuela and the resort village of Kailua-Kona. Imaginary lines stretched in her mind connecting the two towns with Mauna Kea to form three sides of a triangle. If she installed another radio relay atop one of these wind towers, KUMU's radio coverage would double. She searched the nacelle's utility box and found a power outlet. With a little jerry-rigging, this would be an excellent spot for a relay antenna.

Aiva chimed and displayed current weather data. "Barometer pressure 960 millibars and dropping rapidly," she announced. "It appears a storm is developing. I suggest you take shelter." The islands had little warning of any approaching storm. Without its fleet of satellites and array of supercomputers, the National Weather Office had to rely on forecasting methods from a century ago, degrading accuracy and shrinking the forecast period from weeks to hours. With no internet to broadcast local weather data, forecasts had become a luxury lost in history.

Hellen rose to her feet, but a gust of wind caught her and blew her toward the edge of the turbine's housing. Her safety harness cable snapped tight, pinching her chest. She leaned over the side and just about caught her breath. Two hundred feet below, trees in the surrounding forest swayed in the wind. Now and then, the wind abated, giving them a respite, only to return in great gusts. Threatening mammatus clouds raced in. Their strange, saggy pouches made the sky appear as if it boiled. The menacing clouds signaled severe thunderstorms, and she wondered if a tropical depression was headed her way. Off in the distance, the storm broke the sky open, sending sheets of rain on Mauna Kea's western slope. Struggling against the wind, she crawled to the hatch and climbed inside.

She closed the hatch behind her and the howling tempest subsided to a muffled roar. The generator compartment atop the tower swayed with each gust. The stuffy cabin aboard *Ohana* came to her mind. Her stomach rebelled, sending a small burp to her lips.

"We're lucky to have removed the Faraday cage on this turbine before it got too windy," Tanaka said. His homespun mishmash of chicken wire wrapped around the turbines had protecting the stator windings from Helio Hattie's geomagnetic storm but now served no purpose. The wind rocked the central hub, holding the three massive blades back and forth between steel cogs around a thirty-inch-wide gear. The rotor locking latch rubbed against the cog, then eased off with each sway of the hub. She took hold of the manual brake and timed her pull with the gear's motion, waiting until the latch came unloaded. With all her strength, she heaved on the latch handle and the brake sprung open.

At the resounding noise, Tanaka did a fist punch into the air. "Wow, Wonder Woman, how did you get the brake released?"

Hellen's elation died, and her chest swelled in panic. The hub rotated, picking up speed as the three huge blades bit into the wind. "Shut up and help me get it locked again."

Tanaka's hands pushed with hers and they threw their weight behind the handle the moment the next cog in the gear clicked into position. The latch engaged and the hub ground to a stop with a loud bang, vibrating the compartment. Hellen let out a long breath and rested her hand on Tanaka's shoulder.

"It'll be easier with less wind," Tanaka said. "I think you solved our biggest problem. Now, let's bug out before the storm hits us."

By sunset, Tanaka dropped Hellen off at Cloudcroft. The storm strengthened, and sheets of rain swept against her face. Tree limbs snapped and slammed against the side of the house. Many of the windows on the first floor were boarded up with plywood. A few of the solar panels had blown off the roof and lay scattered across the yard. Hellen collected the nearest panels and stacked them in the barn. On the last trip, a panel caught a gust of wind like a kite and lifted her off her feet. She let go of it and fell onto the gravel driveway. Scared witless, she raced inside the house and dumped her soaked jacket onto the hallway floor. She called for Elle and Suzu, but they didn't answer.

Charlie bounded down the stairs but stopped short at seeing her. He smiled and didn't turn away from her. It was a heartfelt delight she had hadn't expected. If nothing else came out of this misadventure, at least their bond might mend.

"It's a wonderful surprise to see you again. Why aren't you at Uncle Donovan's?"

"With the storm brewing, I thought Elizabeth needed company. She's here alone. We boarded up the windows and secured the barn. But the storm is driving the horses crazy."

"Just you and Elizabeth? Where's Suzu and Elle?"

"They left for town this morning but haven't returned."

She frowned. "They must have their hands full with preparing the CD Command Post for the storm. I'm glad you're here. Have Donovan and Malia treated you well?"

"Sure. I'm staying at Malia's cottage—it's next to the hospital. My volunteer work at the hospital keeps me busy, and I help Malia with her herbal garden after our shift. You know, I think I want to be an EMT. Crazy, huh?"

"Sometimes our fears lead us to unexpected opportunities. Look at me, an acrophobic engineer who works atop wind towers."

Charlie picked her coat up and shook the rain off, sending water flying in all directions. The ceiling lights appeared dimmer than usual. Hellen strode to the back porch to check the power management panel. The wind turbine had tripped the supply circuit breaker, possibly for over-voltage protection when the wind picked up. The battery charge status read twenty percent.

With the solar array out, they'd not have power for long. She returned inside and switched off the lights in every room. From the pantry, she retrieved a set of flashlights and a box of candles.

"Where's Elizabeth?" she asked Charlie, lighting two candles. Although eager to see her again, she dreaded the inevitable cold welcome. The last time she had seen her, the night she told her everything, was over three weeks ago. So much had happened.

Charlie took a candle and waved it under his chin, casting spooky shadows across his face. "She's stalking coqui frogs in the deep forest."

"Come on, Charlie. This is serious."

"The storm scares her. She's hiding in her room. But isn't this cool? Even the coqui frogs have battened down the hatches. We never get storms like this in Colorado." He braced his hands on his hips, his voice mimicking Kikaida, his favorite superhero from an alternate dimension. "Don't worry, Mom. I got this."

She kissed his cheek. "You're only the second man who ever told me that."

Charlie's smile vanished like the wind. "Do you miss him?"

She brushed his wild curls with her fingers. "Of course I do. But he'll return in a few weeks."

Charlie nodded. "He'd better."

Hellen walked upstairs. The CB radio in Elle's study sputtered with activity as their neighbors prepared for the storm. Since Helio Hattie, CB radios had replaced cell phones. Those with radios listened all day and helped each other out. Luana reported she had lost power to her freezer, and Papa Kani offered to store her meat and goat cheese. Manu radioed he had spare plywood. Josie's dog was on the loose. And the Mahelonas needed more petrol for their generator. But those without a radio were isolated, cut off from their 'ohana.

Hellen stood at her daughter's door and hesitated before knocking. "Elizabeth, it's me. May I come in?"

Elizabeth cracked the door and peeked at her. "What are you doing here?"

Hellen braced herself, wondering if she should go back downstairs. "I came home to help you guys weather the storm."

She opened the door and placed her hand on Elizabeth's sleeve. "I've missed you, love."

Elizabeth averted her eyes and moved her wrist away. "I'm scared. When's this wind ever going to end?"

"If it's a tropical storm it should pass through by tomorrow."

Elizabeth shut her eyes and flung herself onto the bed. "I'll never get to sleep."

Hellen sat beside her, the first time in weeks she had felt this close to her. "Come downstairs and stay with Charlie and me. We'll defend the fort together."

Elizabeth stared at her with glistening eyes. Her frown relaxed, and she made a reluctant smile, as if she had changed her mind. "Maybe later," she said. Hellen stood and held her hand out to her daughter, her throat thick with anxiety. *Please don't turn away from me.* Elizabeth shook her head and rolled on her tummy, her back to her. Hellen waited at the doorway, taking her daughter in with her eyes, hoping she'd change her mind. Frustrated, she returned downstairs and walked to the kitchen.

A bird squawked from the lanai, its screech piercing the air and making Hellen and Charlie jump. They ran to the porch and found a black raven. Its right wing broken, it staggered over the floor. The wind caught its upturned wing and blew the bird sideways toward the door. It hopped inside and filled the air with a mixture of hoarse clicks and grating caws.

"What the hell is that?" Elizabeth shouted from behind them.

"Elizabeth. Quick. Grab a laundry basket or box from your room."

After Elizabeth returned, Hellen took a towel from the bathroom and covered the basket's bottom. She crept to the bird from behind and snatched it with both hands. The bird's calls pierced Hellen's ears, its body squirming in her fingers, wrestling to get free. The bird settled down once Hellen placed it in the basket. A cup of birdseed and a bowl of water finally silenced the winged noisemaker.

"Let's move it to a quiet spot in the living room," Hellen said. With care, they lifted the basket and placed it by the fireplace with no more protest from the exhausted raven.

Beyond the window in the back door, the wind roared through the forest, pressing hard against the trees, and the rains gouged random channels into the dirt lane leading to the barn. A small uprooted bougainvillea tumbled across the lawn like a tumbleweed. A nest, perhaps the home of her raven friend, was torn from the top of a dead tree and sailed across the paddock like a straw hat. A book lay spread on the porch steps, its pages soaked.

"Shit, that's my calc textbook." Elizabeth pushed Hellen aside and ran out the door. Her foot slipped on the wet floorboards and sent her feet out from under her. She twisted to regain balance and screamed as she fell. On the verge of tears, she held her ankle. She tried to stand but fell on her first step. Hellen ran and helped her into the house. With Elizabeth's arm over her shoulder, Hellen guided her to the nearest chair. She slipped off Elizabeth's shoe and gingerly peeled off the sock. Elizabeth's foot recoiled at her touch but gave no more protest. With the last of the ice and a kitchen towel, Hellen wrapped a cold compress around the injured ankle.

Elizabeth's eyes welled up, her hand covered her mouth. "This really sucks. Now how am I going to get around?"

"I've an idea. Stay here while I get an athletic bandage."

"Like, where else am I going to go?"

Hellen found a sport bandage in Elle's bathroom closet and returned to the kitchen. With gentle fingers, she took the compress off and wrapped the bandage around Elizabeth's foot and ankle, making her wince with each turn. After she taped the last wrap, she went to the stove and fixed a pot of tea. The wind shouldered against the windows, making a low-humming noise, a song of frightened glass. Hellen poured two cups and added a spot of honey. Elizabeth took a sip and gave a slight nod. They sat together, saying everything without words, their first honest moment in weeks. The tension in Elizabeth's face relaxed, her body no longer trembled. She inspected her bandaged ankle and looked back to Hellen, opened her mouth to speak, but said nothing.

Hellen sipped her tea and waited. On her second sip, she couldn't stand it any longer. "What?"

"Nothing." A small smile flashed across Elizabeth's face, a sign of mitigation or satisfaction—Hellen wasn't sure. "I'm just glad you're here," she said at last.

"Me too, love." A bubble of relief swept through her chest. She reached for Elizabeth's hand and let out a deep breath when Elizabeth clasped her fingers. Her hand was warm and nostalgic as if they were always friends. Tears traced down both their cheeks, little streams of mutual love.

Charlie walked in, carrying a pair of smartphones. Elizabeth snatched her hand away, the moment lost, but Hellen would remember it forever. She took a breath and collected herself.

"What ya got there, Edison?" she said to Charlie.

He pressed the home button on one phone before handing it to her. His thumbs twittered over his display and a message alert popped on her screen: *Think like a proton.*

She grinned and texted back to him: *Be positive.* Hellen held her palm against his chin, letting her eyes tell him how much she loved him. Charlie tried unsuccessfully to deflect her kiss. Elizabeth squealed her excitement and ran her hand through Charlie's hair. "You're brilliant. Now, we'll have our phones back."

His face blushed as red as his hair. "No, not yet. It works cell-to-cell, not like a telephone network. I set up a SPAN, a Smart Phone Ad Hoc Network. By configuring their OS to connect on a peer-to-peer basis, our phones can now talk to one another through their Wi-Fi antenna."

"Where did you get this hack?" Hellen asked.

"I got an app from an NCEL tech. Remember that 'bring your

kid to work day' you dragged me to last spring?" He took the phone from Hellen's hand and opened the app for her. "All I did was transfer my app to the other phone set up on the SPAN. No big deal."

He showed her how to exchange the app across OS platforms and she added the app to her tablet.

"I sense two new networked devices," Aiva said. "Is the internet coming back?"

"No, Aiva," Hellen said. "You're on a peer-to-peer network, like a party line."

Aiva's hourglass icon spun around for a few seconds. "I've found four other 5G network devices on 100 megahertz. Connecting now."

"What's she up to?" Elizabeth asked.

Hellen laughed. "She's making new friends."

"Farthest peripheral device detected. Now expanding to ten cellular nodes."

Hellen beamed as Aiva displayed a growing web of connections across town. "I think she's building a cell network using a bootstrap from each adjacent phone along the chain."

"Autonomous Smart Phone Ad Hoc Network complete. I've established a text message exchange protocol across all available cell phones."

Hellen couldn't believe her eyes. The network map grew to dozens of phones connected by different-colored lines showing battery status.

"Jesus," Elizabeth whispered, "she's a queen bee with a hive of drones."

"Give that girl an inch, and she'll take a yard."

Green Valley Farm

The next day Gus Conroy stood at the entrance to the lava tube leading down to his batu lab. The rain poured from the cave's archway like a cow pissing on a flat rock. Helmut shuffled back and forth, circling in vain to find a dry spot to lie down. Tropical storm Lester had passed a hundred miles west of the Big Island, but it still slammed Puna with its fury, bringing driving rain and flooding to most low-lying areas. The gale force winds uprooted many of the trees around Gus's compound and tore off his barn roof.

But the rain and wind damage didn't dampen Gus's spirit. This morning, he had run all over hell's half-acre, making plans for seizing control of the PGP power plant, taking advantage of the chaos in Lester's aftermath. He organized a raiding party, alerted the PGP boys, and announced his plans to assault the power plant at midnight. While the little people of Puna-Whoville hunkered down in their homes, his boys would drive right up to the gate with no resistance, like the Grinch at Christmas.

At the appointed time, his convoy of three trucks pulled up to the south entrance of the power plant. The security lights cast yellow cone-shaped beams through the rain. John and Henry stood by the gate and waved him in.

Gus stopped by the gatehouse and whistled for them to hop in his SUV. "You boys were right. We ain't seen anybody in these parts. Looks like clear sailing so far."

"There're only two guards on duty tonight," Henry said. "They're at the main entrance on the north side of the plant but shouldn't pose any problems. A couple of your guys can handle them. They'll never expect an attack from inside the premises."

Gus led his convoy up the steep road to the power plant control room, dropping his partners off at the main door.

"Me and the boys will sweep the area clear and take care of the guards. You take the mobile generator truck and power up the plant."

"Right," John said. "Henry will operate the generator, and I'll man the control room. Should only take four or five hours. We'll stay in touch with these walkie-talkies." He checked the squelch on two FM-band radios and tossed one to Gus. "One more thing, one of our informants at ConHEL told us they plan to black start the Kohala Wind Farm soon."

"That won't happen. A batu head on their payroll owes me big time. We'll arrange an accident during the startup."

Gus sent three of his Samoans down the road to the main gate while he circled the plant grounds looking for any interlopers. On the second pass, he picked up the mokes at the front gate after they silenced the guards. Henry called it right. The rent-a-cops never saw his men coming for them.

The rest of the operation went as planned. Everyone knew their job and carried it out with little commotion. His gang had taken control of the power plant without firing a single shot. The PGP boys had run through the black start procedure with the generator truck providing ample power.

At dawn, Gus lit a Cuban stogy and took a deep drag. In the distance, Helmut went berserk, barking from around the corner of the building. Gus chased after him and ran right into a rent-a-cop standing beside Helmut, trying to kick the dog loose from his trousers. The guard must have been sleeping out of sight when Gus made his rounds. While Helmut stole the man's attention, Gus casually took his Smith & Wesson 9mm out of his raincoat and fired a single shot into the guard's temple. The shot echoed from the surrounding buildings and sent Helmut scurrying away.

John's voice came through the radio. "We've nominal power from the electric turbine. We're back in business."

Well, that just dills my pickle. Operation Robin Hood had begun. He grinned and took another drag from his cigar. A most satisfying night, indeed. A load explosion resounded within the generator building, followed by shouts of alarm. The lights lost power and darkness returned. *Well, shit. Murphy strikes again.*

Kohala 'Āina Foundation, 29 July

Hellen arrived at Elle's daily civil defense meeting out of breath and drenched from the morning rain. Fortunately, no one had turned up yet. After brushing out her wet hair, she threw it into a ponytail. She didn't understand why Elle had asked her to attend and wished she had stayed at Cloudcroft today. Cloudcroft needed her, and she needed her children. After weeks of separation, brother and sister were back on speaking terms, even with an occasional healthy spot of sibling rivalry.

The past two days had flown in a whirlwind of work repairing the wind damage to Cloudcroft. The work pushed her to her physical limits, but she loved every minute. Charlie worked alongside her, repairing broken windows and clearing two downed trees. Elizabeth remained indoors, nursing her sprained ankle. A part of Hellen welcomed her injury, bad as it might sound, but it gave her a chance to care for her daughter. Elizabeth still resisted at every turn, but her reluctance soon turned into a game between them.

Elle arrived for the meeting before the others, gliding in with a self-possessed confidence. How did she keep at it, day after day? Perhaps the crisis helped Elle find her stride.

"What's up?" Elle asked brightly.

"Certainly not the rain, that's been coming down in buckets."

"Thanks to *Apuhau*, Lester just kissed us on his flyby. I hope Cloudcroft didn't suffer too much damage."

Hellen grinned at how everything in Elle's world spun with its own birthright. The storm had terrified Elizabeth, but Elle had turned to the Hawaiian god of storms. In her mind, the weather, not forecasting, had Buddha nature.

"Charlie calls it 'Lester the Molester'. It wreaked havoc with the out buildings, tearing apart the chicken shed, sending the birds to kingdom come. And I can now add chainsaw lumberjack to my resume. I'm sorry to say your wind turbine is out of commission. And our four-legged friends didn't much care for the storm. The lightning and driving rain spooked Lulua'ina so much she came down with colic, poor thing." She gave a long yawn and stretched her arms above her head. "I spent most of last night walking her around the paddock to get the gas to come out."

"Thanks for managing Cloudcroft while I deal with Lester's aftermath. How's Elizabeth?"

"Sprained her ankle, poor dear. Charlie made a set of crutches for her, fashioned from the handles of a post-hole digger."

"Sounds like she's a captive audience to your loving on her."

"I love it, she tolerates it."

Hellen took out Elle's abandoned iPhone from her coat pocket and presented it to her, as if it were a precious gift. Its home screen glowed in the dim room, displaying a picture of Suzu's muted smile. Elle's eyes grew wide and her mouth dropped open as if she were seeing an old friend come back to her.

"We can thank Charlie. He configured the phones to connect with one another without a cell tower to relay their signal. Aiva did the rest. As soon as I can set up repeaters around Kohala, we'll take another step toward a normal life."

Hellen showed her how to place a SPAN message and sent Elle a text: *Aloha.*

Elle smiled at her phone and texted back: *Charlie real akamai! Acorn fall not far from tree.* "This is a game changer," she said. "Does Brett have one?"

"Not yet." But the chance of talking to him, even by text, sent her mind reeling. She ached for Brett again, for those passion-soaked days on *Ohana.* She hadn't heard from him since dropping him off at Bradshaw and worried if he had come though the storm unscathed. Why did they have to fall in love again in the middle of this mess? An incongruent nexus of intense desire and sadness overwhelmed her. Elle's warm hand came to her shoulder, and she almost lost control. This moodiness drove her crazy; she was reveling with a zest for life in one moment, falling into a depression in the next. She slumped her shoulders and wiped her eyes.

Elle let out a sympathetic sigh. "You look exhausted."

"I'm okay." She paused, not looking up. "Lately, I've ridden an emotional bungee cord."

Elle's hand lifted Hellen's chin up, their faces separated by inches. "Remember the red thread. It stretches and twists, but never breaks. Trust me. Just hold on."

But heat threaded Hellen's throat. She had found the raven dead in the laundry basket that morning, another victim of the storm. It was like a part of her had died with the bird. They shared the same persona: a tool master, a clever mind, a penchant for hasty action without forethought.

Elle reached inside her purse and retrieved her makeup bag. "The ladies' room is across from my office. Take your time. I'll save you a seat."

Hellen washed her face and leaned her hands on the bathroom counter. Her reflection shocked her—haggard, even sad. She hesitated as she reached for the door. Elle was right; she needed to flow with the stream and stop worrying, stop trying to steer the future. It'll work out. Her right hand fiddled with her red braided bracelet. Given to her after Elizabeth's birth, it remained her private connection with Brett even after her marriage to Sam.

Elle had reserved a seat for her at the crowded conference table. Elle's hand rested on Hellen's knee beneath the table and her tension eased. Her brother—an unexpected visitor—sat across from her. His broad grin belied the tension in his eyes. She hadn't seen him since Charlie went off to live with him, another responsibility her brother had assumed with little complaint. Charlie loved shadowing Donovan and Malia at the hospital. The lad had grown up too fast since sailing from San Diego. With a strange awareness, she accepted that her project of raising him had come to a premature end. Crisis made children grow into adults before their prime.

Elle walked over to a white board and wrote "45" with a red marker, the number of days since the solar storm. "First, let's hear the progress reports. Donovan, I assume you are standing in for Malia. Can you lead off?"

"Sure, we completed our EMT first-responder training for our local *kumus* and converted fire stations and schools into temporary health clinics. The new annex at the Maunakea Astronomy Institute has added another thirty beds for convalescence. Ann Jacobs, KMC's director, returned from O'ahu yesterday and is up to speed on our triage plan."

"Congratulations and mahalo nui for your help during the crisis," Elle said. "I know how hard you and Malia worked to keep the hospital running. I hope you two enjoy some personal time together."

Elle held her gaze on him as if they shared a secret. Hellen wiggled her eyebrows and waited to hear the latest gossip on her brother, but Elle returned to her agenda. "Joe, what do you have to report on the storm damage?"

"Most is limited to soil erosion and downed trees. The wind farm already had locked their turbine rotors before Helio Hattie, limiting wind damage to the power plant."

"That leads me to some great news." Elle tapped Hellen's wrist. "Despite the storm, the Navy still plans to deploy a nuclear submarine to provide us with auxiliary power."

Hellen scooted to the edge of her seat and leaned her elbows on the table. "When do we expect them?"

"They plan to arrive at Kawaihae in five days. Will you be ready? We only have them for forty-eight hours before they proceed to Hilo."

"Sure, we'll make it work," Hellen said with less confidence than she had hoped. Tanaka's team had worked around the clock reconnecting power lines and transformers, but the storm had set them back five days. Her mind raced through the dozens of steps needing to come together: removing the remaining Faraday cages, hooking up the harbor shore power to the wind farm grid, and unlocking the rotor blades. There was zero chance of getting all this done in time even if they worked twenty-four seven. With only a five-day window, everything had to proceed without Murphy's Law getting in the way. Restoring power had become a personal mission as much as a public one. Her children grew hungrier with each passing day. Food shipments only trickled in by air transport. They needed to open the commercial port in Kawaihae Harbor for importing bulk food shipments and fuel-oil.

By the time Hellen's attention returned to the present, Elle had adjourned the meeting and most people had left. Elle rested her hand on Hellen's wrist. "You still alive in there?"

Hellen wished her Man from Maui were at her side. Brett's presence brought her solace, one of his many talents. Like flying. Yes, that was it! She recalled how helicopters had flown wind techs to offshore turbines.

As Elle stood to leave, Hellen grasped her hand and pulled her back. "Wait! Can you ask Bradshaw to help us out? If Brett could air-taxi our crew around the wind farm, we'll be ready when the sub pulls into port."

"I'll check with them, but I don't see why not. Come on, let's go home. I've not slept in my own bed in days."

21

Bradshaw Airfield, 03 August

Brett picked up his dispatch logs at squadron ops and drove to Hangar Seven at the far end of Bradshaw Airbase. The RAF jockeys had assigned them to the outfield, perhaps a show of force in their inter-service rivalry. His helicopter crew chief, CPO Mason Jones, had already towed the Merlin HC3 out to the helo pad and was halfway through the preflight inspection before Brett arrived. Jones was several inches shorter and many years older than Brett but still in better shape.

Seeing the Merlin felt like coming home again. Brett had over three thousand hours in type and looked forward to flying helo again after weeks of patrolling the Hawaiian skies in the Cessna.

Brett walked up to Jones as he removed the tail rotor tie-down straps. "You beat me to the aircraft again, Chief."

"Yes, sir. And I always will," Jones called back to him as he gnawed on a wad of chewing gum. "I sleep in the hangar, sir. Haven't you figured this out yet?"

"Jones, you need to get a life or a wife. Either one would make you easier to get along with."

"I would if I thought you did a proper preflight, sir. You

brown shoe noodle-wingers just kick the tires and light the fires and off you go." Jones stuck his head inside the engine intake nacelle. "What's the mission today, sir?"

"It's not another patrol run around this rock," Brett yelled up to him. "It sounds kinda fun, actually."

"Fun?" Jones called from atop the ladder. "That's against RAF regs."

"It's just you and me, pal. To save payload, Air Ops has issued a waiver to let us fly a single pilot with one crew chief."

"What's the flight plan?"

"We're heading down to Kawaihae Harbor to pick up a team of workers and ferry them up to a nearby wind farm."

"Sounds like we're spending the day playing air taxi, Commander. Are there landing zones by each tower?"

"We'll find out when we get there." Brett glanced at his watch. "Now, let's start the motors and spin up the rotors. They want us wheels up within five minutes."

After receiving their ATC departure clearance, Brett headed west to Kawaihae Harbor. Jones wore a big grin as the landscape drifted below them. They flew "nap-of-the-earth," low to the ground, the terrain a blur of motion. Damage from Lester lay everywhere, trees fallen, roofs torn, fields flattened, signs ripped from their posts, yet the wind farm looked intact. He wondered how the towers came through the storm intact. Someone had thought ahead. They arrived at the harbor within twenty minutes, and Brett flew a wide, right-hand circle to survey the landing zone through his side window.

"Jones, look," he said over the crew intercom. His sailboat moored on the far side of the harbor, and a submarine lay alongside the long concrete pier. Several thick black cables were strung out to the boat. Two new cargo ships had also arrived.

"How's the sub getting shore power?" Jones asked.

"Perhaps just the opposite. Maybe they're using their reactor to provide power to the marine terminal."

"That's why we're here?"

"We're about to find out."

Brett descended and came in low over the water to check out *Ohana* and make sure she rode okay on her mooring lines. As he approached the landing zone on the pier, a longshoreman with orange paddles marshaled him to the LZ. Brett pulled back on the stick and made a smooth touchdown, but kept the rotors spinning at standby RPMs so they could load the passengers and bug out quick-time.

Jones slid the cargo door open and eight wind techs climbed in with harnesses and hard hats, filling the passenger cabin. Another one banged on the copilot door while peering into the cockpit. Brett released the remote door latch and the rotor blast slammed the door open, almost sending the wind tech to the ground. The tech gripped the door and stepped into the cockpit. Smaller than the others, the woman wore a blue ConHEL jumpsuit and aviator sunglasses under a ball cap brandishing a "BIC"—Bitch-in-Charge—moniker. Not comfortable with civilians flying up front, Brett turned around to see if they had any space left on the passenger bench. No such luck—full house today.

Brett glanced back to his instrument panel and adjusted the throttle to decrease rotor RPMs. An incessant tapping on his shoulder screamed for attention. *Damn it, leave me alone, can't you see I'm busy?* The needle on the turbine inlet temperature rose out of the green. "Ma'am, there's no room in the back for you," he shouted over the rotor noise without looking away from the TIT gauge. "You'll need to take the copilot seat."

The control stick came alive in his hand. His heart skipped. What's the source of that rotor vibration? The wind tech nudged him again and wiggled the stick. "And keep your bloody hands off the controls," he yelled.

The tech took her sunglasses off and beamed back at him.

Brett's jaw dropped. "How did you get here?"

Hellen shouted over the rotor noise, "Who'd you expect, Amelia Earhart? And don't call me ma'am. I thought we were on more personal terms, especially after our last night together." With a giddy lightness, she bent down, removed his boom mike, and gave him a long, warm kiss, accompanied by a loud chorus of catcalls and whistles behind her. After she released him, she flashed a playful smile and snapped her fingers into a trigger sign. "Gotcha."

Brett laughed and turned his head to an airman. "Jones, get a flight helmet for her."

A crewman with a salt-and-pepper crew cut and sharp military bearing helped her don the bulky headgear and strapped her into the copilot seat. She gave a light touch on the stick between her thighs. "So, how do you fly this whirligig?" Through the helmet headset, her voice had a strange modulated sound.

"With two hands," he said through the intercom.

She feigned a pout and slumped her shoulders. "Great. This flight isn't going to be much fun, is it?" Her headset speaker erupted with a chorus of laughter. Her fleeting fantasy evaporated. Now wasn't the time for such extravehicular activities.

"That's enough out of you clowns," Brett said before he flipped a switch on the control panel, cutting off the racket from the intercom circuit.

"Hellen, what's the deal?"

Her mind cleared, and she focused on the task at hand. "I'm your air boss for the day." She pointed to her ball cap embroidered with the red BIC. "We have to prep the wind farm by tomorrow. The submarine is here to provide startup power to the wind farm. You'll ferry us to each tower, so we can prep the turbines for startup." She pulled out a map and shared it with him. "I'll guide you around, pointing out the next tower in line. This might take all day."

"We've got two hours 'till I'm bingo fuel," Brett said. "After that, we must return to Bradshaw for refueling. This may take longer than you think."

They reached the first wind turbine within minutes. Hellen pointed to the clearing near the tower's base, and Brett descended to a landing. He flipped several switches and fiddled with the controls as he looked out his side window. The adjacent trees swayed from downwash of the helicopter's rotors. After two wind techs jumped out and ran clear, Jones gave a thumbs-up gesture and slid the passenger door closed.

"What exactly are they doing in there?"

"Tanaka locked the blades in place before Helio Hattie hit. Our guys need to disengage the rotor locking brake by hand at the top of each tower."

Brett nodded his head. "That explains why the storm didn't take the wind farm out."

They hopped from one tower to the next repeating this same procedure until reaching the fourth tower, tucked in among a grove of tall trees.

"Hellen, I can't land here. What do you want me to do?"

"Can we hoist a man down while hovering?"

"Sure," he said, smacking on his chewing gum. "To fly is heavenly, but to hover is divine."

Hellen shot him a wry smile and pointed to the wind turbine. "Okay, hotshot, can you maneuver near that small platform at the top of the tower?"

"If the hoist cable is long enough—won't want it wrapping those blades. Rule number one in flying: don't fly into solid objects."

His dark helmet visor obscured the upper part of his face. Still not accustomed to hearing disembodied voices through the intercom, she wasn't sure if he was joking or if these egg-beaters often ran into solid objects.

"Can I talk to the crew? I want to speak to the plant manager who is riding in the back."

Brett threw a switch above him. "Now you can. Go ahead."

"Tanaka, can you hear me?" She twisted around and waved at him.

"Yeah, what's up?"

"We can't land here, but maybe we can hoist our men down and expedite the tower prep."

He looked down at the tower a hundred yards below and shook his head. "No, never done anything like that. Doesn't look safe."

Hellen unbuckled her seat belt and crawled to the passenger bay. The wind techs sat on a bench facing her with stoic faces. She tried to get eye contact, but these ancestors of Japanese warriors who had won the last world war glanced out the window, or at their wristwatch, or the cabin ceiling, anything to avoid her eyes.

All brute and not guts. From her backpack, she retrieved a SPAN cell phone repeater she had packed. Days ago, she had built a waterproof housing for it and welded a small solar panel to the top. After checking the power dongle, she turned on the phone and searched for a signal. At this height, dozens of other phones came alive on Aiva's SPAN network. She stuffed her home-brewed radio relay back into her backpack and hoisted the bag over her shoulders. "Brett, I'm going down. Try not to kill me. Jones, help me with the personnel hoist."

Jones pursed his lips and gave a curt nod before strapping her in. His hand squeezed her shoulder to assuage her fear, before he guided her out the side door. She swung free from the cabin, twisting on the hoist cable just below the helicopter's belly.

"Holy crap!" The height sent her heart racing. She fought to control her growing panic, but the rotor downwash blasted her face and shoulders and terrified her. Suspended in midair, high above the forest canopy, her acrophobia kicked into overdrive and her body became rigid. "Jesus Christ," she cried out, "what did I get myself into?"

The harness pulled taut. She tilted her head back to check on the helicopter thirty feet above her. It surged and dragged her sideways toward the upright wind tower blade. The whip of the hoist cable dropped her stomach to her knees. "No, no, no, no," she said under her breath as the sharp white blade careened toward her. "Brett!" The wind tore his name from her throat. The blade was taller than a four-story building and closed in on her fast. The line jerked and whiplashed her head. A loud ping resounded along the cable. She looked up just in time to take the hit on her shoulder. Pain jolted through her body as she tried to force breath back into her lungs. The line snapped her back again before she caught her breath. Swung free, she tilted her head back to get a view of the helicopter. The cable jerked again, pulling her back toward the blade's base like a pendulum. "Oh god!"

She timed her approach and landed on all fours atop the nacelle. A quick release of the hoist cable and she was free. The helicopter peeled away and hovered nearby. She opened the access hatch and climbed inside the dark compartment, a welcome sanctuary from the hell she went through to get down here. Using the same technique, she developed before the storm, she waited for the gearbox cog to unload, then threw her weight against the latch handle. With a loud clunk, the brake assembly released the rotor. She climbed topside and rested. The three long blades carved arcs skyward, their sweeping motion filling the air with a low wind noise. On the flat surface atop the nacelle, she affixed her SPAN cell repeater with self-adhering Velcro tape. The display came alive and Aiva acknowledged the signal with a text: *Welcome aboard cell unit 137.* A network map on her tablet grew twofold and her joy masked the pain in her shoulders.

The trip back up to the helicopter wasn't as horrific as going down. Brett must've seen his mistake and didn't send her into bungee madness again. She climbed into the crew cabin, slid out of her harness, and gave the wind techs a shaka sign. Their wide eyes threw her into a fit of laughter. Although she had come close to death in the sling, her crazy trapeze stunt had worked. If she could do it, they sure as hell better try.

With a weak grin, Tanaka gave her a thumbs-up. "Great idea, Hellen. It'll save us time climbing the two-hundred-foot ladder inside the tower. Let me call my crew on Tower Three and let them know what we're doing."

Jones patched Tanaka's walkie-talkie into the radio panel, allowing him to speak through his headset and transmit the plan to his men. After a few calls, Tanaka nodded. They were ready.

Brett hovered about one-hundred feet above the next tower's catwalk, just clear of the long rotor blades. Hellen's chest shuddered as she replayed the scene in her mind. Seeing Brett deftly control this immense machine so close to the tower thrilled her. Once in position, Brett let go of the controls, making her jerk back with a start.

"Jesus, who's flying this thing?" she screamed, wondering if he had flown hands-free while she had dangled above certain death.

"Relax. I've put it in auto-hover mode and switched aircraft flight control to the hoist station." He pointed behind them. "Jones will use a small joystick to fine tune the helo's position over the drop zone. That way, these mokes won't have as much fun as you did. Sorry about all the excitement on your joyride, but we couldn't get it to operate when you were on the hoist."

She wasn't sure if she wanted to laugh or smack him, but the rest of the drops went with no incident. With her drop and lift idea, they unlocked and prepped all the turbines in only two hours, allowing them to head back for a late lunch. As they flew in a wide arc and passed over the entire wind farm, Hellen admired their handiwork, each turbine turning its blades out of synch with the others, like pinwheels dancing in the breeze. She recalled how 'Ehulani constructed a windmill for her tribe. Another prophesy in Elle's *Wayfinders* had come true.

They returned to the harbor within ten minutes, and Brett swooped into a landing on the pier. Hellen found a crew of Paniolo cowboys waiting next to a black barbecue pit. She introduced herself and helped them grill the steaks, fanning the smoke from her stinging eyes. The wind techs looked hungry, so she wasted no time. With everyone served, she sat beside Brett to enjoy her dinner.

"God, this is delicious. I've not had a steak in ages." Brett licked his fingers and wiggled his eyebrows, sending her into helpless laughter. She loved everything about this man, even his sloppy table manners.

Tanaka rose from his seat and raised his water bottle in a toast. "Hellen, you really earned your pay today. Your suggestion of air-hoisting the men to the towers got the job done in a quarter of the time."

Blood flushed Hellen's cheeks. The world had changed since that rainy day she met his killer corgi. Now able to leap tall wind towers in a single sling, she was one of them. Brett bent over and kissed the back of her neck, making her giddy again, releasing the flood of tension built up over the day's operation. He was a fresh breeze, breathing life into her exhausted body.

"I'm loving this," he said. His mirthful eyes shined as if he held a secret. "Ah, the things I do for king and county."

"Yes, indeed. 'Ohana nui." She nibbled his earlobe, making him jump. "Here, take this." She retrieved a SPAN-enabled cell phone from her backpack. "Charlie built an app to let our phones text to one another without cell towers."

Brett's eyes lit up. "For real?"

"Just remember, no more hiding. I expect to hear from you every day."

He raised his eyebrows with a who-me-expression planted

on his face and turned on his phone, his fingers flying over the keypad. A text alert chimed on her phone and the glowing screen displayed his message. *God made man and then rested. God made women and then no one rested.* She tussled his hair. "You're learning. Just stay on your toes and try to keep up with me."

"How's Charlie doing these days, still with Donovan?"

"Having the time of his life working as a medical volunteer." In her mind's eye, her son sauntered along the hospital's corridors in blue scrubs, helping patients and getting an education. Like an aspen grove whose many trees spring from one sprout, Charlie learned the trade from his uncle, launching his dream of becoming an EMT.

"Sound's great," he said. "It'll be good for him. You know, I really missed you guys. I can't wait to get our lives back."

"I'm so glad you said that. I was afraid—"

"I forgot about you? God, I think of you and the kids all the time. Remember those days aboard *Ohana*, sharing stories and laughs, sailing under an endless blue sky?"

His words made her heart sing. She moved in, touching his nose with hers, exchanging a honi kiss, breathing in the moment with closed eyes.

"Aloha nui loa," Brett whispered.

"I love you too," she said, leaning her forehead against his.

The setting sun peeked under a low bank of scudding clouds, emblazoning his face with a golden hue.

"So, you must've met Elizabeth. How'd it go?"

"Not as I had hoped. She needs time. I'm sure she'll come around."

"I feel bad about not introducing you. Staying on the boat may have been overreacting. But you're right. She'll come around and accept you." *Time will close the distance.* She was never closer to Elizabeth than the night Lester blasted through the islands. Intense fear had changed Elizabeth, softened her anger, and restored some of her trust. She only hoped the truce would last.

"Ey, you got plans tonight?" he asked with nonchalance.

"No. I'm all done here," she said. "And Charlie's with Donovan, so I'm a free woman."

"Can I talk you into cloud dancing with me?"

"You mean taking me up in that whirligig again?"

He cringed. "Come on, knock it off. She's a fine machine. Brand new."

She took off his ball cap and slapped his chest with it. "You want us to join the 'mile-high club,' don't you? I remember Elle telling me all about that form of aerial intercourse."

He smacked his forehead with his palm. "Jeez, let up on the throttle, will ya? Besides, I fly with both hands on the stick and both feet on the pedals. You're safe from me on this junket."

She pulled Brett's elbow. "Okay, you smooth talker. Take me into the clouds."

Hellen sat in the helicopter's front left seat, waiting for Brett and Jones to finish checking the machine over before they took off. Dark, gray clouds rolled in from the sea, engulfing the hillside east of the harbor. A light rain fell on the windshield, making little tapping sounds. Brett climbed into the pilot's seat and strapped in. He deftly engaged the jet engines and the rotors spun up into a whirling blur, slicing through the air with a high-pitched whine. She marveled at Brett's ease in handling this vibrating eggbeater. How Brett flew blind in this soup was beyond her, but she trusted him all the same.

"It's a fine Navy day," he announced over the intercom. "We'll climb above this goo in no time."

"Roger that," Jones replied from the cargo bay. "Side door closed and secure, Skipper."

She glanced out the bulbous windshield as the ground slipped away. Once clear of the pier, Brett banked the helo and flew seaward. They flew into the low clouds and her world came unhinged. Her body told her she tumbled sideways, but her eyes had no reference to the horizon. She flailed her arms about in search of a handhold. She grabbed the control stick, causing the helicopter to lurch backward. The stick snapped back and forth in her hand until she released it.

"Hellen, stay off the controls. I've got the aircraft. We'll be topside in a second. Fold your arms, close your eyes, and just sit there."

"What's going on, Skipper?" Jones shouted from the rear. His hand squeezed her shoulders with a reassuring grip. Breathless, she reached around and clasped his hand. The vertigo overpowered her, much worse than her seasickness on *Ohana*. Her skin tingled, and nausea gripped her with fear.

Jones handed her a sick bag. She couldn't hide anything from this old salt. Within seconds, they popped out of the clouds. She opened her eyes to a brilliant blue sky. The sharp horizon gave her a visual reference and reduced the vertigo. Her stomach settled after many deep breaths and she patted Jones' hand, signaling to him she felt better. The sight gripped her soul. She recalled the scene in Elle's book where 'Ehulani rode with Aukai on the back of a giant hawk. They flew with amazing speed just over the cloud tops. The sky's blue dome fell upon a wispy, jagged blanket of clouds rushing below her. A magic carpet ride. *My god, how will I ever describe this to Charlie?*

"Brett, this is incredible. I now see why you love flying so much."

Bulbous cloud tops rushed by twenty feet below them, lit by the orange sunset, casting long shadows to the east. "Welcome to my office," he said. "Like the view?"

They climbed over Mauna Kea's slope. Over the radio, Brett called to someone named "Bradshaw Approach" and they jabbered in aviation speak, a language reduced to terse phrases of only nouns and verbs.

Their brief ride ended at the south end of the base and Brett landed on a yellow "H" painted on the concrete pad in front of a set of wide hangar doors. Jones tidied up the passenger cabin while Brett went through his checklist to shut off the engines, a series of pushing dozens of switches and buttons.

The jet engines wound down, and the rotors drifted to a stop. Brett jumped out of the helicopter and placed a pair of wooden blocks under the wheels. Typical of the British; they spent millions on a helicopter missing a parking brake. Jones came forward to the cockpit and squeezed her shoulder. "Brett's been driven hard over the past week. You two go have some fun tonight." He turned and stuck his head outside the cabin door. "Commander, I got the aircraft. Now get the hell out of here, sir."

Brett drove her to his barracks in a gray SandRat. More dune buggy than SUV, the military vehicle sat two in a chassis that ran hard over the road. He pulled up to his bunk house and invited her inside. She entered the dingy shack, a small and sparsely furnished relic of the Sino-Japanese War. No critters yet; a good sign. Brett lit a kerosene lamp and the room filled with a golden glow. Her shoulders dropped. Bare functional utility drove the inspiration for its design, comprising a single room with a folding table and a twin-sized bed. A dull aluminum door led to a small bathroom. In the corner stood an old iron Franklin stove, the type she hadn't seen since her childhood.

"You cook on that pot-bellied beast? Where's the kitchen?"

"We eat in the mess hall at the other end of the base. Don't worry, I'll grab some chow and bring it back here for us. In the meantime, enjoy a warm shower, compliments of the RAF."

"Aye, aye." Hellen waved an informal salute, but wasn't too excited about eating "chow," which sounded more like pet food. She ambled into the tiny bathroom and groaned at the RAF's sense of interior design. A small oval mirror hung over a stainless-steel sink. With no place to sit nor a cabinet to store toiletries, the bathroom's layout must have been designed by a man.

The hot shower, the first in many weeks, washed her qualms away. After drying herself, she smiled at her reflection in the

mirror, a younger version of herself. Food rations had an unintended benefit, she hadn't been this thin since her college days.
She washed her grimy jumpsuit in the sink and hung it over the
shower curtain rod to dry. The sound of Brett's SandRat
returned, and the front door opened. She looked around and
slumped her shoulders. *Great, didn't think this through.*

With no clothes to wear, she tapped her lips with her index
finger and looked around. The towel wrapped around her chest
was still damp and too short to cover her hips. Brett's flight
jacket hung on the hook behind the door. She put it on; the cool
leather rubbed her skin; its colorful squadron patches adorned
her chest and arms. Pressing her nose into its black seal fur
collar, she breathed in Brett's essence. The open leather flight
jacket tickled her skin and sent goose bumps over her arms and
hips. She fixed her hair in the mirror. With no hair dryer, she tied
it back with a Gibson knot, surprised how easy it was with wet
hair. Why hadn't she thought of that before? In the mirror, she
pinched her cheeks and rubbed her lips with a damp facecloth to
give them a natural crimson flush, "cho-cho lips," as Brett had
called them. Maybe someday she'd write a beauty guide, a
collection of hacks she learned during the blackout. *Lights out,
game on.*

She opened the door and found Brett sitting by the wood
stove, working the flames with his back to her. She tiptoed to
him and tapped him on his shoulder. "What do those red
pennants on your whirligig read? 'Remove Before Flight.'"

He spun around and almost fell into the fire at the sight of
her. She gave herself up to laughter and fell on top of him. Her
first ride in front of a fire was a wild one. The force of it
surprised her. Their passion had a renewed desperation to it,
rivaling their first days in Lahaina two decades ago. Or was it
always there, lying dormant, waiting for a spark to renew it? His
desire radiated off him like heat from a fire. It was glorious to see
she still aroused him, after what had happened the last time with
him on the boat, the night she drank herself silly and lost control.

To her infinite pleasure, Brett wasn't a one-and-done sort, but lingered, like a burning amber set aflame again by the wind. His breathing changed, growing louder, and his heart pounded under her cheek. She felt her chest snag, her face flush with heat, and her body quiver. For hours they returned to each other, over and over, one flesh, one body.

Afterward, they lay together by the fire. Brett's fingers ran through her long hair and sent warm shivers along her spine. Hellen never had felt this sort of abandoned, fevered passion until Brett came back into her life. She could hardly breathe, the connection between them was so intense. Copernicus was wrong; their own Earth, their 'ohana, and Brett's hand were the center of the universe. Her mind telescoped to their future together, filled with evenings like this one.

"So, have you forgiven me?" she asked him, sure of his answer but unsure of her impunity.

He took a deep breath and raised his eyebrows as if working through a deep existential question. Just an answer, that's all she wanted. Yes or no. Please.

"Do you forgive yourself?"

"For years, I tried to justify hiding her from you. But no excuse can ever make up for your lost time from her."

"Tell me more about her. I want to know everything."

Hellen leaned her head and sorted through a lifetime of memories. "She's brilliant, top of her class, has my fascination with science and your Polynesian grace, as if she cherry-picked our best traits. She finished high school a year early and entered the University of Hawai'i last year, majoring in physics."

Brett smiled and rubbed his hand along her arm. "And friends?"

"She keeps to herself, another trait she shares with you. She's a true Akamu. In fact, that's why I gave her your surname."

"What, why not Callahan?"

She fiddled with the red, braided bracelet around her wrist, reliving the morning Elle had given it to her, the day Elizabeth came into this world. Elle had said a couple tied together by a red thread were destined lovers, regardless of place, time, or circumstances. The link may stretch or tangle, but never breaks.

"After she was born, I wanted a way to honor you. And hide my identity."

His eyes glistened. "You'll not hide anymore. Together, we'll atone for our past and build a better future."

His words swept away her last smoldering feelings of self-doubt. Brett was her future, a future waiting in the shadows all these years, a future foretold by Elle. Hellen's fingers twisted the necklace holding her father's Claddagh wedding ring. Since the day Elle had given it to her, she had always worn it around her neck, a reminder of the man she never knew, the man who loved and protected her. She removed the ring and slid it onto Brett's ring finger.

"It's a perfect fit," she said with amazement.

"Always was. We should have married years ago."

Nose to nose, they exchanged a honi kiss, shared their aloha for each other, and sealed their *Noi Male*, their vows.

22

Hellen awoke the next morning and found Brett sitting at her bedside with a tray holding English muffins, scrambled eggs, cut mangoes, and a cup of tea.

"Sweet," Hellen said in a sleepy voice. She stretched her arms above her and let them drop over his shoulders. "This is the first time a man has brought me breakfast in bed."

He raised an eyebrow.

"No. Really. I'm an honest, breakfast-in-bed virgin. Bonus points for you, pal."

Brett's bloodshot eyes and greasy hair made her wonder how she appeared. "Didn't get much sleep?" she asked, worried he had reservations about last night.

"Yeah, you could say that. I've been thinking…"

Her eyes broke contact with him; she hated when guys started their sentences that way. He opened his mouth as if to say something but looked away. Seconds passed.

"First, I forgive you for everything in the past," he said at last. "Please don't carry the weight of guilt anymore."

"Thank you." She closed her eyes and pulled him in with her trembling hands laced behind his neck. "I'm worried about the kids," she whispered. "Believe me, I've seen and heard what's going on around us. These are crazy, dangerous times."

"Me too. I've seen the widespread violence building on the island. No place is safe, not even Cloudcroft."

"I know. The creepozoid who attacked me in the hospital is still loose. If he hurt Charlie or Elizabeth, I'll never forgive myself."

"Maybe you and the kids can move to the base. The other military families have relocated."

"But we're not a family yet."

"Yes, we are. Besides, they'll not likely ask for marriage certificates." He gave her a wry smile. "Rogers already thinks you're my wife, remember?"

Hellen recalled the day she had dropped Brett off at Bradshaw and closed her eyes. Despite their vows to each other last night, her dream of an 'ohana with Brett seemed out of reach. So many questions. How would Charlie react? He had grown attached to Brett but becoming Brett's stepson was a much different proposition. And Elizabeth would likely escape to the independence of college dorm life. And where would they live? Cloudcroft was only a temporary arrangement, exposed, and not permanent.

"Okay. Look into it," she said with no conviction. "Sounds like we're safer at the base than in Kamuela." Living at Bradshaw might be safe, but it wasn't the future she wanted for her children. And when would they ever settle down? She clasped her hands together. Rebuilding after Helio Hattie had become a long string of challenges, each with its own flavor of obstacles.

"You don't sound convinced. What's wrong?"

"I don't know. There's too much swirling though my head. The kids' safety. Our future. I can't even think about marriage now. At least not until we restore the power grid. Once we have power back, a lot of problems go away. The port reopens, allowing food, fuel, and medical supplies to come in. People's lives can return to normal, relieving the constant stress from the blackout."

"Let me keep an eye on the kids. You need to focus on getting the wind farm back."

Her muscles relaxed, and she smiled at him. He meant well, and she wanted to believe him but wondered how he'd find the time.

"Charlie's with Donovan for now. But Elizabeth…" Her voice faltered. "Make sure she's safe."

"Trust me." He kissed her before heading to the shower.

Hellen dressed in her blue ConHEL jumpsuit, now dry. She requisitioned Brett's leather flight jacket again to fight the morning chill. Brett threw on his olive drab flight suit and left the cabin. By the time she gathered her things and stepped outside, Brett stood beside a classic motorbike, a backpack slung over his shoulder.

"A Triumph TR6 Trophy?" Hellen asked. "Nice ride." Kalino had owned the same bike years ago. Its sturdy and traditional design strayed from the more popular "crotch rockets." Its handlebars rose higher, providing an upright, confident, and relaxed tandem seating.

Brett nodded at the bike. "I traded one of *Ohana*'s spare VHF radios for it, and it has become somewhat of a project during my down times between missions."

"So why haven't you come to visit me in all these weeks?"

He shifted his eyes from her. "After overhauling the second cylinder and replacing the fuel pump, I finally had it running just a couple of days ago. It's a real fuel miser, sipping only one gallon for every fifty miles, great economy for the apocalypse."

She smirked at his lame gallows humor. Without asking, she straddled the bike and stomped on the starter. The loud throaty engine and vibrating seat stirred her. "Hop on," she shouted over her shoulder. "Just point the way."

Brett chuckled and slid on behind her. She took his hands and wrapped them around her lower ribs and took off. The wind blew her long hair, streaming it into Brett's face. After passing through the harbor's main gate, she revved the RPMs and headed down Saddleback Road along the southern slope of Mauna Kea. They reached the harbor in half an hour, arriving before any of the wind techs. As they rode along the dock, she pointed to the submarine. Its sleek black hull floated with only a small portion above the surface, giving it the shape of an ominous Orca whale.

She parked the bike on the pier next to the sub. A steel gangway led to the boat, whose tall dorsal fin held a temporary canvas banner that read: "HMS *Endeavour*." Before stepping onto the gangway, Brett positioned his khaki garrison cap on his head, adjusting it to a precise angle, making her laugh. *He's a tinker-tailor sailor alright.* He led her onto the sub's fantail and turned to salute the Union Jack waving in the breeze. Hellen mimicked his actions.

"Just stand there," he whispered to her. "Civilians don't salute." She smirked at him and played along. He next saluted a naval officer standing at the end of the gangway. Brett pulled out his military ID card and requested to come aboard. The duty officer spoke into a portable telephone rigged inside a small canvas tent set up on the sub's spine. A submariner in a navy-blue jumpsuit came topside a few minutes later.

"Commander Akamu," the man said, saluting Brett. "I'm Master Chief Holloway, the Chief of the Boat. I understand you want to come aboard. Can you tell me what business you have with the *Endeavour* today?"

"COB, I'm the helo pilot who flew the support mission down here yesterday." Brett placed his hand on Hellen's shoulder. "And this is Dr. Callahan, who supervised the plant readiness and requested the service of your nuclear tea kettle. We came early, hoping to look around your sub before we head up to the operations center."

"I see. Well, it's a pleasure to meet you folks. This is an interesting mission you cooked up for us, Dr. Callahan. I'm sorry, but we aren't rigged for visitors."

"Actually, I'm not interested in a tour," Hellen interjected. "I just want to speak to your chief engineer if that's possible, sir."

The man winced at her. She'd never understand the strange habits of these Navy boys.

"Ma'am, please don't call me sir. I work for a living."

Now it was her turn to wince. "And don't call me ma'am, I'm too young for that."

"I'll see what I can do about scaring up the ChEng. Standby."

He returned within ten minutes with a younger man dressed in a frumpy khaki uniform, looking like he hadn't slept in days.

"I'm Commander Wilson, the chief engineer. What can I do for you, ma'am?"

"I wrote the operating procedure for the startup, and I just want to put a name with a face."

"I've got about twenty minutes, but I'll answer any questions you may have."

"First, let's start with the power sharing. How should we balance the electric load with you guys?"

Wilson went on at length on how he wanted to share the AC load from their ship service turbine generators with the shore power demand. Brett wandered off and chatted with the duty officer. The sky opened, and the rain sent a chill down Hellen's spine.

"Dr. Callahan, let's get below and wait out the weather," Wilson said.

Chief Holloway lifted an eyebrow at him and shook his head.

"COB, I got this." Wilson motioned Hellen to follow him aft along the catwalk to a three-foot-wide, stainless-steel hatch. "Watch your step. This ladder leads to the aux-machinery compartment, and it's coated with an oily film." She followed him down the ladder to a dim compartment.

"What's that smell?" She wrinkled her nose at a putrid odor of ammonia mixed with diesel fuel-oil.

"What smell?" He took a deep breath. "Oh, that. It's amine reeking from the CO-2 scrubbers. You get used it after a while. Every time I return home from the boat, my wife dumps my sea bag into the washing machine and insists I take a long hot shower before she allows me in bed."

"I can't say I blame her." Thank god Brett flew above the water, not beneath it.

Wilson led her to a thick oval door labeled REACTOR TUNNEL. Yellow-green light from overhead lamps bathed the tunnel's clean white passageway, and the sound of pumps and ventilation blowers filled the air.

"I'm sorry you can't go beyond this point, ma'am, but I thought you might be interested in the nuclear reactor; it's directly below this tunnel. Only nuclear qualified crewmembers can pass through this watertight door. The Rolls-Royce pressurized water reactor is rated for twenty megawatts. The core uses ninety percent enriched uranium and never needs refueling during the boat's expected lifetime."

"That's incredible. It has a much higher energy density than commercial plants. The designs I studied at NCEL had only between two to four percent enrichment."

"Not all of that power is available for generating electricity. About half of plant horsepower drives the screw for propulsion."

Hellen bit her lower lip and went through some mental math. "Still, that means you can power about six thousand homes."

"But we have only two shore power cables, each rated for about five hundred amps. This limits our reverse shore power capacity."

"Our needs are modest," she said. "We only need two megawatts to energize the generator stator windings in each of the wind turbines."

Wilson put a stick of gum in his mouth. "This procedure is

new to us. Shore power is straightforward, but this black startup may not work. I'm concerned we may overload the cables. Honestly, I think we're wasting our time. If it were my decision, I'd never stop in this backwater port in the first place. Hilo is our prime mission."

Hellen wondered if the ChEng had enough gumption to make this work. Her experience with the Brits on other projects had soured her. Her engineering professor at Trinity College had said, "The *Titanic* was built by an Irishman and sunk by an Englishman." If the sub's power supply was slightly out of phase with the wind farm grid, heavy cross-currents would build up, inducing voltage fluctuations and damaging the wind turbines and sub's generator. She took out her phone. "Let's use these to balance electrical loads and synchronize the AC phases."

He looked at her phone with skeptical eyes. "Ship-to-shore radio is more reliable. I'll send one of my engineering officers to accompany you to the plant's control room for the black startup. He'll coordinate things with my reactor operator over our VHF."

"Hellen, come on. We have to go." Brett's voice echoed down from the topside hatch.

"Sorry, that's my ride," she said, winking at Wilson. "Let's hope all goes smoothly."

She gave Brett a quick wave before climbing through the hatch. At the top of the steel ladder, Brett took hold of her arm and helped her topside. The rain had stopped. Patches of blue peeked through breaks in the clouds.

"Did you have a nice tour?" he asked.

"I wasn't sightseeing. I wanted to iron out a few last details with the ChEng before we tried the black start procedure."

Halfway to the pier gangway, a flash of light caught her attention, followed by echoing gunfire. Sparks flew from the submarine's metal hull a few feet behind her. She screamed and Brett grabbed her arm, pulling her forward to the sub's dorsal fin and telling her to take cover behind the sail.

A klaxon blared, filling the harbor with a chilling noise. "All hands, repel boarders, repel boarders. This is the XO speaking. The harbor is under attack. master-at-arms, man the small-arms locker. Set condition YOKE throughout the ship."

Brett pushed Hellen behind the black-metal superstructure, his eyes wild. "Stay right here. The submarine hull will protect you." He left before she registered what his words meant.

Gunshots echoed around the pier. Two Royal Marines with rifles knelt atop a forty-foot-tall fuel tank. They wore combat fatigues and fired scope-mounted assault rifles at an oncoming SUV as it roared down the ramp from the main road. Its driver wore only camo shorts and a baseball cap turned sideways. Behind him stood a huge Samoan in a red bandanna do-rag, clutching a grenade launcher. The SUV sideswiped Manu's golf cart, sending it off the pier and into the water.

"Stay down. Stay down," someone yelled on the sub. "He's got an RPG."

Smoke flared behind the launcher. The missile raced toward Hellen. She ducked behind the submarine superstructure an eyeblink before the rocket hit. The explosion shook the sub in a deafening roar. She covered her ringing ears but lost her balance and stepped backward, skidding sideways on the deck's oily surface. Her feet slipped out from under her, and she slid down along the curved hull and into the water. A cold blankness enveloped her. Bullets pierced the water, sending trails of bubbles around her.

Gus Conroy held a pair of binoculars to his eyes and examined the submarine docked at the pier. From the spine of the submarine hull, a woman in a jumpsuit lost her balance and slid overboard, the same redheaded scalawag he had run into at the hospital weeks ago. Damn, she seemed to be everywhere. He radioed his men to take her out. He'd had enough of this gal and

looked forward to seeing her tits up and six feet under. His cele-
bratory fantasy died when the marine snipers took out the driver
of the SUV, sending it into a pier-side shack. Hand grenades
detonated, sending a plume of orange and black smoke into the
sky. His remaining crew stood exposed on the pier and fired slip-
shod at the sub, their shots ricocheting off the hull like BB
pellets. A Royal Marine marksman in the submarine's superstructure picked off his assault team, one at a time, as if he were
skeet shooting. Gus grimaced and threw his cigar to the ground.

The whole operation was almost comical. He had underesti-
mated the naval security force, losing all five men on his attack
team. It was a case of piss-poor planning spawned from
improper recon. He had no one to blame but himself, and he had
a lot to learn.

He stomped out his smoldering cigar and walked back to his
Vagabond, where Plan B, a Filipino wind tech, sat waiting for
him. The scrawny batu addict owed Gus a month's salary, but
his debt would be paid in full today. Plan B was Gus's last
chance to take out his competition.

They drove along a rugged dirt road and parked under a
monkeypod tree, a hundred yards from the closest wind tower.
Its long, white, slender blades filled the sky. A signpost read
"Kohala Wind Farm—Tower Three. Restricted Area. NO UNAU-
THORIZED PERSONNEL BEYOND THIS POINT."

"How's this going to work?" he asked Plan B.

"I disabled the over-speed regulator. If they try to start the
turbine, the rotor blades will speed out of control, setting the
generator on fire, then kablooey!"

"What about the other towers?" Gus asked, his temper flaring. Crap on a cracker, couldn't this guy count?

"With all of Tanaka's men crawling about, I only got to this
tower. But we're good. They'll start each tower one at a time,
sending feed current to the next. We blow Tower Three; and the
other thirteen downstream are broke dick."

"It better work. It's our last chance."

"Hey, look. What else could I've done?"

With the sabotage set, Gus had no more use for him. He pointed to the wind tower, drawing Plan B's attention away. With a calm fluid motion, he snatched his Smith & Wesson pistol of his jacket and fired a single shot into the man's temple.

"You could've disappeared, you idiot."

Hellen sat in an officer's quarters stateroom, shivering under a blanket. Her wet clothes hung in an adjacent shower stall. Her bandaged arm burned with a searing pain, yet she remembered no one treating her. She removed the blanket and ran her fingers along the bruises and cuts. Her ride down the hull's surface had been much worse than the plunge into the cold water. The hull's black non-skid had torn her jumpsuit and scraped her skin all along her left side. The incident was the third time in as many weeks she had risked her life. Providence's wicked bitch sent her spiraling down into anxiety again. She had everything to live for: Brett, her children, restoring power to her 'ohana, yet she came so close to losing it all. She straightened her back and breathed in the gathering gloom. A soft knock on the door gave her a start, igniting a pounding throb in her head.

"Hellen, it's me." Brett's voice came from behind the door. "I've got some clothes for you."

She wrapped a towel around her chest and midriff and opened the narrow stateroom door. Brett flinched at her bruised legs and pulled her into his arms.

"I'm glad you stayed behind the superstructure," he said. "Otherwise, you wouldn't be standing here right now. You had me worried. After you fell into the water, I feared I lost you."

"Then why didn't you jump in to save me, you chicken-heart?" She hid her smile and took a navy-blue jumpsuit from him, holding it up in front of her. The left breast pocket had embroidered gold dolphins and the upper right arm a ship's patch: HMS *Endeavour*. Another shoulder patch read "Silent Service." She raised her eyebrows at Brett, wondering to whom the suit belonged.

"Compliments of the ship's captain. He's the only crewmember close to your size."

She pushed him out of the stateroom and shut the door. The jumpsuit stretched over her sore legs, much too long for her small frame, but by cuffing the pant legs she made it work. After she combed out her hair and twisted it into a bun, a bumper sticker atop the mirror caught her eye. *Submariners do it deeper.* She rolled her eyes at the Navy's raunchy bravado.

"Is the captain back aboard? I'd like to meet him."

"Later. Tanaka is waiting for you at the wind farm control room."

"But the attack?"

"The submarine sustained no damage, and the crew had no serious injuries. Look, we really need to head up the hill now."

Hellen limped behind Brett through the rabbit maze of passageways. Each step up the ladder leading topside made her wince from the burning pain in her side. After they crossed the gangway to the pier, Brett mounted his Triumph and Hellen climbed on behind him. The sun lay near the ocean's horizon and the air cooled. They rolled down along Queen K Highway for about three miles before Brett turned onto a gravel lane leading to the wind farm on Mauna Kea's western slope. The control center sat near the base of Wind Tower One. Its white blades loomed over her, sweeping out great arcs, making an audible swoosh as they cut through the air.

She took Brett's hand and walked into the control room, a busy hub of activity for the startup. Tanaka's corgi trotted over to her and gave a sharp bark.

Tanaka squeezed through the crowd and came over to them. "Hellen, we're about to start the first turbine. I want you next to me—just in case, you know. You're the brainchild of this procedure."

The closest towers spread out beyond a wide viewing window, standing like sentinels above the magnificent desolation of the barren lava field. Farther up the hill, the towers merged with the forest. Three branches swayed in the strong wind.

Tanaka pointed to a man in a khaki uniform standing in front of a control panel, speaking into his headset's boom mike. "He's a nuke engineering officer from the *Endeavour*, here to coordinate our power demand with the sub's reactor."

The naval officer gave a thumbs-up and removed the headset from one ear. "Mr. Tanaka, the *Endeavour* is ready for the first turbine's electrical load."

Tanaka examined the power plant's status panel and spoke into his radio. "Okay, Larry. We're ready. I'm energizing the stator field windings now."

Hellen waved Brett over to her. "After they get the first turbine going," she whispered to him, "they'll use its output voltage to start the next one in line and so forth until all the turbines are running."

"Okay everybody, we're starting Turbine Number Sixteen," Tanaka announced to the control room.

"Why not start here at the control center?" Brett asked Hellen. "Seems backwards."

"We had to rig temporary power lines to the array, and Tower Sixteen is nearest to the harbor."

Tanaka walked over to the expansive picture window overlooking the towers and called into his radio mike, "Tower Sixteen, power up the pitch actuator."

A voice came from the control room speaker. "Engaging turbine acceleration by pitch control. DC-link pre-charge complete."

"Roger," Tanaka said. "Ramp up the blade pitch position and wait until the rotor speed exceeds twenty-four RPM."

Hellen leaned over to Brett's ear. "They're using the submarine's power to change the pitch angle of the three blades, taking more energy from the wind."

"It's like taking off in a helo," Brett said, "twisting the rotor blades to create lift."

She led him to the observation window and handed him a pair of binoculars. The blades of the wind tower closest to the harbor spun slower than the others.

"DC-Link voltage adjusted," the overhead speaker announced. "Rotor current initialized and stator synchronization is complete. Induced stator voltage matches grid voltage."

"Roger, Larry," Tanaka said. "I'm closing the generator contactors now." He walked over to one of the control room engineers. "Engage the closed loop pitch control and ramp the power demand up to rated level."

The panel operator adjusted a black rheostat knob. "We're taking an electrical load now. We're back in business!" Everyone in the control room cheered. Hellen jumped and gave Brett a long hug.

"You did it," he said into her ear over the loud whooping and yelling. "This really worked!"

"We got ourselves power!" Hellen released Brett and smiled over her shoulder to Tanaka.

"And to think I once aimed my shotgun at you." His eyes twinkled at her.

"No worries. We did this together."

The control room engineers started the other downstream wind towers in the same manner. The process became more routine with each turbine, and most observers left within an hour. Brett leaned against the wall, his arms folded across his chest. This must have bored him, the tedious repetition of starting the turbines, one after another. She leaned into him and clutched his arm. "You can take off if you want. Didn't you say you had a mission tonight? Go get some sleep. I'll catch a ride home with Tanaka."

"No, I'd rather stay," he said. "This is an important day for you."

"Thanks, love." She took his hand. "And I want you here."

During the languid days aboard *Ohana* before the blackout, she had imagined how their life together could survive their different careers, fearing they would drift apart again. She placed her hand on her heart and dreamed of her family sailing together off the Kona Coast. With Elizabeth no longer her secret, there was no turning back.

"Starting Tower Three," Tanaka announced. "We're almost done."

She gave Brett's hand a quick squeeze and felt the Claddagh ring around his finger, but he didn't acknowledge her. He leaned away from her and pressed his face against the window. She playfully tugged his hand again and rested her chin on his shoulder.

"There it is again," he said. "There's smoke coming from that tower—it's on fire."

Hellen braced and stared gobsmacked through the window. Jesus-Mary-Joseph. Black smoke vented from the whirling rotor atop the tower. "Tanaka, Tower Three is on fire," she screamed across the control room.

The wind blew the smoke downwind from the huge spinning rotors, shaping it into a weird corkscrew that trailed hundreds of yards from the tower.

"Kalei, get out of there now!" Tanaka called into his boom mike. "Run upwind of the tower as fast as you can."

Hellen snatched binoculars and peered through them. A small figure ran out of the tower base and up the hill. The rotor blades accelerated, spinning into a blurry disk, its slipstream loud enough to hear inside the control room.

"The rotor speed governor must have failed," she shouted to Tanaka. "Take it offline now."

The whirling blades gyrated, at first with a harmonic motion, then breaking into chaos. One of the three huge blades broke free from its hub, cartwheeling hundreds of yards into the sky in a sickening dance, until it crashed into the ground only twenty yards from the control room, shaking the Earth. The other two blades, now unbalanced without the third, flew from the nacelle and sliced the tower in two, dragging the entire assembly into the ground. One rotor ricocheted off the ground and flew into the next tower, taking it down. As the tower collapsed, its blades shattered against the hard lava field, splintering in missile-like shards, flying into adjacent towers, shredding their blades one by one, until at last, only ten of the sixteen towers stood intact in the debris field.

A voice yelled through the radio speaker. "Control, this is Tower Three. I'm clear of the area, but I almost shit my pants. That was a hell of a sight!"

"Isolate Towers Three through Eight from the rest of the grid." Tanaka glanced to Hellen. "We better defer the startup of Towers One and Two until we can make a full inspection."

"For real," Brett said under his breath.

Minutes later, silence descended in the control room. The wreckage outside reminded Hellen how fate played games with her carefully laid plans. Her heart still raced well after the last tower collapsed. She struggled to breathe. The adrenaline rush fogged her mind. She needed to escape the claustrophobic atmosphere. Saying nothing to Brett, she ran out of the control room.

A strong wind flowed down from Mauna Kea, carrying the menacing smoke cloud out to sea. She took several deep breaths and focused on the debris from the wrecked towers. Mauna Kea's peak stood alone in the twilight. The wreckage left Hellen listless, her stomach cramped, as if she had walked a tightrope and a gust of wind sent her plunging. *Will this ever end?*

Brett joined her in the darkness, his arms wrapped around her waist, keeping her from falling off the tightrope. He brought his face close to hers, but she couldn't muster the enthusiasm to bridge the tiny distance between their lips.

Without warning, the red beacons atop the remaining towers came alive, blinking on and off in the night like Christmas lights. The transformer substation hummed behind her. Power returned to parts of Kohala. Her heart soared at the sight of the lights on Mauna Kea. But within minutes, they extinguished and didn't return, plunging her hope back into darkness.

PART V

HŌʻIKE ʻANA

(REVELATION)

23

Cloudcroft, 11 August

Hellen slammed the pickup's door shut, whacking Tanaka's corgi in the nose. After a quick wave, Tanaka drove off. A waning gibbous moon hung in the western sky, marking more than two lunar cycles since she'd left the mainland. So much had happened. Hellen shook her head at the wreckage of Cloudcroft's solar array left by Lester's winds. Another responsibility deferred when she plowed headlong into restoring the wind farm. She trudged up the path to the house, favoring her right leg. After eight days, the bruises from sliding off the submarine had merged into one long orange-and-brown splotch running the length of her thigh.

Her mind kept returning to the sabotage. Tanaka had found the power supply line to Tower Three's over-speed control unit severed with a clean cut. Who would sabotage the startup? What would they have to gain? It was sick. Six of the wind farm's turbines had been destroyed and a wind tech had almost lost his life. Conroy's face came to mind, and she froze midstride. *God no, not him. Why haven't they found the bastard yet?*

After Tanaka's crew worked for a week to clear away the

debris from the wrecked wind towers, they brought only half the wind farm into operation and Kohala had to endure rolling blackouts. At least some power was better than no power. She inhaled a deep breath and her chest shuddered. After weeks of working nonstop, she looked forward to sleeping in her own bed again.

"Elle? Sorry I'm late," Hellen called out as she slumped through the doorway. The house remained silent. "Anyone home? Elizabeth?"

She walked into the kitchen and her stomach growled for some breakfast, hunger her constant companion now. The refrigerator was bare, even the slaughtered boar all gone. Elle's MRE rations had also run out. The pantry had a couple cans of Sham left, but the thought of eating salty pork made her cringe. She took a handful of overripe fruit and went to her bedroom. She deserved a long bath after today. It was a day that balled up into knots, one problem coiling and tangling into another. After she undressed, she stepped into the tub and submerged herself from the neck down, every pore opening to the warm water. Her skin stretched taut over her rib cage. Her arms and legs reminded her of those celebrity models with anorexia. She spent her whole life trying to lose weight; now it was no longer an option.

The fruit stung her taste buds with a sweet explosion of tang. Mango juice streamed from her lips and dripped down her chin. Delicious. With sticky hands, she opened Aiva and scrolled through old photos of Elizabeth. Her messy fingers left a hazy trail on the screen with every swipe. She quivered at the warm memories: birthdays, sailing together, stargazing on silent nights. A photo of her daughter dressed in a rabbit costume sent her into helpless laughter and water splashed over the bathroom floor.

Suzu's muffled voice came from upstairs, his words in urgent spurts in pace with his heels on the wooden floor above Hellen's bathroom. Although she couldn't make much sense of the conversation, Suzu's tone sent shivers along her spine. The radio squelched and popped with static. She bolted upright, straining to listen. The sound of Suzu's pacing feet abruptly stopped. "When did this happen? And Elizabeth—is she safe?" His voice lowered to muffled confusion again. The radio beeped, signifying her sign-off. For what felt like an eternity, silence fell upon Cloudcroft again. Even the forest held its breath.

A soft knock on the door started Hellen, sending ripples along the surface of the bathwater. Suzu entered with an ashen face and eyes puffy and red. This paragon of strength, the kahuna of the Otoko 'ohana, looked on the verge of a breakdown.

"What's wrong? Where is Elle and Elizabeth?"

"Hellen, we have to talk." Her eyes distant, Suzu took a towel off the rack and held it out to her, denying Hellen any privacy.

Panic threaded Hellen's throat and tingled her fingers. She sprang to her feet, splashing bathwater on the floor. "What? Tell me!" She grabbed Suzu's arm, but the Iron Buddha only gave her a sad look. Water dripped from her body, the drops echoing in the room, making Suzu's silence even more alarming. Hellen took the towel and wrapped it over her midriff, her skin livid with red blotches.

After Hellen dried herself, Suzu helped her into a sarong and took her outside to the back garden. With each step, Hellen's chest tightened with worry. They sat on a log bench at the edge of the forest and listened to the world around them, the wind rustling through the pine trees, exotic birdsong drowning out the sound of her heart beat. Her lips turned rubbery, struggling to form the words her mind could not find. She closed her eyes and waited for Suzu to speak. Like an aftereffect of staring at a picture too long, Elizabeth's face emerged behind her closed eyelids.

Her patience worn out, Hellen broke the silence. "If it's Elizabeth, just tell me—"

"No. She's safe for now. I'm sending Brett for her." Suzu's lips trembled when he tried to smile.

"Bring her home? I don't understand. Where is she?"

Suzu took Hellen's hands in his lap and breathed deep. "Elle left yesterday for Hilo with Elizabeth."

"Hilo? That's crazy. Why did she take Elizabeth?"

"Elizabeth insisted. She was worried about her friends at school."

"Figures. When are they coming home?"

"They were due back last night, just a short trip. They went to retrieve our gold. I thought long about how to tell you..."

"Tell me what? Is Elle okay?" Hellen's chest grew heavier.

Suzu sat in silence. The breeze moving through the pine trees took on a surreal importance. Hellen breathed deep and exhaled in a halting sigh. A shudder reached her clammy hands and made them tremble.

After a long while, Suzu spoke in a hollow voice with words Hellen's mind had already heard. "The riots in Hilo. Elle was..." Suzu covered his mouth with his hand, he couldn't go on, nor did he need to.

Fat tears traced down both their cheeks, and grief's gravity pulled them into each other's arms. Hellen's throat stung with sorrow. Elle. Please not her. Time stopped, the moment frozen. All the hope she'd clung to since arriving to Hawai'i splintered into a million tiny shards, as if someone had shattered a glass door with a sledgehammer. Like the day Kalino died, a rift opened, and she fell in.

Over Suzu's shoulders, beyond the trees, the twin peaks of Mauna Kea and Mauna Loa stood in the distance, lit by crepuscular rays streaming through the clouds, reminding her of how Elle had often marveled at the "Fingers of Buddha."

Suzu's tremors subsided, and he released Hellen and sat upright. "We are like a puff of wind. Our days a passing shadow. Brahmā, come down to us, touch these mountains, and they shall smoke."

The forest's sounds, Suzu's halting sobs, and the pounding of her heart trailed off into another dimension. All sound drained from the world. Hellen's attention telescoped to the small cocoon spun into the nook of a nearby branch, swaying back and forth in the breeze. Before her eyes, the chrysalis split open. The cracks in the hardened shell widened and released a yellow butterfly. It flexed its delicate gilded wings in a slow rhythm, testing the air for the first time before it fluttered over and perched on Hellen's wrist. *Life doesn't capitulate, it transforms.*

Bradshaw Field

Brett rubbed the sleep from his eyes. Moisture hung in the air outside the barracks, dripping in slow streams down the window. Scudding clouds swallowed Mauna Loa's peak south of the airbase. His undershirt stuck to him like a wetsuit. The humidity clung to everything. He checked his watch and winced before realizing what day it was. His first day off since reporting to Bradshaw four weeks ago; he had not set the alarm and slept in. Jones said the helo was down for its hundred-hour inspection and he'd have his bird back by tomorrow. With a lightness to his step, he walked into the shower, picturing the look on Hellen's face when he showed up at Cloudcroft unannounced.

More than a week had passed since the wind farm's catastrophic startup. Except for a few texts, he hadn't heard from Hellen, no doubt busy cleaning up the wreckage. To Hellen, the mission was a bust. No lights meant no "mission complete." And he hoped his surprise visit would snap her out of her funk.

Across the room his phone chimed. He dug it out of his flight bag, but the message ID made him grimace. *Suzu Otoko.*

You need to pick up Elizabeth in Hilo ASAP, Suzu wrote.

His daughter's name glowed on the screen like a ghost. He

had spoken to her only the night before he deployed to Bradshaw.

Not authorized, he typed. *No PAX on CAP FLTS, only cargo.*

I don't follow. Just use your magic. This is urgent, Suzu wrote.

Can you pick her up?

The Mauna Loa eruption has cut off access.

Brett bit his lower lip and wondered why the urgency. Where was Elle? Something wasn't right with this picture. But one thing was certain, his daughter needed him.

OK. Don't worry, I'm on it.

Thank you! I'll see you when you return.

On the walk to Flight Dispatch, Brett gnawed on his chewing gum with more intensity. Unsure of how to explain unauthorized passengers to the squadron overlords, he committed himself to the dubious task, one that might get him an invitation to a captain's mast and grounded, never to fly again. What the hell, it was a brave new world, right? The dispatch sergeant gave him a cold reception. No spare aircraft were available, but he could assign him this morning's courier mission to Hilo, if he wanted it. He cautioned him to stay on the airfield. Riots had broken out yesterday, the worst ever. They had called up Army reservists for crowd control, but the situation was still hot.

After he filed his flight plan, Brett downloaded his approach plates onto his FlightNav tablet. The flight line personnel refueled his Cessna and loaded the courier package and other cargo.

Fifteen minutes after takeoff, he leveled at five thousand feet. A white, amorphous cloud lay beyond Brett's windshield, interspersed with sheets of rain and an occasional flash of lightning. Another fine Navy day in paradise. The trip over to Hilo was in the goo the whole way, forcing him to fly solely by instrument reference. He opened the approach plate and studied it for a moment before setting the final approach course heading into the autopilot. He sat back and stretched his arms, his thoughts drifting to Elizabeth again. Flying home with him might melt her icy exterior, a chance to mend her resentment over his first visit with her.

Twenty miles from Lyman Field, Approach Control gave him a final vector and cleared him for landing. He banked the aircraft, pulled back the throttle, and eased down the glide slope. He broke out of the clouds eight hundred feet above Hilo Bay. Runway Two-One lined up straight in front of him. Below his right wing, a submarine floated next to the municipal pier, most likely using its reactor to provide electricity to the airport and town.

He passed over the runway threshold and landed before the first taxiway. After ground control cleared him to the general aviation terminal, he taxied to a man waving him in with lighted orange wands. Before he had completed his shutdown checklist, a fuel truck pulled alongside. "Thanks, but I don't need a top-off," he yelled from the cockpit. "I've more than enough fuel for the return flight." The extra fuel would have reduced his payload and extended his takeoff distance, jeopardizing his escape. Brett climbed out of the cockpit and a white van approached the aircraft. An RAF sergeant jumped out of the truck and saluted him before taking the courier package. A popping sound of distant gunfire came from beyond the airport, across the bay. He hitched a ride with the sergeant, and gunshots grew louder as they screeched to a stop at the terminal.

"You better make this a quick turnaround, sir. The airport is under ThreatCon Alpha, imminent attack."

Lyman Field's terminal lay deserted, no passengers, no cargo, no aircraft. Brett walked into the flight ops office to get the latest weather and refill his water bottle. The forecast showed barometric pressure falling and gusty conditions during the next four hours. The wad of gum in his mouth lost every bit of juicy fruit, leaving a sour taste. His spit it into a trash can and reached for another stick.

"Commander Akamu?" A soft female voice came from behind him.

A Japanese woman in a black jumpsuit with sunglasses and a wireless earpiece stood in the doorway. She carried a stoic expression and a Browning HP40 sidearm on her belt.

He braced his hands on his hips. "What's this about?"

"Aloha. I'm Kaya Masuda, Elle's special assistant." She stepped aside, and Elizabeth came hobbling around the corner with an elastic bandage around her ankle. She didn't move closer, arms folded in a self-hug, her hair in tangles, her eyes bloodshot. Masuda squeezed Elizabeth's shoulder with her small hand and whispered to her.

"I'm glad you're here," Elizabeth said in Hawaiian with a quivering voice. "I'm scared. It's horrible. Auntie Elle, she…"

"Relax," Brett said in Hawaiian. "I'm here to take you home."

Brett looked at Masuda. "Where's Elle?"

"She died in the riots yesterday," Masuda said in a clipped voice. "That's why Suzu insisted you come for Elizabeth."

The news hit Brett like a cold gust of wind. His muscles tensed, and he staggered to Elizabeth. He hugged her and felt her stiffen, then relax as if in resignation. Her floral scent smelled surreal under the circumstances. His arms pressed close around her shoulders, her silky hair against his cheek. Images of Hellen receiving the news raced through his head. She must be in shock.

"I had no idea," he said, stroking her hair. "God. I'm so sorry."

No longer the self-possessed teenager, she wiped her eyes and looked up to him. "Get me out of here. I want to go home."

"Of course you do." The only personal items they had were two steel briefcases, the same used for sensitive electronic equipment. "Leaving with just the clothes on your back?" He released Elizabeth and walked over to one case and tried to lift it. "Damn, how much do these weigh?"

Masuda stiffened and pulled Brett's arm away from the briefcase. "About sixty pounds each. They contain two thousand troy ounces of gold bullion."

"Holy crap. What are we taking with us, Fort Knox?"

"It's our insurance policy for the future," Elizabeth continued in Hawaiian. "Hasn't Hellen told you? Throughout her life, Auntie Elle made a series of lucky investments. That's why she came to Hilo—to get the gold before the bank collapsed."

Hellen had mentioned none of this. But it explained how Elle had bankrolled Hellen's grad school and Charlie's private education. In the distance, muffled popping sounds rang out, bringing Brett back to the present. Shouts in the corridor soon followed. An explosion rattled the windows.

"Look, we better take off. Can I get some help with these cases?"

Masuda lifted them, one in each hand with apparent ease. "Lead the way, Commander."

Brett supported Elizabeth's shoulder and helped her to the flight line. His aircraft remained where he had parked it, ready to go. With the short turnaround time, he skipped the long, methodical preflight check. More small-arms fire ricocheted against the terminal walls. On the open tarmac, Brett worried they might be exposed to the assault. He hurried to help Elizabeth into the aircraft's copilot's seat.

"Hold up there, pal." An airport security guard ran over to them, an ANR-15 assault rifle slung over his shoulder. "Where's your flight manifest, and who are all these people?"

Masuda set the briefcases on the ground and slid her hand over her sidearm, but Brett shook his head, signaling her to stand down. He flashed his military ID and flight plan at the guard, hoping he didn't take time to study it. Another round of gunfire near the terminal made the guard jump and draw his firearm. "Fine, I can't fuss with you guys right now." He waved them on with his rifle. "You better depart ASAP; the airport is under attack."

An MP vehicle peeled around the corner of the terminal and

raced toward them. It screeched to a stop beside the Cessna and a Royal Marine waved to the guard to jump in. He nodded toward Brett. "Insurgents broke through the airport barrier and are heading this way. If you're planning to bug out of here, I suggest you do so bloody soon."

Masuda stowed the briefcases in the back seat and ran back to the terminal. After Elizabeth buckled up, she rubbed the back of her neck, her eyes closed. Brett stuck another stick of gum in his mouth and started the aircraft engine and taxied to the departure run-up ramp. Elizabeth's seat belt came unsecured when she leaned over. Her trembling fingers fumbled with the buckle before Brett reached over and secured the shoulder harness for her.

Brakes locked, engine at full power, Brett completed an abbreviated pre-takeoff check. The cylinders backfired a couple of times, but he didn't have the time to clear them. He received his takeoff clearance for Runway Two and advanced the throttle to red-line RPMs. Above gross takeoff weight, the aircraft was slow to accelerate. Brett chomped on his gum, his brow sweaty. He glanced at Elizabeth, her eyes terrified, her hands gripping the seat. Outside the Cessna's windshield, the trees at the end of the runway came closer and closer.

A pickup truck filled with armed insurgents raced along the taxiway parallel to the runway, threatening to cut him off. Gunfire flashed from the truck bed, smashing the Cessna's back window. Elizabeth screamed. With less than a hundred yards left, Brett pulled back on the control yoke. They inched off the concrete, and he kept low in ground effect to reduce aerodynamic drag. No longer burdened by the wheels rolling on the concrete, the plane leapt forward. The insurgents swerved onto the runway but fell behind. He flipped the landing gear switch and three clunks came from the wheel wells. After he reached best rate-of-climb speed, he pitched the Cessna into the sky. The trees slipped beneath them with only a few feet of clearance.

After departing Hilo airspace, Brett set his cruising altitude above the scattered cloud tops. Far to the south, a volcanic plume rose thousands of feet above Kīlauea. With smooth air above the broken clouds, he engaged the autopilot and glanced over to Elizabeth, her attention on the ravaged landscape below them. Among the hamlets nestled in Mauna Loa's hillside, smoke bellowed out from several fires. The lack of firetrucks and the sparse highway traffic turned the island into a remote outpost.

Brett tapped Elizabeth's headset and gave her a shaka sign. She only gave a melancholy shrug before she stared back out her window. Brett went back to his instrument scan, his mind pulled between respecting her privacy and giving her emotional support.

"I know Elle meant the world to you," he said at last in Hawaiian.

She nodded but kept her eyes on the window.

"I know it's all hard to absorb. But I hope you know I'm always here for you."

"Yeah, I know," she said in Hawaiian. "I feel so alone in the world right now. After I return to Cloudcroft, it's just the Iron Buddha and me, and he's not much company."

"I don't know her that well. Hellen seemed reluctant to talk about her."

"Too stoic for my taste."

"When we met at Cloudcroft, I felt a strong connection to you, not only because we spoke Hawaiian but also our shared heritage—and the way you looked at me. I hope you'll come to see me as 'ohana someday." Brett grimaced at how inane his words sounded over the headset.

"I believe...I mean I know you're my *makuakāne*. I just need some time...time to get to know you more." Her hand came to his knee.

His chest swelled at the Hawaiian name for father. Up to now, "father" had been only an abstract title.

"We're twenty minutes from Kamuela. Hellen will probably be waiting for us when we land."

She smacked her palm against her brow. "Can't we fly to another airport?"

"Why? It's the closest airport to Cloudcroft."

"I still feel... I mean Hellen is... During Lester, hunkered down together at Cloudcroft, we became closer, but I'm still bitter at never meeting you all those years."

"I hear ya. It'll be okay. Just be cool." Brett scanned the instrument panel, set the Kamuela Airport automated weather frequency in the COMM radio, and adjusted the squelch setting to reduce the static noise on the line. "Do you prefer we stick to Hawaiian?"

"'Ae, let's keep it that way, okay?"

He smacked his gum and chuckled. She read him five-by-five. With Hellen not fluent in their native language, they could openly share their thoughts, easing her anxiety. "Tell you what, kiddo. Let me handle this. I got your back."

She shot him a conspiratorial smile.

Brett spotted the Kamuela Airport beacon sticking up through the low clouds. With no ATC services, he had to make a visual approach. He orbited for a half hour until a "blue hole" opened and allowed him to make an emergency descent to landing. The spiraling dive made his ears pop. Elizabeth reached for a stick of gum from his shoulder pocket and stuck it in her mouth and winked.

They landed on the only runway at the small, deserted airport. Elizabeth patted his knee and gave a thumbs-up. He nodded and taxied over to the terminal reserved for commuter airlines. After the prop wound to a stop, Elizabeth climbed out of the aircraft and Brett unloaded the steel cases from the rear seat. He caught his breath and sent Hellen a text, telling her they had arrived.

"So, you have one of Charlie's phones too?" Elizabeth asked.

"He's an electronics wizard alright."

"Like his mother. Ever feel like a third oar in the water when you're around them?"

Brett paused and stared at her. "I try not to let it bother me."

"Good, me too." Elizabeth reached for his hand and held it. "Let's wait out here for them."

"You're in charge."

"I'm not looking forward to this. She lied to both of us—how can you forgive her? She broke your heart."

"*Ua ola loko i ke aloha—*"

"*He alii ka la'i, he ha Ku'ulani na,*" Elizabeth finished the proverb for him.

"Life is an echo—what you give out comes back," Brett continued in English. "It's like Newton's Third Law—cause and effect—the more kindness and happiness you put out, the more you get."

Elizabeth looked away from him. "I'm not convinced. Auntie Elle was a buffer between Hellen and me; she smoothed out the rough edges in both of us. Not sure I'm ready for solo flight right now."

"I can explain it to you, but I can't understand it for you. You need to find your own path to forgive her."

"Hellen thinks she's real akamai," she reverted to Hawaiian, "but she's not so smart in dealing with people." She tugged at his hand. "Let's get out of here. I really can't go through this right now."

"Eddie would go, 'ae?"

"Yeah, he would," she said. "But I'm no Eddie."

He pointed toward the terminal. "It's showtime."

Hellen burst through the airport ramp access doors and embraced Elizabeth with a lingering hug.

"I missed you so much, love." She nuzzled her cheek against Elizabeth's. "I'm so glad to have my girl back. You're safe now."

Eyes wide, Elizabeth stuck her tongue out in a mock choke. "*Kōkua ia'u,* Pāpā," she said over Hellen's shoulder.

Her plea for help tugged at his heart even though it was at Hellen's expense. "Hellen. For Christ's sake, give her some air."

Hellen stood back, her hands outstretched to Elizabeth's arms, and gazed at her with a brilliant smile.

Like a stoic Māori warrior, Elizabeth frowned at Brett. "And so it begins," she said in Hawaiian.

24

The alfalfa smell, neighing horses, dust everywhere, it all felt as an anchor to Hellen, an escape from the nightmare of Elle's death. Like a lyrical earworm, the stable sounds were a catalyst for Hellen's memories. The times she shared with Elle in this barn flooded back to her. Only afterward, these ordinary moments claimed remembrance on account of their solace.

The overhead lights blinked, setting Hellen's heart rate up a notch. Entropy seemed to control the power grid more than her own efforts these days, always one step forward, two back. And Elizabeth's stiff-arm reception yesterday still stung. Gone was the closeness they shared during Tropical Storm Lester. Elizabeth needed time to grieve, to absorb, to accept.

After feeding the horses, Hellen walked back to the house, bracing herself for the difficult day ahead. Suzu did little to raise her spirits. The Iron Buddha grieved in his own stoic manner, letting the world spin on its own momentum, indifferent to it all.

The kitchen smelled of steamed rice. A clock radio on the counter read nine fifteen and filled the room with a melodious ukulele tune. Suzu stood with his back to Hellen at the cutting board, chopping up fish she had brought up from yesterday's trip to the harbor. Hellen's stomach gurgled, impatient for

Suzu's delicious poke, marinated ahi tossed over rice and topped with lettuce and chickpeas. "Where's Elizabeth?" she asked.

"Still sleeping," Suzu said without looking away from the mincing knife. "I've forgotten how I used to sleep the morning away when I was her age."

"Maybe it's her refuge..."

Suzu turned off the stove and scooped the poke into three bowls. He reached in a drawer and put a key into his robe pocket. "Let's go out on the lanai."

Taking two of the bowls, Hellen followed him to the porch and sat on the steps under the sun. They sat without speaking, nibbling at their poke. Suzu's face turned skyward. A military transport plane banked overhead in a lazy turn eastbound, joining other contrails in the sky leading back to the mainland.

"Maybe we can start thinking about our future," Suzu said. He laid a brass skeleton key beside Hellen, a figure of a unicorn at the end of its handle.

Hellen glanced at the key, more curious than amused. The jet's turbine whine receded in the distance. "Yes, it's good to hear the sounds of civilization again. The recovery is gaining momentum at last."

Suzu leaned back on his elbows, the sun on his face. A genuine smile grew across his lips, taking years off his age. Now that Suzu was no longer locked within a cocoon, he both puzzled and frightened Hellen.

"You're my *kaikamahine*," Suzu said, "even more after Elle's passing."

Hellen let the words rest in her mind, surprised at Suzu referring to her as his daughter with such tenderness. Yet Hellen's heart still ached.

"I miss her," Hellen said. "Elle's memory consumes my every hour, even in my dreams at night. I'll never let go her. I want to touch her warm hands again, hear her soft voice."

"All life is suffering, and all suffering comes from desire."

"The Four Noble Truths don't work for me. Soon I'll not have

Cloudcroft to feed my memories of Elle. I'll miss this place. Brett and I may settle somewhere in Kona—close enough to Bradshaw."

"You're not going anywhere." Suzu sat up and placed the key in Hellen's hand, closing her fingers around it. "I'm giving you the cottage. It's yours to share with Brett and your children, forever."

Hellen held the key, her vision blurry with immense hope. "I don't know what to say. While riding in the backcountry, I often stopped by the little cabin, hoping someday…"

"I'm chipping in ten acres as well. Besides, this way I'll keep you around to make breakfast and take care of the animals."

Hellen embraced him, holding him tight. Suzu stiffened his shoulders, then relaxed and returned the hug for the first time in years, squeezing with a surprising force. Hellen found a permanence after months of uncertainty. With this cottage, her dream of having her 'ohana under one roof snapped into focus.

Elizabeth came onto the porch and gave them the stink-eye. "What's going on between you guys? You're acting weird."

"Good morning, Elizabeth," Suzu said, releasing Hellen from his arms. "I've saved you some breakfast. Bon appétit."

Without a word, Elizabeth rubbed the sleep from her eyes and took the poke bowl. She shoveled the fish into her mouth with chopsticks. After scrapping the bottom of the bowl, she came to life. Her eyes wandered as if inspecting the morning. After the last grain of rice, she gave a curt nod and looked satisfied.

Hellen stood and held her hand out. "Come with me. I've something to show you."

Elizabeth frowned and turned to escape inside. Before she passed through the door, Hellen ran to her and tugged her arm, beckoning her to follow her. Elizabeth pulled her elbow away and stood in the doorway, but her frown relaxed, her visceral scorn melting into a slight nod.

At the stables, Hellen walked into the tack room. She hefted a saddle and placed it in Elizabeth's arms. For the first time since their stormy night together, a fleeting hint of a grin crossed her daughter's face. After saddling the two mares, they headed into the woods bordering Cloudcroft. Fiddlehead ferns covered the forest bed, curled in the shape of nautilus shells. By a stream, they dismounted and walked the horses across an old wooden bridge covered with green moss and rubber vine. Hellen led her mare to a small meadow and released her reins, allowing the Appaloosa to graze. Under a nearby plumeria tree, Elizabeth snatched a white-and-yellow flower from a low branch and tossed it into the water. It floated into an eddy in the current, sending it back to the place from which she dropped it, as if caught in a closed feedback loop.

"This is one of my favorite places on Cloudcroft," Hellen said, placing her hand on Elizabeth's shoulder. "I love this stream. It speaks to me. Each time I cross it, I feel I'm stepping across a river dividing my two worlds."

"I know the feeling," Elizabeth said. A raw honesty lay in her eyes as if she were on the verge of a confession. She opened her mouth to speak but appeared to have second thoughts and averted her eyes.

The cottage stood a short distance along a foot path, never straying far from the stream, nestled among Cook Pines rising from the ground to brush the sky. Hellen took Elizabeth's hand, relieved she didn't pull away, and led her to the porch. No longer cold, Elizabeth's hand held a cozy familiarity. The morning sun sent its yellow rays through the trees, now and then blinding her with shards of sunlight. Branches swayed in the breeze, their needles imitating the hiss of ocean waves. Pine cones dotted the ground like fallen Christmas trinkets. Birds called from all around, and the air held an earthy fragrance, reminding her of the Colorado high country.

They stepped to the front door and Hellen took the key out of her hip pocket. "It's ours now. This is our new home."

"My room at Cloudcroft is just fine, thank you. Besides, I need my privacy."

Hellen swallowed a flush of anger and ran her hand along Elizabeth's upper arm. "Of course. I'm sure you'll be happier living under Suzu's roof, right?" She lifted her eyebrows, smiled to herself, and waited for her daughter to speak.

Elizabeth took the key from Hellen's hand and opened the front door. "Okay, I see your point. Let's look around."

A fortnight after Elle's death, Hellen awoke with another bout of nausea, a heaviness she hadn't suffered since she was pregnant with Charlie. The notion crossed her mind, but she couldn't face that now. She didn't have a fever, nor any other signs of the flu. More likely stress. *Yes, please let it be stress.*

That morning, as with every morning, grief visited Cloudcroft like the mist falling from the low clouds. Suzu spent his days at the Zen retreat, preferring his Buddhist *sangha* over 'ohana. Tanaka no longer needed Hellen, depriving her of a much-needed distraction. Instead, she plowed herself into restoring the cottage. It needed her attention, and she wanted more time with Elizabeth, her lifeline to pull herself out of depression. She recalled childhood memories of working with Kalino around Cloudcroft. She hoped the same magic might change Elizabeth's heart.

The previous week she had worked side by side with Elizabeth. In a manner that became a habit, they shared the same space with barely a word spoken between them. But just being with Elizabeth gladdened her heart, nesting in their new home, cleaning floorboards, painting walls, erecting solar panels, and fixing a water pump feeding from the cistern. In their spare time, they restored the Cloudcroft's solar panels and wind turbine, and they ran cables to neighboring homes. Her improvised microgrid earned her a dozen chickens and a fat hog. With no hay nor grain left, the horses now ranged over the property, keeping the grass groomed better than the push lawn mower she tried to use.

Hellen rode bareback on Elle's Appaloosa through the winding path in the forest. She leaned forward and patted the mare's neck, hoping Lulua'ina's good karma would rub off. Her phone chimed a text alert. She glanced at the screen, and her heart leapt at Brett's name. But the message wasn't what she had hoped for. He had a big mission in the wings and might be out of contact for the next week. She imagined accelerated operations, secret targets, her Man from Maui lost to black-ops.

After she reached the cottage, she tied Lulua'ina next to Elizabeth's horse and went inside to the living room, a pinewood paneled little space with a stone fireplace and traditional lodge-style furniture. The rustic room no longer had a layer of dirt on the windows and the rug looked cleaner than she remembered it from her last visit. Elizabeth must have been busy all morning. Even the fireplace mantel was sanded.

Elizabeth sat crossed-legged on the wood floor, stirring a can of wood stain. She handed a brush to Hellen, and they stained from opposite ends of the mantel. Together, they brushed the intricate leaves and flowers carved into the mahogany woodwork. After an hour passed, each brushing in silence, they met in the middle and bumped into each other's rear. "Sorry," they said in unison and laughed.

Elizabeth finished the last brushstrokes and stood back to inspect their work. "You missed a spot." She brushed the carved leaf Hellen had just stained.

Hellen crossed her arms, pretending to be more annoyed than she actually felt. "So, you've resigned yourself to staying here?"

"I'm getting used to the idea," Elizabeth said, "but don't put my name on the door just yet. Oh, I almost forgot, wait here." She ran into the closet and returned with a wooden shingle. "Here, look what I found this morning." An inscription painted in gaudy floral colors with a cursive scroll read "Elle and Suzu,

1976." Hellen tilted her head, puzzled at how the sign came to this place. She flipped it over and smiled at a faded photo taped on the reverse side. One of her favorites, the picture had launched a thousand dreams over the years. After peeling it off, she held it for Elizabeth to see.

For an interminable moment, Elizabeth stared at the photo, her feet rooted to the rug. Without warning, she snatched the photo from Hellen's hands and held it close to her eyes. "Wait, this picture looks familiar. Who are they?"

"Brett and me on my twenty-first birthday."

Elizabeth's face blossomed. "You were hot back in the day. You guys made a cute couple." Her voice had an excited lilt that made Hellen's heart ache for the time before she had confessed to be her mother.

"We made something else that night."

Elizabeth tilted her head to the side before her face lit up with surprise. She moved her fingers over the faces in the photo, her eyes intent, her lips pressed together. For minutes, they sat together without words. Elizabeth's eyes welled up and she handed the photo back to her. "I'm sorry... I've been such a bitch, lately."

Hellen shook her head, on the verge of tears. "You need never to apologize. You and Charlie are the best things to have ever come into my life. It's I who needs to apologize, love. Since your birth, I ached to raise you, to be there for those special moments in your life, but I was so... terrified." Her words sprang from her heart with stories about her first summer with Brett. All the while, Elizabeth kept asking questions, drawing out details of Brett's outrageous shenanigans. They laughed and cried together and shed weeks of tension. Hellen took Elizabeth's hand, and a hot current flowed through her body as if she'd swum into a warm patch in a cold lake.

Elizabeth wiped her eyes. "After you told me I was your daughter, I was angry... needed to get away. But some things make more sense now. I always had vibes you weren't just

'Auntie Hellen,'" Elizabeth said, making air quotes. "Maybe I get why you jettisoned me."

"Not jettisoned. I loved you; that's why I left you in Elle's care."

They fell silent for a moment. A bird crowed in the distance, and the sun cast long shadows into the room. Elizabeth cleared her throat. "Okay, but do you know why Auntie Elle wouldn't let go of me?"

Hellen narrowed her eyes at her, fearing more incrimination about her addiction, her failed marriage, and her failure as a mother. As if she were a Buddha statue, her daughter sat immobile with the corners of her lips curved slightly upward.

Hellen crossed her arms, her fingers pressed cold against her ribs. "Tell me, then."

"In all my years with her, she never mentioned her parents, always avoiding my questions. Don't you think that's a little strange?"

"That's more than a bit odd. I'm embarrassed to admit I never gave it any thought."

"Brett would say you need to improve your situational awareness." She wore an enigmatic grin and raised her eyebrows.

After dinner, Suzu and Elizabeth meditated in the carriage house. Although invited, Hellen didn't join them. From all the work on the cottage, she had enough sore muscles for one day.

At the head of the stairs, the door to Elle's study stood open. For years, Hellen had never stepped inside. Off limits, it became Elle's private space. A rolltop desk sat in the corner and a leather couch filled one wall. On the opposite wall, books filled every shelf, arranged by subject. On one side, little vases of orchids and plumeria adorned an eclectic mix of textbooks on cosmology, calculus, and metaphysics. A framed letter from the prime minister, dated 1991, thanked Elle for her petition to change the national name from Sandwich Islands to Hawai'i.

The bookcase's other side had a much different personality: books on Hawaiian culture and language, psychology, women's studies, Buddhism, and a picture book entitled *Fifty Shades of Polynesia*. The Iron Buddha seemed to hold many secrets—and pleasures—close to his chest.

The opposite wall held dozens of photographs, old images of Cloudcroft, pictures of their marriage two decades ago, and Elizabeth growing up. She fiddled with the red braid around her left wrist and stared at a close-up portrait of Elle and Elizabeth. Elle's eyes, honey-brown with streaks of gold, matched those of Elizabeth, a coincidence she had always found amazing.

An oil painting of Elle and Suzu hung on the back wall. Depicted in their youth, no older than Elizabeth, they stood arm in arm, looking very much in love. Both were adorned only in jewels, white and yellow plumeria floating in their hair, and lei covering their chests. Elle looked like Elizabeth's twin, same lush lips, stringy red hair, and slim figure, except for the flowing tattoos on her arms and thighs. In the distance, the Hawaiian national flag flew from a tall ship in the harbor. A full moon hung in the twilight above the ship. She looked again—no, it wasn't the moon—but the Earth in muted colors.

Hellen sat on a couch opposite of the painting, pondering its hidden message. Like a metronome, a pendulum wall clock ticked off the seconds; the clock struck ten. After the long day, her eyes became heavy, time for bed. She tried to rise but didn't have the strength.

Aiva chimed a text alert from Brett. *Miss u. How is Elizabeth?*

THX, me too, she typed. *Elizabeth is coming around.*

Meaning what?

Not snarky anymore and distant. Working together brought us closer.

Maybe Elle's death opened a door.

The door's still open. Can you come out to Cloudcroft?

Not yet, but soon.

The front door slammed downstairs. *Got to go*, she typed. *Love you.*

Elizabeth came into the study and plopped beside her, her gold pendant bouncing on her chest. She leaned her head on Hellen's shoulder. A déjà vu emerged. At first, Hellen saw Elle sitting next to her for their daily dharma practice. Afraid she was dreaming, Hellen wrapped her arm around Elizabeth. Like an exhausted mother with her newborn, Hellen cherished this unexpected intimacy.

"When is Brett coming home?" Elizabeth asked, her voice soft and resonant. "I wish he could see our cottage."

Hellen's ears perked up. Yes, it was their home now. Hellen swallowed hard. "Me too, love. He's on duty at Bradshaw—on 'His Majesty's Secret Service,'" she said with air quotes. "I think something big is coming."

She let out a long sigh that set Elizabeth in motion, and her hand clutched Hellen's upper arm for the first time since... she couldn't remember when.

"I love you," Hellen whispered.

"Yeah, I know."

Suzu walked into the room and sat in a lotus pose on the floor. Elizabeth removed her hand from Hellen's arms and sat upright. The moment, short and sweet, had vanished. Suzu raised his eyebrows, never missing a beat. "Elizabeth. I see you've tossed away your shackles of resentment—that's good."

Elizabeth narrowed her defiant eyes and clutched Hellen's arm again. A wave of relief passed over Hellen, its energy released in a long breath. Now both of Elizabeth's hands came to her arm.

"Two hands clap, and there is a sound," Suzu said. "What is the sound of one hand?"

The koan echoed the one Elle gave Hellen the day she had sailed for Hawai'i. "Two hands, like in you and Elle?"

"Not me," Suzu said. "Elizabeth."

Hellen looked at her daughter, then back to Suzu, their eyes single-hearted in their shared secret. "I don't understand."

"Life and death are a part of the Saṃsāra cycle," Suzu said. "Our actions in this life and all previous ones lead to further reincarnation. For the dead, this is a time of passage. Elizabeth, tell me. How does the Bodhisattva stay alive and dead at the same time?"

An image of Schrödinger's cat floated in Hellen's mind. The thought experiment, sometimes described as a paradox of a cat both alive and dead, explored the dilemma of applying quantum mechanics to everyday objects. Suzu's koan was a tip of the hat to Elle's famous paper, resolving the problem by applying the Many Worlds Interpretation, a series of parallel worlds. Not one Earth, but many, each with its own twist on history.

"Upon her death," Elizabeth announced, "all of Auntie Elle's karmic forces accumulated during her lifetime triggered her next rebirth."

"You don't mean Elle's reincarnation?" Hellen asked.

"Yes," Elizabeth said and touched her heart, "not in body, but in spirit—a rebirth. I know she's here." Her words were genuine, her eyes confident. Yet her voice was a strange tone, not one from her teenage daughter.

Suzu's eyes shifted back to Hellen. A small, incongruent smile broke from his masked expression.

The meaning of Elizabeth's words came to light and a heaviness spread over Hellen. Elizabeth's break from science gave Hellen pause. She took a breath and heat threaded her throat. Elizabeth must have meant she only carried Elle's memory. "The scientist in me can't accept Elle's reincarnation." She wagged her finger at Elizabeth. "And you of all people can't believe this. Where's the logic in the concept of rebirth?"

"I don't need empirical logic to believe something," Elizabeth said in an unadorned tone. "As a Buddhist, I accept we can understand the universe in other ways, not just from data. I trust my faith, don't you?"

"And you expect me to accept this on faith alone?"

"No, I expect you'll come to accept it in your own way," Suzu said. "Maybe not now, but someday you will. Zen treats a death of a beloved as a time to understand the heart of Buddhism, the unconditional acceptance of the way things are. There's an impermanence to life."

Hellen tittered. "That's Elle talking. I want to believe you, but I'm trapped behind a stone wall of empiricism."

"Of course you are. You've always let reasoning get in your way. You need to go back and read Elle's book again." She took a deep breath and folded her hands in her lap. "Like a door that closes, and another opens, death is the boundary between the end of one life and the beginning of the next."

"Sure, that's the dogma from most religions. You're born, life's a ball of chalk, then you die."

Suzu's eyes narrowed and he took a long breath. "Samsara cosmology isn't that simple. It consists of realms through which the wheel of existence cycles between death and rebirth. Elle is a Bodhisattva, a person able to reach nirvana and break her chains from the Wheel of Samsara. Yet she returned to this realm to help you pursue your own path of nirvana."

"Auntie Elle brought us together again," Elizabeth said with weepy eyes. Her words floated uncharted in the air like a butterfly, and Hellen felt as if lost in another of Elle's dharma lessons. "She urged you to come here, even paid for your trip. Her death led to a rebirth, our reunion." Elizabeth placed her left wrist on Hellen's, their two braided bands touching. "The red thread..." she whispered.

Suzu took Hellen's tablet from the side table. He tapped on Aiva's display and held up the picture of the Polynesian wayfinders in Elle's book. "Elle had planted the seed of her rebirth in her novel long before you left San Diego. The voyagers' journey is your own journey, Hellen. It's all here: the aurora, the wind farm, your trek up Mauna Kea, and your daughter, Elizabeth."

Hellen's mouth went dry. *The Wayfinders* had struck a chord with her, seeming to predict events in her life. "It sounds crazy, but a part of me wants to believe you."

"You're not crazy," Suzu said. "The world is crazy for not recognizing the hidden reality."

"I sometimes wonder if reality is not what we think it is."

"The Buddha taught us reality is often much different from what we believe. The sun seems to revolve in the sky, yet it's we who are rotating. The Earth appears to be flat when it's actually round. And time isn't what it seems to be."

Hellen nodded her head and swallowed hard. "Einstein told us the past, present, and future are only stubborn illusions."

"Our Mahayana dharma, the *Flower Adornment Sutra*, tells us we have many universes. Buddhist cosmology is a collection of an infinite number of worlds. The dharma speaks about 'The Incalculable,' a string of calculations of endless numbers, ending in the measureless, the boundless, the timeless of many worlds. You can think of it as—what do you scientists call it—the multiverse?"

Hellen played with the red band around her wrist. She had never noticed how each braid intertwined with other, seamless with no beginning nor end. Maybe Einstein and Buddha had more in common than she thought. "While we hold on to the illusion of one reality," she said, "the Many Worlds Theory claims many realities exist. Like a stack of papers, the multiverse is the superposition of countless parallel universes, each carrying a different version of reality and—"

"An infinite number of similar," Suzu interrupted, "but slightly different worlds give us plenty of chances to encounter the unexplainable, such as reincarnation. We die in one universe and are reborn in another." He leaned over and lit an incense stick on the side table, its sandalwood aroma curling around them. "You see? Buddhists may ignore science, and scientists may dismiss Buddhism, but we need both to understand the connection between Elle and Elizabeth."

Hellen let out a resigning sigh. Multiverse was to science what reincarnation was to mysticism, both artifacts of speculation. But she hoped she might someday find an answer to this puzzle. Elle had said many times: the middle way is the only path to enlightenment. And she'd share this path with Elizabeth, as mother and daughter, scientist and mystic.

Elizabeth removed the locket around her neck and handed it to Hellen. She undid the clasped and opened it. Inside, a lock of red hair tied into a loop by a red thread fell on her lap. Also within the locket, a small photo of Elle in her late teens had faded over the decades, a secret hidden all this time. Aside from the photo's age, she'd have sworn it was Elizabeth. Hellen held Elle's lock of hair to her eye and peered at Elizabeth. A fleeting inspiration floated into her mind, the idea that Elle and Elizabeth were connected in some way, maybe even the same person. She trembled and chased the foolish notion away.

25

Gus sat alone in the only cafe open in town, stogie in hand, blue cigar smoke rising into a cloud above his head. Rain fell as it did every afternoon on this side of the island. Drops splattered against the window overlooking the green logo hanging outside the shop. The familiar crowned mermaid with wavy hair glowing in the sign gave him a nostalgic comfort. Patrons came and went, ordering their tea and coffee, a few even wore smiles and joked with Loni, the coffee shop's owner. A month ago, he had restored power to the village and every day he stopped by just to watch people. The sound of their voices, the way they dressed, and the smell of roasted coffee beans almost made him forget the island's sorry state after the fall, after the lights went out. Although Loni couldn't offer anything more than coffee and pancakes, her little shop brought comfort to the little Whos in Punaville. He took another sip of his Kona brew, closed his eyes, and listened to the overhead fans, the klatch of voices, the muffled sound of coffee grinders.

His table lurched, and he opened his eyes. Across from him sat the PGP boys, his engineering partners. They wore ironed duds, dressed unlike anyone else around here, but they needed a shave and a haircut. Their bloodshot eyes gave him the impression they had fallen under the claws of batu again.

"What the hell are you doing here?" Gus said out of the side of his mouth. "I told you to never meet me in public. Now get lost."

Henry looked as if he might lose his breakfast any minute now. "We got to talk."

"Make it quick."

"A detective sergeant from the Hilo CID came by and questioned us this morning," John said. "He learned we had worked at PGP and wanted to know how we got the plant back up. They also asked about you—by name."

"And you're going to tell me you kept your lips shut, right?"

"Something like that," John said in a trailing voice.

Gus squinted at him. John picked his fingernails. His partner, Henry, stared out the window. A 4x4 pickup rumbled past the coffee shop. Gus removed his Smith & Wesson 9mm from his shoulder harness and popped the magazine clip, ejected a round from the chamber, locked the slide back, and peered down the empty barrel. "Care to elaborate?"

"Gus—I swear we said nothing."

Gus returned the magazine and released the slide with a loud click. He laid the gun flat on the table beside his dirty coffee cup, the muzzle facing the men. "Is that all?"

"A submarine docked at the Hilo municipal pier. The Navy's PA officer claims they can supply a third of Hilo's homes until ConHEL's Hilo power plant comes back online."

"When?"

"Next week."

Gus chomped on his Cuban and spit out a wad of soggy tobacco into his coffee cup. The sub was probably the same one his gang attacked weeks ago in Kawaihae Harbor. He gagged on his cigar and hacked up bloody phlegm into a paper napkin. With less than six months to live, his swan song changed its tune. He had only a thousand quid left, his operation wasn't nearly as profitable—or fun—as he had expected. After paying his Samoan gang and the PGP boys, he had scant money left, not enough for the opioids he needed before the curtain fell. Another wave of coughing hit him, sending a searing pain through his chest.

"Okay, Fancy Pants. Thanks for the update. Now get out of here before anyone gets suspicious."

"One more thing." Henry's eyes had the pleading expression of a schoolkid visiting the principal. "John and I think it's better if we pass on the next round, at least until the constabulary backs off."

"Pass on the next round? You think I'm running a poker table at a casino?" Gus's neck tightened and cheeks flush. He fingered his dirty coffee cup, a good cup of Kona gone to waste. Even his Cuban tasted like day-old toast.

"Don't worry, Gus. We won't skip town, just want to melt into the background, you know."

Gus narrowed his eyes at Henry. The pretty boy's brow furrowed and sweat beaded at his thin hairline. Sure, time to cut the cord. Besides, these guys didn't have the smarts to make a clean escape to Honolulu or wherever they planned to fly to. And with them out of the way, he'd stop worrying about whistle blowers.

Gus waved his hand at them. "Okay by me. Have at it. You've trained my men, and we can run the operation on our own now. Good luck to you." He reached over and shook their clammy hands. They bolted from the table and ran out the door without so much as a goodbye. How rude.

Before they reached their car, Gus pressed the transmit switch on his black UHF two-way radio. "Koa. See them fine-dressed gentlemen getting in the car across from you?"

"Got 'em."

"Follow them home, then take care of them. Throw the bodies into Pele's fire."

Hilo, 28 August

At midnight, Brett piloted his Merlin low over the city skyline, lit by lights powered from the *Endeavour*'s reactor. His was the lead ship in Operation TomaHawk, named in tribute to Suzu's nephew. If Toma hadn't identified Conroy, they might never have discovered the mastermind behind the PGP plant takeover. This mission was the most important one since he had joined the squadron. If they failed, the Sons of Samoa would control the power grid for the south side of the island, three times the number of homes than in Kohala.

He swooped in and landed onto the municipal pier and set the throttle to idle RPMs. The *Endeavour*'s Royal Marines ran toward the helo with their gear and ammo. The elite, black-ops Direct Action Platoon came from the Kaneohe Bay Marine Garrison. Stationed there before his retirement, Brett was like a brother to these guys. As the twelve-man squad approached, Brett pulled on the collective-control stick and added throttle to raise the spinning rotor tips, giving the men more clearance to get aboard.

Brett craned his head around and checked the cargo bay to ensure all the marines had strapped in. Two marines sat back-to-back facing outboard either side of the copter and manned 51-millimeter M134 assault guns at each of the open cabin doors. Each marine wore a Kevlar flak vest over dark, urban-camouflage fatigues with about fifty pounds of weapons and ammo strapped to his load-bearing harness. They had wrapped duct tape around their left boot with their blood-type marked in black. To make room for the marines, Brett and Jones had removed the passenger cabin seats before leaving Bradshaw. Those not in the doorways squatted on ammo cans or sat on flak-proof Kevlar panels laid out on the floor. They looked like menacing robots in their night-vision goggles, layers of gear, and thick leather gloves. The landing and extraction lasted less than two minutes. Jones shut the cabin door, and they took off, climbing out of Hilo toward the ocean.

"Black Knight-Seven has Chalk One and we're en route to target," Brett radioed to the mission commander. He flew out to sea and headed south, a hundred feet above the waves, to join with a second Merlin carrying Hawaiian troops from Delta Company. Low clouds shrouded the moon, due to set within the hour. The black featureless ocean racing below him, forcing him to fly only by instruments. He stiffened his back and tapped the control stick with his thumb. He had never flown a combat mission without GPS navigation. A ground recon team had set up radio beacons along the route and at the target's landing zone, guiding him in like the approaches into Bradshaw. The yellow needle sensed the NDB signal and swung to the right, signaling Brett to turn inland. He adjusted his night-vision goggles and flew by visual reference, seeing the terrain in a ghost-like green glow. Lava, erupting from Kīlauea, poured into the ocean, displayed as bright green plumes of light.

They had trained for the mission during the past two weeks, honing their night flying skills. Plan the flight and fly the plan. Like an athlete, Brett ran through each step in the mission profile in his mind's eye, the entrance and egress routes, where the obstacles rose, and what buildings they targeted. SAMs and RPGs heavily defended the mission target. How a ragtag gang of Samoans ever got their hands on the stuff was anyone's guess. Two MQ-5 Raven drones joined the mission and orbited a thousand feet above the target. The pilotless aircraft, designed to bring death from the skies, could fly anywhere. Loaded with 20-millimeter cannons and air-to-surface missiles, they'd make their first sweep over the target to clear the landing zone. A Gray Eagle drone flew in a wide pattern overhead the attack drones, relaying the action live to the mission commander in Hilo.

An AWACS aircraft jammed all civilian frequencies over the Island of Hawai'i for the entire mission. Inside the steady scratch of radio static on the secure-band military channel, a continuous stream of disembodied voices came from the different units setting up for the assault. Brett swept inland, flying low and fast in the nap-of-the-earth, banked right, and dashed northwest along Pohoa Kalapana Road. Puna passed beneath them in its awful reality, a catastrophe ravaged by months of civil unrest in the storm's aftermath. Small fires glowed in Brett's night-vision goggles. Puna's jungle hippies had looted everything of value: solar panels, car tires, farm equipment, and wind turbines. The landing zone NDB needle came alive, and he rolled the Merlin into another right turn and descended through the clouds.

"Two minutes," Brett reported over the aircraft intercom. He imagined the Force Recon squad huddled in the back, checking their weapons, running through their mental checklists, their hearts hammering under flak vests. Brett also prepared for insertion, performing his little ritual of rolling her shoulders, scanning flight and engine instruments, and tapping on the rudder pedals with his boots. He broke out of the clouds at five hundred feet over the compound. The drones swooped in low over the power plant, laying down suppression fire ahead of the helos. Brett pulled back on the stick between his knees for a hard flare, arresting the helo's descent. The maneuver kicked up a thick dust cloud, briefly blocking all visibility. He ignored the pinging of bullets hitting the fuselage, hoping they were only small-arms fire.

"On target, drop ropes, go, go, go," he shouted over the aircraft intercom to the Force Recon team leader. The marines kicked a pair of two-inch nylon ropes coiled near the open doors on both sides. Black Knight-Eight hovered over the parking lot beside the PGP ops building. Chalk One squad slid down to the dirt, one by one from each side of the helo. Brett glanced over his shoulder at the squad leader. "Per Mare Per Terram, Sergeant."

The marine gave a curt nod and dropped along the deployment rope, the last man down. Brett waited for Jones to give the thumbs-up gesture.

"Chalk One is on the deck," he radioed to M-Comm, "Chalk Two deployed from Black Night Eight, returning to base."

"Negative, Black Night Seven. Remain in position to provide air support, over."

"Roger. We'll provide air cover over the LZ." He called to his crew chief on the aircraft intercom, "Hey Jones, WTF? I guess you're now a marine sniper. Man the M134 and point it out the starboard cargo door."

Puna Geothermal Plant Control Center

Gus awoke at three-thirty in the morning to take a leak. "Just like clockwork," he said to no one in particular. "At least some things are still regular."

After relieving himself, he stepped outside and took Helmut for a walk. He lit a cigar and looked for the stars. Another cloudy night. The little dachshund seemed in charge of the walk, and Gus gave him free rein to wander around the PGP compound. Every hundred yards, they passed a set of sandbags surrounding rocket-propelled grenade launchers manned by two mokes, each packing a handgun or rifle. Helmut waddled in and out of the yellow, mercury-sodium beams from the security lights along the sidewalk leading to the generator building. Halfway there, Gus came upon two of his guards, one a Samoan, another haole.

"Can't get much shut-eye," he said. "This damn heat and humidity leaves me soaking in the sheets. Have you checked in with the other guards?"

The Samoan's face lifted to the sky. "Yo, Boss—dis radio must be broke dick. Here, try listen." He turned his walkie-talkie volume up and handed it to Gus. Nothing but static.

"I'll go hunt them down," Gus said. "Maybe the idiots fell asleep."

He put Helmut back on his leash and headed for the other side of the compound. His thoughts returned to his former PGP partners. With them out of the way, he'd no longer worry about anyone ratting out his operation. What's more, he'd also keep all the profits to himself. He let out a long breath and relaxed his shoulders. Bamboozling that fancy pair made him grin.

He reached the backside of the compound and a weird buzzing noise came overhead. His eyes caught a drone flying low, spraying heavy caliber fire along the road. An ominous thumping came from the clouds. Helicopters. Bullets streamed from the first gunship, their tracers piercing the black night like short laser bursts. One copter pulled into a hover about fifty yards away and dropped a pair of ropes. Gus gasped; his cigar tumbled from his lips.

"What the hell. Who are these guys?" he shouted to a Samoan running toward him with a handheld RPG launcher.

Soldiers dropped down the ropes, two at a time. Someone in the copter's open cargo bay door aimed a mounted gun toward Gus and his guards. Before the Samoan could raise the RPG launcher, his body jerked in a staccato rhythm with a short burst of gunfire. Bullets kicked up a trail of dust toward Gus and pressure rose in his chest. He abandoned Helmut and snatched the launcher and ran into the shadows. Beyond the generator building, a small gate in the perimeter fence swung open by the rotor downwash. The dense jungle stood in an eerie glow of yellow smoke, beckoning his escape. He started for the gate. A shot rang out and his left leg seared with pain. Unable to stand, he leaned against the fence. He raised the launcher, triggered its laser viewfinder, and fired at the hovering copter.

———

Brett fought the chaotic crosswinds as he hovered above the generator building. From below and on his left, a white-hot streak of light rose out of the jungle. The warbling tone of the threat detector screeched in his headset. Jones screamed "RPG" over the intercom. Without thinking, Brett slammed his right foot on the anti-torque pedal, sending the Merlin into a violent spin. The maneuver saved them from a direct hit, but the rocket-propelled grenade exploded behind him. The controls shook so hard he couldn't keep his feet on the pedals. The buildings and adjacent jungle whirled outside his windshield. The altimeter needle swung counterclockwise. Multiple alarms sounded through his headset. The TAWS ground proximity alarm blared, "Pull up, pull up." He fought with the controls, tried to auto-rotate, but without tail rotor control, the helo spiraled into the earth with enough force to knock the wind out of Brett. One of the main rotor blades hit the side of a building, slicing through its corrugated siding. Metal screeched all around him.

The whine of the helo's turbines died away, smoke filled his lungs, and a numbing tide crept over his body. He called to Jones over the intercom, but his crew chief didn't respond. The ringing in his ears grew louder, drowning out all other sounds. He shifted his body to check on Jones. He couldn't believe the sight behind him. The crash had cracked the empennage in half just behind the passenger cabin. He snapped his eyes open to a pain so pure he couldn't speak. Seconds dragged into minutes as if his brain were recording everything in slow motion. *Jones, where are you?* A kerosene odor filled the cockpit, sending fear into Brett's heart. Small-arms fire sprayed sparks into leaking JP-5 jet fuel and ignited it. A bright orange ball of fire lit the surround-ings buildings. Smoke drifted into the sky, rising in billowing plumes, illuminated from the fire within. He tried to unlatch his seat harness, but his bloody fingers slid over the clip. Tried again, this time it sprung open. He leaned forward to get out of the seat, but his legs didn't obey. He slammed his fist onto his knee but only felt his hand impacting dead weight, like the wooden numbness of Novocain. When he closed his eyes, a bright spotlight shone inside his eyelids. Searing pain engulfed his head. His brain drifted into a fog. "Oh, shit. Hellen…"

26

Cloudcroft

At the far corner of her sleepy mind, Hellen's anguish smoldered. She tried to sort things out but got nowhere. Fears rising in the night always had more potency than her numbing worries during daylight. She searched for a reason but couldn't pinpoint it. Yet she knew—no felt—a haunting disturbance. She went to Elizabeth's room and found her sleeping. The thought of checking on Charlie crossed her mind, a chance to see him at work at the hospital, to make sure he was happy. Maybe later.

At daybreak, Aiva chimed a text alert from Donovan. *I need to see you. Can you come to the hospital?*

Sounds serious, she typed. *Is Charlie okay?*

Charlie's fine, but come ASAP.

She jumped out of bed and quickly dressed. In the kitchen, Suzu sat with a bowl of rice half eaten, his black samue jacket wrinkled over his slight frame. "What is it?" he asked. "You looked worried."

"Donovan just texted me. He wants me to come to the hospital right away. Can you come with me?"

Suzu nodded and got his keys, not bothering to change.

Without further words, they got into the pickup truck. Hellen drove in silence, fearing the worst. If not Charlie, Brett. Was he shot, or did he crash? He had mentioned an important mission coming up, important being the key word, military speak for dangerous. Stomach cramps replaced nausea, and her heart grew heavy. She fiddled with the braided bracelet around her left wrist, thinking of the invisible link she had with Brett. She wasn't ready for this.

Hellen made a sharp turn into the hospital's ER entrance and came to an abrupt halt. They left the truck in the patient drop-off area and ran inside. Donovan stood beside the admissions desk, his lips pursed together, his eyes dazed. After he laid a patient chart on the counter, he looked away for a moment and wiped his mouth with the back of his hand, a reflexive gesture she remembered him making before doling out bad news.

"What happened? Is Brett okay?"

The mention of his name brought worry to Donovan's eyes. He took her hands in his and nodded. "His helo crashed. He survived, but he's in a serious condition. There's no guarantee he'll live through this."

His words cast a shadow over her. She couldn't bear to lose Brett again, not this way. Her knees buckled. Suzu and Donovan caught her before she collapsed and helped her to a chair.

Donovan held her hand and took a deep breath. "He's in bad shape. He has two broken ribs, a fractured femur in his right leg, and three bruised lower vertebrae in his back. We'll try to get him the best care but transporting him to Honolulu is out of the question. Life is creeping back to normal around here; however, O'ahu is still in chaos." Donovan went over to a water cooler and poured a cup of water for her. "He might recover from these injuries, but I'm more concerned about his brain trauma. His CT scan shows a bulge in an artery in the frontal lobe, pressing against the primary motor cortex. Sometimes an injury like this can tear the tissue and form a dissecting aneurysm. This may be the source of his lower paralysis, or maybe he suffered spinal nerve damage. We can't tell yet."

"And Petty Officer Jones?" Hellen said, her words wooden without feeling.

"He died in the crash. We tried to save him, but we haven't the proper surgical facility. The solar storm claimed another victim. Jones died a hero. Their mission chased the Samoan gang out of the Puna power plant, all captured except for Conroy, the gang leader."

Hearing the name of her attacker startled her. Like a ghost, he had crept back into her life. "But Brett is going to be okay…"

"Hellen, I'm not sure if you are asking me or telling me. We've induced a coma for now. Treatment can vary based on the aneurysm's size and location, and whether it is leaking. According to the CT scan, it's accessible, so surgery might repair or at least cut off blood flow, preventing further growth. But if it ruptures before we can get him to surgery, he may die."

Her lips trembled. She tried to focus on his words, but her brother's voice competed with her panic. His face wavered through her watery eyes. "I want to see him."

"He's not back from the OR yet. You can go see him after he's in the recovery ward."

Donovan droned on, his voice fading into the background sounds of the hospital. Someone shook her arm, and Donovan's words seeped through the fog.

"Hellen… Hellen… can you hear me?"

"Yes, I'm okay. My mind just wandered for a moment."

Donovan clutched her arm and helped her to her feet. He and Suzu guided her onto a sofa in a dark corner of the waiting room. "You can lie here. Just try to relax. I'll get you a sedative."

After Donovan left, Suzu sat beside Hellen, holding her hand, his thumb stroking Hellen's wrist. Donovan returned with a charged syringe. A little prick and a subtle warmth spread through her body, pulling her from the sour present and into a well of darkness. She fell into a slumber punctuated by dreams warm enough to never want to awake. A small, soft hand brushed her cheeks. A face came into view. Elizabeth—no, it was Elle—bent over and kissed her forehead. Floating beyond her closed eyelids, Elle's young face smiled in the sunlight.

By late afternoon, Brett had returned from surgery. The recovery ward was full, but Donovan made an exception and found him a private room. Hellen sat at Brett's bedside, leaning over with her cheek resting on his arm. The health monitor sang its staccato beeps over the long hours. A nurse made her rounds in hushed silence. The ICU room smelled of numbing grief and the overhead lights shone through faded, yellow plastic. Hellen stood from her chair, turned the depressing lights out, and pulled back the window curtains to let sunlight fill the room. Outside the window, the world spun on its own momentum, people walked on sidewalks, birds alighted from a nearby tree. All of this made her horror seem as if it were only a surreal nightmare.

She returned to her seat and took Brett's hand in hers, feeling his elevated pulse with her fingers. She cried in earnest now with hollow gasping sobs emerging from her chest, like breath on a winter day. A sip of water helped to wash down the bile seeping in her throat. The sound of glass breaking on the tiled floor made her jump. She froze, fixated on the spilled water flowing along the cracks between the floor tiles, pooling here and there in random patterns. She let it flow, eager to distract herself from both the horror of the present and the equally unbearable future.

"Are you okay, Hellen?"

She stirred, hearing Elizabeth's voice. She glanced up. Donovan and both her children stood near the door. Not sure of when they had come into the room, she checked the wall clock. Where did the hours go? "Yes, I'm all right. Thank you, love."

"You need not keep up appearances for our sake," Elizabeth said.

"It's okay," Hellen said without much conviction. Her eyes blurred with tears and she reached out her hand. Elizabeth ran to her and held her.

"It's not okay," Elizabeth said. "Life sucks sometimes. Hang on. Remember the hidden reality."

Hellen lifted her head and gave a slight nod. Elizabeth unfastened the gold locket from around her neck and handed it to her. Hellen opened it and removed the lock of Elle's hair, handing it to Donovan.

"What's this?"

"I want you to do a DNA match with it."

"With whom?" Donovan asked. He held on the small lock of auburn hair.

Elizabeth nodded to Hellen before she spoke. "With me."

Honaunau Bay, 4 September

Warm water lapped at Gus's feet. He stepped down two steps carved into slippery lava rock at the ocean's edge, aware he could turn back anytime. The seawater came up to his calves, then his sore knees. This once popular snorkel spot was empty. It was too late in the afternoon for fishermen, a time of day when the fish hid among the coral reef. It seemed as if he were the only one in the whole world. The dense rain forest sloped from Kīlauea Volcano and ended at the shoreline. A rusted sign tacked to a red post warned of the strong currents in the bay.

In the distance, Helmut barked. His Weiner tail wagged at a kid who shared his sandwich with him. The only person in sight at the beach, the boy held Helmut in his lap and nuzzled his cheek against the dog's ears. After a spell, the kid stood and walked away with Helmut trundling behind him. So much for loyalty.

Another step. The water lapped his thighs. A searing pain

came from the gunshot wound in his left leg, rising to his chest, making him gasp. His lips trembled, his breath coming in bursts. He scooted onto an underwater ledge and rested. In time, the stinging heat subsided into a dull ache. He took another step, the water now at his chest. Unsure of what he wanted until the last rock slid beneath his feet, he swam out to the waves beyond the reef.

He swam hundreds of yards before he glanced back. The primitive tiki huts stood against the sun's glare. At this spot, his nightmare had begun decades ago. During the reign of King Kamehameha the Great, Pu'uhonua Village had offered a safe harbor to defeated warriors, and those who committed kapu. Reaching the boundary of this City of Refuge meant sanctuary. Looking back upon his years in this strange world, he felt a kinship with those ancient Polynesians. Like them, he was desperate to find refuge from his hunters. His gang captured, his face plastered on search warrants across the island, he had spent the past week moving only at night until reaching this shore, the water's edge to that damn gopher hole between his two worlds. He was done. Here it had begun, and here it would end, dammit.

His arms ached from treading water. Favoring his good leg only led to more cramps. A wave crested and broke on top of him. Caught by surprise, he swallowed seawater and went into a coughing fit. He wiped the snot from his nose, his fingers sticky with bloody phlegm. He slapped the water and cursed the scythe-wielding skeleton, lung cancer his constant companion now. Exhausted, he floated on his back and closed his eyes. The sun made bright red spots behind his eyelids, streaming across his vision like tracer bullets. One red spot ballooned into a woman's face, a spicy wahine with flaxen red hair. He recalled her face, but not her name. She alone had saved him from insanity, the uncertainty of who he was and where he came from. Years ago, he had met her at this bay, the last time he had snorkeled at this spot. She bumped against him while he swam with a sea turtle in the reef. Her naked body both surprised and pleased him. And her eyes captured him, deep brown with flakes of gold. They swam together and chatted, even flirting despite her having ten years on him. She pointed at the IdentiTag implanted in his upper arm, an artifact from his home world, a world ruled by a surveillance society. She cried out. Before he covered the chip with his other hand, she pointed to her arm. Hidden by a tattooed yin-yang symbol, a biochip like his laid beneath her skin. Surprise, not curiosity, filled her eyes. Indescribable joy filled his heart, proof this wasn't all just a bad dream. No longer the only souls from the Old World, they shared their stories, their accidental sojourn to this world, their fear of insanity. She had arrived six years before him—at this same spot—but gave no hints of how. Another woman, perhaps her friend, called from the beach and waved her arms wide. After a brief hug and goodbye, this mysterious vixen swam away. Their promise to meet again never materialized, but he had always held on to her memory, the new reality, the knowledge he wasn't alone.

He opened his eyes. The shore lay far in the distance, the tiki huts now two specks on a thin black shoreline of lava rock. His gunshot wound no longer stung. His heart pounded. He estimated his distance from the shoreline, close enough to make it back if he tried. But then what? Back to the fox hunt, the cops chasing him all over the island to kingdom come. Besides, he had only months to live. What was the point?

He continued to swim away from land and enjoyed how his body slipped through the waves, helped on by the current. He stopped and tread water. Ocean spread in all directions. His fury at this parallel world floated out from him in a long moan. He found peace at last. Sanctuary.

Enough. He exhaled his last breath and slipped below the waves. The air escaped his tired lungs in a stream of bubbles. Sunbeams shimmered through the water, refracting rays of blue light from the surface as he drifted into the dark abyss. "This is my new home," the redheaded wahine had said. "We can't return to our Old World. So, why not make the best of this one?"

KMC Annex, 18 September

Hellen ran her fingers through Brett's thick black hair, luxuriating in its touch. No longer a military stubble, his mane had grown well past his ears since leaving San Diego. It had only been three months, yet it felt as a lifetime.

Two weeks after his crash, Brett awoke from the coma and a second CT scan showed his aneurysm had shrunk. He'd also regained feeling in his legs, but still couldn't walk. The news of his mission securing the Puna power plant brought a huge smile to his face. He asked about Jones, but she stayed evasive, not sure how he'd take the death of his partner. Three days ago, Donovan had moved Brett from the ICU and into the former astronomer's lodge across the street from the hospital for convalescence and physical therapy. Donovan had said she could take him home in a couple of weeks. But Brett's flying days were over, much to her relief.

Hellen loved Brett's new room, a bedroom suite with bright airy windows looking onto the gardens. The queen-sized bed gave her plenty of room to cuddle with him, brightening his mood and speeding his recovery more than any medicine. During the days, she read aloud from Elle's novel, *The Wayfinders*. By night, she held him in her arms, as he had done for her the night she fell overboard.

After serving him lunch, she sat beside his bed. His doleful eyes touched her heart and sent her back to the summer they met. She opened her mouth to speak but didn't find the words.

"What's that look for?" he asked.

"What look?"

"You've something on your mind. I can hear the wheels

churning."

She reached over to Aiva and activated her music app. After a few stanzas, she smiled at Brett. "Remember this?"

Brett's face lifted to the ceiling, and he closed his eyes for a moment. "It's *Two Worlds Apart*, right?"

Her lips parted, and she caught his beaming smile.

"Okay, you get points for that." She took Aiva off the bedside table and flipped through her photo album. "Bonus question. Where was this taken?"

Brett squinted at Hellen's tablet and pinched open the photo. "Looks like Hōkūle'a in Lahaina. Our first night together, right?"

She grinned and waved him on to continue.

"I wore my naval dress-white uniform to impress you."

"And caught the eye of every lass."

"You're one to talk. That revealing dress of yours was pure eye candy."

Hellen threw her head back and laughed. Like a flickering spark sprung from a fire, the memory returned, at first smoldering before bursting into a small flame.

"And it was the night we made a baby," he said in a weak voice. "On your birthday, no less."

"It was the best present you ever gave me."

She climbed onto the bed, careful to not hurt him, and lay beside him. After they exchanged a honi kiss, she whispered, "Suzu has given us the cottage behind Cloudcroft and ten acres of land. Elizabeth and I spent the past weeks fixing it up. The work also brought us together, a chance to reconcile."

He said nothing, simply smiled at her, and for the first time in all the years she had known him, his eyes welled up. They lay together, her head on his chest, matching her breaths with his. An awareness grew within her, one seeming to stretch to infinity. For once in her life, she felt complete. At last, Brett closed his eyes. His chest rose and fell in deep swells, his breathing turning into soft snoring.

In the darkened doorway, a figure appeared, obscured by the

backlit sunshine.

"Hellen, we need to talk." Suzu's voice came from the cloaked figure.

Hellen's stomach stiffened. She recalled the last time Suzu had spoken those words. With trepidation, she followed him outside and along the path through the campus. Here and there, sprites of sunlight cast through the trees. They crossed the gardens and entered the main building, still deserted of its astronomers. Adorned on every wall, photos and press releases described the observatory's historic discoveries. At the end of the west wing, she came upon the Otoko Education Center. Elle's philanthropy had touched many lives. Next to the conference room door, a seven-foot oil painting dominated the hall, showing seven dancers glowing within a sheer blue nebula veil, the same image in Elle's book.

"You might recognize this piece," Suzu said without turning from the painting. "Elle commissioned it for you."

Hellen read the painting's dedication, "Makali'i—The Pleiades Star Cluster—from the kind donation of Dr. Elisabeth 'Elle' Akamu Otoko (2K13)." Akamu. Hellen lurched her head back. Now she understood why Elle had never revealed her maiden name nor had ever spoken of her parents. Yet, she wasn't related to Brett. Neither he nor Elle had ever mentioned her sharing his last name.

An adjacent sign explained that Makali'i signaled the Māori New Year to Polynesian wayfinders, celestial navigators who sailed thousands of miles across the Pacific long before Magellan. The true meaning of Elle's book snapped into focus. Wayfinding was more than navigating by the stars, it entailed navigating through life. Like the ancient wayfinders, Elle had steered Hellen's life, becoming her hānai mother, funding her schooling, encouraging her to leave Sam, and arranging her reunion with Brett. All these events carried time's arrow in a circle back to Elle's rebirth. The red thread linking her destiny may have twisted and stretched, but it never broke. Hellen staggered back—her own name held this secret: HelleN. In an instant, she saw herself as the bridge between Elle and Elizabeth, both the same person. Here and Now, she stood between two parallel worlds, both the mother and daughter to doppelgänger twins.

"Elle and Elizabeth..." Hellen whispered.

Suzu narrowed his eyes. "Are the same person but born on separate worlds, Elizabeth in this world and Elle from a parallel world. Perhaps the same goes for Toma. Don't reveal any of this to Elizabeth. Doppelgängers should never meet their maker. Let her continue to believe in Elle's reincarnation."

Hellen's chest burned until she remembered to breathe. As if breaking the surface from a deep dive, she gasped for air. "How could I be Elle's birth mother? An artifact of time travel?"

"Nothing so pedestrian. Elle came into my life in 1976. She was a feisty one back then, just like you, or I should say the same as your twin on Elle's world. Yet her homeland wasn't the same America we know." He removed a tattered photo from his pocket. "This was taken the day I found her off the coast of Honaunau."

Hellen held the photo close. Elizabeth's eyes, framed by her dripping hair, stared back at the camera fifty years ago. Like a whip cracking across the decades, the photo sent shivers through Hellen. Elle's wet suit had an American flag sown over her left breast. It had fifty stars.

Kawaihae Bay, 31 October

Hellen stood on *Ohana*'s foredeck and reveled in the dolphins playing beyond the sailboat's bow. The water was clear down to about thirty feet, the sun's angle perfect for watching them dive deep and spring upward to ride *Ohana*'s bow wave. The dark blue water surface broke as each dolphin took its turn porpoising in front of Hellen. Lost in the improv circus, she jumped when Brett's arms came around her waist.

"Boo," he whispered.

She spun around and embraced him. "I chose a bad day for this—all Saint's Eve."

"Don't worry. Only you Yanks celebrate Halloween."

"Maybe it's fitting? After all, Elle was a saint to us." *And a ghost from a different world.*

A dolphin sprang high enough to allow Hellen to stroke its dorsal fin on the flyby. "I love watching these little guys, don't you?"

"I wouldn't call them little. These spinner dolphins weigh over two hundred pounds."

One dolphin leapt out of the water and twisted its body and rose high into the air. It arched over, spun twice, and landed on its side with a loud slap. Cold seawater doused Hellen's shirt. Hellen gave out a cry and blushed, wishing she had worn something less shear.

"Look at them! They're awesome," Hellen said. "Why do they do this?"

"It's a female trying to get the attention of the pod's bull dolphin." Brett held her hips and twisted her to face him.

She shot him a wry smile. "There are easier ways to catch a man's attention."

At the far end of the boat, Elizabeth regarded them with winsome eyes.

"Can you believe it's been only five months since we first sailed to this island?" Brett asked.

"I've thought about it a lot lately. This summer has shaped my life more than any other time."

This summer, on her fortieth orbit around the sun, she had lost many of the modern conveniences she had taken for granted; the Internet of Everything went dead, the lights went out, and the stars returned to the night sky. The summer also revealed hidden dimensions of her life, the kind that sit close beside you every day in awkward silence, waiting for you to notice them. In some ways, it had marked a rebirth for Hellen, a discovery of her true identity, both the daughter and mother of her Bodhisattva. This awareness filled her like the clouds engulfing Mauna Kea.

"Now that the grid is back, are you planning to go back to work?"

She pointed toward her children. "They're my work. I've found what's most important in my life."

"It's nice to have our family under one roof at last."

Hellen's heart warmed at the sound of his words. She looked back to Elizabeth, who raised her eyebrows and tapped her nose with her index finger.

"Mom. Come take the helm for a while," Charlie called from the cockpit.

She walked back to the ship's wheel and wrapped her arm around Elizabeth's waist. Charlie checked the sails one last time before handing the helm over to her.

"See that pink cloud ahead of us?" he asked. "Just aim for it. Don't even think of looking at the compass or else you'll wander off course."

Hellen squinted at the sun and nodded. "I have the helm, sir."

Standing behind the wheel, she waved her son off and stared back to the compass. Another pod of dolphins splashed off *Ohana*'s starboard beam. The jib slacked and flailed against the foredeck stanchions.

"Mom, watch your heading," Charlie chastised. "You're backing the sail again."

She checked her heading and laughed. *No accidental jibe this time.* "That's your father talking. Why don't you and your sister go to the bow and watch the dolphins play?"

Charlie and Elizabeth went forward, leaving Hellen alone with Brett napping in the sun. The kids held onto the jibstay, their heads bent toward the water. Elizabeth's hair danced in the breeze over Charlie's shoulder. Their laughter, carried by the wind, sang to Hellen's ears. Salty tears stung her eyes when she viewed the wide sky, the horizon that stretched into infinity.

The water sparkled in sunlight, every molecule dancing in this radiant parallel universe. Elle had once said, "Profound discoveries come at unexpected moments." Weeks after Suzu's revelation, Hellen's initial shock had evolved into awe. She now saw the world in which she had sailed since her birth was separated from a hidden reality, a world separated from this one by a thin layer like the line between ocean and sky. Elle had traveled between two worlds in spacetime, like a fish jumping from the sea. Hellen's hands relaxed on the ship's wheel, her mind swimming beneath the rapture, the sound of one hand clapping.

Several hours passed with the idyllic waves. By the time they approached the shoals of Honaunau, the red sun inched toward the ocean, sending rays arching through the dusk, the Fingers of Buddha. A light drizzle fell from a lone, dark gray cloud ahead of them, creating a dazzling, double rainbow stretching into the ocean.

Donovan came topside and helped Hellen tack to avoid the lee shore. The racket of grinding winches and flapping sails woke Brett. He grunted and squinted at Hellen before sliding his ball cap over his face and falling back to sleep.

Donovan crossed his arms and gave Hellen the Look.

"What's your problem?" She checked the compass to make sure she hadn't fallen off course again.

"Remember the DNA analysis you asked for?"

"You got the results?" she asked, wondering why they had taken so long.

"They came three weeks ago, but I sent them back to double-check. I'm dying to learn where the hair sample came from. The genome shows an identical twin to Elizabeth, yet epigenetic changes show it's from someone decades older than her." He raised one eyebrow and rubbed his chin.

"Don't tell her, okay?"

Hellen looked away and recalled Suzu's warning a week before the kahuna died of a stroke. Once again, Hellen harbored a secret deep in her heart, one she must never reveal to Elizabeth.

From the far corners of her mind Hellen heard Brett whisper, "Okay, Hellen. Are you ready to do this?"

She gave his hand a quick squeeze and wiped her eyes before going belowdecks. From the forward locker, she retrieved two urns. She returned topside and handed them to Elizabeth. The canisters sparkled under the brilliant sun, Elle's a blue ceramic with engraved constellations, Suzu's an obsidian vase with Japanese inscriptions.

Hellen tied two long, satin ribbons to the stern railing and tossed their loose ends over the boat's transom. The red streamers intertwined and trailed in the breeze behind them. Hellen removed the gold locket from around her neck, a constant companion since the day Elizabeth had given it to her. Elizabeth took the pendant and tied it to Suzu's urn. "Elle gave this to Suzu after they met, the summer she came to this island, the summer of America's bicentennial, the summer they fell in love."

Hellen asked herself how Elle might have traveled to this world and wondered if the answer rested in the future—or maybe the past.

"Any final words?" Donovan asked.

Hellen and Elizabeth shook their heads in unison and tossed plumeria leis into the sea. With a quivering voice, Hellen sang the hymn *New Britain*. They lifted the urns and spread the ashes into the wind. The gray flakes floated in the air, drifting upon the ocean waves before swirling together and mixing into a thin stratum in *Ohana*'s wake.

Amazing grace, how sweet the sound
That saved a soul like me.
I once was lost, but now am found,
Was blind but now I see.

ACKNOWLEDGMENTS

Popular science fiction dealing with the possible aftermath of a solar storm tends to follow a decidedly dystopic plotline. Yet the scientific literature doesn't support apocalyptic notions of an electromagnetic pulse on the scale of a nuclear strike. A coronal mass ejection from a Carrington-class solar flare would likely emit a longer-period, albeit lower energy, EMP. Electrical currents induced by the geomagnetic storm would ravage EHV transformers and longer transmission lines for sure, but residential renewable energy systems and microgrids would likely survive.

The most probable scenario for the solar storm in this book is the aftermath of Hurricane Maria in Puerto Rico. Its isolation from the US mainland and FEMA's failures in responding to the aftermath resulted in a death toll far exceeding Hurricane Katrina. The insights and shared experiences from Mayor Carmen Yulín Cruz and other survivors provided valuable background for this book.

I am indebted to Wayne Hicks at the National Renewable Energy Laboratory (NREL) for sending me lots of interesting information about the effects of solar storms on power grids and renewable energy systems. Thanks also to Laurence Sombardier of the Natural Energy Laboratory of Hawaii Authority for graciously giving his time to educate me on the wind and geothermal power initiatives on the Big Island.

David Deutsch of Oxford University and Michio Kaku of the City College of New York provided me with the inspiration for the premise of a parallel universe. Unlike the Copenhagen interpretation of quantum mechanics in which the Schrödinger equations collapse at the moment of observing a QM event, the Many Worlds interpretation of QM allows Schrödinger's s cat to be both alive and dead; that is, dual outcomes continue to exist after the lid is opened. The cat is alive in one world and dead in a parallel world. For more on the scientific premise of *Mauna Kea Rising*, please see www.mwkelly.com.

Thanks to Nicole Milne and Liam Kernell at The Kohala Center for providing me invaluable information about sustainable living on the Big Island. Perhaps by living on a remote outpost in the middle of the Pacific, many Hawaiians are far more informed on renewable energy and sustainable living than those living on the US mainland. Thanks also to Dr. Samantha Murray-Bainer for her valuable insights into hospital operations.

Any errors or technical inconsistences are entirely mine and not the opinions of the experts interviewed for this book nor those who provided me with background research.

The support of the Chaparral and Cherokee Trail writing faculties has been invaluable to me, particularly Lauren Hyclak, Paul Whipple, Damon Larson, and Shannon Walsweer. Thanks also to Mike Farris, Andrew Sippie, Alicia Canet, and Judy Murray, all of whom read earlier drafts of the book and offered sage advice.

This book could have no finer editors than Rachel Weaver and Lourdes Venard, who helped me to grow as a writer, provided encouragement when I was lost, and added common sense to the whole process.

Most of all, I thank my wife, Patty, for sharing her love of Hawai'i and her support in my getting through this project.

ABOUT THE AUTHOR

Kelly became hooked on science after Neil Armstrong took an epic stroll one Saturday evening in July 1969. He later served as a submarine officer based in Scotland and New England. He is a graduate of the U.S. Naval Academy, Bryant University, and Swinburne University. After leaving the Navy, he spent two decades teaching college physics and astronomy. A member of RMFW and the Hawai'i Writers Guild, Kelly loves reading and writing mind-expanding science fiction. His articles and short stories have appeared in *Pilot Mag*, the *Torrid Literature Review*, *Latitudes*, and Pole to Pole Publishing's anthology, *Twenty Thousand Leagues Remembered*.

Thank you for buying this Hokulei Press book. To receive bonus content and information on new releases in this series, visit www.mwkelly.com and sign up for the newsletter.

Facebook: M.W. Kelly – Author
   Twitter: @mwkelly2001
   Newsletter: www.mwkelly.com
   Goodreads: M.W. Kelly

If you read this book and liked it, would you consider leaving a review on Goodreads or your favorite bookseller? That would be great. I would so appreciate it.

For questions and comments about the quality of this book, please contact us at mwkelly@HokuleiPress.com.

ELLE, THE NAKED SINGULARITY

More from the *Lost in the Multiverse* series:

Elle, the Naked Singularity is science fiction spiked with magical realism, a story in which a college student finds herself lost in the multiverse. Twenty-year-old Elle Akamu slips from 21st century Earth through spacetime into a parallel universe in the 1970s British Hawaiian Islands. She befriends a transgender social worker, a teenage orphan, and a POW survivor in her quest to return home. Lost in the multiverse, she discovers life is about accepting her past, choosing a future, and finding love in her new world.

A fusion of science and Buddhism, the story explores racism, gay rights, and gender inequality in the 1970s through the eyes of a 21st century time traveler. A stranger in a strange land, Elle wrestles with our oldest questions—what is the nature of the universe? And how do our relationships shape our world?

CPSIA information can be obtained
at www.ICGtesting.com
Printed in the USA
LVHW091735200320
650701LV00001B/236

9 781734 693003